KNEE-DEEP IN GRIT

Edited by ADRIAN COLLINS
& MIKE MYERS

GdM

Editor: Adrian Collins
Copy Editor (all stories): Mike Myers
Cover Art, Cover Design, and Interior Layout: STK·Kreations
Interior Art: Jason Deem, Julian de Lio, Austen Mengler

Hardcover ISBN: 978-0-6481784-2-2
Trade paperback ISBN: 978-0-6481784-3-9
Ebook ISBN: 978-0-6481784-4-6
Worldwide Rights.
Created in Australia.

All stories within are reprints of the original fiction published by Grimdark Magazine
between 1st October 2014 and 1st July 2016.

Published by Grimdark Magazine
Unit 1 / 184-186 Military Road
Neutral Bay, NSW 2089
www.grimdarkmagazine.com

For the *Grimdark Magazine* team past and present, whose selflessness
and passion has created something wonderful.

For the *Grimdark Fiction Readers and Writers* Facebook group, who
have backed us for nearly four years now.

For our Patreon supporters, who put their hard-earned cash down
each quarter to make sure we can keep putting out content.

For Victor. An imagination and ability gone too soon from this world.

CONTENTS

FOREWORD
Mark Lawrence ....*xi*

INTRODUCTION
Mike Myers ....*xv*

THE KING BENEATH THE WAVES
Peter Fugazzotto *1*

THE LINE
T.R. Napper *17*

AT THE WALLS OF SINNLOS
Michael R. Fletcher *31*

THE RIGHT HAND OF DECAY
David Annandale *51*

THE NEUTRAL
Anatoly Belilovsky and Mike Gelprin *61*

BRAZEN DREAMS
Matthew Ward *67*

THE KNIFE OF MANY HANDS
R. Scott Bakker *81*

DRONE STRIKES FOR FUN AND PROFIT
Aaron Fox-Lerner *119*

ALL THE LOVELY BRIDES
Kelly Sandoval *129*

SHADOW HUNTER
Adrian Tchaikovsky *137*

A RECIPE FOR CORPSE OIL
Siobhan Gallagher *147*

REDEMPTION WAITS
Mike Brooks *157*

A FAIR MAN
Peter Orullian *175*

BOOMER HUNTER
Sean Patrick Hazlett *199*

THE NU-THAI SCREWJOB
Gav Thorpe *209*

LESSONS OF NECESSITY
T.C. Powell *225*

A PROPER WAR
James A. Moore *229*

THE RED WRAITH
Nicholas Wisseman *243*

THE WOMAN I USED TO BE
Gerri Leen *245*

THE PRICE OF HONOUR
Matthew Ward *257*

RED SEAS, RED SAILS
Victor Milán *277*

ASHES
Tara Calaby *293*

VIVA LONGEVICUS
Brandon Daubs *307*

AGAINST THE ENCROACHING DARKNESS
Aliette de Bodard *321*

BAD SEED
Mark Lawrence *337*

ART GALLERY *351*

FOREWORD

MARK LAWRENCE

K nee-Deep in Grit is Grimdark Magazine's first print collection and brings you 25 short stories, one of them mine!

I'm reliably informed [*] that subsequent collections will sink further into grit, progressing from hip- and neck-deep to 2022's *Floating Face-Down in Grit*.

I'm not at all sure what introductions should have in them. I'm kinda hoping you'll all do what I do and skip this one like all the others! I Googled "an introduction to introductions" but it was less helpful than anticipated. Anyway, I was invited to write an introduction and by the old gods and the new I will do so.

First a word about the magazine. Two years! Tempus fuckit! It seems barely more than twenty-three months ago that Adrian asked if I could contribute a story to issue one. A big round of applause to Adrian and the team for keeping a magazine going in such a tough market and for maintaining such high standards. I've been particularly impressed by the covers too and this print collection is no exception. Stellar work by artist Jason Deem and designer Shawn King.

Short fiction is a hard sell these days…which given the rapidly reducing attention spans out there, and the rising tempo of everyday life, is a surprise. So well done you for being here and supporting it! Actually it's a smart move because much, maybe most, of the innovation in the world of fiction takes place in short stories. Short stories are a much smaller investment of the writer's time, the audience is smart and open-minded, and also small in number, all of which means that it's a format in which it is safe to experiment, and one in which you can fail. By which I mean not that anyone aims to fail, but that you can. Write a book that tanks and in the current world of publishing it probably means your career is over. That's basically it. Write a duff book and you're out. This encourages playing safe, sticking to what you know sells etc. But in a short story you can gamble, and if you lose you get to fight another day. For the reader this means there will be some lows, but some of the highs will be unparalleled!

Anyway, in lieu of a proper introduction I've opted for a stream of consciousness ramble. Enjoy!

I guess the question of the moment is how deep in grit do we need to be? Is knee-deep too much or too little?

Whilst grit in the sense it's used here is more than simply the inclusion of graphic violence and the depiction of bleak worlds to house such acts, I'm going to focus on the violence. The wider picture of grit is of course painted in fifty shades of moral grey and as much about the feel or vibe of the tale as about the checklist of its contents.

This brings me to consider the often brought up notion that violence needs to 'justify itself', that 'shock value' is somehow an oxymoron, and that failure to justify the former and avoid the latter are 'lazy writing'.

When people say, "That <Insert Act of Violence> was only added in for shock value." they are not complimenting an author.

But if they say that something was added in for comedy value... that's rarely a criticism. Take it another step... how about, "You only added that in for interest value," or "Come on, you only wrote that bit to make me feel a sense of wonder and awe." I can't remember ever seeing that.

So what is wrong with shock value?

A story generally comprises highs and lows. Few readers consume books hoping for a constant feel-good tale. The darkness in a book allows the bright spots to shine more brightly. There's less joy in a victory if you haven't come face to face with the consequences of failure first.

So is the accusation of shock value only made by those upset at being more shocked than they wanted to be?

Let's look at the idea violence needs to justify itself. That its consequences need to be explored. That the victim's side of the story needs to be shown and we should be left in no doubt it's a bad thing. No! No again! And no! Stories are not moral instruction for idiots. Every part of writing needs to justify itself and the justification it needs for occupying valuable page space is that it achieves the aim of the story, which is often primarily to keep the reader reading, to keep them invested, emotional engaged, and at the end of the story both satisfied and wanting more. Rather like sex.

Is grit lazy writing? I hope so! Optimal laziness is essentially efficiency. Writing strives to be efficient. Good writing hits the chords in the reader necessary for them to do the heavy lifting for the story. The emotions you want the reader to feel, the things you want the reader to see…almost all of it is already inside that person and the aim of good writing is to hook it out of them with as few words as possible. When one line, out of context, can give someone chills…that's good writing, that's efficient writing…it's lazy writing and it isn't an insult.

When you show that someone is 'bad' by having them do a bad thing…you can call it lazy…but it isn't an insult. When you show someone is greedy by having them eat all the pies…call it lazy but it's not an insult.

The thing is that when 'lazy writing' is levelled as an insult it's done primarily when what the person throwing the term around really wants is for you not to write about the thing you have written about. It's misdirection.

So, returning to grit and how much is enough. It's a meaningless question. How much spice is enough? It's entirely down to the individual tastes of the reader. Everyone finds their own level and it's context-driven. You open a tub of yoghurt and chances are you won't find it's jalapeno flavour. You order a vindaloo and it's going to be hot. Knee-Deep in Grit is a curry house of stories, they're all going to be spicy and if you like your reading bland…you've come to the wrong place. If not, dig in, bon appetite.

^(*) this is a lie.

Mark Lawrence
September, 2017

BEGINNINGS

An Introduction by MIKE MYERS

D oes everything begin with Mark Lawrence? I hope so. A few years ago, I had a mid-life crisis. I had been rereading some pretty grim Hemingway and Saul Bellow, like I'm supposed to (and love), and I said to myself, "I'm getting old, and what I really love to read most of all is fantasy. I want great contemporary fantasy." So I scoured Amazon for just the right book that wouldn't let me down. It had to be a great story, well written, and grim, without any knights on white horses, much less dwarves and elves and other Tolkien rip offs. I finally decided on a novel called *Prince of Thorns*. I read it and thought, *Yeah, that's pretty good*. So I bought *King of Thorns*, and I thought, *Wow. That's fucking amazing*. Grim and ruthless and exciting, with a real bastard for a hero, and beautiful, understated writing. I was hooked. So I decided to Google Mark Lawrence, which eventually led me to the website of a brand new e-magazine that had just published its first issue, featuring...wait for it...Mark Lawrence! I gobbled it up. *Grimdark Magazine, hmm... that's pretty cool. Wouldn't it be cool to work for them, to help publish this lovely, brutal fiction?* Lo and behold, the website said they needed a volunteer copyeditor. I'm not usually the type of guy that reaches out to people I don't know, but I just loved the idea of this new e-magazine publishing dark, violent, fantasy and sci-fi—the kind that makes you think. I applied (at the time I don't think many people were visiting the *GdM* website yet) and got the gig!

We got rolling immediately on issue #2. Adrian Collins, our Head Honcho, sent me a couple of stories to edit, and I was immediately blown away: This Bakker dude is a genius. This story by T. R. Napper is brutal. The characters and worlds these guys come up with are grim and dark and painful and smelly and... beautiful. The sweat and the fights, the technology and magic, the deep world-building, the grimy sex—it's all so fascinating and riveting. While waiting for issue #3, I filled the void with *Emperor of Thorns*; then Daniel Polansky's brilliant *Low Town* trilogy, Abercrombie, Anthony Ryan, GRRM, and I just continued reading grimdark novels, helping edit *Grimdark Magazine*, and loving every merciless minute of it. And evidently, you, our readers, loved it, too. More and more issues sold—we almost broke even once!—and our submission queue runneth over with great stories from writers known and unknown, experienced and novice, all wanting to take part in this thing called "grimdark."

Along the way there have been kerfuffles and outright bloody skirmishes: what is grimdark? Is grimdark even a thing? Seems like everyone wanted to have a say on it. Numerous bloggers, too many to mention, have written about the very existence of a thing called grimdark. C.T. Phipps and James Schmidt of @themightythorjrs held a round table to try to figure out what the hell this thing is. Is grimdark a genre? A subgenre? A sentiment? A formula? Does it have to have certain characteristics? Morally grey characters? Characters making morally grey decisions? Fighting? Violence? Death? A grim setting with lots of mud?

To which I say, who cares? Grimdark, to me, is something you feel in your bones. You read it and feel, *Something bad is happening here, and this guy/gal is going to try anything, good or bad, to get out of it alive. If they make it, hooray! If they don't, hooray!* It's the feeling that counts. The feeling that desperate times call for desperate measures, and there are no right choices—except the choice to read on.

So here we are, bringing you all the stories from the first two years of *Grimdark Magazine*, including the one that kicked off our first issue, the first publication of Mark Lawrence's *Bad Seed*. Just thinking about Alann Oak's bloody evolution gives me chills, but it's the ghost of Darin Reed looking over Oak's shoulder that makes the story fantastic in every sense of the word. Between the covers of this first-ever *Grimdark Magazine* print collection, you'll find top notch grimdark fantasy from well-known authors like Mark Lawrence, Locus Award winner R. Scott Bakker, Nebula Award winner Aliette de Bodard, Arthur C. Clark Award winner Adrian Tchaikovsky, Reddit Fantasy Stabby Award winner Michael R. Fletcher, Bram Stoker nominee James A. Moore, Tara Calaby, Richard Ford, Peter Orullian, Victor Milan, Peter Fugazzotto (whose story *The King Beneath the Waves* knocked me out), and lots more. On the other side of the SFF spectrum we have grimdark science fiction from Writers of the Future winner T. R. Napper, Matthew Ward, Aaron Fox-Lerner, Mike Brooks, and several others that stunningly capture the brutality of our techno-future. We hope you will enjoy reading these stories again if you've read them in our e-magazine editions, or if you're really lucky maybe you're reading them for the first time. Either way, we strive to bring you grimdark SFF you'll love.

Three years after those first nervous days waiting for a reply from Adrian, I'm still here, still nervous that all the authors hate me. Still working with Adrian and the GdM team to publish the best in grimdark fantasy and science fiction. Though we live all over the world, grimdark fiction brings us together. We love to explore the dark and dirty worlds, meet grim and hopelessly striving characters who fight not for the archaic ideal of good versus evil but for survival, for existence, to live to fight another day, and face the challenges of a world that can't be easily separated into moral dichotomies. It's speculative fiction, but it's real. You can feel it in your bones, and it hurts. And we love it.

We are delighted to bring you this print edition of our first two years, beginning, of course, with a foreword by Mark Lawrence because, yes, all things do start with Mark Lawrence. I am happy to still be here at *GdM*, and I am even happier that you, our readers, are still here, stronger and more supportive than ever. Thank you for keeping *Grimdark Magazine* alive in this brutal world of words. We hope to continue to bring you the best in grimdark fiction. Now read on and get *Knee-Deep in Grit*.

Cheers,

Mike Myers
December, 2017

THE KING BENEATH THE WAVES

PETER FUGAZZOTTO

GdM #3

Werting could not break free.

The frigid sea held the boy, his feet churning, tired arms paddling. The rocky shore, so close, taunted him with every swell. His lame foot felt heavy as a stone.

Just as he was ready to give up, a wave lifted him. The water folded and he tumbled head over heels against sand and stone, grey sky replaced by a veil of bubbles and froth.

His hands dug at broken shells and shiny weed and he crawled out of the embrace of the sea. The water pulled at him but it could no longer drag him back. He would not join Hreoth and the long ship in the depths.

Blood and seawater dripped into a tide pool, disturbing the

reflection of his emaciated face, his pale hair, the gash across his forehead.

"Look, the little shit got spit out from the sea. Can't escape us that easy." Oslaf, the only one Werting wished would have drowned, shuffled across the sand. Behind the old man, six others that survived were stripping off sodden furs and breaches, hanging them from branches, and slapping bare skin. One of them gathered salvaged axes and shields in a pile.

"Get wood, Oslaf. You and the waif," said Roogar, his wet, greying beard clinging to the old scars on his chest. "We need fire or we'll die."

By the time the sun slashed orange across the horizon, Werting was finally dry enough that he no longer shook uncontrollably. Fat Henging had found a few mussels and they boiled them in Emod's shiny helmet. The young clan warrior grumbled that the helmet was a gift and it would be ruined.

Werting was still hungry but he knew better than to say anything.

"Hreoth was an idiot," said Emod, glancing in a small shard of mirror and smoothing his blonde beard. "Any fool could have seen the storm brewing. He should have stepped aside for someone whose eyes hadn't failed."

"Someone wearing a shiny helmet?" said Roogar. He sat with his sword on his lap, his whetstone singing.

"Why the fuck not?" Emod kicked the pile of discarded shells. "Three miserable months, village after village, and what? Copper coins and rusted axes."

"Don't forget Maeve." Fat Henging hid his snickering behind a fist. His red hair curled like flames.

"His fucking pet crow. Maybe it's better the fool sunk the ship. We go raiding and we return with a bird."

"No bird now," said Fat Henging.

Roogar shook his head. "Leave it. The man made a mistake. Elders should be respected."

Emod burst out laughing.

Dawn brought dark swirling skies and the eight survivors began plodding north on the shingle.

At first, the clansmen bunched together, laughing and telling stories, but as the day dragged and the rain returned in sudden squalls, they stretched along the beach.

Black clouds, piled thick, ate the sun.

The boy Werting with his lame foot brought up the rear. Ahead of him walking side-by-side were Roogar, Yrm, and Wulf, who had managed to swim to shore with his prized axe. Farther ahead shuffled old Oslaf, his mouth moving in silent curses. At the front marched Emod, his helmet shiny in the gloom, and at his heels Fat Henging and the baby-faced giant, Hrolf.

They were a four-day trudge from the river mouth. Then another two days to the clan village.

Werting wondered how far they were from his own village. If he ran south, would they come after him?

Werting's gaze drifted between the ragged sea and the dark wall of trees beyond the dunes.

Hreoth, the drowned captain, had been the one who kidnapped him. A seven-year old boy dragged from his house. His mother's screams piercing the laughter of the raiders. His last memory of the village, black smoke against a bright blue sky.

Werting stopped walking.

The other men stopped a quarter of a mile ahead when they noticed he was no longer with them. They shouted. They waved. They cursed.

Eventually, they sent Oslaf.

"You stupid little shit!"

Werting turned his head just enough that the blow caught him on the skull rather than his ear.

"Making me walk back to get you."

The sea slid around the boy's ankles. The tide had pulled back exposing writhing sand crabs.

"I should break your other foot."

Werting remembered that day. He had thought that they would not come after him. He was no prize—a malnourished, undersized boy. But his captors had sent Oslaf. When the old man caught up with him in the pines, he smashed Werting's foot with a stone to keep him from running. Returning to the village, Oslaf said the boy had fallen, and was lucky that trusty Oslaf had found him.

Werting and Oslaf were almost caught up to the others when Werting stopped and pointed. From beneath the waves, a ring-whorled prow jutted out of the black waters. A once-golden banner sloughed from the mast.

Yrm squinted across the clapping waves. "A boat of the Spear People. Ruined now."

"Hidden by the tides," said Roogar. He unbelted his sword and pulled off his boots. "I'll see what bounty she holds."

"We'll all see," said Emod, also quickly shedding his clothes.

"I'll watch the gear," said Henging.

"You, too, boy," said Roogar to Werting. "You come help me." Then the scarred warrior was in the waves, wading towards the old shipwrecked vessel.

The boy had his shirt pulled over his head when he heard Emod whispering to Henging. "Acts like the boy's his servant now. Thinks he's captain now. Another old fool to sink the next boat."

The fat man chuckled. "Out with the old. I'll raise my sword for you. Follow you far into the night."

Werting was the last to unclothe. Roogar and Emod had already reached the boat. The others were nearly there. The water slapped Werting's shins. He turned to Henging. The fat man was slipping slimy kelp into Wulf's oversized boots. He lifted a conspiratorial finger to his lips.

Despite the retreat of the tide, when the boy reached the boat, the water was at chest level.

The wood of the prow was sea blackened, mottled with mussels. From beyond the shoals, it would have looked like a rock along the shore. When the tide was fully in, the boat would have been completely submerged except for the mast.

The raiders stood on the boat, laughing and shouting.

Werting pulled himself onto the deck.

Hrolf stood over a chest split by Wulf's axe, spreading a chain mail tunic between his hands. "Look at this, boys."

Roogar hefted a sword in his hand, sighting the line of the blade. "After all these years and it still shines."

The others hacked open the remaining chests. Bladed weapons, coats of arms, and war tack. Yrm's hand emerged from a leather sack, fat coins leaking between his fingers.

Oslaf hoisted an iron knife, its wooden hilt covered in ornate runes, and gambolled from foot to foot. "Look at this beauty!"

Roogar slapped the knife out of the old man's hand. It rattled on the deck then slid past Werting into the dark waters, the heavy iron head dragging it down.

Roogar drove a thick finger into Oslaf's chest. "The plunder is for the men of the Shark Clan, not for slaves."

The clan warriors sprawled on the beach in a loose circle. When they had discovered barrels of mead in the hold, they decided the rest of their loot was not going anywhere.

Werting returned to the fire with an armload of branches scavenged from the forest floor. The woods were dark and cold, a place where the sun rarely warmed the spongy earth. He wondered how the trees did not topple, rising from such rot.

Oslaf squatted among the warriors. They had dressed him up in a woman's fur robe and embroidered slippers taken from one of the chests. A blow from Emod had quelled his protests.

"The bounty of the fucking gods," Roogar howled, dribbling mead into his grey beard.

The others raised their cups.

"Getting hungry," said Henning, his hands spread over his ample belly.

"More lovely seaweed and mussel soup," chimed Hrolf.

"As long as the young king of the world doesn't mind us using his helmet." Yrm sneered.

Emod belched. "Boy, come get my bucket."

Werting came to his side, brushing splinters from his hands.

"Sit, boy!" Emod's breath seeped of sweet honey. "I'll let you prove yourself," he hissed into Werting's ear. "When I lead the clan, any who prove their worth will be one of us. Learn to wield a blade, drive a ship through the breakers. Even you. An equal. The old ways have to go."

"Stop your lover's whispers," said Henning. "Send the boy for mussels. My belly is rumbling."

The sea had receded. Midnight blue crabs skittered around the exposed rocks and the air stank from stranded seaweed. Where the retreating wash collided with the waves, the water hissed. Werting's bad foot ached deep in the bone. The old witch told him it might mend, but he doubted it. Oslaf had crippled him for life.

He would never escape.

Icy water swirled around his waist. The mussels held fast to the hull of the boat. Werting's fingers bled with the effort of prying them free. Then he remembered the iron knife that Roogar had slapped out of Oslaf's hand.

The low tide exposed the vessel, nearly to where the dark wood had splintered on the rocks. He climbed onto the deck and searched. The iron knife rested against a large unopened wooden chest that had been beneath the sea when the clansmen were looting.

The knife was heavy. He swiped at the air, then jabbed. In his mind, he saw the Shark clansmen, his iron knife plunging between ribs and slashing throats. He scraped the blade against the deck and a mussel peeled off. It clanged into the bottom of the helm. Would they take the knife from him when he got back? Emod might let him keep it.

Most likely Oslaf would smack Werting and snatch the weapon.

Oslaf should have been nicer. He too had been stolen from his village.

Werting plunged the knife into the wooden chest imagining it was Oslaf. Then he could not yank it loose.

A shout pulled his gaze to the shore. Roogar was waving him back and rubbing his belly. Emod was kicking Oslaf as the old man stripped bare and stepped into the sea. Even from this distance, Werting could see curses pouring from his lips.

The boy grabbed the knife with two hands and worked it back and forth. Then without warning the chest popped open.

A body lay in the chest, submerged in sea water.

It was a man with a braided beard, hands crossed over his heart, silver rings on his long fingers. He wore a fine chainmail jerkin that trailed to his broad thighs. He appeared to be about the age of Roogar. His eyes were closed, his smooth, white skin like ivory.

On his head he wore a simple gold band with a large red gem set in the middle and a helix of embedded pearls running its length.

Time and water had not touched him.

Werting imagined that he must have been a king and this was the vessel in which his followers launched him out alone over the waves. Maybe he should just leave things alone. He could set the lid back on the chest.

But he wanted, if even for a moment, to wear the crown of a king and imagine that he was free.

He slipped the crown from the king's wet, grey hair.

The king's eyelids lifted. Werting jumped back.

The king's lips parted. His pale bloodless flesh peeled back in strips, to chin and brow. The skin and muscle disintegrated, clouding the water.

Then the water cleared. Where the king once lay, a skeleton grinned.

Werting's breath caught high in his throat. Then a blow knocked him to his knees. Oslaf tore the crown from the boy's hands. The old man climbed to the prow, waving the treasure, shouting to the others to come see what he found for them.

It was Hrolf's turn to try on the crown.

"Ho, ho, ho, look at me. I'm the King Beneath the Waves." The crown perched askew on greasy strands of blonde hair. "I was a great king, but then I died. And my boat sunk."

Werting huddled close to the fire. The stars hid behind clouds. A line of surging white waves crashed against the sand.

"That was inspired." Yrm smirked. "Let Roogar have a turn."

"I'll have plenty of time later to wear it," said Roogar.

Emod snickered.

Hrolf trotted with the crown on his head, pausing in front of

Oslaf. "Old timer's turn."

The crown sunk over Oslaf's skull catching on the tops of his big ears.

"Go on, tell us about the King Beneath the Waves," demanded Hrolf.

Oslaf unfolded from the sand. He adjusted the crown but no matter what he did, it hung at an angle, a shimmering slash against his brow.

"The King Beneath the Waves!" shouted Hrolf over his cup.

Oslaf spit into the fire. "No King Beneath the Waves when this crown sits on my head. Oslaf, first son of Osleuw, scourge of the Ragged Coast, ring giver, boon to his men. No line of kings. Men of the axe and spear we turned back the night. Chiefs knelt at my father's feet, pressed their foreheads to his hand. We ruled the Ragged Coast as was our right.

"Until the treachery of the Shark Clan, the lies, the gift of death. I still hear the screams of my father from the flames of the long house."

Emod cuffed the old man's head sending him and the crown to the shingle. "The strong eat the weak." He kicked Oslaf in the side so hard that bone cracked. The young warrior plucked the crown from the dark sand. "They should have speared you that day. A blight you have been, slave."

"Let Roogar have a turn," Yrm hissed.

Emod scoffed. "Game's over. Old bastard's ruined all the fun. It's late and tomorrow will be a long day hauling our find north."

He settled against a driftwood log, laying the crown on a shield salvaged from the wreck.

Werting curled close to the fire. He tried to sleep but a cold wind licked his neck and his foot surged with pain. The flames of the dying fire flickered in the eyes of the men and a line of light pulsed along the crown. Finally exhaustion swept over him and he slept.

Werting woke to whispers.

"Thinks he's more than he is."

"We can always cut him down to size."

"I'll cut his fucking throat."

Embers rippled orange in the fire. The stench of rotten fish rode on a jolting breeze. Werting's clothes hung damp, the cold soaking to his bones.

He tugged a salvaged sailcloth closer around his shoulders and fell back asleep.

Waves thundered so hard that they woke him again. Stars flickered through a gash in the clouds.

"You can't trust the bastard. He's coming for you."

A grunt.

"Out here who will know? The crabs and the gulls?"

Werting woke to a cramp in his foot. Would dawn never come?

A whisper. "Men of axes and spears. Knelt at my father's feet."
It was Oslaf's voice.

Werting drifted as if the tides carried him away.

The sky had paled but the sea was still black, oddly silent, caught between the pull of the tides. Werting knew it would not last.

"You, of all people, accusing me." Roogar stood over the dead fire, hands clenching his leather belt. The sky was grey, the sun smothered in clouds.

"Where's the fucking crown?" Emod dug at the sand around the pilfered shield. He stopped and pointed a finger at Roogar, Yrm and Wulf. "One of you snuck over last night and took it."

Roogar laughed. "Couldn't it have been Henging or Hrolf?

Or one of the slaves?"

Hrolf scratched his head. "I didn't see nothing last night. Too dark. Plus my eyes were closed."

"Is your head hollow?" snarled Yrm.

Big Wulf rose and cracked his neck left and right. His axe hung heavy between his slack arms. "Why make a big deal out of nothing? We didn't have the crown before yesterday. If I find it, I chop it into six pieces, one for each of us."

With those words, he lifted his axe and drove it down, shearing one of the driftwood logs in half.

A sudden gust swirled the ash from the fire pit. Werting covered his eyes with his forearm. Then rain came in icy pellets.

"Enough," said Emod. "Grab what you can carry and we'll bring a ship back for the rest."

The men quickly layered themselves in armor, stacked their shoulders with shields and spears, and hoisted bags of coin.

It was all going well until Wulf stepped into his boot.

He screamed as he ripped out a foot covered in rotten kelp.

Fat Henging bent over laughing.

Wulf's arms arced, axe in hand, and cleaved Henging from neck to shoulder.

Werting stumbled, hands tearing at the sand, heels digging to scuttle away.

One of the spears from the king's boat, old, heavy, and iron tipped, flew from Hrolf's hand and Wulf staggered, fists wrapped around the rune-carved shaft. He twirled and fell into the sand.

His face landed next to Werting's. Wulf's eyes rolled, white then blue. "Tell her." He cleared his throat over and over and then coughed a bloody glob on the sand.

Werting scrambled away.

The clansmen stood wide-legged, swords pointing. They

clustered—Roogar and Yrm shoulder to shoulder, and Hrolf to Emod. The only sound was the heaving of their breaths.

Werting rolled behind one of the driftwood logs and crouched. His hand closed around the iron knife.

The clansmen circled the fire pit, the rain pinging off helmet and shield.

Oslaf too had hidden behind one of the logs, spitting sand from his lips. It sounded as if he were laughing.

Roogar spoke first. "Never content to be in your place."

Emod answered. "You can't have what isn't earned."

"Doesn't have to end this way, boy. Put your tail between your legs, give back the crown, and we'll forget about all this."

Emod laughed and then spat on the beach at Roogar's feet.

They paced in a circle, swords wagging, eyes sharp.

Then Emod had enough.

He kicked up sand and charged. He went for the smaller and older Yrm, leaving Roogar to deal with the giant Hrolf. But Yrm was not as fragile as Emod had hoped. Yrm dodged to the left, and Emod's sword clanged against his raised shield.

Roogar wasted no time in charging at Hrolf. The baby-faced giant back pedalled, unintelligible words slipping from his smiling lips. Roogar came in hard, sword arcing over his shoulder.

Werting could see the path of the sword and imagined raising his own weapon overhead to block the blow. As soon as Roogar's sword made contact with Hrolf's raised blade, the wily veteran kicked the giant just below his breastbone. Then they were tangled.

Oslaf dragged himself along the sand, a trench marking his path. His icy fingers peeled at Werting's arm. "Watch them kill themselves. Our day will come. All these years of suffering."

Werting tore himself from the old man's clawing hands.

Wiping the rain from his eyes, he watched the two pairs of

battling men: lips snarling, glistening teeth, the screech of metal, sand billowing around shuffling feet, a scream, a sword dropping, the spray of blood, a knife in a fist, the pounding of flesh, cracked lips whispering a prayer into another's ear.

Only two remained: Roogar, one ear half torn from his bloody scalp, and Emod, drops of bloody rain gathering in his smooth golden beard like rubies.

The warriors circled, kicking sand, flicking swords, and tossing curses.

"I'll eat your heart." Tears dripped down Roogar's cheeks. A stain of blood seeped from his gut and down his thigh. "All this for what?"

"Your days are done, old man."

Roogar spit blood. He stumbled, sword wavering, the point dropping to the sand then lifting.

Emod shook his head. "This day."

Oslaf jeered from behind the log. Werting hunkered down next to him.

The next time Roogar stumbled Emod charged, screaming as his weapon slashed downwards. Roogar lifted his sword diagonally over his head with both hands, his left supporting the blade. Emod's sword sheared metal and Roogar's fingers flew into the sand.

Roogar screamed, reversed his blade in his good hand, spinning it around his head and cut hard into Emod's exposed neck, sending the young clansman crumbling to the sand.

Roogar stepped on Emod's chest to pull free his blade. He lost his hold on the blood-slick grip and fell hard on his back. He lifted his hand. Blood pulsed out of the stumps of his fingers.

"Oslaf, a binding cloth." His other hand fished around the wound in his belly and came out dripping with blood. "Hurry now."

The old man tottered around the log and knelt beside the fallen warrior.

"I won't forget this, slave."

Oslaf smiled wide, his thin hair heavy with the weight of the rain. The old slave straddled Roogar's chest, knees pinning arms, and squeezed the fallen man's throat.

The rain cracked against the flat black sea.

Oslaf dragged Werting by the wrist into the cold waters. "Took it while they slept."

The boy's lame foot clipped a stone beneath the rising sea. He bit his lip to conceal his curses.

"Thought one or two of them would survive." Oslaf laughed into the swirl of clouds. "All these years biding my time. I've spit in their food. Gnawed holes in their shirts. Sand in their boots."

"Let me go," said Werting, jerking his arm. The grip on his wrist constricted, so tight that he felt the bones might snap.

"We're free now. Don't you see?"

They reached the black-hulled boat. Water lapped at its hull. The tide had not yet reached the high mark.

"I hid the crown where we found it. We'll be rich, boy."

Oslaf led him to the submerged chest. The old man gave a toothy grin, then ducked beneath the waves.

The rising sun, pale but sneaking out from the thickest of the clouds, transformed the ocean into a mirror, and Werting saw himself, a boy, tousled hair, freckled, still unshaped, a boy who could become anything.

Oslaf broke the surface, the crown held aloft, and jerked to a stop.

His smile vanished. "Take the crown, boy. My foot's caught."

The band of gold was heavy in Werting's hand, as if it fought to return beneath the waves.

Oslaf ducked down and then emerged again. His eyes bulged. Water ran from his nose and mouth. "Give me the iron knife. The planks are like stone."

The boy stepped back towards the prow of the boat.

"Werting. The knife!"

Dark strands swirled through the ceiling of clouds. A squall descended battering the shivering boy with icy rain and wind.

"Give me that fucking knife, boy."

The tide climbed the hull.

"Werting, my little friend, please."

Hours later, when the sun began to descend, Werting slid down the deck and stared into the waters. Oslaf's eyes were wide open and a minnow peered out of his gaping mouth. Werting's own reflection wavered over him. They looked nothing alike.

Then the boy looked down at the chest. The skeleton of the king rested beneath the waves. Werting took a deep breath and ducked into the frigid, dark waters.

As he placed the crown back on the skull, he saw flesh returning to the king's face, his beard sprouting, and his eyelids closing.

Werting did not linger.

Instead, he dove off the deck and swam towards the shore, the sea unable to hold him back.

THE LINE

T·R· NAPPER

GdM #2

T his is going to hurt."

George held the goateed man in an arm-bar, face down on the canvas. The man managed to turn his head to one side and gasp, "No."

George bent down, easing the strain on the arm for a moment. Sweat rolled down his brow, from the tip of his nose onto the man's back. He whispered, "Yes."

"BREAKER…BREAKER…BREAKER…"

The waves of the chant broke across his concentration. The floodlights centred on the cage burned his eyes. But beyond, in the twilight of the stadium, he could see it was packed, as usual. Most had come straight from work, wearing the red and fluorescent yellow coveralls of the operators, or the blue and yellow of the mine technicians. There were a smattering of brown faces in the crowd, but that mob usually stayed away from fight night. Understandable. Emotions always got a little high by the end.

In the front row were the dark-suited executives, on their feet with the rest of the crowd, punching their fists in the air. A glassteel partition separated their comfortable faux leather seats from the plastic provided to the rest of the crowd. The redhead—Langer— was there of course, in his regular front-row spot, his white shirt soaked through with sweat. He pointed his rust-red akubra at George's opponent, bringing it up and down, like he was trying to break the man's arm himself.

George shook his head against the noise, against the heat of the room. The air conditioners were on full blast, but five thousand sweating, jostling bodies made the atmosphere dense, inescapable.

George looked down at his opponent.

Fight Night couldn't end with a submission. One fighter had to be unconscious, incapacitated, or dead. George ended most fights by breaking his opponent's arm. The Corporation gave a medical exemption for injuries received on Fight Night, fixed the fighter free of charge. Even used nanotech to knit the bones, have them back at work in a couple of days. A break was the easy way out. Merciful even.

Except for this moment.

George levered the arm until he felt the snap vibrate through his hands, sharp and final. He let the limb drop. The goateed man writhed on the canvas, clutching at his elbow.

George stood to his full height, his lean muscles coated with sweat. He looked around at the crowd, faces all in shadow.

"BREAKER...BREAKER...BREAKER..."

The tumult grew; they chanted his name over and again. George didn't acknowledge them. He walked to the side of the cage.

His corner man passed him a towel and water bottle over the top.

"Too easy."

George drank deeply then handed the bottle back. "Yes."

He mopped his face with the towel and waited for the announcer to make it official. Then he walked over to the steel gate. It clicked open. He ducked his head as he stepped out. Two fighters, stripped to the waist, waited to enter for the next bout. George moved quickly up the stairs between the stands, away from the cage. The crowd reached out to him, patted him on the back, called out his name. He let the sound wash over him. The hands he brushed aside.

The Cochlear Glyph implant behind his left ear—silent during the bout—started broadcasting as soon as he left the cage. As he glanced up at the giant scoreboard above the stands, the c-glyph whispered the odds for the next fight. When he looked away, the feed switched to the murmurs of the commentators discussing the match. The only time the implant was silent was in the ring. How he looked forward to those rare minutes, when the itching in his mind finally ceased.

George made his way to the change room and sat heavily on a hard-plastic bench. He held out his arm while his corner man undid the bindings on his fist.

"Know what that fight was, George?"

"I wouldn't really call it a fight."

Burgess smiled. He had a round face. Pleasant, some would say, if not for the tell-tale redness of his neck and bloodshot eyes. "Not many would." He threw the first wrap away and begun work on the second. "That victory made you the most successful cage fighter in the free zones."

"Is that so?"

"They've been talking about it through the Interwave all week." Burgess tapped his finger behind his left ear, against his own c-glyph implant. "Haven't you been watching? You certainly can't help listening to it."

"I've learned to tune it out."

His corner man laughed. "No wonder you're still sane." He paused, pulling a small capsule out of his shirt pocket. "Different strokes."

George pointed his chin at the pill. "That shit will rot your brain."

"Probably." Burgess shrugged. "But what difference does it make here?"

"All the difference in the world."

Burgess raised his eyebrows. "Really? I'm not the one spending all my spare time getting kicked in the head."

George smiled. "I'll kick you in the head free of charge. You'll get the same result as that shit," he pointed at the powder, "and save yourself some money."

Burgess returned the smile. "And you wonder why you don't have any friends."

"I never wonder. Friends are a liability."

"So is having broken the arm of half the people you work with."

George grunted. "Ha. True enough, true enough."

His corner-man cracked the capsule between his teeth, closing his eyes for a few moments. When he opened them again he seemed to find it hard to focus. "This can't last forever George."

"What?"

Burgess scratched the side of his face slowly, pointed vaguely at the room. "This."

George looked at his fist, flexing it. "Yeah. I know, Burgess. I know."

George sat alone at one of the long tables in the mess hall. A score of rows were in the hall. Each could seat more than a hundred. The morning diners moved around him quickly, ate quickly, departed quickly. No one wanted to be late. In the distance were the cyclical tunes and bells of the slot machines.

George took a bite of corn bread and scooped some beans. He grunted. Not much flavour in either. The entertainment screen built into the breakfast counter murmured at him through his implant. He ignored it. The endless stories of imminent war bored him. He didn't want to look at the betting markets either: the line on live female births next year in Sichuan Province, or the line on soya tonnage harvested in Hunan for June. Nor was he interested in placing a few credits on the temperature range down in Perth on the next Wednesday, or the odds of rain falling in the Free Economic Zone any time in the next six months. Weather investments weren't his thing. None of the markets were for that matter. All except for one. Fight Night.

George tapped the scratched touchscreen, flicking past the markets and newsfeeds until he found the icon for solitaire. George was halfway through his second game when three ascending tones sounded in his ear. The voice of the c-glyph, flat and uninflected, followed. "Probationary Citizen George Duulngari. You are required at an executive meeting in the gaming hall in three minutes."

George glanced down at the time-stamp on the counter screen. "If I do that, I'll be late for my shift."

"Your shift has been cancelled, courtesy of Vice President Langer."

George raised an eyebrow. "The redhead himself? I'm honoured."

"An understandable reaction."

George returned to tapping his finger on the solitaire game, sipping at a cup filled with a thin, bitter liquid they insisted on calling coffee.

After a minute: "Mister Duulngari. Why are you not proceeding to your meeting?"

George indicated the entertainment screen with his hand. "Just savouring my day off."

The c-glyph Artificial Intelligence couldn't see him gesture, of course, just force of habit. He'd never got used to having conversations with voices inside his head since arriving in the zones.

"For every minute you are late to a meeting with an executive, you will be given a productivity penalty," said the voice, with the rhythm of a metronome.

"Cheers. You're very efficient."

"Efficiency is productivity's midwife," quoted the voice.

"So is the whip."

The usual response from the AI when perplexed by a statement was to act as if it hadn't heard it—pretty human in that regard as well. "You are now one minute late for your meeting. A productivity penalty has been applied to this quarter's pay."

George sighed and stood, wiping his mouth on his sleeve.

The sound of the slots was deafening as he entered the large archway at the rear of the cafeteria. Five thousand machines spewed sound and fury into the dark, cavernous hall. To one side of the door, an image of Langer shimmered into life. He was half a head shorter than George, and nearly a full body wider. He wore his usual tailored black suit and rust-red akubra. His trousers were a couple of inches too high, the grin on his face a little too wide.

"Breaker, so glad you could join me."

George walked over. "Are you a projection of the actual Langer, or are you one of his day copies?"

The simulation of the man shrugged. "Not relevant. If you're speaking to me, you're speaking to Langer. We carry the same authority."

"So you're a day copy."

The too wide grin was shortening. "The vice president receives a download directly from his day copies every twenty-four hours, summarizing all our decisions. In the five years he has been in his position, he is yet to change or even question one of those decisions."

George looked him up and down. "They certainly feed you well in the executive."

Langer's eyes flashed. "You want to play it that way," he said. "That suits me fine. I'm here to discuss business, not enjoy the stellar conversational skills of a cage fighter." He pointed at one of the aisles between the slots. "Let's walk."

The vice president moved into the gloom. George hesitated for a moment before falling into step.

"You're the most successful fighter in the history of the free zones, Breaker," he said, though his tone didn't make it sound like a compliment.

George said nothing.

"You've become something of a legend here in Free Zone Three. But this success has its consequences. The odds for your fights have left you almost unbackable these days. Pretty soon no-one left will bet on you."

"I will."

Langer nodded, but not in agreement. "Sure. I've seen your record, same as everyone. You've made good money on yourself, especially at the start. But these days you face diminishing returns." He stopped, lifted his akubra up with one hand and wiped a gleam of sweat on his forehead with a white handkerchief.

He pointed at George with a closed fist. "How'd you like to make some real money?"

George winced and started moving again down the aisle. Rows upon rows of faces, brown and white, sat at the machines with eyes glazed. Or closed. The players held one thumb out, pressed on a glowing red pad on the front of the slot, making the reels spin and spin again. George felt a tugging on his implant as he passed each machine, each one reaching out, asking him to play: the familiar ache returning for a moment.

Here in the hall, if he closed his eyes the nanos attached to his optic nerves would activate. A perfect, three dimensional image of each machine would appear in the darkness behind his eyelids. A few lines of script would provide the current jackpot on the machine, the comps accrued from playing. A woman, chosen by complex algorithm to appeal to George's tastes, would sit smiling in front of the glittering, hypnotic pattern of the wheels. The vision of the room would be crystal clear, clean and bright, with smiling patrons and carpet that didn't stick to the soles of the shoe. No wonder so many played with their eyes closed.

George waved a hand at the banks of machines. "This was all I did when I first arrived, got into it real quick. But that's the way the Corporation set it all up, right? It's just this or the dope."

Langer placed his handkerchief back in the top pocket of his jacket. "We're in the middle of the desert. People need to be entertained."

George stared straight ahead as he walked. "I'd work twelve hours, come back and play for four more, then collapse into my bunk. I'd wake up in the morning and my implant would be urging me to play. I'd see the slots behind my eyelids, floating, waiting. But I didn't need any encouragement: I'd always get an hour in before work. I could never stop thinking about it when I wasn't playing and I never wanted to stop when I'd started. It got to the point where winning or losing didn't matter anymore. Even though, of course, I was losing everything. In the first two years here I never slept with a woman, got in a fight, or popped an ice-nine."

Langer shrugged, glancing over the machines as they passed. "This isn't a nanny state. People's personal choices are their own."

George stopped and looked at the man. "Then it got really bad. I went at it for three days straight, lost for three days straight. Missing work. I couldn't distinguish between playing the slots and dreaming about them. What was real, what was imagined. So exhausted I had some sort of seizure, thrashing around on the floor until they sedated me and put me in the infirmary. I remember how the Corporation gave me a few days off to 'recuperate.' You know where your mob sent me?" George clenched his fists, his knuckles cracking.

Langer's eyes had glazed over. "I don't know where we send the addicts and the weak. And I really don't care."

"You piece of shit!" George threw the punch he had wanted to throw for six years, his fist driving into Langer's face. His hand, of course, passed clean through, hitting the face of the slot behind. The machine rocked, a crack appearing across the screen.

Though a simulation, Langer jumped back a step, mouth parted in surprise. George stepped close, his voice low. "You gave me a free hotel room. At a casino in the rec-quad: a fucking casino." He pointed a bloodied fist at Langer. "You want me to throw the fight?"

The surprise had already slipped Langer's face. His eyes went hard, like water over smooth stone. "In the third minute of the second round."

"Why? Hope Corporation owns every slot machine in the free zone, half your workers go broke on them before their contracts are up, and then you own them, too. You are the book for Fight Night. So you're winning every time I win anyway. You don't need the money. Even a big score on this fight is trivial, for the Corporation."

"Nothing is trivial, here."

"What does that mean? Why this fight?"

Langer looked him over, eyes shining in the reflected glow of the machines. It really was a very good day copy. "I might be a vice president, Breaker, but in the end I'm just a company man. I'm a company man because I always put the Corporation first. It'd be smart to show everyone that you can too."

"Yeah, it would," said George, looking down at his hand. One of his knuckles was split and bleeding.

There are a hundred types of pain in the world; it's impossible to avoid them all. As far as George could figure, the only choice you had about it was which one you'd embrace. He looked up. "Here's your answer. Fuck you."

Langer shook his head, eyes gleaming under the shadow of the akubra. "Just wait until I find out about this. You've made a very big mistake."

"Wouldn't be my first." George turned and walked away.

When they pulled the bag from his head the light blinded him. He coughed, barely able to breathe in the heat and thin red dust. His body ached from where they had beaten him with their force batons. After they had dragged him from his bunk, late at night, and set upon him.

Behind him stood a half-dozen security personnel, black sentinels silhouetted against the maddening heat. A second figure stood directly next to George. As his eyes adjusted to the light he saw it was Burgess. One side of the corner man's round face was swollen, his bottom lip split. He smiled weakly. "You might be right about that 'liability' thing."

Less than a metre in front of them, the edge of the yawning chasm of the Great Yandi Pit: one kilometre deep, maybe five wide. The wind whipped at their clothes, pulling at them, beckoning them toward the abyss. A black Humvee rested nearby on the crushed red rock. The door slid open. Inside sat the vice president, in the flesh. He held the akubra in his hands. He seemed to be adjusting the brim.

"I'm asking you twice: lose your next fight, George."

George's voice came out in a croak. "Not going to happen."

Langer looked up, nodded at the guards. One stepped forward and brought his force rod down on the back of Burgess' head.

George turned. "No."

Burgess pitched forward. He was looking at George with bloodshot eyes when they struck him. He seemed surprised. His mouth was open, trying to speak.

George looked after him as he disappeared into the depths of the pit. His chest heaved. It felt like he was choking. "Motherfucker."

"Why, yes. Yes I am," said Langer.

George tried to speak, but let out a sob. He fell to his knees.

The redhead watched him from the cool shadow of the vehicle. "Really, George? That's all it takes? One dead drug-addict? Maybe you're not the man I thought you were."

George coughed, cleared his throat. The ground was warm under his knees, the sun stinging the back of his neck. "You're the one sitting behind ten men. Come over here, little man. Come over here and I'll show you who I am."

Langer smiled. "That's more like it. You'll need to bring some of that to the ring for your next fight. But not too much." He turned and swung his legs over the side of the seat, so he was facing George, "We have a problem, Breaker. It's the audience. The punters, the…" he gestured with his left hand, "the people. They love you. And fear you. These are powerful things, powerful emotions. The problem as I see it is this: you didn't earn these things by yourself—far from it. You're a freeloader. You've manipulated our system. The one we invented, built, and paid for. An operation like this, like Hope Corporation, isn't an accident. It's a work of art. You see, what you're doing, by using the system to your own advantage, is taking us for a ride. And there are no free rides here in Hope Corporation. The user pays."

The vice president ran one finger along the brim of the akubra. "This law is immutable. The user always pays."

George watched him in silence.

"So you'll throw this fight," he pointed at the pit with his hat. "Or you'll follow your friend. And if we do have to put you in, well...everyone will think you're just another jumper who couldn't take the heat, the desert, and the time. Another brown stain baking at the bottom of the Yandi, soon forgotten. We win either way."

The redhead placed the akubra on his brow carefully. "So, what's your answer?"

George closed his eyes for a half a minute. When he opened them, he looked at the place where Burgess had been standing.

He slowly got to his feet. "I'll take the fight."

He'd drunk hard after Yandi. Missed work, knowing they wouldn't care. Wouldn't dock his pay. Wouldn't say a thing. And he played again. Yeah, he played. Six years of living clean, saving his pay, betting on himself on Fight Night. A small fortune.

In three weeks it was all gone. The last of his liabilities sunk into the slots.

So when he stood, finally, in front of the tumult, he felt light as air.

"BREAKER...BREAKER...BREAKER..."

The crowd was as big, as loud as it had ever been.

A fighter with a heavy jaw looked at him through slitted eyes. He moved forward slowly across the canvas, watching George from behind two large fists.

George stood, arms by his sides, watching the man. He smiled a small smile.

The man paused, lowered his fists slightly. "What? What are you grinning at?"

"This is going to hurt."

AT THE WALLS OF SINNLOS

MICHAEL R· FLETCHER

GdM #6

I rode at the Captain's side, sweat pooling in the folds of my fat and soaking my shirt. I watched him from the corner of my eye. He sat slumped in the saddle, his once crisp, blue uniform crimson with the blood-red dust of the Sinnlos Desert. My heart broke and I had to look away. His parents had died the day we rode from Grauschloss, slain in the Theocrat's latest cull of the old-guard families. Their lands and holdings confiscated, the Captain's entire family were hung in the traitors' cages to starve and rot. We'd ridden past them as we left the city; he hadn't spared them a glance. He dared not. Had they not disowned him when he'd joined the ranks of the Theocrat's army, he would have shared their fate. But years of impeccable service did not lift him above suspicion. Trust is something the Theocrat commands and demands, not something he gives. I couldn't help but think the Captain had been sent to Sinnlos to die. I knew why I was here but dared not share that truth. My silence felt like betrayal.

I knew the Captain's sins as he knew my own. Sometimes I think our friendship was based on that knowledge more than anything else. How could either of us judge the other without condemning ourselves? Not that we didn't condemn ourselves. Far from it. Much as I loved him, *I* was contemptible. Beyond redemption.

Belief defines reality, and the beliefs of the deranged can be truly dangerous. We, the broken, could believe something so utterly it altered reality. The mental instability that was my source of power made me the ruin of a man I am today. The Theocrat found use in that ruin. He fed that ruin, reminding me of my crimes, fuelling my self-hatred, to make use of the manifestations rising from my insanity. In those moments when I was not in sway to his power, I loathed the man. I wanted to punish him for his casual manipulation of my emotions.

I wanted to *burn*.

The rest of the time I loved and worshipped him. It made thoughts of treason difficult. Almost impossible.

The Captain's horse looked more depressed than its rider, who examined the blackened fingertips of his left hand as he rode through the blowing bloody dust. The once proud warhorse dragged hooves that seemed too heavy to lift. Its back sagged where it had previously been ramrod straight. Its saddle and skirt were caked red with sand and horse sweat and chafed the poor beast's sides raw.

Behind us strode a platoon of Dysmorphics, massive parodies of physical perfection. Muscular arms and legs, thicker than many trees, pumped in perfect unison as they kept pace with our exhausted horses. Watching their eyes dart as they measured themselves against their comrades, I imagined their thoughts: *Are his arms bigger than mine? Is my left leg more muscled than my right? Do I look lopsided? I'll have to work on that when we break for camp tonight.*

Small minds in big bodies. At least that's what I told myself. It was unfair that they might manage such bodies and intelligence while I fell well short of brilliance and was both fat and ugly.

These men weren't under the Captain's command; they merely followed us as we marched to meet with the army already surrounding Sinnlos. Unlike myself, the Captain had left Grauschloss with a distinct lack of orders. My own orders were twofold. I was to spy upon my only friend, watch for signs of disloyalty, and deal with him should the need arise. Finally, if all else failed, I was to turn my Hassebrand powers against the Empress of Sinnlos.

But I had plans of my own.

The Empress was the one person who could challenge the Theocrat's iron grip on the hearts and minds of his subjects. As long as she lived the Theocrat would know he wasn't untouchable and that fear would temper his choices and actions.

I think the Theocrat wanted the Captain to fail this test. Or was this a test of my own loyalty?

I ran a hand across my bald pate and through its greasy fringe, all that remained of my black hair. My hand came away dripping sweat and gritty with russet sand.

"Captain?"

For a moment I thought he hadn't heard me as he continued to stare at his fingertips. Finally he looked up, turning lifeless grey eyes in my direction.

"Yes?"

I nodded at the hand he held before him. "Is that…" I couldn't finish the question. The Captain had been depressed for so long I could barely remember what he used to be like. I had long worried he might become suicidal.

"I think so," he said, his voice devoid of emotion.

"Oh," I said. "Is that…everything?"

"So far." He rubbed fingertips with a greying thumb. "I'm numb." He twitched the hint of a smile. "*It's* numb," he corrected.

"Oh." What else could I say? That I was sorry? What good would that do? Could I offer him my love and support?

I opened my mouth to extend what comfort I could and the Captain turned away. He gestured forward with blackened fingertips. "Sinnlos. We'll reach the wall by nightfall."

I squinted through the swirling sands and made out the towering walls. Not surprising I hadn't noticed them; they were the same gods-awful red as the blowing sands.

I had been right, the Captain was suicidal. What I hadn't foreseen was how that desire would manifest. He didn't merely desire death—he craved the punishment implicit in a slow, rotting death. The Captain, whom I once would have sworn was a pillar of sanity, was a Cotardist. He'd surrendered all hope and was decaying before my very eyes. I swallowed my helpless anger.

I dared no unchecked emotion.

I had wondered if the Captain regretted abandoning his family to serve the Theocrat.

I had my answer.

Behind us the Dysmorphics sang songs of blood and plunder, stomping and clapping in time to their chants. They too had spotted the distant walls. Their songs failed to lift my spirit. Judging from the grim look on the Captain's face they didn't do much for him either. Behind those towering walls lurked the Empress of Sinnlos, a Delusionist of great power. How would her delusions manifest?

When all else failed, when armies lay shattered and dead, I would be called to face her, the Delusionist Empress of Sinnlos. Me. Gehirn Schlechtes, Hassebrand of the Theocrat's cadre of the dangerous and deranged. If my will held strong I would turn my back upon my Theocrat and do what I must to keep her alive. Then and only then would I allow myself emotion.

And I would burn the Theocrat's army.

For two months the Theocrat hurled troops at Sinnlos.

No new orders came for us and I stalked the camp at the Captain's side, sweat soaking my robes in comic juxtaposition to his dust-stiffened uniform. The dark stain of rot on the fingers of his left hand spread past the second knuckle.

I watched the Theocrat's army dwindle as countless lives were thrown against the red wall and once again swell as replacements arrived. The Dysmorphics were never called forward and remained in their own separate camp. So many Dysmorphics in one place, it could be no mistake or coincidence.

The Dysmorphics were an inhuman force.

They would be ash in the wind.

The Captain and I took our meals together, the only real human interaction I had. Sometimes he would fumble with his fork before cursing and passing it to his healthy right hand. Raised in a family of wealth and privilege, this minor breach of etiquette pained him beyond all reason. Once he paused in mid-meal to stare down at the chipped plate.

I sat across the table, shovelling army gruel—a mash of fried beans and what might have been goat—into my face. "Sand gets in everything, eh?" I said between mouthfuls.

He didn't answer and instead rose to his feet, spun on a booted heel, and left without a word. But not before I saw his eyes. I wanted to follow my Captain. My friend. Instead I remained sitting, finished my meal, and hated myself for my cowardice.

Uniforms tattered and frayed in the relentless desert wind and paled under the unflinching sun. Men shrank inwards on themselves, their skin leathery and desiccated. The camp was dry like old bones. An entire world poised on the brink of ignition.

I dreamt I was flint and steel.

Still no orders came for the Dysmorphics. When the Captain had no need of me I would watch them as they exercised obsessively, compared muscle measurements, and fretted over their perceived inadequacies. Rubbing my round belly and thinking about my small eyes and bald head, I wondered why I could not share their insecurity. I'd much rather be a parody of fitness than the very definition of slothful gluttony.

Each night I thought about burning those bright lives. Each morning I awoke soaked in sweat and hoarse from screaming.

Early in the fifth month a cadre of the Theocrat's personal guard arrived. They were a small squad of only four members. The Captain sent me to greet them and, though my ego grumbled at being given such a lowly task, I went.

I approached slowly to have more time to examine them. There were three men—one of them towering seven feet tall and shaggy with coarse brown hair—and a single heavy-set woman. She couldn't have been much over four-and-a-half feet tall but was thick with muscle. Her hair was black and hewn short and her eyebrows twitched and arched as she conversed with her squad. A dark lust rose up within me before sobbing and retreating back into whatever seldom visited part of my soul it came from.

They saw me coming, ceased their conversation, and turned

to await my arrival. The smallest of the three men grinned at me showing black gums and teeth filed to sharp points. I ignored him.

Go ahead. Taunt the fat man. I'll burn you to ash.

I stood before the huge man—who else could be the leader of this squad?—and stared up into his face. His brown eyes were surprisingly gentle.

"I have been sent to welcome you to camp," I said.

He merely watched me with sensitive eyes.

The third man muttered something sibilant under his breath. When I turned to face him he blinked nictating secondary lids over yellow slit-pupil eyes. His nostrils flared as if tasting the air and he nodded towards the woman. I turned to face her.

"You are in command?" I asked.

She shrugged. "I am Asena of the Theocrat's Therianthropes." She stared at me with the ice blue eyes of a northern wolf.

I'd heard of the Therianthropes, these shape-shifting animal-spirit warriors.

"I am Gehirn Schlechtes," I said. "Hassebrand." Like any dog, these shape-shifters would only learn respect once they learned fear. "Come."

I turned and headed back towards the main camp. They'd follow or not. Going out of your way to accommodate the insane is rarely worth the effort.

They followed, Asena quickening her pace to walk at my side. Her booted feet kicked up plumes of rust-coloured dust that spun away like fleeing spirits.

"The walls of Sinnlos still hold," she said, stating the obvious.

"The walls still hold," I agreed. Even in the day's heat I felt the warmth of her, breathed deep her animal musk. Much as I wanted to shy away I dared not. "Tell me of your squad," I said to distract myself.

"The big one is Bär. The one with the teeth and bad temper is Stich. The other is Masse." Her blue eyes glanced up at me, the eyebrows arching in mute humour. "Stich is the dangerous one." She grinned, showing pronounced canines. "He's *crazy*."

"And Hassebrands aren't dangerous at all." I'd meant it to be a casual joke but sounded tight and defensive.

"Has the Empress shown her strength?" she asked, ignoring my pathetic attempt at humour.

"No. We won't see her until the Theocrat commits something of his own strength." We both knew what that meant: We *were* his strength in this battle.

"It won't be long now," she said.

The siege dragged on. Men hurled themselves at the wall and died, their corpses left to rot and swell in the desert sun. Asena sought me out often. I could never be sure if she saw something of a kindred spirit in me or if she simply avoided her fellow shape-shifters. I had not the courage to ask. That this strong, confident woman could see anything at all in me beggared explanation.

When I dined with Asena, as I often did, the Captain took his meals alone. Did he see this as abandonment or betrayal? I would have. I dared not risk my tenuous friendship with Asena, but saw no way for that friendship not to come between me and the Captain. He made no mention of it and seemed not to notice I was rarely available. Meanwhile, the stain grew to encompass much of his left hand. He took to wearing leather gloves and sometimes I caught hints of the sweet stench of rotting flesh. Each night I told myself I would talk to the Captain on the morrow, and each day cowardice won out. What would I say? Guilt gnawed the frayed edges of my soul.

One night Asena followed me to my tent after dinner and we

sat talking until the sun rose the next morning. She seemed to be waiting for me to say or do something but I couldn't imagine what. Or rather I could but dared not. She left the next morning with a sad smile but followed me again the next evening. Since I hadn't slept a wink the night before, I dozed off only to wake with her curled at my side, sleeping peacefully. For the first time in years no nightmares haunted my sleep. Unwilling to awaken her for fear she might leave, I neither moved nor slept for the rest of the night.

The following day the Therianthropes and Dysmorphics were summoned. The Theocrat was impatient with our lack of progress.

With Asena called away to receive her orders, I sought out the Captain. I found him watering his horse, stroking the animal with his bare right hand and whispering into its twitching ears. I saw how the horse's wide eyes followed his left hand, and I hoped the Captain didn't notice. His uniform had become rigid with red filth, his brown hair grown wild to his shoulders. I wouldn't have recognised the once dapper Captain should I bump into him in a crowd.

I cleared my throat and saw his shoulders tense. He stopped stroking the animal and slid the glove back onto his right hand. But not before I saw the bruised colour of the fingertips. How do you ask after someone's sanity? I wanted to hug him close, to shield his wounded soul with the fat bulk of my body.

"I heard the Theocrat sent new orders," I said instead. Coward.

The Captain turned to face me with lifeless grey eyes.

"Have you received orders yet?" I asked.

Seven months without word. Happy as I was not to push my already fragile sanity with heavy use of my Hassebrand power, I felt unwanted, unneeded and unloved. Such is the power of the Theocrat. He abuses your love and worship until you hate him. Then, when he casts you aside, you feel abandoned and can't wait to once again serve. Even though I plotted against him, I felt forgotten.

"No," said the Captain, staring at his gloved hands.

"We should pack up and go home," I joked.

The Captain stared at me, unblinking, and I could have kicked myself when the realization hit. Home. The Captain's parents were dead. He had no home. I hated my self-centred thoughtlessness.

He offered a wan smile. "Tomorrow we send in the shape-shifters and Dysmorphics. Go and see the woman." He shrugged apologetically. "I'm sorry, old friend. You deserve more." He turned away from me then, pretending to examine his horse. The animal shied when he reached to stroke it with the left hand. "If we face the Delusionist tomorrow, you must be ready. We know nothing of her. Nothing of what she believes. Nothing of what she fears."

"I am ready," I said with false bravado.

"You've been happier of late," said the Captain, turning to once again face me. "Careful it doesn't weaken you."

What a world I have created for myself where confidence, security, and happiness are weaknesses. "Not to worry," I said. "If I am called forward to face the Delusionist, it means the Dysmorphics and Therianthropes have failed. It means Asena has…" I steeled myself with a shaky breath. "Fallen."

The Captain studied me for a moment. "Losing her will hurt," he said softly.

"The pain will make me strong." I said this as if it were a reason to fall in love. It was terrifying to even admit the *possibility* of love.

But for Asena, I would burn the world.

"The Theocrat, is he worth it?" the Captain asked.

I thought *no* but said, "Does it matter?"

"We all have choices," said the Captain. "You could take the woman away from here. You might find some brief happiness."

His words trod dangerous ground, far too close to my own treasonous thoughts.

"You could come with us," I said, meeting his flat grey eyes with my own.

"I stay." He lifted his gloved left hand. "I'm rotting. Death will be a release."

"If you stay, so do I." I would not abandon my friend.

That night Asena and I didn't talk after returning to my tent. She curled up in the protective bulk of my body and slept as I stroked her hair. If I cried there were no witnesses. When I awoke she was gone. Once again I had slept dreamless and untroubled. There was a scrawled note on my side-table.

You and I, we are a pack of two.

When I found Asena she was already out on the field beyond my reach. The Dysmorphics, armed with blades too heavy and bows too thick for normal men, faced the wall. Heavy iron shields hung upon their broad backs. They marched forward, followed by Asena and her Tiergeist, stopping well beyond the range of the Sinnlos archers.

As if in anticipation of the coming battle the wind died to nothing. The air hung still and stifling. The corpses of the fallen littered the field but were piled highest at the foot of the gargantuan, stone-and-iron gate set into the Sinnlos wall. Too large to have been made by men, that gate could only be the result of focused delusion. The Empress shaped the very fabric of reality with her self-deception.

A dusting of rust-hued sand covered the bodies. There were thousands. Tens of thousands. And we had yet to breach the wall. They were certainly almost all our dead.

"Gods," I whispered in shock. All those lives, spent for nothing. I could stop this pointless death, but only at the cost of more death. I squinted at Sinnlos' bloody wall, trying to make out the tiny figures poised upon its crenellations.

My attention returned to the Dysmorphics as they bent their massive bows to string them. Even at this range I could make out obscene muscles straining with effort. Bows strung, they nocked arrows and took aim. I looked back to the wall and the miniature figures there. Too far. Far too far.

As one the Dysmorphics released. Long arrows hung forever in the sky before falling upon the wall. I watched in awe as bodies toppled and fell in eerie silence. I counted to five before the first corpse reached the base of the wall, landing in a cloud of blood-red dust. Calmly, as if they had all the time in the world, the Dysmorphics nocked their second arrows and took aim. Again they loosed and I watched the graceful arc of the arrows as they rose to kiss the sky before falling to rain death upon the wall. Fewer bodies fell this time as the defenders took cover. A third volley resulted in no more than three tumbling bodies and the wall looked deserted.

At a signal I neither heard nor saw, Asena and her Therianthropes dashed toward the gate. The Dysmorphics unleashed another volley. Asena was almost to the gate before the cowering archers on the wall realised what was happening. Though the Dysmorphics kept up a steady barrage, the Sinnlos archers, leaving themselves exposed, loosed volley after volley at the charging shape-shifters.

What could three men and one strong woman possibly do? This made no sense! They were being thrown away, discarded. This was suicide.

Without breaking stride Bär and Asena *twisted*. Their bodies contorted and bent at impossible angles. Bär grew as he ran, shaggy grey-shot brown hair exploding to cover his body; within two paces he was a colossal grizzly bear racing on all fours. Stich and Masse remained human and ran at Bär's side, sheltered by his mass from the Sinnlos archers. Asena fell forward and I thought she'd stumbled. My heart lurched, and then I saw her as a loping grey northern wolf.

A fire of rage grew within me. What the hells was the Theocrat thinking sending these four in alone? My pulse pounded hot and loud in my ears.

Arrows fell upon the Therianthropes. Bär was hit several times but didn't flinch. Stich and Masse were unhurt and Asena easily dodged everything that came near her. I held my breath as they reached the gates. Asena and Bär slid to a halt and stood poised and motionless at the foot of the gate. What could they do now? They were easy targets.

Then Stich and Masse *twisted*. Stich's skin turned glistening black as he crumbled and fell apart like a house of cards. A mound of wriggling scorpions took shelter under Asena. Masse shredded like someone peeled long strips of flesh from his body and collapsed into a writhing mass of snakes. He took shelter under Bär.

Asena staggered as arrow after arrow slammed into her unmoving body. Even Bär sagged under the weight of the onslaught, his shaggy pelt thick with shafts. Then, as Stich and Masse dwindled and disappeared, I understood. The two found cracks and holes in the gate through which to enter Sinnlos. Asena and Bär had merely been there to provide cover while they worked. I could only imagine the chaos happening on the other side of the gate as the defenders found themselves swarmed by deadly snakes and scorpions. Would they panic and flee, or stand strong?

When Asena buckled and fell, a sob wrenched from deep within me. Bär moved to shelter her with his body. There were so many arrows in him he looked like a massive porcupine. I could see long streamers of thick, ropey blood leaking into the red sand below him. I stood paralysed as Bär shuddered and collapsed beside Asena. I watched the dying bear struggle to protect the wolf before being racked with one last convulsion. As I blinked away dusty tears the two bodies again *twisted* back into their human forms. She looked so small against the backdrop of Sinnlos. So fragile. So broken.

I hadn't even realised I'd started to move forward until a firm hand on my shoulder held me back. I spun with a snarl, ready to burn whoever dared touch me. The look on the Captain's face stopped me.

"Not yet," he said. "Don't rob her death of all meaning. Don't take that from her."

The Captain wrapped me in a tight hug and crushed the anger from me. I could never hurt him. I don't know how long we stood in that embrace, him giving me the comfort I hadn't managed to offer in return. When he finally released me we turned to face the wall. The distant screams of men reached our ears and, at that very instant, the Dysmorphics dropped their bows. Half drew sharp climbing pitons while the others slung heavy shields. As one they charged. Misshapen muscled legs drove them at such speeds the Sinnlos archers were unable to score more than a few hits. When they reached the gate half leapt to climb, pulling themselves hand over fist, while the rest took shelter under their shields. In seconds the gate had been scaled and the Dysmorphics dropped out of sight on the far side. A moment later the gate cracked open and the Dysmorphics waiting outside surrendered their shields, ignored the arrows raining down upon them, and bent their backs, pulling wide the massive stone-and-iron gates.

With a roar the mass of the Theocrat's troops charged.

The Captain and I watched as men swarmed the gate, were briefly repulsed by the rallying defenders, and then pushed forward to disappear within.

"She gave us the city," the Captain said.

I nodded dumbly as tears blurred my vision. Was I too late? Had the Theocrat already won?

The Captain patted me on the back, prodding me into motion. "Let's go and see for ourselves this grand city of Sinnlos."

"We have orders?" I asked.

He paused for a moment, looking uncomfortable. Maybe even ashamed. "*That,*" he gestured towards the gate with a gloved hand, "is where you will be needed." He wanted to say more I but didn't care enough to press him. Asena was dead.

We walked together, picking our way between the scattered bodies. Even through the thick blanket of crimson sand I saw the Theocrat's colours on the dead soldiers' uniforms. As we approached the open gates we heard the echoing screams of death within. Asena's body was hidden beneath the corpses of the Dysmorphics who died opening the gate. Even massive Bär was buried beyond sight. A glint of golden motion on the wall caught my attention. I craned my neck staring upwards, shadowing sun-stung eyes with shaking hands.

There, atop the crenellations above us, stood the Delusionist Empress, lithe and sleek, sheathed in liquid gilt. The dress, woven of strands of fine gold, clung seductively to her every curve. Only when she turned to look down at us did I see the abject terror on her face. Her wide eyes stared straight through us and I realised she saw only the piled corpses.

I remembered then the Captain's words. *We know nothing of her. Nothing of what she believes. Nothing of what she fears.* I thought I understood something of what the Empress feared most. She was a Comorbidic, and suffered from multiple disorders. Not only could she build a city worthy of the Theocrat's jealous hatred from nought but dust and delusion, but she was also a Phobic. I understood why we had not seen the Delusionist Empress before this moment.

She feared change.

Eternal Sinnlos. It made sense now. She'd built this impregnable city in an attempt to make something unchanging. Undying.

Of course the Theocrat had to bring it down.

A battleground is a bad place for a Metathesiophobic. The Empress' keening scream grew from an inaudible whine to a deafening wail as she watched the destruction of her city. Lost within that terrible scream I could almost make out her words. She gestured at the empty fields beyond her mighty wall, imploring, begging, "Please no," but there was no one out here except the Captain and I.

And the dead.

Once they had lived, but we changed that.

She changed it back. But insanity allows no finely tuned control and the more powerful we are, the less control we have. It is the curse of the delusional.

One moment we were certain of victory and the next men streamed from the gate, fleeing something terrible within. The Captain and I stood directly in their path. Neither of us moved and we would surely have been trampled had the retreating men not seen the rising dead.

"Gods," the Captain mouthed silently.

We watched as thousands of corpses pushed themselves from the bloody dust to stare about in mute, dawning comprehension. They looked even more terrified than the living, but that didn't stop them. The dead launched themselves at the Theocrat's troops with no thought of self-preservation or defence. I don't know what drove them: the Empress' delusions or the realization of their own plight and the death of all they had dreamt and planned. They dragged men down, ignoring the vicious wounds they suffered as they did so. The slain rose once again to join the fight. The wind picked up, spinning the sharp sand and obliterating sight and sound alike. It was impossible to tell friend from foe, the living from the dead. Red grit covered everyone and everything.

This was not the Delusionist Empress launching her counter-attack. This was the apex of insanity, the tottering pinnacle of power, that moment when delusions take a life of their own and run wild, beyond all control.

Numb with shock and loss I watched the massacre as if from a safe distance. Why had the Captain brought me here? My thoughts were interrupted by the shattering roar of a grizzly bear. Those closest to Bär's corpse were sent spinning away like scattered toys as the bear swung paws the size of a man's chest to devastating effect. Through the chaos I saw him, already ragged and trampled, his shaggy fur, matted with blood and dust, hanging in shredded knots. Too many arrows to count protruded from his mangled pelt.

If Bär once again stood…I choked down the surge of hope. This wasn't Bär, at least not in any way that mattered. If anything remained of the shape-shifter its mind was damaged beyond recognition.

"Asena," I said.

The Captain stared at me with dawning comprehension.

He said something, screamed it into the wind. I didn't hear it.

"I'm sorry," I whispered. "I can't see her like this." It was both denial and prayer. It didn't matter that Asena was already dead, if I saw her I wasn't sure I could do what had to be done. This was it, the moment where I could turn the tide against the Theocrat's troops and save the Empress.

I saw two ice-blue eyes in the blowing sand. The deafening clamour of battle faded to nothing, drowned by the roaring beat of my heart pounding in my ears. The hot wind and scorching sun were nothing compared to the heat building in my veins. I boiled from within. A sudden gust occluded the blue eyes in a maelstrom of crimson dust.

The flames of my silent scream engulfed the pain, bright and sharp. I let loose my guilt. I loosed my hatred of the Theocrat for bringing me to this hellish place and I loosed my anger at myself for so desperately wanting to please him. My guilt for lying to the Captain, my love of Asena and self-loathing for thinking I could ever be happy. The desperately clenched grip I kept on my emotions—all that stood between me and raging insanity—crumbled and fell apart.

I let loose the fire.

The blowing sand turned to molten glass and rained blood-red upon the field of war. Bodies ignited and blew away like so much papery ash in the gusting winds. The gate and wall ran like thick blood, sagging and then collapsing under their own weight.

Still I burned.

I had no thought of stopping. I would burn until there was nothing left of myself or the world around me.

He must have been standing safely behind me, for the Captain saved my life at that moment. And damned himself to a hell of decay and corruption.

When I awoke my skull throbbed and my thin fringe of hair was crusted with blood. The Captain stood over me, looking down with a sad, apologetic smile. I felt cold. Empty.

"Sorry," he said.

I stared past him into the clear blue sky. It was so nice to see something other than gods-damned red.

"Help me up," I said. "Take me back to my tent."

"Sorry," he said again. "The tents are gone." He looked away, scanning the horizon. "It is all gone."

I lifted a hand and with a grunt of effort he pulled me to my feet. We were surrounded as far as the eye could see by a rolling sea of red glass.

"Why?" I asked. "Why did you stop me? I want to die. I *know* you want..." I trailed off unable to say the words. Surely he must crave an end even more than I.

This time only his eyes spoke the apology. "The Theocrat asked me to stay with you. He asked me to stop you if you were going to...burn yourself out. Those were my orders. The Theocrat says he is not ready to lose you yet. He said he has further use for us both." The Captain paused to take a ragged breath. "He said he *needs* us."

Emotions battled for supremacy. I hated the Captain for stopping me but loved him for saving my life. I loathed the Theocrat for sending me here but had never been so happy as the moment the Captain told me I was still needed. Was it better to be needed and used than not to be needed at all? Probably not, but such is the power of the Theocrat. His need crushes all other desire. His selfishness makes us selfless.

"I was supposed to kill you if you turned treasonous," I admitted to the Captain.

"I know."

"The Delusionist?" I asked.

"Dead."

No one remained to challenge the Theocrat's supremacy. He'd won, and the cost meant nothing to him. I looked at the endless sea of red glass. How many dead lay buried under there? Did some live on undead, trapped and struggling?

"The Theocrat," I said, "this can't be allowed to go on."

The Captain held up his rotting arm, flesh peeling from bone. "I suppose a goal might give me something to live for," he said with a crooked smile. "Shall we pay him a visit?"

I nodded.

Side by side the Captain and I walked across the sheet of crimson glass toward Grauschloss and the manipulative bastard who was our Theocrat. Sweat pooled in the folds of my fat and I watched the Captain from the corner of my eye. Had Asena been part of the Theocrat's plan? Why had the Captain sent me to greet the Therianthropes? Had he pushed me at her, all the while knowing she was to be sacrificed? It wasn't beyond the Theocrat to use her simply to drive me to a point where I would lose all control. Had he known of my plan to betray him?

The one question I dared not ask myself: Did Asena know?

I shoved the thought away and walked alongside my only friend.

I think I have one last fire building within me.

THE RIGHT HAND OF DECAY

DAVID ANNANDALE

GdM #5

They were building the mound when she arrived on the battlefield. The corpses were piled higher than the trees that girded the plain below Barragano, but there were many more yet to be gathered. The executions had not started yet. All in good time.

It was midday, but overcast, clouds hanging low and so dark that they bathed the land in a hard twilight. Smoke rose from campfires and from inside the walls of Barragano. The stench of blood, thick and pungent as grief, rolled in waves over the field. The Grey Queen breathed in the smell and contemplated the growing mound. She must not take the loss for granted. The sacrifices must be noted and given meaning.

She was conscious of how rote the ritual was becoming for

her. *Make note of that too*, she thought. *Watch yourself. This should not be easy.*

And it was not. But perhaps not as hard as it should be. More and more, not hard enough at all.

She had ridden alone to Barragano. Leaving her mount in the forest, she crossed the plain on foot, taking in the measure of the defeat. Most of the corpses in the field had been dragged there before being added to the mound. The deaths had occurred in the near approach to the walls of Barragano. The fortified city sat on a basalt plateau with sheer cliffs to the north, south, and east. Down the steep westward slope, a single road twisted through jagged outcroppings. It was a slow route for any army leaving the city. For an attacking force, it was a death trap, and the only choice. Barragano had never been taken.

And the Grey Queen's army had never been defeated. She had not felt the need to take on Lord Harrad before. But he had forced her hand by sending large raiding parties over her borders. So she had ordered her forces to topple the seat of his power. They had failed. So she had come to do what was necessary.

A command tent was set up midway through the field. The mound stood between it and the road to the fortress. The Grey Queen entered. Two of her generals, Temis and Gascon, were waiting for her. They were both wounded. Temis had a head wound. Blood soaked her cloth bandage and streaked down the right side of her face. Gascon's left arm hung limp. The arrow that had pierced it through the elbow had been broken at either end, but not removed. There was no point in doing so.

They bowed. She nodded, then said, "Tell me."

"We were defeated by the land," Temis said. "It was impossible to move troops up faster than Harrad could take them down."

"Our siege engines were burning before they were a third of

the way toward the gate," Gascon added.

"Was the enemy reinforced?" She hadn't seen any of Harrad's banners in the field.

"No," said Temis. "The Barragano contingent was more than enough."

The Grey Queen sighed. The hope had been to force Harrad to recall his divisions, ending his incursions. Most of the raids were occurring within a day's march of here, but they were spread out. She wanted the lord's army concentrated, arriving in a single force to combat the threat to the seat of power. A single battle would have ended Harrad's threat. As bloody as that struggle would have been, it would have been preferable to the alternative she now faced.

Really? Would you really have preferred not to be involved? The voice, venomous and eager, was her own.

Yes, she answered herself. She was unsure if she made the assertion out of desire or an eroding sense of obligation.

"Then he has left us with little choice," the Grey Queen said. "You've arranged a parlay?"

Gascon nodded. "We have. He has agreed to meet you at the base of the slope."

"Good. I will attempt to reason with him."

"If he fails to listen, we will not fail you," said Temis.

"I know you won't." She smiled. "And you have my thanks for the sacrifice you will make." She heard the solemnity in her tone. That was good.

But her smile. Had it been mournful? She worried it had been eager.

Soon, said the hungry voice.

———

Harrad strode down the final stretch of the road to the base of the plateau. Just past the final bend, his squad of archers stopped and took aim. Beyond where the Grey Queen waited, her own archers were in position. If one ruler was killed, the other would not draw another breath. The precaution was hardly necessary. The Grey Queen's reputation for honour in negotiations was beyond reproach. And Harrad had no intention of triumphing through assassination.

He evaluated his opponent as he crossed the patch of rocky ground towards her. She wore no armour except for a gauntlet on her right arm. Her robes, true to her name, were grey, but he was surprised to see the material. There was nothing royal about it. The robes were linen, as if she were wearing a shroud. She bore no crown. Instead, her robes had a hood, which she had put back. Her gauntlet, Harrad now saw, had no joints. It appeared to be carved from granite and held together by metal bands. It must have been very heavy and allowed no movement of the fingers. It looked like a brutal sculpture.

He had trouble guessing her age. She was older than his forty, of that he was sure. She had been on her throne when he was born, and how long before that, he didn't know. Her hair was the colour of iron. Her face was lined with experience. But her posture was as straight as his. And when he was close enough to see her eyes, they burned with both the judgement of age and the energy of a young conqueror.

"Your troops fought well," Harrad began. It was true. This had been the first time he had seen the Grey Queen's army for himself. The ferocity of their siege had surprised him. It confirmed the truth of the reports, coming back from his expeditionary commanders, that victory over the small town garrisons was possible only through overwhelming numbers. The campaign was still in its early days, and the siege of Barragano was the first major encounter between the powers. His victory was decisive, but there had been moments when it had seemed the flood of soldiers streaming up the road would exhaust his arsenal. It had been like attacking the tide.

Harrad looked at the immense mound of bodies. His gut twisted. It was a monstrosity, not a funeral pyre. Soldiers climbed to the top, crushing limbs beneath their feet, hauling more corpses, tossing them to the peak. Most of the dead had been collected now. The troops not involved in the assembly of the mound lined up at its base.

"They are still fighting," the Grey Queen said. "I am here to offer you a last chance to surrender."

Harrad choked on his astonishment. He stared at the Grey Queen. He must have misheard. She gazed back, calm.

At the mound, executions began. The rank and file walked forward, one at a time, and the commanders ran them through with their swords. New bodies were added to the hill.

Harrad blinked. "You're demanding I surrender at the same time that you are killing your troops for being defeated?"

"My soldiers are sacrificing themselves to our cause. This is the last and greatest gift they will grant me. And yes, I am demanding your surrender. The day has seen enough horror, don't you think?"

"Your position is absurd. You will soon have no army at all."

"Another is being raised as we speak. It will push you from our lands. But none of this is necessary if you withdraw."

The wind shifted, blowing the smell of the bodies Harrad's way. He grimaced. "You are very sure of yourself."

"I am sure of the loyalty of my people."

"Are they loyal or afraid?"

"I give them peace and security," the Grey Queen said.

"That does not answer my—"

"You brought war," she continued, speaking over his objection. "You must understand, Lord Harrad. Your ambitions do not concern me. You may do what you like, but not in my lands. You have invaded, and when war comes, we will win, no matter what the cost. That is the precondition of our security." Without turning her head, she gestured at the executions. "This is part of that cost. Yours will be greater."

Harrad shook his head. "I believe you're quite mad. It is clear to me that your time has passed. But it does not have to end tonight. This is my counter-offer. Finish your demented ritual and leave. If you or any of your forces are still here by tomorrow dawn, I will attack."

Her expression did not change, but the fire in her gaze burned darker. "You have a family, I believe."

"I do," he said, confused.

"They are here?"

"They are."

"Then for their sake, I ask you one last time, Lord Harrad: will you surrender?"

"Of course not."

"I see." She raised her arm as if the stone gauntlet were weightless and pointed the open hand towards the massive walls of Barragano. "Then you should return to your city." She paused. "Go to your family."

The executions lasted until nightfall. By then, the mountain of bodies had doubled in size. The Grey Queen stood at its base and acknowledged her soldiers as they bent their knee to her before they were killed. The deaths walked up the ranks until only Themis and Gascon remained. Gascon handed his sword to Themis, bowed to the Grey Queen, and said, "I rejoice in the peace that is coming."

"Thank you," said the Grey Queen.

Gascon straightened. Themis plunged the sword into his heart.

He fell.

"Will you ascend with me, your highness?" Themis asked as she took the corpse's arms.

"No. I am sorry, but I must play my part in the labour."

"Of course."

It took close to an hour for Themis to drag Gascon to the peak of the hill and descend once again. Then she stood before the Grey Queen and waited.

The Grey Queen looked at Themis' face. Beneath the grime and the blood, it was pale in the torchlight. *Are they loyal or afraid?* Harrad has asked.

Both, was the answer.

And did that matter? Did it change anything? Would it stay her hand?

No.

Do you act from necessity or desire?

And again: *both*.

And again, it didn't matter.

She drew the dagger from her belt. Like her gauntlet, its blade was fashioned of old iron and older stone.

"You honour me," Themis said.

"You deserve no less," said the Grey Queen. "And it is you who honours me. All of you do."

Themis kept her eyes open. The Grey Queen stepped forward and drew the blade across the general's throat. Themis's blood sprayed over the Grey Queen. It ran down her face, was absorbed by the linen of her robes, and the red vanished into the grey. She caught Themis as she slumped forward. She held the general until the blood stopped flowing. Then, with her left arm, she hoisted the body over her shoulder, sheathed the dagger, and began to climb.

Limbs shifted beneath her feet. Dead flesh muffled the crack of bone. Eyes were deep hollows in the dim light, shadows staring into the dark. Her boots slipped on blood-matted hair. *In my name,* she thought. *Each death. In my name.* Not the name she had been born with, though. She had lost it so long ago, she could no longer remember what it had been.

Honour the dead. Do what must be done. And then face the consequences of that act.

The other voice, the hungry one, was silent for the moment. It had retreated behind a smile now that the moment had almost come.

She reached the peak and placed Themis at the top. The Grey Queen stood on a mountain of death. It was soft with flesh and hard with bone. To the west, she looked down on the darker patch of the forest. To the east, the torches on the ramparts of Barragano were wavering pinpricks. Above was the dark of pure void. She could feel the weight of the clouds. They pressed down, massive with the tension of a storm that refused to arrive.

The storm would be hers to unleash, and there would be nothing cleansing about it.

Still facing Barragano, she crouched. With her left hand, she unfastened the gauntlet. It slid off her arm with a squelch.

Below the elbow, her right limb still had the shape of a forearm and hand. It ended in five fingers. But it was a deeper grey than her robes. It was mottled, and the patches suppurated. It was boneless. It coiled and flexed. Then she touched a serpentine finger to a splayed hand jutting from the corpse mound.

Putrefaction radiated from her hand. It spread throughout the hill of the dead. It ate into the bodies. They rotted. They dissolved. The mound trembled and began to settle. It turned to sludge beneath her, and she dropped into a mire of deliquescing flesh. Down and down, deep into a morass of bubbling muscle, of bones that broke into jagged splinters, crumbled, and then jellied. Deep into the stench of grey, the enveloping sea of grey, the grievous cost of grey. The sludge pressed into her nose, her mouth, down her throat. She took it in, but did not drown. She absorbed the gift of her people.

Every body. Every life. Every dissolving scrap of flesh a sacrifice to her. The great dissolution poured into her. It fed her, filling her with the inevitability of decay.

At last she sank to the ground. The mountain fell away, turning into a viscous liquid covering the plain, and flowing to her, oozing into her pores, coating her limbs with fragments of bone and pieces of curling skin. She began to walk towards the slope. She struck out her right arm as a viper attacks, and the decay that was now hers rushed forward.

It was unseen and swift as the wind. It was unstoppable as a wave.

For the first few seconds, as the rot climbed the slope to Barragano, the effect was subtle. There was little vegetation. Lichen turned to dust. Stone eroded and softened. Then the Grey Queen's gift touched the walls. The screams reached her a moment later. They began on the ramparts. Their volume grew. The Grey Queen listened to thousands of voices crying out as corruption took them. The choir was ragged. Soon it was wet, choking with rattling throats.

She wondered if Harrad was on the walls when her grasp came for him. Or if he had listened to her, and was with his family. She wondered if her admonition had been cruel.

No matter. Wherever he was, he would know, in his final moments, that what he loved died as he did.

The Grey Queen found her gauntlet. She slithered her arm back inside.

The human voices fell silent. They were replaced by the thunder of collapsing structures as timber rotted to powder and mortar flaked away. The Grey Queen wound her way up the road, and when she reached the gates, they had fallen down, corroded with rust. The walls of Barragano stood, but they had crumbled under the attack of sudden centuries.

The Grey Queen passed into the city. There were many piles of rubble. It was almost all stone. There were few traces of anything else. But she walked through the open spaces, her feet kicking up the dust. She was waiting now for the dawn, when she would see the full extent of her works. There would be some fragments of bone still, some faint physical memories of the bodies.

Some of them would be very small.

She had brought ruin, and she must own it. She would make herself look at the brittle remains of civilians. She would force herself to confront what she had done. She would think, not of the soldiers she had defeated, but of the innocents she had slaughtered. This was the most vital act of all. This knowledge, and the grief it brought, was what kept her from misusing her power. It was what kept her from revelling in the glory of decay.

This was what she told herself.

This was how she lied.

THE NEUTRAL

Written by MIKE GELPRIN
Translated by ANATOLY BELILOVSKY

GdM #1

The bus straddles the runway a hundred yards from the terminal. I cross the runway toward it, toward the four barrels aimed straight at me through broken windows. The front door is open, and I peer in. Two dozen eyes, wide open in shock, stare back: all women and children. The only men alive are the ones holding the AK-47's.

"Who's in charge here?" I ask. "Come on out. Let's talk."

From the darkness of the vehicle a huge unshaven man emerges to stand on the bus step in front of me. His hairy hands fidget like an errant schoolboy's, and an ugly scar twitches across his left cheek. He throws his rifle behind his back, steps off the bus and crowds close to me, our bellies practically touching each other. I watch his face relax a fraction, though his sweat still reeks of curdled fear. For him, my shadow is the safest bit of real estate anywhere in the world. I am his shield and his safe conduct. I am a Neutral—an ambassador, indispensable and untouchable. I can be killed, of course; but the killer won't live long after. The Brotherhood guarantees I will be avenged. To harm a Neutral is to draw a death sentence. Whoever does so—criminals, terrorists, policemen or decorated army generals—the Enforcers will find them and gun them down alike, wherever they hide. I maintain absolute impartiality, my only purpose is to bring this standoff to a bloodless end. Both sides know this.

"We need an airplane," the unshaven man informs me. "An airplane with a pilot and a full tank of fuel to get us to Venezuela. Plus ammunition, hand grenades and food. And half a million dollars."

"Fine," I reply. "Let the hostages go. The trade is authorised."

In Venezuela, I collect the Brotherhood's cut, standard twenty percent.

Late at night I refuel in a small bar in downtown Caracas, pumping as much alcohol on board as I can convince my body to hold. These four robbed a bank, shot two cops and a young girl clerk behind the window. Then they killed the bus driver and with my help held up the authorities for another half a million. If not for me, and for the Brotherhood I represent, the cops would have their heads. And they would have had the heads of the four dozen mothers and children.

I keep on drinking till memories recede; they keep their distance for a while but then, as usual, the past intrudes upon the present, and I see faces I struggle to forget. Ten years ago, Ellen and Kate took a plane home. A gang of hijackers had different ideas: reroute to Yemen and set free a dozen guerrillas locked up in five different countries. They didn't get what they wanted, and I didn't get my family back. The plane fell into the Bay of Biscay and I became a widower—a childless one.

I joined the Neutral Brotherhood two months after that.

I cross the yard and enter the school building. In the hallway just beyond the door lies a dead girl, barely twelve years old. Down the hallway is a dead boy, about the same age.

"Here." A gun-holding silhouette appears at the gym door. "Hey, Neutral! Over here!"

I step into the gym and stumble over another body, a woman in a jumpsuit, probably a teacher. Twenty children huddle together in the remote corner guarded by two armed men. Two more gunmen sprawl on the mats, smoking: weed, judging from the smell.

"Listen, Neutral, we need a speedboat with a full tank, enough to get to Haiti," says the red-eyed man with dilated pupils and shaking hands. "Plus three hundred thousand bucks in twenty-dollar bills. And a navigator."

"No problem," I assure him. "It's a deal. Let the hostages go. The boat is on its way, I'll navigate."

We walk outside, the rest straggling behind us. Once out in the sun, his grin widens as he takes a deep breath of air. Free air, as long as supplies last.

I come back the next day, grab a litre of whiskey and lock myself in my hotel room. Those five broke out of jail. Shot the guards first and the kids in a nearby school later. Neutrals aren't allowed to show emotions on the job, but off duty anything goes. I light a cigarette, belt down another shot, and close my eyes. *This is what I do*, I remind myself. My job is to be neutral, absolutely, totally and unconditionally neutral.

For the first nine years, I held the lowest rank: I worked as an Executioner, dispatching to the great hereafter those marked for death by the Brotherhood. Few Executioners live long enough to be promoted, but I did, collecting a dozen violators in process. Now I am a Neutral. My life is a guarantee of the safety of both the kidnappers and the hostages. Those who break a promise to the Brotherhood sign their death sentence. The Brotherhood never forgives and the Executioners never give up.

Neutrals don't have to carry weapons any more, but most of us do, just the same. My little backup Beretta in its ankle holster is no match for any of the weapons I've faced so far, but its weight in the ankle holster is a welcome reassurance.

The other comfort Neutrals enjoy is the option to retire. I am not ready for retirement, not just yet. Not as long as I can make a difference.

After two hours of bouncing in an ancient all-terrain clunker, we reach the destination. My blindfold comes off, revealing a burly man wearing oversized sunglasses between his creased forehead and a carved-in frown.

"Come out, Neutral," he says as he holds the door.

I step out of the jeep and squint at the landscape. I see three dilapidated straw huts elbowing each other in a small clearing amidst the jungle. I see a boy in khaki shorts who crawls out from one of them and runs toward us.

Under my arm I hold the bag with two hundred thousand dollars in cash—a buyout for the girl the men kidnapped three weeks ago. First, they demanded a hundred thousand, but when the family supplied the money, perhaps more quickly than was prudent, the gang sent them back her pinky and doubled their ransom.

More thugs crawl out of the huts, eight in total. They call

themselves the Forces of Liberty or some such bullshit, but I see nothing in their faces to suggest fanaticism or obsession: some faces are blank, some smirking, one with what looks like a petulant pout. The khaki-clad boy, a rivulet of drool running down his chin, whispers something to the burly man. The man turns suddenly and snaps a vicious blow to the boy's face. The boy almost topples over, but doesn't let out a sound. Neither do I. I don't really give a damn.

The man turns to me.

"Sorry, bro," he says. "The deal's off."

"The deal's on," I reply. "I've got the money, you've got the girl. Where's the girl?"

"Dude, like I said, the deal's cancelled," the man says. "Don't worry, you'll get the Brotherhood's payment anyway. Forty thousand green ones, as promised."

"What's the problem?" I ask.

"It's like this," the man says, "the boys are alone in the woods, they haven't seen a female for months." He pauses; his scowl does not change. It has not changed since I had seen him: a scowl of annoyance with life's petty disappointments. "So, you know," he continues, "they overdid it a bit."

"Where is she?" In my heart a suspicion rises. "Show me the girl!"

"My boys are gonna take you right back, bro," he says.

"You don't get it, you moron?" I step close to him, belly to belly. "Show me the girl. Now!"

"Easy, bro, easy," the man backs down. "Okay, I'll take you, no problem."

He heads into a hut and I follow.

The girl is sprawled on the floor, dead. The ragged remains of her dress barely cover her small skinny body. Her face is a mask forever twisted in agony and terror. My knees tremble and I have to hold on to the wall to keep from hitting the floor next to her. Instead I stand there wishing I could still cry. She is about as old as Kate was, *then*. The last time I saw her.

I am a Neutral. And as long as I'm alive, so are those who tortured her. As long as I'm alive.

I think I'm ready to retire. Yes. It's time.

I bend as if to tie my shoe, retrieve my gun from its ankle holster. The men step back, their eyes wide in confusion. I raise the weapon to point at my temple.

"No!" the man hollers, lunging forward. "Don't!"

I pull the tri—

BRAZEN DREAMS

MATTHEW WARD

GdM #4

The vault door was a featureless slab of white stone. It ran floor to ceiling, with suggestion of neither join nor crack in its pristine surface. There weren't even seams where it met the tunnel walls. In fact, Elida wouldn't have known it was a door at all, but for her companion's insistence.

Pulling back from the control panel, she threw a glance in Vortane's direction, the weight of her airmask making the motion ungainly. The grav-boots were worse—every step felt like walking through molasses—but at least they hadn't needed to bother with full containment suits. He was running a gloved hand along the surface of the door, as if he could unlock its secrets by touch. Even with the airmask half-covering his thin, watchful face, he radiated quiet intensity.

"I think I can open it," Elida said, wincing at how tinny her voice sounded through the comm circuit.

"You're certain?"

Elida bit back a response that teetered between irreverence and exasperation. Vortane loved to pull her strings. "Of course not," she said instead. "I've never seen anything like this."

Vortane raised an eyebrow. "You remember when I recruited you? I recall you saying that there wasn't a lock you couldn't open."

How could she forget? She'd been desperate to get out of the Camarelles slums, and had talked up her skills considerably. Of course, she hadn't known who or what Vortane was at that point—he'd just been a saviour, cutting her loose from a term as an indentured factory worker. "I wouldn't know about that."

"Just like you don't know about any of this?" The comm channel's static couldn't hide his wry amusement.

"When it comes to this Forgotten Age stuff, guesses are all I have. I can bridge the connection. I think it'll open the door—if it *is* a door…"

"It's a door."

"…but there's always the possibility it'll trigger something else instead."

"What sort of something else?"

Elida shrugged. "An antiquated alarm, defensive system, emergency coolant venting? Could be anything."

Vortane seemed to consider for a moment. "Well, who wants to live forever? Do you? I certainly don't. I'd get bored."

A warbling chime cut across the comm channel. Grimacing at the sudden noise, Elida stabbed a button on her airmask's cheek-piece, and the sound cut out. "That was the shuttle's proximity web," she said, trying to sound surprised.

"So it was," said Vortane. His voice was calm, but he tapped at the ruby amulet hanging around his neck, just as he always did when unsettled. "A drifting asteroid isn't the place for a chance meeting—someone must have followed us. I must visit Bendick after we're done here and…reacquaint him with the precepts of client confidentiality."

Elida caught his tone and was glad it wasn't directed at her. "Do we continue?"

"Of course. It's at least a mile back to the surface, so we've a little time yet. Who knows? We might find something suitably… welcoming…inside."

He smiled, leaving her in no doubt that he knew exactly what was inside the vault. Arrogant devil, always confident he had the answers. She'd give a good deal to see him wrong-footed, but only under the proper circumstances. "Understood."

Reaching into the control panel, Elida pressed the end of her multitool across what she hoped was the correct circuit pairing. There was a sharp *crack*, and a shower of sparks pattered off her airmask's faceplate. There was no alarm, just a deep, mournful rumble.

Turning, Elida saw that the face of the door was no longer smooth. A series of concentric circles had appeared in the stone. They twisted clockwise and counter-clockwise, then irised outwards.

Synthflame torch held high, Elida followed Vortane across the threshold. The crunch of gravel beneath her boots was replaced by the hollow *thud* of metal. Looking down, she saw brass floor tiles gleaming where her footsteps had scattered the accumulated dust of centuries. Swirling shapes were embossed into the faces of the tiles, and torch-cast shadows pooled in the grooves.

Deeper and deeper into the vault they went, until Elida could no longer see the entrance. There was just the patch of floor illuminated by her torch and the bobbing will o' the wisp of Vortane's synthflame ahead of her. His stride was careful, unhurried. Apparently he didn't care that he had pursuers drawing closer all the time. Arrogance again, she decided. Probably he thought he'd be able to talk his way out of it.

"Take a look at this," he called, voice crackling across the comm channel.

Vortane was standing next to a wall when she reached him. No, not a wall, Elida realised, a pane of filthy glass, framed in ornate brass. Similar panes stretched away to her left and right. Pressing her torch against the glass, she peered into the space beyond and stifled a gasp of horror.

There was a man-like shape inside. He—if it was indeed a "he"—wore a tabard of plain black cloth over ridged metal armour. He stood hunched over, his spine arched upward. A cluster of cables protruded from his back, and vanished in the darkness of the vault's ceiling. It was clear that the cables were the only things holding the figure in place—without them, he'd have slumped forward against the glass. Elida crouched, trying to glimpse his face. He had none—just a smooth, white mask. She looked again, and realised that what she'd first taken to be armour was, in fact, his "skin"—an exoskeleton of riveted brass plating. "Mechtrites?" She peered into the next cell, and saw another figure identical to the first. "Why are there mechtrites here?"

"Why not?" asked Vortane. "Did you really think they were just for serving drinks?" He tapped on the glass. "No, they had to come from somewhere. Those we're used to were simply left behind after the old war. I've been searching for a place like this for a long time."

Elida wanted to look away from the mechtrite, but found that she couldn't. The sight made her skin crawl, but she found it fascinating, all the same. When she'd been a young girl in

Camarelles, a troupe of mummers had strayed beyond the gleaming inner-city towers. They'd only managed a single performance before one of their number was stabbed and the others robbed blind, but she still remembered the mannequins they'd brought with them, great gangling things taller than a man, manipulated from above by a web of strings. The similarity was striking. Lost as she was in bittersweet recollection, it took a moment for Vortane's words to register. "What do you mean?" she asked. "What 'old war'?"

There was no response. Elida turned to see his torch bobbing away to her left. Presumptuous sod. Three years together, and still he couldn't bear to share his secrets. In the beginning, she'd thought he didn't trust his gutter-born protégé. Now, she was convinced that he simply couldn't bring himself to shed his veil of mystery, not even for a minute. She supposed it was wise. After all, it wouldn't do for folk to learn that the great and powerful Vortane, spymaster of Clan Balanos, was a fraud.

Oh, he was good at ferreting out secrets, she'd give him that. Whispers and rumours were Vortane's weapons, and she'd seen him wield them well. The Camarelles lawkeepers had spent five years trying to bring down the dockside gangs, but had never found evidence to convict the headmen. When the clan finally sent Vortane in, he managed it in five days. Nobles were no safer than gutter-born. He'd broken Lord Atalan by uttering a single line from a Lowtown address. To this day, Elida didn't know its significance. A mistress? An undesirable business partner? Vortane had said afterwards that he hadn't known the nature of his lordship's secret either, just that the address would provide the needed leverage. Atalan's own fears, and Vortane's reputation, had done the rest. That had been Elida's first and only glimpse beneath her master's veil, but it had been enough to tell her that being a shadow was nothing more than a confidence trick. She'd learned confidence tricks running with Roth's gang, and gotten good at them, so how much more did Vortane really have to teach her?

Presently, she realised that the line of cells wasn't straight, but curved, like the rim of a wheel. They reached the end of a row and descended a wide stair. She had the sense of other cells passing to her left and right, row upon row cloaked in musty darkness. Just how big was this place?

"You see," said Vortane, toying with his amulet, "the clans have forgotten so much. There's a tendency to assume the past *was* much as the present *is*. We see mechtrites serving drinks, or bearing gaudy palanquins, and consider ourselves fortunate to have been bequeathed such helpful mechanical slaves."

It struck Elida that he was being unusually garrulous, the triumph of the moment overriding his natural caution. That was fine with her. Perhaps he did have one last thing to teach her, after all. "So what are they really?"

"What else did our ancestors leave for us? They're weapons."

A squat, toroid console sat a short distance from the foot of the stairs, its surface covered in a forest of switches. The console itself appeared to be panelled in a rich, dark wood. How it had survived the passing years, Elida couldn't begin to guess. In the centre, accessed through a split in the console ring, was a chair. It was curiously ornate, made of black metal that looked almost like polished stone, the outer edges filigreed in silver. It seemed more like a throne than the command chair it presumably was.

Vortane crossed to the console, his manner that of a child loose in a confectioner's. "This is more than I'd hoped. The interface seems intact, and…" He stabbed a finger down on the console. A thousand bright pinpricks burst into being high above, bathing the chamber in warm, yellow light. "Yes, yes, yes! It still has power after all this time. Incredible, simply incredible. I found one before, you know, on one of Singoria's moons. The chamber had collapsed, destroying almost everything." He set his synthflame torch aside, and tapped absent-mindedly at his amulet. "It was a waste, a terrible waste."

For the first time, Elida was able to get a proper sense of the cavern's size. In the dark, she'd had no idea just how far they'd descended. Now, she saw the brass-framed hibernation cells rising above her like the tiered seats of a stadium, each ring contained by curlicued rails and tattered velvet drapes. There must have been hundreds of mechtrites. A body could live a dozen lives of luxury just from the sale of what was in the chamber. If the mechtrites were indeed weapons, as Vortane said, then their contribution to Clan Balanos' war effort would be incalculable. No wonder he was so glad to find them.

Vortane busied himself prodding and poking at the consoles, practically hopping from foot to foot with excitement. Vortane, destroyer of the rich and powerful, giddy as a child. Elida had never seen him this way. It was pathetic. Giving him a wide berth, she slipped past the console to take a closer look at the chair. Close up, it looked even more like a throne, what with its high back and quilted seat. Like everything else in the chamber, its creators had made the effort to conceal function with form, hiding its cabling within its ridged frame. She ran a finger along the edge of an armrest, brushing dust to the floor, and pictured someone sitting in the chair, issuing orders to subordinates labouring away at the console. "Nice chair."

Vortane didn't look up. "If my research is correct, that's the command interface. It's the hub that sends the mechtrites their orders. They're capable of some limited self-awareness, of course, but they're really more of a hive."

"You mean, they obey whoever sits in that chair?"

"That's the gist of it, certainly. The detail's a little more involved."

He looked up as a sharp, clattering sound echoed down through the chamber—the kind of noise that might be made by a boot punting a loose piece of stone across the tunnel. "There must be a way to close the door from this side. Help me look, would you?"

Elida ignored him, unable to take her eyes off the chair. The plan was the plan, but this? Well, this was too good an opportunity to pass up. There was no point thinking about it—that would just give doubt time to grow. Taking a deep breath, she twisted around and sat down in the chair.

"Wait, what are you doing?" Vortane shouted. "Elida?"

The expression on his face was priceless, a mix of fear and betrayal. For once, she'd surprised him. That alone made it worthwhile. That alone…

Elida felt a sudden spike of pain between her shoulder blades. Darkness clouded her vision. She awoke a heartbeat later, woken by a raw, agonised scream. Her scream. Panic welled up inside her. She tried to pull away, but her body wouldn't respond. A second spike followed, this one at the base of her skull. She managed to stay conscious this time, and felt metal scraping her spine. She screamed again. When the sound faded, the pain went with it, and she could move once more.

Gasping for breath, Elida slumped forward. She didn't fall far. Something held her in position. Choking back a growing sense of revulsion, she reached up to her neck. Her probing fingers found a small, metal disc fused to her flesh and a tangle of cables extending back into the throne. What had she done?

Vortane watched her from a few paces away, his expression unreadable. "I warned you before about rashness, Elida. You should have listened."

She ignored him. Even the memory of pain had faded now, and with it the worst of the revulsion. She felt dizzy, euphoric. Her vision fragmented, overlaid with a thousand glimmers of light. Elida blinked her eyes closed, but only the image of Vortane faded. She was left with a thousand not-quite-identical scenes of smeared glass and bright brass. The mechtrites. She was seeing through the mechtrites' eyes while they slumbered. It was more than that. She could feel their minds communicating with hers, the babble of voices like an ocean breaking across a shore. She focused on one voice in particular, and told it to awaken. In one of the scenes, the glass panel shattered as a brass hand crashed through it. Elida focused on another voice, and another. Grinning, she sent the same command again, and again.

She opened her eyes to see Vortane watching her thoughtfully. "I don't suppose you're rousing the mechtrites to help repel our intruders, are you?"

Elida laughed, elated to be in a position of power for once. "Why would I? We go way back, Roth and me—from before I wasted three years with you."

Four mechtrites clanked down the steps and took up position behind Vortane. Two seized the shadow's arms and held him fast. Infuriatingly, he didn't seem at all concerned. The other two took up flanking positions behind her throne.

"You should know that I'm very disappointed in you," he said.

"I guess I'll live with that."

He watched her, a thoughtful expression on his face. "Will you? Yes, I suppose you will."

Elida scarcely heard him—she was too busy rousing other mechtrites to wakefulness. Her gamble had worked out better than she could have expected. Not only had she denied Vortane control of the mechtrites, she could now order them aboard Roth's transport, saving the considerable effort of carting them away.

Through their eyes, she could see Roth and his lads making their way down through the tiers. There were twenty of them in all—far more than necessary, as things had turned out, but it had seemed prudent not to take any chances. One of the newcomers, startled by a mechtrite, whipped up his pistol and started screaming incoherent threats. Elida suppressed a sigh and ordered the mechtrite to freeze. She switched her comm to the frequency Roth was using. "Calm down. I have them under control."

"And what about him, love?' asked Roth, reaching the foot of the stairs. The sights of his pistol didn't waver from Vortane. "Is he under control?"

Elida quashed a spark of irritation. Roth was easy on the eye, in a rough and rugged sort of way, but he'd never been that bright. On the other hand, he had connections—connections that she'd need. Mechtrites weren't exactly something she could sell on a market corner. She scratched at the back of her scalp, trying to stop a sudden itch. It didn't help. Instead, the sensation grew worse. It felt like it was on the inside of her head, not the outside. "Does he look under control?"

Roth opened his mouth to reply, but Vortane cut him off. "Ah, Roth Taricon. Second-rate fence, third-rate hired gun. Used to run with Briadon's gang, until that unfortunate misunderstanding two years back. I suppose the idiots clanging around up above are the rest of your rabble? Mackon, Drost, etcetera, etcetera?"

Roth scowled. "How did…"

"Tell him nothing," said Elida. She'd seen Vortane try this before. Conversational ranging shots; not intended to illicit information by themselves but to identify weaknesses in resolve. She couldn't see how it would help him, but that didn't stop it being annoying. "In fact, I don't think we need to keep him alive any longer."

"What, kill him?" asked Roth. "But he's a shadow. That's trouble. Lawkeepers is one thing, I don't need the clan looking."

Vortane raised an eyebrow. "Oh, that's a compelling point, if made with questionable grammar. What do you think, Elida? Prepared to give it all up?"

"Shut up," she snapped, and turned her attention to Roth. "If we let him live so he can talk about what we've done, that's going to end better for us, is it?"

"Sorry Roth," said Vortane. "I'm afraid she's not going for it. It looks like the lovely Elida is looking to leap a few rungs higher on the underworld ladder." He leaned close to Roth—or at least as close as he could, given that his arms were still pinned. "Between you and me, I don't think it's going to work out."

Elida glared at him. The itch at the back of her mind was getting stronger, making it hard to think. "I said, 'shut up.' Roth, kill him."

Roth looked from Vortane, to Elida, and back to Vortane again. He lowered his gun. "No. No, I don't think so. You want him dead, you do it."

Vortane nodded approvingly. "Good choice, Roth. Cowardly, but with a hint of principle. If you leave this asteroid, you'll go far."

"Enough!" Elida shouted. "I'll do it." One of the mechtrites left the side of her throne, and advanced towards Vortane.

"You're not going to kill me."

She laughed. "Appealing to my better nature?"

"Oh no, I've spent three years looking for that and found not a trace, despite the search." Vortane's voice hardened. "It's not an appeal, or a prediction; it's an instruction. You're *not* going to kill me."

"We'll see about that." Focusing on the mechtrite, Elida ordered it to snap her former master's neck. The command wouldn't form, the thought dissipating like mist even as it took shape. It was like having a word on the tip of her tongue, but a hundred times worse.

"Having trouble?" asked Vortane.

Elida tried to send the command to another mechtrite, but again the order slipped from her mind before it was fully formed. The strange itch was getting worse, like raw static arcing across her brain. She screamed in frustration. "What have you done to me?"

"You did it to yourself. Let me go."

"No," she said. Nonetheless, the command coalesced at the back of her mind.

The mechtrites released their grip. Vortane took a step towards her, then stopped as Roth jammed the barrel of his pistol into the shadow's temple. "What's going on?"

"I don't know." Elida's mind was filled with a gabble of thoughts. She couldn't tell which belonged to her, not anymore. The scene of Vortane and Roth seemed no more distinct than the images being relayed from the mechtrites' eyes. For a moment, she forgot who she was. A surge of panic brought the memory floating to the surface. Elida Tyren, she was Elida Tyren. But that wasn't quite true, was it? She could feel another consciousness writhing around in her mind, cold and clear, where her own awareness was growing increasingly hazy. Elida felt it probing at her memories, her feelings.

"I'm afraid Elida's not quite herself anymore," said Vortane, the sound seeming to come from far away. "She's part of the interface now, a living, breathing component of the mechtrite hive. Their queen, I suppose you could say." He raised his amulet between finger and thumb and shook it gently from side to side. "And the queen only obeys someone who has one of these."

"Give it here!" shouted Roth. "Give it here, or I'll kill you!" He ground the pistol into Vortane's temple, forcing him to tilt his head.

The shadow sighed. "I'm sorry, Roth, but you should have stayed a coward. There's no room for heroes in our little drama, only the dead and the damned." He shifted his gaze, and Elida felt his eyes boring into hers. "Kill him. Kill them all."

What? No! But the command was already sent. She saw Roth's finger tighten on the trigger. Then a mechtrite clamped its brazen hand around his, the sound of cracking bone almost lost beneath his scream. The mechtrite released him, and Roth collapsed to his knees, screaming and cradling his mangled hand. The mechtrite reached down and clamped Roth's head in both hands. There was a sodden *crack*, and Roth's scream stopped.

Desperate shouts rang out to take its place as the mechtrites hunted the rest of Roth's gang amongst the hibernation cells. Elida saw it all through the mechtrites' eyes: every crushed skull, every snapped neck, every torn throat. Some of the gangers fought back, guns blazing as they pumped plasma bullets into their remorseless pursuers. Elida felt a flash of sympathetic pain with each impact. One mechtrite went dark entirely, fading from her mind. Its destroyer had little time to celebrate his victory. Two more mechtrites closed in from behind and tore him limb from limb. A small part of Elida shuddered at the gruesome scene; a larger, alien part revelled in the satisfaction of a task well done.

"What is it doing to me?" she breathed.

Vortane glanced down in distaste and brushed a dribble of brain from his robes. "Replacing you with something more...tractable. You see, the interface needs a human host to convey instructions to the rest of the hive. As I understand it, a mechtrite's brain simply can't handle the strain of autonomy—that's why so many go mad. But a human mind can, once it's been adjusted."

"This...this...was always your plan." Even the small effort to speak was almost beyond her, suffocated by the presence in her mind.

"Let's say rather that I gave you the opportunity to disappoint me. I would gladly have found someone else." For the first time, a hint of anger touched his expression. "I'm a shadow, you stupid child. Did you really think a gutter-rat like you can sneak around behind my back without my knowing it?" He shook his head. "I thought you had potential; I wanted to raise you up, give you an honourable cause that you could serve willingly. No matter. You'll still serve, and serve faithfully, won't you?"

"Yes," said the new mechtrite queen.

Deep inside her mind, Elida screamed.

THE KNIFE OF MANY HANDS

R· SCOTT BAKKER

GdM #2

· PART I ·

Glory drinks blood and vomits history.
—Ajencis, *The First Analytic of Men*

High Spring, 3801, Year-of-the-Tusk, Carythusal

Violence hangs from you in sacks when you triumph in the Sranc Pits. Cruelty is contagion.

For this and many other reasons, Thurror Eryelk stood apart in the crowded confines of the Third Sun, a tavern renowned for the diversity of its clientele. Since time immemorial the place had been a notorious caste entrepot, a place where 'gold danced', where decisions made atop silk pillows became deeds in the gutter. Caste-nobles populated the incense-fogged gallery along the back, reclining in their divans, tipping their heads back in laughter, or leaning forward to peer across the commotion. Merchants, menials, soldiers, and even priests packed the thundering trestles below, raising toasts, arguing business or love or politics. Prostitutes either sashayed into groping hands or slapped their way clear of them. Naked adolescents—Norsirai slaves—held their serving trays high, slipping as if greased through the raucous gauntlet of patrons.

Eryelk relished his solitude near the entrance. Truth was, he had been famous the day he first set foot in Carythusal, for his red hair as much as for his unnatural frame. *Ratakila*, the swarthy Ainoni called him, 'Bloodmane', and without exception, they were wary. They could sense it in him even then, the Incarnal, the patter of some unseen pulse, beating as quickly as murder. They could see the necks his great hands had broken. What they witnessed in the Sranc Pits would simply confirm their immediate suspicions. Something was not quite right with Thurror Eryelk, the new *Inris Hishrit*, or 'Sacred Hewer', the most recent champion of the Sranc Pits.

But the well of fools, as they say, knows no bottom.

"Are you the new Hewer?" a voice piped from his side.

"*Earth and muck*," the Holca cursed in his native tongue. He turned from his reverie, assessed the man who accosted him. He was one of those sharp and oily picks—the *hard* as opposed to the talking kind, bearing murders that only drink could blot from their conscience. He wore the *ciroj* tunic of a trader, a saffron that had been bled yellow by sun and wear and too many washings. His jet-black goatee looked like something dried and hardened. He even sweat the sweat of some disreputable caste-merchant, vicious for drink.

But the man was anything but—Eryelk could *see* it.

All sorcerers bore the Mark of their sin.

"Are *you*..." the man pressed in a drunken slur, "the new *Hewer*?"

The new champion of the Pits clamped his teeth. He scanned the crowded tables about them, found what he was looking for leaning against the nearest of the Third Sun's many columns. He graced the rat Schoolman with a look of pale-skinned cheer, turned square to the man, watched the fact of his physique cloud the fool's charade.

Arms like knotted pythons. Shoulders as broad as a greatbow was long. Chest as deep as a sarcophagus. His war-girdle could strap a saddle, yet he was lean, striate. Elephantine legs, sunburned beneath his mail skirt. Without exception, his presence awed all those near or in his shadow. He poked the man in the chest the way he did whenever some vengeance-seeking relative accosted him, not because he thought the man was such, but because this was what the pantomime demanded. This was the great sickness afflicting Carythusal, the fact that everything devolved upon mummery.

"The Men I kill are all condemned to die," he said. "Scamper off to Sarothesser, pick. Your grudge is with your King."

The nameless Schoolman's head wobbled about some incredulity. A moment passed before Eryelk realised the man was *laughing*.

"You have no inkling, barbarian."

The barbarian's second heart kicked deep in his chest. *Boma-bom.*

The first of the Flush crept into his pallor, line upon web-thin line, a scribble of faint crimson across his skin. Were this pick the mere drunkard he appeared to be, the matter already would have been concluded. But he was not.

Eryelk scratched his close-cropped beard. Humour sorcerers, a dear old friend had once advised him. Humour them so far as your life is worth. Play along with their games, *especially* in Carythusal, home of the accursed Scarlet Spires.

"If your grudge is with your King, why throw number-sticks against me?"

The surrounding uproar slipped into oblivion, and the slow pounding of his warrior's heart—*boma-bom-boma-bom*—climbed into its frame.

"Because I *saw* you..." the Schoolman replied with a queer softness. "I saw the *Queen* cast you her blessor."

The Holca followed the rat-like glance at his waist, saw the pale white ribbon jutting from it, laying like a thing wilted against his hip, the text inked along its length plain for anyone to see.

In his soul's eye, he glimpsed her, Queen Sumiloam leaning like a golden beacon from her box.

Boma-boma-boma-boma...

"Tell me," the rodent continued. "Why the mask? Why hide your face in the Pits when no man could mistake your frame?"

The memories came flooding back. He had stood as he always stood in the blood-drenched aftermath of the Incarnal, alone, surrounded by the pulped wreckage of what had once been living. In the Pit, looking out meant looking up. The concentric tiers were so steep that the audience hooked themselves to their seats. They would stand leaning out against the hemp ropes, row after row, forming a sleeve of dendritic gills, and it would seem the Pit was some kind of obscenity from the deepest sea, a cold encrustation about tissue hot and living, filtering whatever nourishment provided by his murderous deeds.

"It is my other face."

Boma-boma-boma-boma...

The rat was amused. "Aye. All Men need spare faces in Carythusal!"

Even Palatines stood so hooked—the Steep-of-the-Pit, as they called it. Only the balcony of the Surmantic Vigil allowed spectators the luxury of reclining, let alone coming and going at their leisure. And only the guests and family of King Sarothesser

IX set foot upon that allegedly sacred floor...

"You speak of the necessity of deceit," Eryelk scoffed. "I speak of *truth*."

As old as Ancient Shir, they said. The Sranc Pits, a ziggurat gutted for the sake of death.

Boma-boma-boma-boma...

The rat's whiskers twitched in surprise.

"*Truth?*" he snapped. "Oh...you mean *lies that win*."

They knew him not at all, the Holca realised—or nothing of the Incarnal, at least. They improvised. They had merely seen the Queen cast him her blessor, then had waited the following day to approach him here, at the Third Sun, where the crowds might set him at greater ease—or restrain him.

They—the Scarlet Spires. One could not walk the ways of Carythusal without catching some glimpse of their towers above the burnt-brick ridges of the city. They were impossible to miss, especially when the red enamel plates scaling them caught the sun. He himself saw the highest tower, Marakiz, ablaze every morning on his way to train at the lyceum. From pit to pinnacle, it seemed, Carythusal was drenched in blood. And as much as its inhabitants craved the bloodletting of the Sranc Pits—as much as they celebrated the likes of him (if only from a cautious distance)—they genuinely *feared* the Scarlet Spires, the greatest and most dreaded sorcerous School in the Three Seas.

"I despise jnan," Erylk lied. Spoken by a foreigner, this meant, *Tell me what you want.*

Boma-boma-boma-boma...

"Our Blessed Queen..." the rat said, his manner even more narrow. "How should I put it? She has summoned you to recline upon her favourite couch, hasn't she?"

"How should I know?"

Boma-boma-boma-boma...

"Would you like me to tell you what it says?" the sorcerer said, gesturing to the ribbon. Apparently only rats were literate in Carythusal.

"I can read your chicken tracks," the Holca grated. He need not look at his hands to know how the skin reddened.

Boma-boma-boma-boma...

"So what?" the rat scoffed. "The *Queen of Ainon*, the infamous *wife* of Sarothesser IX—the sacred pustule himself!—tosses you her blessor and you...what? *Forget* to read it?"

They knew him not at all.

Boma-boma-boma-boma...

What remained of Thurror Eryelk grinned in the way that made mothers weep. "One cannot forget something suffered by another."

The rat laughed, chirped some gibberish in a tongue that sounded like cackling geese.

Boma-boma-boma-boma...

"Oh yes... The *other* you."

Boma-boma-boma-boma...

"Such a clever rat," he grated.

Boma-boma-boma-boma...

"What did you say?"

Boma-boma-boma-boma...

"The rat that burns other rats, that would rule over other rats, become tyrant of the rat nation..."

His voice—his *hatred*—had become as a grinding mill.

Boma-boma-boma-boma...

"Silence, cur!"

Boma-boma-boma-boma...

"... that would worshipped as the Rat of Rats..."

Boma-boma-boma-boma...

"Insolence! Do you real—"

The Purple Coin, they called it, the killing floor…

The bottom of the Pit.

Ratakila whirled, seized a passerby, cast him into the astonished sorcerer. He dove on the forward edge of the eye-sheering glare, rolled, leapt toward the nearest of the Third Sun's columns, hammered the cheek of the swart fool standing there—the one who harboured the pin-prick of oblivion against his breast. The man spun about, trailing blood, spittle, his left eye on a string.

The first of the sorcerous words twisted sound and decency. "*Umma tulutat ish…*"

He wrenched the man's jerkin up as a rapist might. "… *kiapris hutirum…*" He gouged the Chorae from the corpse's navel. "… *thiri…*" He clenched the iron marble in a great red fist…

"… *totoalas!*"

Wricked it loose.

A region of lightning, vertical forks flickering in and out of existence, both blinding and miniature, making the air snap in lieu of thunder. Men fell dead, shaking for a light-skewered instant, slumping. Ranks tripped over benches and tables fleeing the perimeter. The entire tavern scrambled back, away, horrified faces carved in intermittent white. One man tumbled screaming to the floor, battling his blazing robes.

Boma-boma-boma-boma…

The Holca warrior barrelled through it unscathed, his famed greatsword, Vampire, drawn and swinging.

Teeth closed across glaring light.

Again.

"*Uh! Even the mask reeks.*"

"*Aye. Sulphur…*"

Feminine voices, young and old.

"*Sorcery?*"

"*That is why we did what we did.*"

He was what he was, once again.

"*He breathes like a bull…*"

"*Enough. Silly girl, why do you gape so?*"

The Incarnal always returned what it took.

"*His very look offends the eye.*"

"*And draws it.*"

The World always came seeping back.

"*He is not natural.*"

"*No. He is Holca.*"

Sometimes more simple, sometimes more complicated.

"*Holca?*"

Always wet and mangled.

"*You are an ignorant child. A whore should know her Men!*"

He had been running. He could feel memory of it. The pinch
deep in his breast. The warmth in his thighs.

"*This kind in particular…*"

He could not so much as twitch, yet he felt the flutter of chill
fingers across his abdomen.

"*He isn't a Man… He cannot be!*"

He smelled incense… No. Perfume. Perfume and the scent of
air…burning. Pillows as supple as sod.

"*He can and he is. The Holca reside high on the Wernma, the highest,
where the Sranc rule the nights.*"

What had happened?

"*In ancient times a child was born to them, a child possessing* two
hearts. *Wiglic. Have you heard of him? Of course not.*"

Obviously he had survived the sorcerous rat…

"*The days were fearsome, and the Holca tottered on the very scarp. Wiglic saved them. So mighty was his strength that the wombs of all their wives and daughters were yoked to his pole, indentured to his seed.*"

"*Oh…that Wiglic.*"

"*You jest, and yet still you gawk like a girl in flower!*"

But had the rat survived him?

"*He has two hearts?*"

"*So they say…*"

And what was wrong with his blasted limbs?

"*If I put my ear to his chest?*"

"*Perhaps you might hear.*"

How had he found himself in the care of these women?

"*But is it…is it safe?*"

"*Now it is. But later, who could say?*"

Even his tongue and lips were denied him!

"What do you mean?" the younger asked, her voice wincing in horror.

"The Sarcal simply robs him of motion," the old woman replied, her voice growing distant. She had left the chamber…or whatever housed him.

Thurror Eryelk wrenched at his musculature with a savage effort of will. Nothing. What had once been an effortless extension of his being was now as smooth and insensate as glass.

"You mean he can…can *hear* us?"

The old woman laughed from some socket in the unseen structure.

"If he has *awakened*."

"So…so…there's a chance he might c-come back *after*?"

A barking laugh signalled the old woman's return. "Eh, Holca?" she called from a floating point above his face. "When you return to wreak your vengeance, ask for Isil'alma—"

"*What are you doing?*" the girl cried.

The old woman's laughter was husky and rueful, canny and matriarchal. Eryelk knew her kind. She had learned the secret that escapes so many of those who live into the white of old age, the understanding that *mischief* is what keeps the soul hale and vital. And since all mischief risks injury, she could not but indulge some small, carping yen for cruelty in its expression.

"Such a simple girl!" she chortled, her voice still hot above his face.

The woman would have made a good Holca grandmother…

Were she not a rat witch.

"Were you kicked by a mule as a child? Did your father cane your head?"

An injured huff.

"No-no-no, my child…" she said, floating back into the near void to inspect him. "You need not fear this beautiful monster…" A breath filled with longing and spite, onion and cheese.

"What one gives to the Scarlet Magi never comes back."

Earth and muck.

Perhaps he had not survived after all.

A crew of mail-armoured men had arrived hard on the old woman's revelation. They treated him roughly, cursed his bulk with marvelling apprehension. He heard wheedling female voices, the kind of how-dare haggling to which the helpless are prone, the laying out of conditions on an unconditional transaction. Huffing and muttering in unison, they tossed him into the back of a muck-wain. Naked, he could chart the continents and archipelagos of shit scabbed across the bottom with precision. He could feel well enough, but he could not in the least *move*.

He shook and bounced like a corpse once the wain began kicking over ruts and debris. His eyelids relented, at least, revealed crescent-moon glimpses of his nocturnal transit, parades of ancient brick facades against starry black, all crammed into wending canyons. A particularly nasty slap of the planks sent him onto his side, and he found himself staring down his cheeks at the image of the crimson-canopied palanquin that followed them. The carriage sat upon black-lacquered yokes long enough for some twenty or more bearers, but possessing only twelve, slaves that in no way resembled slaves, armed and armoured as they were. Sorcery riddled the whole of the conveyance, an intimation of disgust that the Holca could sense through scissoring black. Even concealed by silken drapes, the sedan's occupant smouldered with nauseous clarity—and the horrific truth of Eryelk's circumstances as well.

The Scarlet Spires had him.

The most violent Son of Wiglic was no stranger to doom. Ever had danger been a matter of curiosity to him, be it infested forests, piracy on the Seas, or mercenary wars. One could not be born with gifts such as his and not come to a bloody end. Even now, paralysed by sarcal, a captive of the most cruel and powerful of the Schools, he did not fret so much as wonder. Only *ignorance* had caused him any real fear in his life—a fact that Stitti, his mentor and surrogate father, had found endlessly amusing. To know was to fear, the old pick would say (making no secret of his own cowardice). To be *ignorant*, on the other hand, was to be *immovable*, to possess the inexhaustible courage of the oblivious. One cannot fear what one does not know. This was why so many grew besotted before battle. This was why the learned were so craven, the civilised so servile...

No man craved both wisdom and peril as he did. His was an *upside-down soul*, the Sranc slaver insisted, one that, combined with a Holca frame, made him as rare as nimil. "If only you had *will*, boy, *discipline*, the whole Three Seas would tremble!"

If only.

The barbarian could smell the river. Carythusal had to be mucked like any other stall crammed with beasts, and the River Sayut, for all its sluggish immensity, could not but become a sewer. "Why else would the Scarlet Magi built their towers so high?" the wags in the street said. The wheels hissed and smacked across mudded ground. With the yokes extending so far past the bearers, the palanquin resembled some immense beetle scuttling in the gloom, chitinous and raw. Warehouses, windowless and ancient, loomed over its passage.

The air grew hard with moisture. The palanquin stopped with the muck-wain. The armoured bearers bent at the knees and stepped from the yokes—and yet the conveyance hung as before. The slaves were mere ornaments, Eryelk realised—likely a means to avoid outraging the pious masses. Ekyannus XIV, had been baying for the destruction of the Schools for years now, ever since becoming Shriah of the Thousand Temples.

Water slurped about unseen pilings. The barbarian sensed more than saw the armoured Bearers close about the wain. The gilded litter, meanwhile, sank to a point less than a cubit above the ground. The occupant batted aside an embroidered flap, unfolded like an ancient crane stepping clear of the sedan. He strode directly to Eryelk, his manner brisk despite his stooping age. The Nail of Heaven burnished his hairless scalp, etched the ragged lines of his mien.

Thick lips parted about a lozenge of white incandescence. Lanterns flashed from his eyes.

"*Scir-hirammal topta ez...*"

And in the heartbeat that remained to him, Thurror Eryelk realised that Stitti had been wrong. Some Men did share his lust for knowledge *and* peril.

Sorcerers.

———

Air lathed his body.

His Clay-father, the one who had struck him from his mother's hips, had died when he was but four years old. Moiar, his name was. Eryelk remembered nothing of him, though his uncles never ceased commenting on his uncanny resemblance to him.

The waters lay beneath, snakes twining under black-silk sheets.

His Breath-father had been the Master of the Kumrûm, the only slaver entrepot above the Sixth Cataract, high enough on the River Wernma to border the traditional tribal lands of the Holca. Stitti, his name was, Heramari Stitramoses. For all the local prestige he enjoyed, he was an outcast among his own, forever barred from his native Carythusal, where he had been nothing less than the Royal Scribe, a master of thousands, not to mention the way history would frame his sovereign. Barons, even Palatines, had come to him grovelling for favour—that is, until the circulation of several tracts (written in his distinctive hand) had sorely offended the Ainoni King.

Scaled towers loomed naked from veils of haze.

Moiar had been Stitti's most prolific supplier. The Sranc Pits were well named, for they were nothing if not bottomless gluttons, devouring hundreds of the raving creatures every week—more during holy festivals. It behove any slaver to court the favour of his suppliers, especially where *Sranc* were involved. Thus did Stitti and Moiar become fast friends. And thus did the young Eryelk, by dint of some scandalous arrangement no one would explain, become Stitti's ward upon his father's death.

The famed crimson gleamed black in the light of the Nail, horns soaring into the void.

And so a Holca boy on the savage rim of civilization learned everything there was to learn about the great, diseased city of Carythusal—and its most notorious and fearsome denizens.

They swelled into scaled immensities, blotted all vision...
The Spires!

They had practiced until their welts bled. They crossed their training swords in observance of jnan, then, their limbs humming, meditated upon the hearth fire.

There was a carelessness to the way Stitti spoke, a deceptive air of thoughtless rummaging, as if he searched for something precious belonging to someone he did not like. "Of the cancers that pock the City, the Scarlet Spires are by far the most wicked, the most deadly. The Collegians say they have begun plumbing the Hundred Hells, communing with unclean spirits. Pray that you never have call to deal with them."

"And if I should be so unlucky?"

"Humour them, boy. Humour them so far as your life is worth."

"And if my Heart does not allow it?"

He was always chewing gow-gow seeds, always holding thoughts between his teeth, pondering...

"Then your flesh shall be your pyre."

Somewhere... Yes. He was somewhere.

"All who know of Carythusal," a voice crooned, "know at least two things..."

Somewhere dark.

"The Sranc Pits..."

He hung suspended, ankle to ankle, wrist to wrist, so that he resembled a nude diver.

"And the Scarlet Spires."

Iron often communicates its strength through mere touch. Eryelk needed only become aware of the chains and manacles to know they could not be broken.

Even still, something about the voice antagonised.

"The Pit and the Spire. Which is more *wicked* I wonder?"

And so the most violent Son of Wiglic wrenched, hissing for effort. Great sheets of muscle twisted and flexed, all of it braced against the fulcrum of his monstrous will. Veins mapped the swales and striations of his musculature. It seemed the ceilings should come crashing down from the gloom, such was the huffing violence of his exertion.

His chains did not so much creak.

The voice continued as before, unaffected by his display.

"Between us, who has heaped damnation higher?"

The speaker stood immediately behind him, he realised, the way priests do during invocation—the way the Gods were rumoured to do.

"Is it you, the darling of the mob?" the voice asked, moving through nowhere. "Or *me...*"

His captor at last strode into the circuit of what could be seen, appraising him like a slaver on walkabout.

"The devil."

Shinurta. Eryelk's eyes balked for scrutinizing him, so septic was his Mark. Never had he gazed upon a soul more soiled for the commission of sorcerous blasphemies. The Grandmaster was every bit as tall as rumoured—as tall, if not taller than the Holca freebooter himself. He wore an inexplicable robe, black silk wrapping him in burial swathes, his shoulders so narrow that Eryelk might almost believe that a boy stood perched upon another beneath his clothing. But the man's great and ghastly head dispelled the illusion. He was a chanv addict, his skin rinsed of his race's swart pigment, so that the tepid meat of him could be seen through his skin. His irises gleamed crimson. What hair he had left was white and intermittent, here matted into locks, frayed and greasy, there thinning into bare scalp.

"Do you know *why* they celebrate you so?"

Shinurta. He seemed an old acquaintance, so often had Eryelk heard his name mentioned. The rabble of the Worm called him the Moth, and he looked as much, his great head perched on a bundled and stoop-shouldered form. The caste-nobility called him the Secharibi, a name derogatory enough to appease the Collegians, but not so contemptuous as to offend the Schoolmen.

Kwi Shinurta, the Grandmaster of the dreaded Scarlet Spires.

"Why is it, I wonder? Why does the mob prize the rapacious Hand, yet loathe the rapacious Intellect?"

The Holca barbarian glared down at his horrid captor, still swaying for his earlier exertions. He spat the taste of sour garlic from his mouth.

"The wise trust what they can *fathom*," he grated in reply.

"Yes!" the Grandmaster hissed, smiling not so much in surprise as at the recognition of shared insight. "What is easily grasped is easily wielded! *This* is the why the mob loves your kind, Hewer! Why they populate so many fancies with souls such as yours. Even small boys 'fathom' you. You are a knife that fits *any* hand…"

Shinurta chortled for some obscure reason, caught drool on his thumb. "They despise my kind because we fit no hand save our own. *Treachery* is the very essence of Intellect—they know this the way cattle know wolves. The rapacious Intellect is the treacherous Intellect, one that can at most humour the thought of fatter souls…"

"And what of it?" the Holca snarled.

An offended peer.

"But this is why *you're here*, is it not?"

Eryelk dragged his bearded chin across his shoulder. "What do you mean?"

Shinurta gazed at him with flat constancy, a look fearless in the mild, bottomless way of those astride death.

"You are here because *you could only be a traitor* among your people, your race."

The most violent Son of Wiglic glared at the Grandmaster of the Scarlet Spires.

Boma-bom.

A compassionate scowl crept into the mien, a clutching of myriad muscles about the eyes and mouth.

"Such a curse," the Grandmaster said, "despising what one is. It eats souls…makes lives thin."

Once, in this thirteenth summer, Stitti found him whetting his knife. "War, is it?" he had asked.

"They called me pick."

A laughing huff. "They call *me* pick."

"You *are* a pick!"

"Earth and muck, boy. And you? What are you?"

"I'm *Holca.*"

"And yet you read. You write. You train in chirong. You even play benjuka!"

"So then I *am* a pick!"

"No. You are more. More than a pick. More than a Holca.'

"More? Why not *less*?"

"Indeed. Why not?"

"Curse your rat riddles!"

"Then *go*, slake your fury, avenge your honour, bring down bloodfeuds upon my House, ruin the poor pick who has made you so much more than your kin!"

These words had slapped him as surely as any palm.

"I must do something!"

"Aye," the canny slaver said, "*laugh*. Move near them, show them the trim and temper of your soul. Look at them and *think*, do not say, '*Poor…rancid…savages…*' They will feel it, but since they cannot hear it, they will be confused. Confusion is identical to terror."

"You mean do what you do! Play rat-pick word games—play *jnan!*"

The slaver shrugged. "I merely refuse to squander my time on the stupidity of others."

"You do more. You try to make that stupidity *work* for you!"

Cackle. "And this is a *bad* thing? How do you think a man such as me has won so much respect among the Folk?" He shook his head the horse-like way he always did when confronted with some absurd point of Holca honour. "Make a flag of their idiocy, boy! Laugh to show strength, to communicate their woeful insignificance. Move near to make them bristle, to bodily demonstrate their inferiority, to show how quickly their courage strikes bottom. And think contemptuous thoughts to better embody yo—"

"Outland madn—!"

"*For them!*" the diminutive man roared with sudden violence. "Not for us! Not! For! Us!"

A moment of mutual breathing.

"Look, boy. I understand how such words cut—even hack at y—"

"*What one is,*" Eryelk cried, "*determines what one must do! Ajencis* even says as much!"

But the old slaver was already shaking his head. "*Philosophers,*" he spat. "It's their curse to confuse their skullpan for the sky—bah! Forget Ajencis. When a Man has a heart such as you, he is never such a fool as when *he asks what he is…*"

"No…'

"*Yes.* Trust me, boy. The self is known only so far as it is *mastered.*"

"No!"

"No? No? Why am I not *surprised.*'

"There is *blood*, Stitti—blood! Blood always has its say."

The most violent Son of Wiglic jerked and wagged for paroxysms of laughter, a sound that boomed through the black, cracked into ambient echoes across unseen walls. He laughed all the harder for the way Shinurta's obscene face pursed.

Boma-bom...

"Earth and *muck!*" he roared on a carnivorous grin.

The Grandmaster of the Scarlet Spires retreated a step, such was the heat of his animal ferocity. For all the convolutions, all the disfigurations, the sorcerer's soul remained a mannish one, and could not but genuflect in the presence of such a frame and manner. The barbarian chortled.

"What is it, rat? Numb to demons yet cowed by the likes of me?"

Boma-boma-boma-boma...

A smile hooked the whitish lips.

"You are not a thing of proportion," Shinurta sneered. "You disgust."

A monster-headed sorcerer—a *chanv-addict*, no less!—complaining of *proportion*? Thurror Eryelk howled some more. He had seen Shinurta's ilk before, men who called themselves wise, simply because they could think ways others could not. But thoughts were like rivers: the more they forked, the more they made swamps of what was sensible ground. Wisdom was naught but cunning made grand, a weapon forged to win empty battles.

"Who?" he boomed at the Grandmaster. "Who was it I killed at the Third Sun?"

Boma-boma-boma-boma...

The red eyes narrowed.

"So it's true. You do not recall what you do, when Gilgaöl seizes your soul."

"What was his name?" Eryelk barked.

"Nagamezer."

"And what is the punishment for killing one such as he?"

Boma-boma-boma-boma…

Another sneer, rendered grotesque for the glutinous film that passed for his skin.

"Nagamezer…lingers," he replied, smiling as if at the memory.

Boma-boma-boma-boma…

"So I relieved you of a rival! Excised what you could not!"

Boma-boma-boma-boma…

The Grandmaster of the Scarlet Spires grinned as if at some leprous secret.

"Rival? Nay. Simply a fool… Nagamezer saw you as another errand to discharge. He *earned* the judgment you delivered."

Eryelk glared at the hideous figure.

"But you must destroy me, nonetheless."

"Not at all."

Boma-boma-boma…

"Surely you aren't surprised," the putrid face said. "Carythusal is ship at sea, barbarian. Eternally so. Sometimes it founders for the riot of waters, and sometimes it founders for the riot of Men. Certes, she houses both a King and a Grandmaster, yet *it is the Mob* that rules her most, the countless souls packed in her obese belly…"

What was happening?

Boma-bom.

"And as much as it recoils from the likes me," Shinurta continued, "the Mob *adores* the likes of you."

Earth and muck.

Could it be?

"My brothers say the Pit has not seen your like in *generations*… that if I kill you, I would be remembered for nothing else…"

A sudden, translucent sneer seized the face. "You! A trifle! A mummer! A Norsirai sell-sword!'

Thurror Eryelk broke into a bull laugh, saying, "You would much rather be remembered as a rat without skin?"

Boma-boma-boma…

"You *provoke* me?" the Grandmaster of the Scarlet Spires spat, as wondrous as outraged.

"Destroy me! Make yourself immortal!"

"Ware your words, Holca. The Mob casts away their baubles!"

Boma-boma-boma…

"*Kill meeee!*" the barbarian roared. "Lest I kill you!"

A stalk of sorcerous words reared into the chamber…

And with that, the floors seemed to plummet, dissolve into a Pit more profound than any he had mastered.

Boma-boma-boma…

• PART II •

The Soul has a thousand directions, the World one.
—antique Nilnameshi proverb

High Spring, 3801, Year-of-the-Tusk, Carythusal

Monstrous dreams.

His face burned for the inferno, the great temples imploding about smoke…

The bodies burning like sacks of pitch.

Then…hard ground against a jaw of plaster. A web of sunlight cast across glimpses of gloom. A gaggle of nearby voices across the throb of thousands…

A market somewhere? One of the greater avenues?

The most violent Son of Wiglic squinted against the brilliance, raised a great hand to obstruct it. He spat an unholy taste from his mouth. Sulphur lingered in lieu of memory.

What had happened?

They had dumped him in an alleyway, he realised. *"Earth and muck..."* he growled thrusting himself to uncertain feet. He leaned against a blackened wall to gather his wind, legs, and wits. He was relieved to find his gear and his body intact. Even his broadsword, Vampire, hung from his hip. The pommel looked scorched, but the edge was as keen as always.

He staggered to the mouth of the alley, blinked across the crowded thoroughfare. The heat was sweltering, at one with the urban clamour. The Kiro-Gierran temple complex rose over the colourful current and countercurrent of passersby. Dozens of temple-prostitutes languished across the monumental stair, gossiping behind demure hands, naked beneath sheer black habits. He was on the far side of the River Sayut, in the Mim-Paresh quarter, where the residents could afford to worship Gierra and—most importantly— where unconscious warriors could expect to awake. Thieves would be hawking morsels of his flesh by now, were this the Worm.

His musculature hummed for exhaustion. His joints ached. His wrists and ankles stung for the skin his struggles had stripped from them. His thoughts roiled. The Spires! Shinurta—the fat-headed Grandmaster himself!—had interrogated him. Eryelk had been abducted by a *School*, the worst of them, then released like a fish fat with roe. He knew Stitti would advise him to run, to put as much distance between him and the devil-mongers as he could. Forget all delusions of honour and pride, he would say. Earth and muck, boy! Drink and whores were cheaper medicine than vengeance. Cheaper by far.

But he was Holca still, and it *rankled*, the indignities he had suffered—the outrage of being chained naked!

Never had he endured such…*humiliation*…

Boma-bom.

Never!

And there was something else…an ache or horror…something that pitched and yawed within him, an inner vertigo that became more distinct as the mist rose from his senses and his reflexes. They had *stained* him, somehow, *polluted* him with their wicked craft—he could feel it!

He was lurching down the street before he realised what he was doing. Stalls lined the street opposite the Temple of Desire, and he wasn't long in finding a coppery. He swatted aside the cringing proprietor, seized the largest plate sporting the finest polish. The work was crude, his image was smeared, puckered about dimples, but even still, it was clean, uncorrupted, untouched by the nauseous *wrongness* of sorcery's telltale Mark.

He stood dumbfounded amid the shining clutter… Why? He had killed one of their own, shamed the dread Scarlet Spires in their very own city—why would they simply release him?

He left the owner wailing among his copper wares, wandered down the thoroughfare, his thoughts reeling. As always, a wave of startled looks preceded him, and a wake of whispers and gestured charms trailed him, but he scarce noticed.

Vermin should be amazed by the likes of him.

He had wandered all the way to the Heaps, the ancient spice market of Pruvineh, the greatest in the Three Seas, the wags in the Worm said—as old as Shir itself. The expanse was military, stalls stacked into far-flung regiments, and immense enough to afford a clear view across the shoulders of Carythusal. There, above the marmoreal estates and pleasure gardens of the Hermitagic, the famed mosaic walls of the Palaparrais gleamed in the evening light, winking violet, black, and gold: the great palace that Sarothesser built, and that his corrupt descendants had soiled for more than 400 years.

He looked to his war-girdle, saw Queen Sumiloam's favour still hanging there, her blessor, the white ribbon that caste-noble Ainoni women would tie about their left thigh inked with messages for their husbands and lovers. He snatched the thing—what the first sorcerer, Nagamezer, had wanted from him—realizing that he *still* had no clue as to what she had inked across it.

They know of you at the Creeping Postern.
Come, Hero.
Not all has been conquered.

And he smirked wondering. Had the Queen cringed upon writing this, or had she merely thought herself clever?

Shinurta was wrong. Carythusal was better known for things quite apart from the Sranc Pits and the Scarlet Spires, things less dramatic, yet nonetheless more pervasive. Plague. Spice. Women. Cosmetics. Slaves. Narcotics. These were far more likely to accompany reference to the ancient capital of Ainon. She, as perhaps no other city, had earned her many monikers: the Diseased City, the City of Flies, the Whore of Nyranisas. Not a port on the Three Seas accepted her traffic without inspection.

Eryelk should know. Stitti's death had wrecked not so much his heart as his *aim*. The same bloody wandering that had delivered him to the shrieking crowds of the Pit had also delivered him to the *Momus Gale*, for a time the dread of commerce across the Three Seas. He had won the ship the way he had lost her, playing numbersticks, and since gambling enjoyed all the piety pirates denied the World, he found himself a fool captain aboard a ship of murderers, thieves, and rapists.

And so he learned what Carythusal was to the wider world plundering ships bound to and from her antique bosom. The pirates of Cern Auglai were renowned for acts of outrageous brutality. Some merchant captains set their own boats afire, burned themselves, rather than throw numbersticks against their rapacious fury. The crew of the *Momus Gale* had no doubt that their souls lay beyond reprieve, and so they sucked as violently as they could from the teat of brief life. They were Takers in every way, and woe to those with wares to be taken.

They were condemned, and it was simply the lot of damned souls to crow about the damnation of others. So they described the Carythusal they needed to balm their own blistered hearts, or to stitch the mercurial rifts that arose between them. For them, she was a place where the fires of damnation licked as a whore's tongue, anything but the gleaming marvel that Stitti had described. *That* Carythusal, the man liked to say, "was simply what happened," a consequence of Men outliving their ancient customs and laws. "Souls are born *old* in that city, boy. Wonder never fights clear of boredom. Men so crowd the edge of fashion that everything is either dead or dying…"

Carythusal was simply what *came after*, a civilization that had run out of blank scroll, and so began to overwrite what was written. It was a place where *anything was allowed* so long as it did not impede commerce, where *aimlessness was not a crime…*

Where indulgence, rather than deprivation, was held to be holy.

A city of wicked Takers.

Where the Virginal Queen could openly boast of wanton liaisons with white-skinned lovers.

The Creeping Postern turned out to be a gate hidden in a wooded cleft low upon the Assartine Hill. The guards cavorting there had known him, and snapping into sudden and improbable discipline, they escorted him across the palace grounds. Humid gloom ruled beneath the age-old cypresses. The guards did not so much as glance at him on the way—to protect the dignity of their whorish Queen's suitors, the barbarian supposed. No one bothered to check the blessor he held clutched in his right hand. His weapons did not seem to be a matter of concern. They brought him to an outbuilding constructed of ancient Shiradi blocks, many of them bearing weathered suns and ciphers, lines of cuneiform text, as liable to be upside down as sideways or right-side up. He was delivered to a low-ceilinged lounge, not so much lavishly furnished as amply. A man dressed in white, gold-trimmed vestments—the garb of the Thousand Temples—stood awaiting him.

"I am Ûsulares," he said in a crystalline yet deep voice. Despite his shaved jaw and cheek, he spoke as a native Ainoni—from the Secharib plains, Eryelk guessed. "Shrial Emissary to the Blessed Queen."

Whale-oil tripods burned between the chairs and settees, allowing the barbarian to study his assessor closely. He had no real lips to speak of, but he possessed a well-groomed beauty reminiscent of Sranc.

"Priest?" Eryelk asked.

The merest nod.

"Collegian?"

A scowl darkened the fine features, but it was merely ornamental. Ûsulares' eyes twinkled with anticipation—relish even.

"That abomination, Shinurta," he said, "did he speak of me?"

Eryelk felt a twinge of surprise, even though he knew the whole city had heard of his abduction by now. All the better, he decided.

"No."

"And the Blessed Queen? Did the blasphemers speak of Our Celestial Lady?"

Eryelk furrowed his brow. "The first one did."

"You mean Nagamezer. The one you killed in the Third Sun."

A trill of wonder inflected the man's voice, and Eryelk realised that Ûsulares genuinely *admired* what he had done, as he should. The man belonged to the famed College of Luthymae, the arm of the Thousand Temples charged with the prosecution of sorcery. Ûsulares almost certainly possessed the Gift of the Few, the ability to see the Mark, and like Eryelk, he had elected to eschew the accursed power it promised. Unlike Eryelk, however, he had chosen the God of Gods over anything his own hand might deliver. He had gone to Holy Sumna to train and meditate upon the Tractate and the Chronicle of the Tusk, to become a lifelong guardian against the greatest and most terrifying blasphemy of all. Sorcery.

"Shinurta claimed that Nagamezer survived," Eryelk amended.

"He didn't, but there's no way Shinurta could admit as much. As far as the city is concerned, Nagamezer has to be alive, otherwise the Spires would be releasing someone who had murdered one of their own."

The barbarian shrugged. "Regardless, he demanded I let him read *this...*" Eryelk brandished the white and wilted blessor.

The Collegian's gaze clicked to and from the ribbon.

"And after, when they questioned you in Kiz?"

"They squeaked like the rats they are, but they said nothing *of her.*"

"Did you witness blasphemous acts?"

The most violent Son of Wiglic snorted.

"You're the Collegian. You tell me."

Thurror Eryelk had found his way to many caste-noble couches since arriving in Carythusal. The path to Queen Sumiloam's differed only in luxury and scale. After his interview with Ûsulares, he was taken to the baths, where a small host of slaves scoured all trace of the city from his hair and skin. A pallid scribe inventoried all his belongings before absconding with them. He was then taken to a familial shrine, where he took an oath of discretion before some nonsense idol. More than two watches had expired before two enormous Sansori eunuchs at last led him, dressed in nothing more than a traditional white Shiradi kilt, to meet the Blessed Queen.

The ornamental splendour of the palace proper stupefied the Holca barbarian. The eyes thirst for gleam the way the mouth thirsts for water, and for a soul born upon the very fringe of civilization such as his, the parade of great foil plaques and bejewelled prizes beggared all he had hitherto seen. But he was not so foolish as to be *awed* by the display. Stitti had always insisted he recall the *misery* that lay beneath flagrant luxury: the slaves whipped, the artisans maimed, the temples looted. "Why else would your kin die to sell me Sranc? Murder, boy. Murder is the mortar of all great works…"

The Palaparrais, he reminded himself, was as much a crypt as a palace. Men had been ground to meal in its making.

Only the pleasure garden contradicted this intimation of death and foundation. Too much earth. Too much life. Lotuses braided the black pools; orchids hung humid in the gloom. Golden censors hazed the porticos with sandalwood and myrrh. The eunuchs led him down a path through the premeditated undergrowth. Walled in by their black-skinned bulk, he marvelled that rats could grow so big. A bucolic grotto opened amid bamboo and silkwood, a circular depression ringed with sumptuous couches, and centred by a black-lacquered table no higher than his shins. High-hanging lanterns waxed behind paper screens. An alternating motif of dragons had been painted across them, throwing ferocious shadows across the coin of marble, violet and crimson. The scent of ambergris and moss haunted the air.

A young man—a boy, really—and a woman he immediately recognised as the Queen reclined across pillows set at opposite sides of the table. A bared sword threaded the golden receptacles that crowded the table between them.

Both eunuchs fell to their knees, scowled fiercely when he remained standing.

The Queen frowned, but the boy seemed not to care in the least. He fairly exploded to his feet, crying, "Such an honour! You make a temple of our floor, Sacred Hewer—*a temple!*"

Sumiloam swivelled her frown toward the youth. "This is my husband's eldest, Horziah," she said, camel eyes aflutter. "I fear he insisted that he meet you."

"And I am dazzled!" Horziah cried. "*Look* at him, Stepmother! Is he not ferocious to gaze upon?"

Eryelk noted that it was *his* sword, Vampire, lain so negligently across the table.

"Hmm. He is indeed."

"You are *stamped*, Northman. Struck in the very mould of War!"

The most violent son of Wiglic snorted. Some Ainoni saw religion in the Pit, something more exalted than apes whooping for the sight of blood. Horziah was one of them.

"How many have you killed, do you think?" the adolescent yammered. He did not so much walk as float toward him. "I'm sure the likes of you keeps no count, but if you had to guess, how many would you say?"

Earth and muck. He understood jnan better than this greased rat.

"Sranc or Men?" the barbarian asked.

Horziah would not survive his vicious inheritance, Eryelk realised. His nature was too daft, too *good*. The Blessed Queen hugged her bare shoulders, for the same premonition of doom, perhaps—though her eyes remained fixed on Eryelk's bare torso…

"Come-come, Horziah!" she cried, her voice bearing the gentle ire that souls reserve for simple kin. "You've had your look now!"

"Perhaps we can dine *after*, then?" the boy asked him plaintively. "There's so much I would love to discuss!"

Eryelk stared, witless. For the first time he noticed the semi-circle of figures kneeling behind the surging bamboo—almost a dozen slaves, tucked in their shadowy stations, awaiting the opportunity to appease some whim—eagerly no doubt.

Rats were easily trained.

"We co-could drink…" the Prince continued.

The Sranc had been screaming in their pens that night. But Eryelk's ears had always been unnaturally sharp—"Like a skinny's," Stitti was forever saying. He heard the creak of timbers above, the scuff of boots below. He slipped nude from bed, his hairless hide sizzling for sensation. Grabbing his dead father's sword, he scampered down the stair, crept through the gloom of the dwindling hearth, through the kitchens, and into the scullery. There he found the slave-trader dressed all in black, fussing over a sack.

"Where did you go?" Eryelk asked, his voice shredded for slumber.

Stitti whirled, his eyes shining white from a black-painted face. "Boy? Back to your rack!"

"Your face is sooted. You're covered in blood."

A long pause.

"A sacred rite of my people. One that cannot be spoken of."

"Who?" the boy pressed. "Who was it?"

"Earth and muck. Back to your rack!"

"*Who did you kill?*"

Another, even longer pause.

"Kaman Phiraces," Stitti said, not so much as blinking. "For a grudge he did not even know existed."

"Phiraces… From the trade mission? But they only just arrived."

"The grudge has dwelt here for years."

Young Eryelk regarded him narrowly. "You do not sweat. Your eyes do not dart for apprehension… This is something you have done before!"

The very relentlessness of his gaze answered the question.

"It is time you learned," Stitti said.

"Learned what?"

"Chirong."

"Chirong?"

"There is more than jnan, boy. More than manner and manoeuvre. More than gaming the benjuka plate."

The young barbarian lowered his sword—at last. "What are you saying?"

The Ainoni's gaze sharpened. He nodded in the manner of patient and ruthless men.

"There is blood."

Queen Sumilaom indulged her eldest stepson—the Crown-Prince, no less—but only so far as his muddy wit required. Horziah was one of those useless sons, a boy with a talent for nothing more than dreaming of talents he would never possess, a man who would never be more than a boy in the presence of men. Insulated by his station, forever chasing the lure of his fancy, Horziah simply could not apprehend the grim truth of his place in history and the world. His stepmother went so far as to dismiss him *with* her waddling eunuchs, and he remained oblivious!

"My husband's eldest, I fear, is an idiot."

Eryelk was always bold with women he was about to bed, no matter what their beauty or station.

"You risk much, speaking to him as you do."

She scanned the silent semicircle of attendants about them, for a heartbeat merely.

"He cannot see for squinting," she said.

The Holca snorted. "But others can. Skulls like his are stoked as easily as they're cracked."

"What are you saying, barbarian?"

"That you've grown lazy in a world that only *seems* to indulge careless whims."

"You call *me* lazy? Your *Queen*?"

He stood with the stern, statuesque immobility he always used to cow his caste superiors. Let them pull on their invisible strings— their jnan. The truths of strength always wins out.

"No," he replied. "I call *Sumilaom* lazy..."

"You what?"

"Sumiloam. The woman who possessed the cunning, the care, and the patience to conquer such a place as this." He leaned over the foot of her settee, felt the reciprocal tremble that passed through her body. "*That* woman, I wager, would do more than scowl at *your* recklessness."

Her eyes narrowed in shining reappraisal. Perhaps, like Horziah, she had loved him *before* he had arrived. Perhaps she had lain at night yearning for this encounter. But if not, there could be no doubt that she loved him *now*. Sumilaom was a murderess and a mummer, and with but a single declaration he had exposed her, torn away clothing far more intimate than her glorious, olive skin.

"So it's true," she said, speaking more with her breath than her voice. "What they say about you."

"What do they say about me?"

Her smile was girlish for embarrassment.

"That you *woo* as ferociously as you war."

He placed a great, scarred hand upon the couch's gilded backbone, loomed above her.

"Truth," he said, "can only seem ferocious to a race so bent as yours."

Heat thickened the grotto between them. She raised a palm, ran it down the *idea* of his chest and abdomen, rather than touch the blushing skin. Her left knee drifted outward, at once fleeing his proximity, and inviting.

She swallowed. "Tell me, Sacred Hewer, is a flower depraved for blooming brighter, broader than those scattered wild across the meadow?"

In the corner of his eye he saw a shadow flit through the lattices of growth, then slip into place among the others arrayed about the grotto's servile perimeter. Another slave?

He pinned her breasts beneath callused fingers.

"Not depraved," he growled over her moan. "Merely weak."

She slipped his embrace, danced to her feet.

"Come, Barbarian," she cried in mischief, her laughter as husky as any man's. "Fill Sumiloam with your wisdom and your cunning. Find reward in serving your Queen!"

Her hair was jet black, pinned and piled into caste-noble absurdity. Her face was more frank than fine, more athletic than fair—it was her *eyes* that rendered her exceptional, brown and glistening, as large as those on ancient Shiradi statuary. She wore a *kitsari* of brocaded white-silk that covered her shoulder to ankle, save, of course, for the long, open seam that ran down her left—the side of desire. When she twirled to lead him to one of the larger divans, this one nearer the meridian of shadowy slaves, weights in her hem drew the whole out in a conical sweep, and the dress opened like the curled pages of a book, revealing the oiled glory beneath.

He blinked—saw Shinurta convulsing with laughter, his great head roped in meat that should have been hidden.

Eryelk's grin faltered, for a heartbeat merely.

"*Come*, Acclaimed Champion," Queen Sumiloam of Ainon purred.

Blood or seed, the saying among his people went. Blood or seed.

"Hew your Blessed Queen."

Something had to be spilled.

She cried out when it happened…and then they lay, pulse raw upon pulse, their nudity trembling as a gold sheet beneath hammers.

"What are you?" she gasped, baring her teeth about his ache.

"Holca," he exhaled.

"Yes… But what…are Holca."

"A boy…" he began, only to pause at another crazed image of Shinurta. "A boy with two hearts was born to our people in ancient days. His name was Wiglic."

She gingerly squirmed against his pubis. Her eyebrows climbed into a pained crescent as her focus faded.

"I am his most violent son," he concluded on a bull-deep exhalation.

She looked up, made to smile, but swallowed instead, puffed an errant lock from her eyes in a manner that only further inflamed him.

"And why…" she gasped. "Why have you come my city?"

His first Carythusali lover had been a widow far into her barrenness. *Menace*, she had told him. Menace was what had made him her most prized narcotic. The fear that such mighty seed might take root within her.

Fear and wonder.

"Because only *it* can contain me."

A cry climbed from her timid exertion.

"Because only Carythusal is so mad as to make me sane."

And it seemed almost religious, speaking such words in the strangling thickness of coitus... Making such declarations.

Shinurta cackled in his soul's eye. Claws combed the ginger haze across his abdomen.

His stomach lurched. His second heart flexed into a brandished fist.

Boma-bom.

"You mean depraved," she whispered.

Chitinous limbs rattled.

He rolled upon her so that she might writhe beneath the splendid might of his form, feel *manhood* in all its stamping glory, brown skin crushed against red, crying out for the girth of him, murmuring, *Slow...slow...* her thighs pinned open by his hips, as she made sounds of sobbing wonder, and he huffed breath like a dragon, arching as she enveloped the throat of him, wincing for the purity of his bliss—

This! *This* was what was happening!

Scales slapped skin.

Boma-bom.

She panted, swallowed as if to wrap breath around more than heaving thoughts.

The barbarian blinked, saw Shinurta hunched, a greased grotesquerie toiling over his loins. The world kicked and yanked about chains and manacles—

What did they do to him?

Bom-bom-bom-bom...

No! No! This! *This* was what happened!

The most violent son of Wiglic roared, indulged her with a spearing thrust, filled the cup of her insatiable appetite, filled it unto overflowing, and so made shy boys of all her previous lovers...

Her painted husband most of all.

Sumiloam wailed in delirium, laughed in wonder.

The Holca barbarian winked at the King of Ainon where he stood in the bower, pretending to be one of the slaves. This! This! This was what happened.

His skin flushed red.

Bom-bom-bom-bom-bom-bom-bom...

Chained to a thread above Hell. Choking sulphur. Bolting terror. Something horrid convolving about his hips, climbing, mounting...

Bom-bom-bom-bom-bom-bom-bom...

The Queen grunted, slathered him with her bliss, and *Ratakila* howled for ardour, cackled for absurdity. His second heart pounded from his very summit.

Bom-bom-bom-bom-bom-bom-bom...

He roared as a dragon, a demon, in release, in terror.

Bom-bom-bom-bom-bom-bom-bom...

And Shinurta wheezed for hatred and fury.

Bom-bom-bom-bom-bom-bom-bom...

"Strike your foul image upon his very pit!"

Sumiloam sobbed for...for...

Bom-bom-bom-bom-bom-bom-bom...

Screaming. Thrashing. Bestial glimpses of spider eyes and puckered cunnies.

Bom-bom-bom-bom-bom-bom-bom...

"Ravish him!" the Grandmaster screeched, keened.

Bom-bom-bom-bom-bom-bom-bom...

"Sack his flesh! Blast him with shame! Rape! *Rape!*"

Thurror Eryelk awoke on the riverbank, curled about Vampire beneath a rotting dock, clothed only in filth and blood. Carythusal, when he at last dared crawl out to observe it, burned in every quarter, a vast smoking scab beneath shrouded skies. And though he remembered nothing save making love to the Queen in the grotto, he could see the print of what had happened in the gore that robed him…

The shrieking memories would not be long in coming.

Shinurta had no need to curse him, he realised. He need only trust the curse that was his blood. He need only *know* him to transform him into a knife for yet another hand…

And so Eryelk fled Carythusal, knowing even then that he would return, that he would pluck his vengeance only when it had grown ripe…

As Stitti had taught him.

DRONE STRIKES FOR FUN AND PROFIT

AARON FOX-LERNER

GdM #2

I was flying high on my first successful kill when I saw the message. I'm sure that there were others before it, but this was the first that I noticed. "Hello to the Predators!" it read in thick white letters painted upon a sloping red roof.

At the time I didn't give any thought to who might have written that or why. I didn't think about how there might be other messages like it, messages meant for me or any other drone pilots. I just saw an enthusiastic missive that fit my elated mood. I was too busy feeling that rush to worry about the message.

A few months before, on my sixteenth birthday, I'd come downstairs and seen the full software and supplemental hardware controls for my very own drone, a brand new MQ-88 Predator. I knew it was coming; I'd already spent over a year taking classes and doing all the certification work, but I was overtaken by excitement nonetheless.

A couple weeks later I got accepted into The Order of the Red Condor. TORC was a pretty old and well-established clan with a solid record, but they took on a newb like me because they'd been barred from the leader boards for two years after a scandal. Some Chinese national had used these crazy complex IP scramblers and VPNs to run missions with them and they got blamed for letting a non-citizen take part in American military matters.

Once they were allowed back on the leader boards they needed fresh blood, metaphorically and literally, so they took me on. TORC was running missions in Indonesia before and doing well enough to be considered for the top leagues blasting Islamists in the Middle East, but post-scandal they've been relegated to Ecuador. I tell other kids at my school that I officially compete in the UAV leagues and they all automatically think of Pakistan or Afghanistan. But most of us who aren't in the A leagues are stuck with the world's many petty conflicts.

Hell, before I joined The Order of the Red Condor I didn't even know there was a war in Ecuador. Well, officially it's not a war, just a Continuous Military Situation. I spent hours on Wikipedia trying to fill in as much context as I could before my drone shipped out, researching the conflict between the National Military Government and the Pan-Andean Alliance, not to mention the indigenous separatist movement happening at the same time. Even given all that, Ecuador's still one of the more stable countries in the region, having ridden out the water and gas crises relatively well. The National Military Government's a US ally and they paid Hallwater/USAF Inc. for their services as a Class C Location, so it seemed to be a pretty good starter area.

I began with a few uneventful weeks there. I'd circle above Ambato and the surrounding areas at an altitude too high to spot from the ground, keeping an eye out for anyone matching the tags of wanted insurgents or flagged for suspicious behaviour. I didn't have much luck. The most I got to do was identify a couple of suspects and forward the footage to the image analysts.

I lobbied my parents to allow me to stay up later so I could have a better time span to work with, but they refused. Then I tried Lloyd, my class psychiatrist, but he agreed with my parents that allowing me to stay up that late would upset my sleep schedule, which would have a negative effect on my stress levels and ability to focus. I was annoyed, but I still felt like I owed him. He'd helped convince my parents that it was worth it for me to get certified as a UAV pilot. It's funny because he used to try and get me to participate in sports or group activities, and I'm really not the type. I even wanted to switch psychiatrists, but Mom and Dad were worried that having a different psychiatrist than the rest of my class would alienate me. But once Lloyd found out that I was interested in UAVs he was actually really helpful, saying it was a way for me to realise my worth in society and ability to function within the larger world.

Really I'd rather be piloting my Predator than hanging out with any of the kids from my school anyway. There's nothing they can give me that would match the thrill of piloting in the field. Well, maybe sex, but with the girls at my school I'm about as likely to get laid as I am to get a million dollars. Honestly, though, I imagine that even sex isn't as exciting as pulling off a successful kill.

Which brings me back to what I was doing when I saw the message. I was on a standard surveillance run above one of those sad little towns up the mountains a bit to the east. I had a pretty good image of the region despite minor cloud cover and I got an auto-alert on what might be suspicious movements. It was two guys setting up a mid-sized mortar, apparently to fire at the troops stationed in Ambato.

So I got the go-ahead and bug-splatted the two of them in a hot second. Because I killed two baddies in one strike I even got a multi-kill bonus. I watched the smoke flower on my screen and practically floated out of my chair with it. Who knows how many people they would have killed if they'd successfully set up and started firing?

I kept my surveillance up hoping to double tap, but no luck. The only people who came by were kids and then some old people, the men in fedoras and suits, the women wearing hats and dresses whose bright colours scanned weird on my screen. After circling the scene for an hour I realised that no insurgents would be coming, so I circled around back to the base by Ambato and kept an eye on the screen for anything else that might pop up. Nothing did, except for those white words, sprawled across the roof, greeting me and my drone.

After I noticed the message I started seeing more, all written on the roofs around Ambato. One said "Wat (their spelling, not mine) is your model?" Another also asked "What kind of drones do you have?" Others just said things like "you are in the USA" or "I think UAVs are very cool."

The first message was a funny little thing. It matched my joyous mood after my first kill. But now it was different. There were too many of them to take for granted. It wasn't an amusing random thing anymore. It was a mystery. The questions began to ride along with me over the city. Every time I cruised over Ambato I would start looking for messages. And I'd find them. Who was doing this? Why? I had to know the point of these things left all over the city for me. I had to know who was behind them. I didn't find any clues until my third kill.

The strike was against a PAA operative who'd been tagged but disappeared from view for a few weeks after that. I was doing routine surveillance when my auto sensors picked up someone matching his stats. He got into an old white Honda retrofitted to be electric and I tailed him for long enough to confirm and then blasted him.

As always, I circled the area after I bug-splatted him, hoping to score a nice double tap bonus on top of it, but no luck. Just your standard neighbourhood gawkers. And then I saw this kid, a little younger than me. He came out right after the explosion and started staring up into the sky and waving, jumping up and down like he was trying to get my attention. Of course I was at an altitude too high to see, but he still kept acting like he knew I was hovering right above him. I found it weird enough that I tagged him for further surveillance and uploaded his general stats.

The next couple of weeks I didn't follow up on him, though. There was a surge of infighting between the PAA and an Indigenous Autonomy group, and it spilled over into the Central Highlands. It was great for the clan because both groups were on our kill list. Any struggles between them pull them out into the open, where we can strike easily.

One day I was running standard surveillance after school when some indigenous terrorists tried to bomb a secret PAA convoy headed up towards Quito. They failed to pull off the bombing but in doing so gave away the convoy as smugglers. Two missiles, both cars down. I circled overhead for half an hour and caught a known Indigenous Autonomy agent checking out the aftermath. I bug-splatted him, and thus clinched my first successful double tap for extra points and a special merit badge.

This made me man of the hour with the crew. The whole spat kept us busy for a bit, but things calmed down again soon after. Once I was back doing routine surveillance over Ambato I began to notice even more new missives written across the city, facing up to the sky for my benefit. I had a flash of arbitrary intuition and decided to pull up any footage with the general descrip tags of the kid I'd seen earlier.

It turned out I was right on the money. After cycling through footage of the kid going to school or Internet cafes by himself I started pulling up videos of him writing messages on the rooftops around Ambato. Multiple occasions of him clambering onto old buildings with a big brush and a bucket of white paint.

I started watching for him, keeping an eye out when I was actively piloting and pulling up tagged footage when I wasn't. One day I saw a message saying that he thought my strike on the white Honda was very well done. A message specifically for and about me. I had to remind myself that it wasn't completely about me, he didn't know my actual identity. I was just another anonymous drone pilot in his eyes. That strike could have been carried out by anyone.

I think he started to stick in my head because he reminded me of a younger version of myself. I remember how fascinated I was when I was a kid, waving at the low-flying police drones overhead, staring up at the sky and wondering who might be looking down from a higher altitude. I would watch him acting all enthusiastic in the same way and wonder if he could be in this kind of situation, then why not me?

I brought him up at one of TORC's weekly recap meetings, but no one else cared. They just shrugged it off. Not like he was ever going to make the kill list. Just some weird kid with a weird hobby. So I was the only one who was interested, faithfully following every new message like a serialised update. He told me that his name was Ignacio, and he wished he could have his own home drone set up like me.

I pestered piss_em_gbye, the clan founder, about it a couple weeks later, asking him if he'd ever seen anything like this kid before. He hadn't, but he didn't really care about him either. I asked how he wasn't confused by this kid. Didn't he think the whole thing was odd? Maybe he was a spy, I suggested. I found it weird that this kid in Ecuador could speak English. But piss_em_gbye dismissed my concerns and explained to me that Ecuador used to be a pretty stable country. It wasn't too crazy for people there to know English, even now, years after we sponsored the coup and they got drawn into the whole region's military struggles. He told me to just forget about the kid.

I kept flying missions and tried not to bother about it, but I couldn't stop thinking about Ignacio, watching for his messages. I'd never considered any of the people on my screens as anything more than targets before him.

I realised I had to break myself of my obsession with him. I'd even started neglecting standard surveillance so I could track new messages and watch his movements. I convinced Lloyd to recalibrate my meds, but it didn't help any.

Making matters worse was the fact that it felt like Ignacio was actively reaching out to me. He left a message asking me to email him, writing his address on a dark grey rooftop. His missives got more personal, telling me how he wished he could be in the American league, how we get way better drones than the Ecuadorian army or the PAA. He asked me if I had a Predator MQ-88. It was his favourite model.

It was like he knew all about me, knew I was watching. It was so tempting to just pull up my browser and email him, simple as that. I started dwelling on it and realised that something wasn't right. There couldn't be some kid down there who was as obsessed as I was. Who just happened to know English and was almost my age yet also lived in a neighbourhood officially marked as borderline hostile. As if he were another me living in another country, in the middle of a combat zone. It didn't make any sense. I told myself that he was trying to get me to email him so he could infiltrate the league or hack my address or something. It didn't seem right otherwise.

This element of suspicion didn't make things any easier for me, though. Instead I grew more interested in his motives, wondering if he really was a kid just like me or if he was the pretence for a hacking team or a spy. I watched my collected footage of him and would gaze at his email address in my contacts bar, never pressing enter, just typing and staring.

Then some PAA operatives managed to detonate a car bomb outside a police station while I was on surveillance duty. Six dead, eight wounded. I missed it.

Everyone in the clan was really good about it. They keep telling me that none of the operatives had been tagged, that their behaviour didn't set off any alarms on the auto-sensors. But they didn't know why it really happened. I wasn't paying attention when I was supposed to. I was watching Ignacio.

I'd become familiar with his schedule. He'd go to school every day and spend a lot of time afterward on the Internet. He'd go outside and stare up into the sky, climb around on buildings, or write messages to me. I never really saw him interacting with other kids. I'm pretty sure his parents worked somewhere else. They seemed to be out of town for weeks at a time. I was watching him at the exact moment the bomb went off.

Six dead, eight wounded. And it was his fault. The way he distracted me, the way he wormed his way into my head. Six people are dead, eight of them were sent to the hospital because of him. Because of what he did to me. He was ruining everything. I realised I couldn't let it continue. I had to do something.

Eventually, I found a way to take care of it, fitting my solution into a great multi-kill I had on three indigenous insurgents who tried to set up an IED in Ambato. Instead of bug-splatting them right away I tracked them as they got into their car and left. They were already close to Ignacio's neighbourhood, and I kept waiting until they were right in the thick of it.

The second missile hit their car. The first one went straight into a modest little brick building nestled among the ugly concrete boxes and tin shacks. It only took one missile to turn the house into rubble. Ignacio was inside. He'd just gotten back from school.

Now obviously killing a non-com meant minus points on the rankings, but I'm hardly the only person with an accidental death on my record. It's par for the course when you're part of the UAV leagues. They happen to everyone eventually. And the multi-kill bonus I got practically negated the lost points on the leader board anyway. I would have liked to move onto the Class B leagues with a clean record, but like I said, no one pilots UAVs seriously without occasionally bug-splatting a non-com. It just happens.

I mention the B leagues because The Order of the Red Condor is doing so well that we're likely to move up a league at the end of this year. If everything goes well then TORC could be back in the A leagues by some point next year, and at AAA level they actually start paying you semipro rates for your kills.

My parents met with Lloyd recently and they all agreed that joining the UAV leagues has really helped me raise my self-esteem and engage with the world. Mom and Dad are still sceptical that I'll ever be able to surpass the level of a sporadically paid hobbyist (if that) and go pro, but I aim to prove them wrong. They talked with my school counsellor and agreed that it's a laudable goal as long as I've got a backup plan. I'm doing well in school, and I even started hanging out with a couple of guys in the grade below me who are doing their own certification courses. I feel at peace with myself again, like I'm truly becoming who I'm meant to be. Everyone agrees that this has been really good for me.

ALL THE LOVELY BRIDES

KELLY SANDOVAL

GdM #3

Sariana's touch is gentle as she slides the last ruby pin into Lydra's hair. Still, Lydra flinches. Soon, Sariana's sure fingers will draw a blade across Lydra's throat. Will she be so gentle then? The knife is more difficult, in Lydra's experience. When she slit her own Mistress's throat, her hands would not stop shaking.

That was five years ago. Her Wedding Day. She remembers the blood on her skin, warm as the Lord's smile. She remembers believing he loved her. That she would be the one he kept.

For a time, he let her believe. He danced with her on the surface of Bride's Lake and visited her bed. Everything bloomed. Now the farmers complain of their weak harvest, and she shrivels as his hunger consumes her. She believes very little, anymore.

She studies her reflection. Her dress is black, for mourning. Sariana wears red. A wedding gown.

"You look very beautiful," Lydra says. A Bride should hear such things. And, despite herself, Lydra likes sweet-tempered, gentle Sariana. They were friends once. Or nearly so. The Chosen are bad at friendship.

"Thank you, Mistress." Sariana doesn't meet her gaze.

"Are you excited?" It isn't a kind question. "The Lord is waiting."

Sariana shakes her head. "I thought, with you—. I thought he might—"

"He might love me?" Lydra tries to smile. But she is too tired and too hungry. "Yes. We all believe that, don't we?"

She can't remember her life before the temple. She can't remember the priests taking her or her first days among the Chosen. But she remembers when the priests told her she could be the one. That if she only loved the Lord enough, he would love her too.

"He does not love," Lydra says and Sariana flinches.

In three years, five if she's strong, Sariana will sit before the mirror, dressed in black. Jamyr will pin rubies in her hair, readying her for sacrifice. Jamyr is to be Sariana's handmaiden. Jamyr, then Leshta, then Trinel, then Roni. The priests brought Roni a year ago. She's six.

"The priests say he's looking for a Bride who truly serves him." Sariana's voice has a desperate edge. "A partner."

"The priests are priests. To them, he is only a god." Lydra adds another dusting of false colour to her cheeks. "He will be your husband. Then you will see what it is to serve him."

"I'm scared," Sariana whispers.

"We all are."

Of the two of them, Lydra imagines her fears are greater. She touches her neck. It's still whole, still smooth. Her fingers are sharp sticks of bone and the paint doesn't hide her pallor. But she is whole.

Sariana's skin glows with health. She holds out Lydra's crown, the rubies suiting her complexion better than they ever did Lydra's.

"Thank you." Lydra settles the crown on her hair. It feels heavier than yesterday.

"You look lovely." Sariana lies well. The Lord will appreciate that. Perhaps he will love her, find sustenance in her quiet kindness.

Lydra, too, was kind at the beginning. It was easier, then. She was more beautiful and less hungry.

"Do not hope for too much." She tries to sound gentle. "He is not as you imagine."

She has lain in his arms, heard him whisper of death and godhood.

"We are both sacrifices in the end," he told her. "You feed me. I feed the land."

"You live," she said.

"I suffer."

She knows his suffering. His endless hunger sits like a worm in her belly, devouring her by inches. His fingers, corpse cold, have stolen the warmth from her flesh.

The people grow wheat and grow fat.

In time, fresh, beautiful Sariana will be sallow-skinned and sunken-eyed. Sariana, and all the girls who come after. All the girls who don't want to die.

Lydra doesn't want to die.

"What else can I do?" Sariana asks. Lydra has no answer.

Sariana pours wine and offers her the cup.

The wine is a deep, bruised red. Lydra lets it touch her lips. Sweet. It hides the laudanum well.

"Perhaps I'm wrong," she says. "Perhaps it's better to love him… for a little while. Buy yourself a few months of joy."

"I love our people." Sariana sets her shoulders and lifts her chin. "That's enough for me."

"Love them while you can, then. Love their hunger. It's all they'll offer you."

The discordant clang of the noon bells fill the air. Lydra stands in a sweep of black silk and leaves the nearly full cup on her dressing table.

She used to believe she'd face the blade bravely, even smile as the Bride slit her throat. Her own mistress died cursing, and Lydra never forgave her. She forgives her now.

At the Bride's door, the Chosen gather. Jamyr wears pink. The rest wear white. Little Roni is crying.

"Hush now." Lydra crouches and grasps the girl's hands. Her own hands won't stop shaking. "You must be good."

"Are you really going away?" Roni asks.

"Yes."

"But why?"

"Because that's what the Chosen are for. It's Sariana's turn to be the Bride."

"Will I go away?"

Lydra feels the disapproving weight of Jamyr's stare and doesn't care. What good will lying do?

"Yes, Roni. All the Chosen go away." Lydra stands and straightens her skirts. "We're ready."

Jamyr opens the Bride's door.

The Grand Hall is built for first impressions, with vaulted ceilings and pillars of iron. Lydra's people have gathered to witness. They stand as close as they dare to the aisle of red silk. She looks for herself in their round, healthy faces. They have thrived as she has withered. And now they've come to watch her die.

How easy it must be for them. A Bride, killed slowly, then all at once. A small price to pay for a generous god.

Beyond the crowd, the Lord waits on his iron throne. A grey-robed priest stands beside him, holding the knife. The priest keeps his gaze locked on the Lord. The Lord watches Lydra.

He smiles, showing straight, white teeth. She used to like his smile. Now, she looks away and focuses on her feet. One step. Another.

He will settle in Sariana like a tumour. She, too, will think he loves her.

They stand before him: the old bride and the new. Lydra kneels, pressed down by the weight of his gaze. He touches her cheek and she shivers. What remains of her warmth leaves her.

She does not want to die.

She looks up at Sariana, meaning to smile, or to curse her, or to beg. Sariana takes the knife in a shaking grip. Her eyes are bright with tears.

She'll botch it, cut shallow. Lydra will bleed out slowly while the Chosen watch and the Lord gathers Sariana into his arms.

She reaches up and grips Sariana's wrist, trying to steady the knife as it grazes her throat.

"I'm sorry," Sariana, whispers. "I don't want to."

But she will. They all do.

Lydra hates her, and herself, and all the lovely, obedient Brides who came before.

She squeezes, digging brittle nails into Sariana's fine, soft skin.

The knife drops, hitting the silk covered stone with a muffled thud. Lydra wraps her fingers around the familiar hilt. It's heavier than she remembers, warmer to the touch. She stands, still holding Sariana's wrist.

They were friends, once. And she's so very gentle.

Lydra takes her by the chin. "You serve your people," she whispers. And she slits Sariana's throat in a single, steady stroke.

The parting of skin and muscle. The rush of warm blood over her hands. The dull sound of Sariana's body hitting the stones. None of it surprises her. She has done it before.

She wanted to live then, too.

She ignores the gasping crowd, the cursing priest. Only the Lord matters now.

He laughs. She remembers the sound, all velvet and heat, from long walks by moonlight. She's pleased him. The worm of his hunger eases its grip as he gains new strength from Sariana's death. Lydra takes her first full breath in months.

She had forgotten what it meant not to hurt.

She turns away from Sariana's corpse, looks past the crowd to the Bride's door. Roni sobs silently, her fist stuffed in her mouth. Jamyr stares at Lydra's bloody hands. Lydra understands the relief in her expression. Jamyr need never learn the weight of the knife or the heat of fresh blood.

"I thought you had tired of bringing me gifts," the Lord says.

Lydra refuses to mirror his smile. She won't play at banter. Not while Sariana grows cold between them.

"I am not as tired as you might have wished," she says.

"And what will you do now? Host my hunger for another five years?" He reaches forward and touches her gaunt wrist. "I fear you haven't the strength for it."

She studies the crowd. A slack-jawed farmer gawks at the Chosen. The woman next to him links her fingers in the sign against evil. The man, she decides. He can be first.

"You need not hunger. These are prosperous times, Lord. There is plenty of life to offer."

"And will you offer it? A god can't take what his people won't give."

She smiles at last. "I am ever your loyal Bride."

She will bring them, and slit their throats, and feel the warm flush of health return to her skin. She will bring as many as it takes.

She will live.

SHADOW HUNTER

ADRIAN TCHAIKOVSKY

GdM #1

To each of the Insect-kinden, a totem: source of their power, shaper of their nature. Beetle-kinden were tough men and women, able to endure and prosper anywhere; Flies were small and swift and skittish; the people of the Spider were elegant and clever and not to be trusted. Moths, the mystics, claimed to know all the secrets of the old darkness, while the Dragonfly-kinden claimed the light, and claimed to be better than everyone else as well. And the Wasps?

The Wasp-kinden were savage and angry. Their totem gave them wings, and their hands flashed with gold fire as they slaughtered each other, generation on generation. And while that ferocity was turned inward, tribe against tribe, family against family, nobody much cared. Nobody even noticed, when one chieftain beat and bribed and challenged until all the people of the Wasp were facing in the same direction, under the same rule. When all that boundless energy and ambition was abruptly turned outwards, all the armies and walls of the world could not stand before it.

The Empire, they called it, and it swept across all the little city states, the Ant and Bee and Beetle-kinden, enslaved their people and called them the Empire too. And then the Wasps went looking for bigger game. For a decade now they had been swallowing great chunks of the ancient Dragonfly Commonweal, teaching those high-minded people just who was better than who. The Dragonflies were a people of many talents: farmers, artists, swordsmen, archers, mystics. They were Inapt and they fought in the old way—honour duels and massed peasant levy. The Wasps were soldiers, every single man of them—they had slaves to do the rest for them. Being Apt—mechanically-minded—they fought with crossbows and siege engines and primitive war automotives, ripping up the history of a thousand years and sending the loot home to the Emperor.

What happened, then, to a man of the Wasp-kinden who no longer wanted to be a soldier? What happened to a man who, by dint of extreme conniving, effort and brute luck, was released from the adamant bonds of military service to make his own way in the world?

Should never have taken this job, was Gaved's thought on seeing the forest. He was a man who preferred to trust his instincts, but he also preferred to eat. Being a freelance Wasp-kinden in an occupied land where every other man of your people wore the uniform made it hard to find work. Patrons were scarce when you were hated by the locals and despised by the invaders.

Then he had met the Moth, tucked quietly in the corner of an army drinking tent: raucous, full of off-duty soldiers and half of them still in their black and gold armour. That one corner had been an oasis of stillness and quiet, and there the Moth had been. They were a relic of another land's mystical past, the Moth-kinden, eking out a living on the edges of the Apt world. Like all the Inapt—like the Dragonfly-kinden that the Wasp army had recently bludgeoned into surrender—the Moths were a people who could not grasp the principles of machines, of logistics, of the modern world. They were the last tattered scraps of the past.

This man of the Moth: grey skin, blank white eyes, slender enough that a burly Wasp like Gaved could have broken him in half, yet somehow his soft voice had slid past all the rowdy jabber of the drinkers. "I have work for you."

And here Gaved was, following the only employment he had been able to find, doing the bidding of one Moth by hunting down another. Somewhere in this tangle of thorn-barked trees there was a second man of that grey kinden, and Gaved was tasked with bringing him out.

Or kill him, the instructions had gone. *Tell him it is better to be dead, than to be what he is.*

He had trawled for rumours about the forest his quarry had holed up in. A dark place, he was told; a bad place. The locals had never gone there, the army had not needed to fight there. Probably it was somewhere the Dragonflies thought was magic, not that a Wasp would care about that. More recently it was a haunt of bandits, because the war had left a lot of armed men with nothing to do.

Gaved didn't mind bandits. He preferred them to soldiers, most of the time.

They ran into him at the same time he ran into them, both sides freezing in surprise. Gaved had his hands out instantly, his palms warming with the Wasp Art. A thought from him and golden fire would be spitting from between his fingers, showing these locals just why his people were feared.

He saw a man and a woman, both Dragonflies, lean and golden-skinned. The woman wore a few pieces of iridescent armour, no doubt prised from a dead noble's body. She had a sword, and perched on one wrist was the hunting insect of her kinden, a dragonfly two feet long with a carapace of glittering metallic blue, huge eyes regarding him and all the world impartially.

The man wore a ragged greatcoat and he had a short bow in his hands, which concerned Gaved far more than the sword or the insect.

"Good day, fellow travellers," he said, one hand covering each of them. He tried a smile, but his smiles were seldom reassuring. He was one of the dreaded invaders, after all: a big, pale man with the red weal of a burn-scar about his neck and chin, from when he had finally decided to leave the army and go freelance.

"What do you want here, Wasp?" the woman demanded.

"I've come looking for someone." Better not to say *hunting*. It had so many negative connotations.

Gaved saw the archer's hands twitch, saw a moment's glance pass between them, and then the Dragonfly man said, "He's after the Moth."

It was plain that "the Moth" was no friend of theirs. The tension leached out of the moment.

The woman's name was Eriss; the man was Kael. They never used the word *bandit* but that was plainly what they were. More, they'd another dozen friends who plied the same trade. Or they had, before coming to this forest.

"Because your army wouldn't come here," Kael grumbled. "Even your Empire can't make the trees pay taxes."

"But *he* was here already," Eriss added. "We didn't realise at first. We'd made camp. But there was something…"

"Nobody slept," Kael took up the story. "Not well. We started to see…shadows, ghosts. Then he came to our fire. A Moth. A magician."

Gaved raised a doubting eyebrow.

"Scoff all you want, Wasp; what do your people know?" Eriss snapped. "He walked in and told us we were his, and our chief couldn't speak, not one word. Kael and me, we got out, just slipped away. We thought the others'd follow us when they could. Nobody did."

"This is a place of evil magic from the old days," Kael added. "A death-place. We should never have come here. Your people wouldn't understand."

They were going back to find their friends. Gaved was going to face down their enemy. Common cause was made.

The Art of the insect-kinden gave many gifts. It let the Ant-kinden speak to each other, mind to mind and allowed the Wasps to sting, to each race its own blessings. Gaved could fly a little, too, the shimmer of wings materialising from his back when called on. The Dragonflies were better, born to the air.

The forest was dense, the interlaced branches of the canopy a fortress that even the Imperial army had not fancied bringing down. The bandits' preferred road was the high one, from bough to bough, making short hops through the uppermost fingers of the trees.

Eriss had sent her dragonfly ahead to scout, the agile insect hovering and darting over the dense foliage. When it returned to her, she would speak with it, gleaning what it had seen from its simple mind.

The first two times she sent it out, it found traces of the other bandits' progress through the woods, heading for the very heart of the place. The third time it was on its way back when the canopy came alive and reached for it. In sight of its mistress, what seemed just green leaves and branches unfurled toothed arms and clawed for the insect. Gaved saw a triangular head with bulbous, gleaming orbs for eyes and mandibles beneath like scissor blades: a mantis, one of the great forest mantids, and this one surely fifteen feet long.

For a long moment they stared at one another: the three humans and the monstrous insect, with the dragonfly waiting on above. Then the mantis cocked its head at them and let itself drop, vanishing into the gloom of the forest below.

They thought like men, he had heard it said. They hunted and planned and held grudges. And sometimes, said the old tales, they served magicians.

Soon after, they found the rest of the bandits.

They were in a clearing, sat in a circle, as though they had decided to stop for some conference of thieves. Except they were dead. Except they were splinted up, propped on bloody, jagged shards of cane and wood. Some even had arms spiked out as though caught mid-gesture. Some had open mouths, and Gaved could see the splinters that had been driven in, to keep their jaws in place. It was a ghoulish tableau, and what was worse was the empty place. All those dead eyes, all that arrested body language, led the eye to one spot about the circle, as though some chairman of the damned had only that moment stepped away.

Kael and Eriss were frozen, staring. Gaved himself was watching for the Moth, because a man with this sense of showmanship would not miss his entrance.

And sure enough, there he was: stepping in to take his place at the circle, the grey-faced man of slender build, bundled in a threadbare robe. His blind-looking eyes took in his visitors and he smiled.

The Moth. The same Moth. The same man that had sent Gaved here; there was no mistaking.

Then Kael had his bowstring back with a shout of fury, and Gaved was already moving, running around that grisly circle, hands out, but holding off—

His forbearance made Kael the target, so that when the mantis's strike lashed out of the shadows it was the archer who was snatched away, gone in a heartbeat and a cry. The huge insect loomed above them, from shadow to killer like a trick of the light. Its razor mouthparts were working busily as it chewed at the stump of Kael's neck.

Eriss should have run, then, but she shrieked and hacked at its nearest leg, her dragonfly spiralling up and away overhead. Gaved saw her blade smash one of the mantis's stilt-like limbs, and it raised its killing arms in threat, Kael's remains still dangling.

Gaved's hands flashed, his sting searing across the clearing. One bolt charred across the creature's thorax, another crackled past the creature's head, even as Eriss lunged forwards and sunk her blade up to the crosspiece into the insect's abdomen.

And it was shadows; it had only been shadows. Gaved stared, seeing the patterns between the trees that had looked as though a monstrous mantis was there, wondering how he could have been fooled by it. And yet Kael was dead and dismembered, and Eriss's sword was gone...

Gaved saw the Moth was already beside her, reaching out. One thin grey hand caught her collar and the other drew a dagger across her throat with a butcher's economic skill.

Then those white eyes turned to Gaved, who unleashed his sting.

Or he had meant to. There had been no other thought than that, before the burning gaze caught him. Moths had their own Art, and abruptly this one was in Gaved's mind, holding him rigid, trapping his will as the thin figure picked its way towards him, bloody blade held reverently.

"Why have you come to this place of power, little Wasp-kinden?"

He could not be sure whether the voice was in his ears, or just in his head.

"This place of magic—and there are so few left anymore. The iron armies of your people trample and trample, with your machines and your progress; with the brightness of your lamps. A poor scholar must travel a long way to find somewhere that has even a vestige of the old days about it. And who can say what the quality of such a place might be?" The Moth was right before him now, the wet coldness of the blade resting on his cheek. "And yet we must make accommodations. We magicians cannot be choosy, in this latter age…"

The Moth turned the blade, so that the thin, hard line of its edge was against Gaved's burn-scarred throat.

Then the dragonfly stooped, glittering wings battering madly at the grey face as it tried to avenge its fallen mistress. The magician staggered away, clutching at it, shielding his eyes, and abruptly Gaved could move again.

He sent a sting-shot at the robed figure, only catching the Moth a glancing blow, even as the man snatched the dragonfly from the air, crushing its delicate wings between his fingers and tearing them from the insect's body.

Those white eyes were on him again, and although he had a hand out, he could not loose his sting. But the Moth's hold was imperfect: he could speak.

"You sent me!" he got out. "You came to me and sent me here! You told me, 'Tell him it is better to be dead, than to be what he is.'"

The words struck the Moth hard. For a brief moment there was realization on that grey face. Those blank eyes took in the scene around them: the gruesome parliament, the utter bloody madness of what had been done under the forest's influence. No wonder some part of him had rebelled, seeking what little help could be found in this occupied land.

Then Gaved's hands blazed again, and this time he struck true, and just in time. He had seen the twist of cruelty coming back to the man's face, the moment of truth already passing.

Standing there, with nothing but that conclave of the dead for company, he felt a tired emptiness inside him.

With a wary eye out, in case that mantis had been real, and not just shadows, he set about relieving the corpses of their valuables. One thing was certain: he wasn't getting paid for this job.

A RECIPE FOR CORPSE OIL

SIOBHAN GALLAGHER

GdM #3

T he streets were swamped with foreigners, all bundled up, their pockets bulging with trinkets from lands beyond the city of Fride. Tavin squeezed his lithe form between smelly bodies—and oh, did they reek. Had these people never heard of a bath? His hands gently touched the outsides of their pockets, fingers tracing for anything of value.

One woman—at least he thought it was a woman: she had the round face of a motherly figure, despite the whiskers on her chin—eyed him with suspicion. He smiled reassuringly to her and said, "You seem lost. Might I direct you to one of the fine shops here at the Lane?"

The woman snorted and pushed past him, elbowing him in the gut.

"Well, that was rude," he muttered, rubbing his stomach. Admittedly, the rate of successful pickpocketing by day was rather poor. But it was either by day, or compete with the will-o-wisps after nightfall, and those wisps were a good deal more skilled than him. Maybe he'd try his hand at one of the shops, where customers would be too busy browsing to notice their pockets were getting lighter.

Extravagant Oils of the Arcane sounded promising, and pricey. Tavin struggled to the shop's entrance, which was nothing more than a gaping hole in a brick wall with a rag of gauze draped across it. The shop smelled marginally better than the crowd outside. Its shelves were stacked with odd-shaped bottles, from swan necks to spirals to multi-pointed stars. They weren't the typical oils like olive or puffertoad: some bottles read *Cat's Eye*, *Tick's Blood*, *Tumbleweed-Roe*, *Eckle-Feckle*... What in all the dark regions was *Eckle-Feckle*?

Tavin continued to pretend-browse till he came across a squat creature—a goblin, maybe, hard to tell with such an oversized coat—holding a bottle in each hand. He stood beside the creature, eased himself into a kneel, plucked one bottle from the shelf that read *Turnipickle Numb*, and asked the creature, "I've never tried this brand before. What do you make of it?"

The creature only glanced his way, grunted.

Tavin took up another bottle, *Languid Lavender Lady*. "What about this one?"

This time the creature didn't even acknowledge him. So he reached around it for another bottle, drawing back his hand close to its backside, fingers deftly probing pockets.

"Yes, I think *Walking Sage* will do." He walked away with a single coin to show for his effort. A solid coin, but only a worth a night's stay at the inn. On to the next...

A hand clamped down on his shoulder, spun him around. He shut his mouth on the yelp that wanted escape. He had to stay composed, act natural, like he belonged here. The man's hand weighed on Tavin as did his gaze, especially that intense right eye that looked about to pop out. The man's skin was tanned in another land; he wore a black box hat and an extravagant silk robe.

"Come with me," the man said, grabbing him by elbow.

"Hey, wait—! I didn't—"

"You're not in trouble."

Well it certainly *felt* like he was in trouble. The man dragged him into the back room and slammed the door.

"Look, I'll give it back," he said. "It was a joke, really."

The man snatched the bottle from him and it set on a stand. "You seem like an unsavoury fellow."

"Umm, thanks?"

"I need a person like you to do something for me."

"Well, if there's pay…"

"There is. Good pay."

Tavin relaxed enough to allow himself a smile. "All right. What ya need?"

"Chins."

"Chins?"

The man nodded. "They're the key ingredient in corpse oil."

"I would think you'd need *corpses* for corpse oil."

The man chuckled and slapped him on the back so hard he nearly stumbled. He rubbed the sore spot, frowning. All this jostling was going to get him bruised.

"Chins! I'm all out, and I need to make a new batch for a very special customer. She can't wait and neither can I. So you go out and get me some chins."

"When you say chins…"

"Human chins, they make the finest corpse oil. Twelve of them. They have to be fresh, bone and all."

"I see…" Tavin rubbed his chin, now very aware of its value.

"So you'll do it?"

"It's just chins? I don't have to kill anyone, right?" He might be greasy, but he was no murderer.

"Of course. You can live without a chin."

That was right, you *could* live without a chin; it wasn't like they were vital for anything. He rather liked the idea, and could think of quite a few drunkards who didn't need their chins all that much.

His skill at chin harvesting wasn't much better than his ability to pickpocket. There was the matter of removing the chin, which was much messier then he'd imagined. His attempt with a dagger was woefully unpleasant. As he tried to cut through the bone, blood made the chin and jawline too slippery to grip. The drunkard was bound and gagged, but nonetheless he thrashed. Tavin knocked him out with the very bottle the man had been drinking from, and went looking for a saw.

The saw was too loud: the sound of steel grating bone drew the attention of passersby. A hatchet finally did the trick. One swing cut through tissue and bone with no noise to spare. Of course his aim wasn't always true, sometimes striking ground, or worse, an ear or a nose. He was very sorry whenever that happened and apologised profusely, promising to buy his chinless victims an ale. They were out cold when he made the promise, but he thought the gesture counted just the same.

Nevertheless, he made great progress, collecting eleven of the twelve chins he needed. Then the rumours came and washed clean the alleyways of drunks, beggars, prostitutes, and other undesirables. Only the revenants stuck around, but no one cared about them and their midnight whining. Besides, they had no chins.

So he went scouring the residential district for that one last chin, then he wouldn't have to pickpocket, or beg, or sleaze his way into a warm bed at night. There had to be a loner living around here somewhere. A foreigner would be the obvious choice, but they lived in packs, dozens of them under the same roof. With a loner, there'd be no bothersome witnesses.

The poor district's dirt roads bled into the pockmarked cobbled streets of the middling district—and here there were actual windows in the houses!—and from these shoddy streets to the pristine ones of the wealthy district. The wealthy district made for an uneasy stroll, for the guards were most vigilant: not a vagrant or even a stray mutt in sight. He kept to the shadows and bushes, watched and waited. It had to be here that he'd find a loner, because who else but the affluent could afford to live on their own?

As always, he was right. On the second evening of his wealthy district watch, he passed by a two-story house and saw a gentleman on the deck, observing the stars through a fancy telescope. And by the forsaken gods, did this gentleman have a chin! A magnificent chin, jutting out like a flesh spade. It had to be three inches long, maybe as long as his pointer-finger. He tried lining up his pointer-finger with the chin from afar, before realizing that he was still the middle of the street, and people were looking at him funny.

He hurried away, breathless and slightly dazed.

Later that night, when all were assuredly asleep, Tavin returned to the home of the gentleman with the big chin. He went around to the back, peered inside. From the dim glow of a fireplace, he could make out an immense clutter: papers, books, gadgets of brass and iron. Some seemed very impractical, like the system of ropes and pulleys that ran from the ceiling to an armchair. A wife or sister wouldn't have allowed for such a mess. That was a good sign.

He took two thin pieces of metal from his coat pocket and stuck them into the keyhole. Tinker, tinker…*click!* The door swung open. He tiptoed down the hallway, passed the open living room with its fireplace, and—

The world whiplashed him. His neck sore, blood rushing to his head, a pinching pain around his ankle, everything upside-down. From the corner of his eye, he saw the pulley system at work, the armchair used as a counterweight.

When did wealthy people set traps? That seemed like an odd hobby, unless this gentleman's house had been broken into previously. In which case, what terrible luck.

"Ah, finally," came a nasally voice from upstairs. A moment later, Tavin was approached by the great-chinned gentleman, who looked less fancy up close; more like the sickly, bookworm type that everyone picked on. Still, he admired the chin.

The gentleman smiled, puffed out his chest as if this were his grandest moment. "No more chin-stealing for you."

Tavin almost stopped breathing. How did the gentleman even...? Never mind. He needed to keep calm, act natural, like he belonged here—sort of.

"How do you know what I'm stealing? Maybe I liked that stupid telescope of yours."

"A telescope wouldn't sell for much, and other homes have nicer things than mine. But I have something that would only interest a certain kind of thief." The gentleman pointed to his chin, then—to Tavin's great disappointment—he broke the chin off.

"So you put a fake chin on to lure a thief?" Tavin said, disgusted.

"When I first heard the news, saw the pictures of those poor chinless drunks in the newspaper, I *knew* I had to put a stop to it. Because you can replace goods, but not chins."

Tavin's temples throbbed ever harder. His head filled with blood. The rope choked the circulation at his ankle. "Well that's very noble of you. But since I'm not here for your chin, how about—"

"I'm making a citizen's arrest!"

Tavin snorted. "There's no such thing here in Fride."

"What?" The gentleman frowned. "I thought… Oh well, I'll just call the guard."

"You do that, and I'll just tell them you're in on it too."

"They wouldn't believe that. I caught you attempting—"

"You just caught me. That's it. Could say it was a deal gone sour and you were gonna turn me over. Then it becomes 'he said this—he said that.' Guards would shrug and just hang us *both* on the gallows-tree walls." While explaining this and seeing the frustration twist the gentleman's face, Tavin slowly reached behind his back for the hatchet tucked into his belt.

"They wouldn't—" the gentleman said.

"Oh yes they would. They do it all the time. Why do you think the executioner never gets a day off?"

"That's barbaric!"

"Welcome to Fride."

Hatchet in hand, he struck the rope where it was tied to the armchair—his aim much, much better with all the practice. He landed hard on his head, felt the bump already forming. Blood sloshed around his eardrums as he stood, a dizzy haze over his vision.

The gentleman gaped at him in silence. Tavin held the hatchet high, all the more menacing because he stood a good half-foot taller than the gentleman.

"All right," Tavin said, "let's make a deal. You don't mention this to anyone and I won't kill you."

"That seems hardly fair." The gentleman pouted with all the petulance of a spoiled child.

"Or we can both go to the gallows. It's up to you."

"Hmph. Fine, you filthy chin-stealing—"

"Shut up!" The sloshing inside his head had become a full-on headache, and there was a knot in his neck, and he just felt awful all over, like he'd been trampled on. If he wasn't short a chin, he'd swear off chin-stealing this very instant.

Though maybe…

"Let me see that." He snatched the fake chin from the gentleman's hand.

"Hey!" The gentleman stood up straight, only to slouch away from the hatchet.

"What's this made of?" He rolled the fake chin around in his fingers, getting them all greasy.

"Bacon fat and pig's skin."

It looked quite real. Maybe he could fabricate a twelfth chin from the other ones he'd collected, substitute the bone for a bit of pig joint. He'd gotten to know chin anatomy pretty well. He could pull it off.

"All right, I'll be off." He bowed, slipping the hatchet back into his belt. "You have yourself a lovely evening."

The gentleman rudely slammed the door behind him.

The shopkeeper of *Extravagant Oils of the Arcane* greeted him with a crushing handshake. Tavin gave the shopkeeper the bag, then rubbed his poor fingers. The shopkeeper counted out the chins, held up a misshapen one for inspection. Tavin held his breath, crossing his toes inside his boots. The shopkeeper nodded in approval, and everything inside Tavin unwound.

"Nice, nice, nice," the shopkeeper said, collecting the chins into a cooking pan.

"So how about my pay?" Tavin said.

The shopkeeper tossed aside the empty chin bag, retrieved a heavy pouch from his robe and dropped it in Tavin's hand. Through the fabric he felt nice thick coins, the kind that could buy access to just about anything, legal or illegal.

"You know," the shopkeeper said, "I could keep you on."

"What? For more chin-stealing?"

"Not always. There's other kinds of stealing. Or maybe disposing."

"Ehh, I dunno..." He still felt miserable and was looking forward to the bathhouse, a massage and a nice feather bed.

"I can make you partner. You'll get some of the profits."

"Decent profits?"

The shopkeeper gave a toothy grin. "Why do you think I needed the chins? One of the most expensive oils I sell."

A steady income would be nice. He'd never have to pickpocket again. Maybe save up and buy a house of his own—or better yet, leave this city far behind. He'd heard there were some nice tropical places in the east.

"Then I agree."

The shopkeeper made to shake his hand again, but he drew back and instead offered, "How about a gentle pat on the shoulder?"

Next time he would define 'gentle', as the shopkeeper whacked him on the shoulder. He clutched the spot like it was bleeding, masked his pain with a smile. Had to keep up appearances, after all.

"Where you going?" the shopkeeper asked, as Tavin stumbled out of the back room. "Need to show you how corpse oil is made."

"Uh, I really don't—"

"Come, this will be good practice."

The shopkeeper grabbed his arm, pulled him back into the back room.

"Ah, ah, ah. Not so hard."

For all of the shopkeeper's smiling and chuckling, that intense right eye of his made Tavin uneasy, as it focused unwaveringly on his face...or was it his chin?

REDEMPTION WAITS

MIKE BROOKS

GdM #5

What the shit is *that?*"

It was a fair enough question, Ichabod Drift reflected. The galaxy was full of wondrous things, and some of them really were quite odd-looking. Such was the case with the edifice hoving into view through the viewshield of the *Keiko*, the somewhat battered *Kenya*-class freighter of which he was captain and proprietor.

"What does it look like?" he asked. Amir McGillicutty screwed up his face, as though considering the question caused him physical pain.

"Looks a bit like some bastard built a giant flying church."

"Some bastard did," Drift confirmed, "but in space, bad things can happen to good people. Or bad people. Just to people in general, I guess."

"Basically, it's not a church anymore," Tamara Rourke said. Short where Drift was tall, curt where he was loquacious and with her black hair cropped close to the skull while his hung in violet-dyed lengths to his shoulders, Drift's business partner didn't like anyone wasting words. She looked up from the terminal screen she was studying on the other side of the cockpit. "We've got clearance for Bay 23, Jia."

"Gotcha," their pilot acknowledged, adjusting the thruster settings.

"So if it's not a church now, what *is* it?" Amir persisted. He was younger than anyone else on the crew except Jia, and despite Amir's collection of useful skills, Drift was already starting to find him slightly wearing.

"Best to let them explain," Drift said, tapping a flashing icon. The holodesk sputtered into life and two white male figures appeared on the dash, about one-eighth of real size, in the pre-recorded welcome message which had been hailing them. One was tall and stocky, with long dark hair tied back, a beard extending an inch beyond his face, and antiquated clothes that wouldn't have looked out of place on Old Earth, including a ridiculous tall hat with a brim. The other was shorter, slighter, and clad in a bodysuit of some modern poly-u fabric, with one side of his head shaved, the hair on the other side left combed over, and a mechanical eye not dissimilar to the one that occupied Drift's right socket.

"*Greetings, and welcome to the House of the Redeemer,*" they chorused in unison.

"*I'm Captain John,*" the taller one continued.

"*And I'm Captain Jack,*" his smaller companion added. "*At a mighty three miles long, this is the largest pleasurehouse in the galaxy…*"

"*…and since it is conveniently positioned in international space, it's not subject to any laws except our own. And we have just one law:*"

Have Fun."

"*Remember,*" Captain Jack concluded, giving a thumbs-up, "*you can't be redeemed unless you've sinned!*"

The transmission winked out, leaving Amir frowning at the holodesk. "Is this for real?"

"You bet your life," Drift told him. "Which you can, in there, although I wouldn't recommend it." He activated his comm. "A, you ready to roll?"

+Yes bro, I'll be right up.+

"Roger that." Drift stood, shifting his shoulders in an attempt to loosen them a little, while the crenelated majesty of the former house of worship passed lazily beneath the *Keiko*. He looked at Amir again. "You know what your job is?"

"Yeah, yeah," Amir muttered. "I walk in with you, I keep an eye out for anyone sneaking up or scoping us while you're talking to the mark."

"Don't take it lightly," Rourke said. "A void station like this is effectively lawless. If you want to walk out, you'll keep your wits about you."

"Feel free not to walk out," Jia added from the pilot's chair, without looking around. Drift frowned at Amir in silent warning not to rise to the bait. Jia normally only verbally sparred with her brother Kuai, their mechanic, but she and Amir had apparently gotten off on the wrong foot.

If it came down to it, Drift knew which one he'd be booting. Amir was useful, but Jia was gifted. Egotistical and almost completely uncontrollable, perhaps, but certainly gifted.

He hustled the kid out of the cockpit and into the boarding hall with no further exchanges of venom. Jia expertly brought them alongside one of the long docking tubes and Drift used the slight delay to give final instructions to his crew.

"The contact's supposed to be on the third gambling floor, standing at Roulette Table 5," he reminded them, checking his hip holsters. "We won't have long to get this done before that Brazilian *cabron* turns up for what he thinks is his job, so we'll have to move fast and slick. I make the approach, Amir watches our back. Big A lurks, and makes an entrance if needed."

Apirana Wahawaha, the crew's enormous Maori bruiser, nodded his heavily-tattooed head. "You got it, bro."

"Tamara is backup in case something unexpected happens," Drift finished. "If it all goes south, disperse and meet back here. Clear?"

There were assorted nods and mutters of assent.

"Very well then," Drift beamed, popping the airlock behind him open to the pressurised tunnel beyond. "Let's do something illegal."

The docking tunnels always led to areas of the House that catered to fairly tame pursuits, so as not to scare away first-time punters. Drift and Amir walked through brightly-lit malls and passed eateries, bars dispensing alcohol and soft narcotics, and flashing lights advertising rooms of coin-operated gambling machines. Soon enough they reached a bank of elevators, the doors of which hissed softly as human traffic passed in and out.

"What does *that* mean?" Amir asked, gesturing at a large sign on the wall. An arrow pointed upwards with the word 'CHANCE' next to it in a variety of languages. Below it an arrow pointed downwards next to variations on the word 'CERTAINTY'.

"Directions," Drift told him, heading for one of the cars, which had just arrived. "Upwards is gambling. Downwards is…well, see for yourself."

The doors slid aside and a small group of people staggered out. They were in various stages of undress, and the one in the lead—a pale-skinned, thickly-bearded man with a turban—was bleeding from several neat lines on his bare torso.

"Oh," Amir said weakly.

"Pleasures for the body and the mind," Drift said, slipping into the empty car with Amir on his heels. "Word of advice, though: don't go too far down. Some people don't come out again."

"You don't say," Amir replied, eyes still fixed on the unsteady revellers until the doors closed and obscured them from view.

"And if you go right to the top, you can end up betting on what happens right at the bottom," Drift added, shunting an unpleasant memory aside. He'd never gone back to that particular contact a second time, and not because they'd paid badly. He wasn't too proud to admit that some things turned his stomach. "They've got cameras. We're only going a little way up though. Good, honest games of chance."

The third gaming floor had a more subdued lighting scheme than the malls they'd passed through below, and a colour scheme of rich burgundy (including velveted walls, which had always struck Drift as an odd choice of décor). He led Amir in a casual wander between the tables, trying to look as though he was searching for his game of choice. In fact he was scanning the roulette tables, looking for the mark.

There—blonde tresses done up in an intricate style and held in place with a pair of black hairsticks. Drift closed his natural left eye for a second so as not to get the unpleasant blurring sensation that reminded him of the wrong end of being drunk, and kicked up the zoom on his right. The girl expanded in his vision: late twenties perhaps, barring surgical or chemical age treatments, in a tight black dress and bicep-length matching gloves. Just as their information had said.

"You got her?" Amir muttered from beside him.

"*Si*." Drift pulled the zoom back to a natural level and began walking again, lifting a glass from a robotic dumbwaiter's tray as he did so. "Any eyes on us?"

"None I can see."

"Keep watching. You see A?"

"Hard not to spot him," Amir snorted. "He's circling round to our right, about thirty yards away. Isn't he kind of conspicuous?"

"Sure," Drift admitted, "but that only matters if anyone who happens to be watching us thinks he's with us. Which they shouldn't, given we entered separately."

They were approaching the roulette table. Now Drift was closer he could tell she wasn't there for the gambling: she wasn't paying close attention to the table or the wheel, or even chatting with the other players. Instead, she was sipping her drink in the too-small doses of someone who wanted to fit in but didn't want to get drunk, and was trying to look all ways at once. She saw them approach, of course, but didn't look twice until they were on top of her. Drift was almost hurt: he felt he normally warranted a second look.

"*Olá, senhorita*," he greeted her amiably in Portuguese. "Amanda, I believe?" Her dress wasn't actually black, as he'd thought from a distance. Instead it had a faint, rainbow-touched sheen to it which was probably supposed to be captivating but actually reminded him of an oil spill. She wore no jewellery except a pair of square, overlarge silver-edged sapphire studs on her ears. All in all, she didn't look as much like the image of a sophisticated, high-class gambler as she probably hoped.

Unsurprising, given that so far as he was aware she worked in a weapons lab.

She turned completely away from the table to face him. Appearance aside, her blank expression would have done a professional poker player proud. "Do I know you, sir?"

Her accent was precise, cut-glass British, and another act so far as Drift could tell. "Just looking to conduct a little business, ma'am."

Her eyes narrowed and she began to turn away from him. "You're on the wrong floor. The prostitutes are further down."

Damn. He caught her arm, but she squirmed free and backed off a couple of feet, glaring daggers at him. One or two other players glanced up at them, but only for a second: other people's squabbles weren't any of their concerns.

"You're drawing attention to us," Drift murmured, trying not to look around. That was Amir's job, he just needed to stay focused. "My name is Ricardo Moutinho-"

"No it's not," she replied, her eyes furious. "I've seen a picture, and you're not who I'm supposed to meet."

Double damn. "My money's just as good," he said, essaying a winning smile, but he hadn't counted on her nerves. This wasn't an experienced go-between, this was a nervous lab tech out of her depth and too scared to see the advantages of compromise.

"I'm not alone here."

He snorted. "Bullshit." Her eyes widened slightly, and he knew he'd guessed correctly. He took a step closer, trying to exude an air of confidentiality and common purpose instead of intimidation, despite his height. "You can't risk anyone else knowing about this deal, so you have no backup. Please, this will work out better for us both if you-"

"Keep away," she snapped. "You'd better know, I can handle a man twice my size if I need to."

Drift sighed. Sometimes you just had to play hardball. "It's not your lucky day then, because I brought one *three* times your size."

"*Kia ora,*" Apirana rumbled from behind her. At closer to seven feet than six and well over three hundred pounds, the sheer sight of Big A had defused many a potential fight before it started. He'd wandered closer as the conversation progressed, and bless him, he'd ended up exactly where he was needed and right on cue. Almost-certainly-not Amanda actually squeaked in alarm at the sudden appearance of a wall of Maori but then did the one thing Drift simply hadn't counted on.

She bolted directly away, swerving between the gaming tables and making for the nearest exit.

"Shit!" Drift recovered himself in an instant and scrambled after her, ignoring the cries of protest from around him. She really was painfully amateur at this, he thought as he nearly clattered into a tray of drinks held by another robot. The first rule of dealing contraband, whatever it might be, was to avoid attention. Even in a place like the House of the Redeemer, where the law held no sway, you'd still want to keep your activities on the down-low lest someone else decided you had something valuable and muscled in.

Which was exactly what he was trying to do, he supposed, but at least he had a bit of class. He'd been perfectly willing to pay for the goods if she'd had the sense to negotiate.

Amanda was fast, he'd give her that. She made it to the exit before he could gain much ground on her, then darted left out of sight down the corridor. It took him a couple more breathless seconds to reach the doorway, just in time to see her back disappearing around another corner.

The comm crackled in his ear. +*Jesus, Ichabod, what did you* do?+

"I overestimated her," he told Rourke curtly, without slowing down.

+*You* over*estimated her?*+

"I thought she was smarter," he replied. "Got any suggestions?"

+*Stay on her. I'll cut her off from the elevators: we'll get her one way or the other.*+

He rounded the next corner, and was startled to find Amir

pulling level with him. He'd never expected Apirana to join the chase—the big man could build up a reasonable head of steam in a straight line but wasn't what you'd call nimble—but he hadn't expected the kid to think quickly enough to keep up with him.

"Just shoot her!" Amir shouted as they pounded through startled punters and staff, leaving a trail of spilled drinks, scattered *hors d'oeuvre*, and sulphurous swearing in their wake.

"No!" Drift was a little surprised at the vehemence of his own objection, but damn it if he'd resort to murder *and* theft. That was just…uncivilised. Besides, despite the Captains' welcoming speech, the House had its own enforcers to make sure all 'fun' stayed where it was meant to. If you started causing trouble outside of the lower levels…

Well, then you might run into the likes of the two men in gold-trimmed, navy blue uniforms around the next corner, who were turning in the direction of Drift and Amir at the frantic urging of Amanda. Drift caught a brief glimpse of the triumphant smile spreading over his quarry's face before his attention was caught by a pair of gun muzzles being raised with bad intentions.

Drift dived instinctively, using his momentum to throw himself into a roll across the plush carpet. The crack of gunfire assaulted his ears, and he came up by the far wall with a pistol in each hand. His first left-handed shot went wide but the second one caught one of the guards in the shoulder, while his first right-handed shot lucked out and hit a knee. The right-hand enforcer screamed and fell, his gun dropping as both hands clutched instinctively at the shattered joint; the one on the left staggered and swung his weapon in Drift's direction, but Drift's next shots stitched a line across the man's chest and put him down.

His response had been automatic, and it was only once he'd fired that he realised how unusual it was for House security to shoot first and ask questions later. However, when he looked around to check on Amir, an explanation presented itself: the kid's gun was in his hand and the kid himself was on the floor. The young idiot must have already had his weapon out, and that would have been all the reason security needed to drop him.

"Damn it!" Drift scrambled to Amir's side, but there were two holes in the kid's chest leaking dark stains over his flight suit. That was it: the *Keiko* didn't have the sort of equipment or personnel to save someone from even one bad chest wound, let alone two. It was a shame, but Drift hadn't made a living off the galaxy for as long as he had by being overly sentimental. If the kid had only been winged, he'd have dropped his pursuit and trusted Rourke to get the deal done, but Amir had just transitioned himself from asset to deadweight and the *Keiko* had no room for deadweight.

A clatter of swing doors snatched his attention back to Amanda, who'd dived through them once her improvised ambush hadn't turned out as she'd planned. Even worse, Drift could hear shouts and running feet indicating that additional security had been nearby and had heard the noise. The entire thing had only taken seconds, and there were still other people standing around the corridor in shock. Drift's eyes latched onto one, a middle-aged man with a ferocious beard and moustache and a bandana, which probably hid a bald spot but also gave him a vaguely piratical air.

"Catch!"

Drift threw his left pistol underhand at the man, who caught it reflexively. Horrified realisation was just beginning to creep over the poor bastard's face as Drift crashed through the double doors in pursuit of Amanda, which was when three more enforcers rounded a corner with guns drawn. It wasn't *exactly* Drift's fault if they jumped to inaccurate conclusions.

"Wai—"

The man's protestations were cut short by gunfire as the doors of what turned out to be a kitchen banged shut behind Drift. Other witnesses might clue the security into what had actually happened, but for at least a precious few seconds the guards would think they'd killed their colleagues' murderer.

He needed to use those seconds wisely. There was another set of doors on the far side and, judging by the startled body language of the chef and waiter who were just turning away from them and towards him, it was pretty obvious which way Amanda had gone. Both staff shrank back from him as he sprinted forward, pistol still in hand, and it occurred to him as he burst out into yet another corridor that he'd probably better holster his remaining weapon again before he ended up going the same way as Amir.

"A little help?" Rourke's voice rasped from his left.

Amanda was facing him, a kitchen knife at her feet and her hands desperately clawing at the arm wrapped tight around her neck from behind. The arm itself was attached to Tamara Rourke, who was glaring at him from over the other woman's shoulder.

"Any time you're ready…" Rourke added, a trifle breathlessly.

Rourke was deadly, but Amanda was struggling desperately against her grip. However, all Drift had to do was haul her hands away from Rourke's forearm and allow his business partner to sink the blood choke in properly. The struggling lab tech slumped to the floor a couple of seconds later, her brain briefly deprived of oxygen.

"Which hand was she holding her drink in?" Rourke asked without preamble, releasing the hold.

"Uh…the right," Drift replied. He'd learned not to query Rourke's choice of questions when time was a factor, because there was always a good reason to them.

Rourke bent down and grabbed Amanda's right ear stud, then simply wrenched it loose. Drift winced: that was going to sting like hell when she came around in a few seconds.

"Let's go," Rourke told him, her long coat flaring behind her as she hurried past him.

"You...what makes you think that's it?" Drift demanded, catching up with his partner with a few long strides.

"She left her bag when she ran from you," Rourke replied, not looking at him as they tried to put some distance between themselves and Amanda's temporarily unconscious form without appearing too suspicious, "so it had to be on her person somewhere. Subdermal transport doesn't lend itself well to an inconspicuous handoff, and a hidden pocket in that sort of clothing wouldn't be much better. No other jewellery, so the ear studs seemed anomalous and overlarge unless being used to conceal something. A right-handed person would instinctively put the more valuable of two otherwise identical studs on their right ear, as it would feel more secure there." Her dark-skinned hands twisted together around the earstud and there was a faint *click* before she slid the stone aside to reveal a small, black square of plastic laced with metallic lines.

"Presto. One payload."

"You're going to be wrong, one of these days," Drift told her through a smile.

"And then you'll get to say, 'I told you so'."

"I doubt I'll want to." He chewed the inside of his cheek for a moment while Rourke discarded the stud's separated halves and slotted the data chip into her pad. "Amir didn't make it."

Rourke's mouth twitched, but her stride didn't falter. "That's a shame. He was useful. What happened?"

"The girl set security on us," Drift replied. "They got him. I had to, ah, take steps."

Rourke's eyes flickered to him for a second, then back to the pad in her hands. "Wonderful. The stairs, then?"

"They can't lock those down," Drift agreed. "How's it looking?"

"Dangerous," Rourke said, blueprints scrolling across her pad's display.

"Good," Drift nodded. "That means someone will want to buy it." He keyed his comm. "A, you there?"

+*Right behind you, Cap.*+

Drift looked over his shoulder. Sure enough, Apirana was visible a little way back in the corridor, moving through the House's other punters like a freighter through a fleet of tugs. The big man had clearly remembered Drift's instruction to return to the ship if anything went awry.

"Good," Drift said, looking away again. "Pick the pace up a little though, I know we're an odd-looking bunch but I'd rather stick together at the moment. We're taking the stairs."

+*You got it.*+

Apirana caught up with them just as they turned onto a wide staircase which was a little too deserted for Drift's liking. The House of the Redeemer was huge and therefore hard to police, but the captains took an understandably dim view of people killing their staff and Drift would have preferred a little more cover.

"Where's Amir?" Apirana asked as they began to descend.

"Took a couple of bullets from security," Drift muttered, trying to pitch his voice loud enough for the big man to hear him but without anyone else picking up what he was saying.

"Seriously? Damn, bro." Apirana's big face soured. "I kinda liked him. Nothin' you could do?"

"Two to the chest." Drift shook his head. "All over bar the shouting."

"Shiiiit," the Maori sighed. "Tell me you at least got what we came for?"

"*Si*, thanks to Sherlock here," Drift said, gesturing at Rourke.

She looked at him blankly.

"Who?"

"What, you don't...?" Drift looked at Apirana, who seemed equally mystified. "*Madre di Dios*, does *no-one* appreciate the classics anymore?"

They were fifty yards away from the hatch of the docking tunnel the *Keiko* was attached to when the press of people around them suddenly sprouted guns.

"Whoa, what..." The instinctive progress of Drift's right hand towards his remaining pistol was halted by the intimidating, cold presence of a barrel against his temple. "*Jesu Cristo*, man!"

"No such luck, you Mexican *babaca*," a voice snarled. Its owner appeared in Drift's eyeline, tall and weathered with a thick, dark moustache and generous stubble.

"Moutinho," Drift sighed, his heart sinking. "Is there a problem here?"

"You tell me," Ricardo Moutinho spat. "Actually, wait, how about you don't speak? You think I didn't see that piece of trash you call a ship lurking around Jörmungandr?"

Drift frowned. "I had business with Church and Camden, just like you."

"Which happened to bring you here? I don't think so. Somehow, you got wind of the job I took for them and thought you could sneak in and take it first." The Brazilian snorted a laugh. "I sorta admire your balls...but not enough to let you get away with it. Hand it over."

"I don't know-"

"I'll happily redecorate this hallway with your brains," Moutinho said. "You're capable, Drift, I'll give you that, and I don't reckon you'd be heading back to your floating rustbucket unless you'd got what you came for. You can hand the chip over to me right now and you get to walk away, or we kill you and then search your corpses. One way is easier for both of us."

Sadly, Moutinho wasn't an idiot. Drift sighed. "Tamara?"

"There aren't *that* many of them," Rourke replied, gesturing at the half-dozen thugs that made up Moutinho's crew. She was standing totally relaxed, with no evidence of the tension Drift was feeling other than the diamond-hard glare she was shooting at Moutinho.

"Yeah, but me and A aren't as tough as you," Drift pointed out truthfully. "Just give it to them."

"Damn it, Drift." Rourke pulled the chip from her coat pocket and tossed it to the floor at Moutinho's feet.

"*Don't* stop covering her," the Brazilian ordered, squatting to retrieve it while keeping his eyes fixed on Rourke. He handed it to the woman beside him, a dark-haired tough with a face like a knife blade. "That was too easy. Check it."

His crewer slotted the chip into her pad, then frowned. "Looks like...ponies?"

Moutinho's face creased in disbelief, and he craned his neck to see over her shoulder. "*What?*"

"Seriously. It's episodes of some sort of animated pony show. The shit *is* this?"

"A decoy," Moutinho snapped, turning his attention back to Rourke. "Nice try. The real chip, *now*. And your pad."

Rourke glowered at him, but tossed him her pad. Moutinho pulled the chip out, dropped the pad and stamped on it until it broke, then passed the new chip to his crewer. She placed it in her pad and nodded in approval. "This looks like what we're after."

"Wonderful." Moutinho clicked his fingers and the gun barrels levelled at Drift, Rourke, and Apirana lowered. "One last thing,

Drift: how did you find out about this job? And don't try to tell me Church and Camden sent you here as well: the twins aren't dumb enough to set both of us after the same thing."

Drift shrugged, not bothering to hide the hollow feeling in his stomach. They'd lost Amir for nothing. "Where's that redhead navigator of yours? Back on the *Jacare*?"

Moutinho's eyes narrowed.

"I mean, I don't like to brag, but if you'd taken off as soon as you'd been given the job then even I wouldn't have had time to loosen her tongue." He managed a smirk. "As it were."

"Bull*shit*."

"Seriously, I mean, why would a navigator get tattoos on her *ass*? She sits in a chair, that's her job, that's got to hur—"

"Oh, fuck me," the woman to Drift's left said, shaking her head. "He's telling the truth, boss."

Moutinho's moustache quivered as his mouth moved beneath it, but finally he forced a smile. "Well, thanks for the heads up, I guess. And for doing my work for me. But if I find you sniffing around one of my scores again, I won't be so friendly." He turned and walked away, presumably towards where the *Jacare* was berthed. His goons followed, but they kept their guns drawn and their eyes on Drift and his companions until they'd rounded the next corner.

"Damn," Apirana said, slamming one giant fist into the other palm.

"Good call on the navigator story," Rourke said to Drift. "A better idea than admitting we bugged the twins' office, and you've got the rep to make it believable."

"Nice try on the bait and switch, yourself," Drift replied. He attempted a smile. "Kuai's going to be mad you lost his ponies, though."

"Shame they didn't buy it," Apirana muttered.

"Don't be so sure," Rourke said, the faintest hint of a smug smile cracking her lips. She pulled another data chip from her pocket. "I switched the chip in my pad while they were looking at the first one."

Drift stared at her, hardly daring to hope. "But they checked it!"

"They didn't know exactly what they were after," Rourke said. "They got weapon plans alright, but it was a copy of the ones we stole from New Ghayathi a few months back."

"The same ones we sold to Church and Camden last time!" Drift laughed. "Hah! Moutinho's going to try to sell the twins something they've already bought!"

Apirana grinned. "I take it we ain't gonna go back to Jörmungandr for a bit, then?"

"That wouldn't seem wise," Drift admitted, leading the way towards the docking hatch. Suddenly everything had fallen back into place. "Besides, the twins are only going to be middlemen taking a cut; they've got no use for weapon blueprints themselves. When we first planned this I was thinking about trying to find a buyer at the Great Soukh, but Tamara had a better idea."

"I've got some contacts in the less reputable parts of the USNA government," Rourke said as the airlock hissed open. "They'll be *very* interested in what we've got here, and where it came from. And when I say 'interested', I mean 'willing to pay well'."

"Hear that, big man?" Drift said, slapping Apirana on the back as the Maori ducked his head to pass through the doorway. "A *government*. We're practically doing good!"

Apirana turned to him. "You see this face, bro?"

"Yeah."

"This is my 'I don't believe you' face."

"Oh, come on!" Drift said, securing the airlock behind them.

"*Someone's* going to make money off this, it might as well be us!" He sighed happily. "'Cry havoc, and let slip the...'"

Rourke and Apirana looked blankly at him again.

"Oh, never mind."

A FAIR MAN

PETER ORULLIAN

GdM #6

Pit Row reeked of sweat. And fear.

Heavy sun fell across the necks of those who waited their turn in the pit. Some sat in silence, weapons like afterthoughts in their laps. Others trembled and chattered to anyone who'd spare a moment to listen. Fallow dust lazed around them all. The smell of old earth newly turned. Graves being dug constantly for those who died fighting in the pit. Mikel walked the row, one hand on his blade, the other holding the day's list.

He passed a big man sitting in a spray of straw. The fellow wore several brands across his chest. A prisoner. More than forty fights. Each win burned into his flesh with a simple hash. He'd die in chains. Or die in the pit. Blood caked his left foot below an iron manacle that had torn up the flesh of his ankle. Dust clung to his sweaty skin. The prisoner didn't look up at Mikel, any more than he blinked away the fly drinking at the corner of his eye. But there was something foreign about the man. And something menacing. *Indifference?*

Further down, a young man practiced thrust and parry combinations, his boots lifting more dust into the hot haze. The fellow narrated each movement, the tone of his voice like a man trying to convince himself he'd survive the pit. Mikel hated this type. Not because they sought glory. No one was that stupid. It was desperation. The pup had a bit of training and had almost certainly wagered on his own victory, hoping to turn a few thin plugs. The young man's sad, nicked sword told the story of his need.

Across from the pup came a hissing laugh. Mikel turned to see an old pit survivor. Jackman. An incomplete fellow. One arm. Wood stump beneath his left knee. A face that whitened around scars when he smiled. The bastard kept a list of his own. Odds for bettors. He limped up beside Mikel to watch the pup dance.

He said nothing for a long moment, then took a deep breath through his nose. "Smell it?"

"Just you." Mikel turned to finish his round.

Jackman caught him with his one good hand. "Pup's already dead. He just doesn't have the sense to lay down in the grave yet." The hissing laugh followed. "Ten seconds for ten coins."

Mikel gave the pup another look. The young man would never best a pit fighter. He'd die wearing the surprised look of a man who'd thought too much of his own skill. Mikel stared into the milky eyes of the odds maker, anger burning at the truth of it.

"Maybe," he finally said. He pushed two thin plugs into Jackman's dirty palm, taking the odds, and crossed to the pup. "Your sword arm is slow. Don't use it to attack, only defend. Then jab with your knife hand. You're faster there. Be patient. Winning is more important than looking heroic."

The boy stared, confused, but nodded. Mikel clapped his shoulder and returned to the row. And the list. Jackman called after him, "Don't go frustrating my odds, you whoreson! Leave the row alone."

Toward the end of Pit Row, he found a man with thin shoulders seated on a tree stump. List said he was a debtor. In front of the man knelt a woman beside two children. The young ones stood quietly, around them all the feeling of goodbye.

The man had calloused hands, but no weapon. The list shared no further details.

Mikel approached. "I don't see a blade. Do you have one?"

"Was told they'd give me something," the man said, his eyes still fixed on the ground.

"What are you good with?" Mikel asked.

He finally looked up. "I'm a cobbler."

"A debtor," Mikel added.

"Money was for a roll of boot leather and some mink oil. And they took me in the morning on my day of payment."

The cobbler didn't need to say more. It was a common practice. Take a borrower before he can pay all. Especially one with an interesting story for the pit. Makes better theatre. Spectators root louder, bet emotionally. And what better story than a simple boot maker fighting against impossible odds for his wife and children. Would love prove stronger than an opponent long acquainted with this theatre court? And when the cobbler died, his death would stir a moment's regret in its witnesses. And all would feel blessed not to be in the pit. All would feel a moment's humanity.

Keeps the pit fights from becoming routine. Keeps its patrons from disinterest.

And it wasn't fair. None of it.

"You ever handle a weapon? Ever fight?" Mikel asked, surveying the man's family.

"I make shoes," he replied.

These children would be fatherless by dusk. For the price of a hide and some bootseal. *Deafened gods.* Mikel stood silent and shared a knowing look with the man. The cobbler knew it, too. Only the little ones might be unaware.

This fellow was not a gambler. Not a whore-monger. Not a spender beyond his means. He was a cobbler who'd bought material enough to earn a week's keep. And fallen behind.

Sent to Pit Row for sport. For good measure. For the law. For the entertainment of those who walked on marble floors and drank water chilled.

Deafened gods.

Mikel stared at the cobbler's little girl and thought of his own daughter. Soon to reach her cycle. Soon to visit one of those homes with marble floors and chilled water...

...Mikel let that alone for now.

He took out his writing lead and scratched out the man's name.

"What are you doing?" the cobbler asked. "It'll go worse for me if I don't—"

Mikel raised a hand to silence him. "Go home."

The cobbler stood, looking Mikel in the eyes for a long time. Then he proffered his hand in thanks. The surprise of it almost caused Mikel to smile. Almost. The man had a grip every bit as tight as Mikel's own. He then gathered his family and left Pit Row.

Mikel looked back at the list and wrote his own name into the blank.

Sword and shield held loosely at his sides, Mikel stepped into the pit. Blood old and new stained the dry ground. Around the perimeter, the bodies of the fallen lay strewn, reminders of the stakes. The pup was among them. Behind Mikel, the door shut and the cross-brace slammed into place. A moment later, a boulder of a man ducked through the opposite door. When Mikel's opponent stood up straight... *Silent gods.* The cobbler had drawn the pit fighter with the branded chest.

He remembered thinking the man looked foreign. The branded giant stood an arm's length taller than Mikel. His limbs twice as thick. In his broad face resided that *indifference.*

He's Inveterae, Mikel realised. Inveterae were a race from beyond the Pall Mountains. Some said they felt no pain. No emotion. *The perfect pit fighter.* Mikel now noticed brands over much of the rest of the man's skin. This Inveterae was either a decorated soldier or a traded commodity with a long history of owners. Or both.

They were called to the centre of the pit to face the prince and his coterie. Mikel realised he might be recognised by one of the platform captains, so he scooped up some of the blood-drenched earth and smeared his face and beard with it, making it appear an elaborate ritual.

When he and his opponent came foot to foot, a chill shivered through him. Not fear of the match. Or even of dying, exactly. He'd felt the closeness of mortality before. This was different. This was the feeling of standing next to a creature who didn't fight with fear. Or aggression. Or anger. Or even to win, necessarily. This was the feeling of a fighter who simply put down whatever stood up in front of him. Without care. Without concern for himself.

A perfect killer.

Mikel would never best him. Any more than the cobbler would have.

Together they turned to face the prince. Aron was the prince's given name. He'd dubbed himself Aronal—the *al* appended by most of the new aristocracy to suggest they served *all* the people. It was a feeble and transparent attempt at democracy, further betrayed by the prince's attire. Aronal took great pleasure in how he dressed. Loved clothes that proved difficult to acquire. Especially boots, which he had polished several times a day.

Aronal held a long pause, drawing attention to himself. A hint of a smile turned his lips up at the corners. All self-congratulation that smile was. Smug as every last hell. Mikel hated the sight of it. Especially because the prince had a way of turning it beneficent when he needed to.

Aronal began to announce the match. "It is civilised of us to resolve our disputes…"

Mikel heard very little, instead seeing the young girl beside the prince. Today's offering. What was she, twelve? Maybe thirteen? A fledgling woman come to her cycle, and so taken into the prince's company for his entertainment. Until he tired of her. The Monarch's Privilege. The girl stared out with deadened eyes, looking small.

"…from the land of the Bourne. Never defeated…"

Mikel's own daughter would reach her cycle soon. Would she sit here like this young one? Would she watch death with dead eyes? Would she have to learn such things so early and hard and lose something of herself?

"…against a simple cobbler. A good man who fell behind. Whose family…"

That's when Mikel noticed two young boys behind the prince. Each with the same dead look in their eyes. Around them sat men and women in stainless clothes, woven of Soren Silk, sharing quiet conversation and amusements. They were a new caste. A new ruling class, whose rule was lawlessness for themselves.

And yet they kept the peace.

They took their privileges, but the roads were safe.

And I'm a part of it. I carry their lists.

Because the law mattered. Keeping people safe mattered. And so sacrifices must be made. It was a fair trade.

But early arrest wasn't fair. A cobbler against an Inveterae wasn't fair. Mikel had taken the boot maker's place thinking his own skill against a pit fighter would be a fairer match. Maybe even that he'd have the advantage. He was a skilled wrestler, after all. And this pit, where he'd competed, had once been a place of high sport. And he usually won. Nowadays, though, he mostly taught his little ones how to defend themselves. And today he'd be fighting an Inveterae. Even his skill didn't make it a fair match. He would leave his wife a widow and his children fatherless.

He'd seen these pit fights a thousand times. The prince or another of the new aristocracy would tell the story of the fighters in dramatic detail, while blood-thirsty revellers listened in rapt attention. A few tattered pennants would flap in the breeze like tired accompaniment. And at the end, instructions for the match would be laid out. A few simple rules. When to start fighting. An invocation to honour.

Mikel listened closely now. Waiting.

Prince Aronal raised his palms toward them, like a grateful benefactor. "The match will start when I say 'begin'."

Without moving his feet, Mikel swept his sword up and thrust it into the Inveterae's throat. Blood sprayed from the gaping wound, splashing across his hand and arm. The Inveterae dropped to his knees as the crowd gasped. Growled complaints rose on the hot afternoon air.

Mikel drove the blade deeper into the other's flesh, pushing the Inveterae to his back. Blood covered the giant's neck, but it made no attempt to fight back or remove the blade or staunch the flow.

When Mikel came near, that *chill* shivered through him again—the Inveterae's indifferent eyes hadn't changed. They looked at him, as if waiting to die. Though he thought he saw something else. A small flicker of acknowledgement. Gratitude maybe.

Then the blood stopped flowing. The Inveterae's eyes stopped seeing.

"You're a coward," called the prince. "You've disrespected our rules—"

"No," Mikel said, turning. "You said the match would start when you said 'begin'."

Aronal considered for a long moment. A small smile crept upon his lips. "Clever." He raised his arms to the pit theatre. "Our match champion," he announced. "And the day's fastest win by more than a full minute."

A roar ascended all around as Mikel walked from the pit to find Jackman. The pup had beaten the odds; Mikel had twenty plugs to collect.

Night came on full as Mikel patrolled the Tides. Sever Ens wasn't a port town. It had no harbour. But it had a traveller's district. Cheap rooms. Cheap food. And a plug bought you a seat at any table of odds. Whores were easy to come by, too. Male whores made double the rest, as they tended to have a broader tolerance for risk. The Tides was where drifters rolled through Sever Ens. Where people washed up on its shores and away again as if drawn by one of the dominant moons.

Mikel walked the south side of the market street, keeping a close eye on idlers. Experience had taught him idlers in the Tides were either flimflam men, or marks. Trouble either way. On each side of the street, every thirty paces, stood a thick post topped with a lamp—an attempt to discourage pickpockets and the like. The lamps created pools of darkness that needed to be managed closely.

At the edge of light thrown by one of these street lanterns, an old man strolled. Men do, sometimes, when their luck has been good at the tables. Stupid thing. Beating one set of odds makes them confident enough to walk as if they haven't anyplace to be. Mikel wondered, though, if it wasn't as simple as feeling a little contentment. The fear of debt once removed—if only for an hour's time—allows a man to imagine happiness. And happiness is rarely hurried.

Into the old man's path stepped a street scamp. Gunnysack jacket. Smears of coal on his cheeks. Part costume for a mark, part disguise against a man like Mikel.

The waif—maybe twelve years old—petitioned the old man. Mikel couldn't hear the words, but he recognised the tone easy enough. A palm went up. Suspicion in the old man's shoulders fell to compassion, and his hand went into his pocket.

The lad pointed to the mouth of the alley. Mikel started to run after them. The old man followed the scamp into the shadows. By the time Mikel rounded the corner and turned up the alleyway, the old man was surrounded by seven waifs—three boys, four girls. Each held a knife.

"Enough," Mikel called, rushing to the old man's assistance.

Behind him—as he knew would happen—three more scamps closed in to block his retreat. Didn't matter. Alley kids folded when you crushed the will of their leader. Mikel needed to quickly identify which one led this gang. Then either talk him out of his prize or pound him senseless.

"They've robbed me," the old man said, pointing to a boy who wore a satchel over his shoulder.

Too easy, Mikel thought. The leader wouldn't be wearing an obvious telltale.

"Doesn't concern you, coat," said one of the girls. "You can go back the way you came. No harm. But if you stay to play hero, you're getting cut."

Men who carried the city's lists—like Mikel—or walked patrol, or kept the peace, were called "coats". Not because their coats matched, as a uniform might, but because they had a coat in the first place. Authority to act in the name of the ruling seat was a piece of paper folded into a waxed pouch against his chest.

"No one's getting cut," Mikel said, nearing the circle. "And no one's getting robbed. Return the coin, and I won't drop you into a work camp."

These kids wouldn't have parents. Not in the sense that it would be a threat to invoke their names. And jail was out. Scamps were too young for that. But the work camps. Worse than jail they were. And Mikel didn't make idle threats.

"You've not walked a turn in the Tides in a while, have you, coat." One of the girls turned to face him. Hers was a different kind of confidence. It wasn't the same as the Inveterae's, but it lived in that direction. Scary as every last hell to see that look on one so young.

"Tides are always the same," Mikel replied. "Just like you." He swept an arm at the lot of them.

Before she could reply, the old man leapt at the boy with the satchel and clubbed him in the side of the face with a hand-length cudgel he'd had hidden beneath his belt. The boy went down hard, his head cracking on the cobblestones.

Immediately, another boy leapt onto the old man's back, taking him in a choke hold. Another swept the man's legs, dropping him to the alley floor. A second girl pounced, slicing two of the old man's fingers clean off. He screamed and grabbed his hand, squeezing back the blood.

The girl in front of Mikel never moved. Never took her eyes from him. And Mikel had had enough of this gods-damned business. He started toward her, his sword ready. Two steps and she flashed her hands. A half-moment later something entered his cheek with a searing pain. Mikel stopped and pulled a long, sturdy pin from his face. A third of it coated with blood. Delicate fletching made it something slightly more than a sewing needle.

"I would have put that in your eye, but I don't want you coming back." The girl casually raised a second pin between them, staring at him over its tip. "Take it as a warning, and get the hell out of my alley."

The old man on the ground moaned, still held tightly in a choke hold. That's when Mikel saw it, the pendant hanging on the old man's chest—the prince's seal. This was a member of Aronal's coterie. An official man.

That's also when Mikel realised the old man hadn't come into the alley for charity's sake. There'd been an unseemly proposition. It hadn't been compassion that relaxed the old man's shoulders. It had been the ease of filling an appetite. The carnal kind. For this old man, it seemed Privilege wasn't enough.

But Mikel wouldn't leave him here. Didn't matter the circumstance or danger. Ten against one. Not fair. Even if they *were* kids. Though, perhaps it would be two against ten, assuming the old man could be expected to defend himself if Mikel pushed this.

He stared at the girl and her pin for an uncomfortably long time. He meant to make them uncertain about what he'd do. Mostly, he was thinking about her age.

"How old are you?" he asked, his voice softer now.

"I don't work on my back," the girl said.

"Twelve?" he asked. "Fourteen at the outside?"

She frowned and spat at his feet. "You want part of the take. That it? Because you know you could put a couple of us down before we cut you through. And you think we won't make the tradeoff?"

He shook his head. "You took to the streets rather than—"

"Men and women who wear silk don't have Privileges in the Tides." She twirled the pin deftly between her fingers.

But that was bluster. The law had every name on a list. Every name. Save drifters. And Mikel was paid to keep drifters moving in and out. These scamps and gillers were refugees who'd escaped the Privileges. For now. And to survive in the Tides, they ran together and fleeced whomever they could.

It made sense to Mikel now, where it hadn't before. The packs of children. The crime. The killings.

He studied the pin he'd pulled from his cheek. He guessed this scamp's mother had given her a leather sewing kit as a means to provide for herself when she left her to the Tides—to escape the touch of Privilege.

My silent gods, he thought. Anna, his daughter, would be this age in a few years' time.

"Easy," he said, and reached into his coat for a bag full of coins—his take from Jackman on the pup's odds. "Let him go, and I'll make him square with my own money. You keep your take and go the hell home."

The girl's eyebrows arched in surprise, then her eyes narrowed. "What trick?"

Mikel ignored the question. "I'll see him to a physicker for his fingers. And if we meet again, I'll go hard on you for this." He waved the pin and tossed it aside.

"Maybe we'll take your coins, too," she said, her fingers tensing on the pin in her hand.

"You're welcome to try," replied Mikel, hefting his bag to jingle the coins. "But I won these by frustrating the prince's odds maker at the pit. So these are winnings that stole wine from Privileged bellies."

The girl laughed, and lowered her pin. Then she took several steps toward Mikel, coming up close to see him clearly through the shadows. "We're not looking to be saved. We don't need your sympathy."

Softly so that the others wouldn't hear, he said, "That's horseshit."

She smiled.

"I've made a fair offer. Are we made?"

The girl motioned with her hand, and the scamps disappeared into the alley. She backed slowly away, looking frailer in the darkness with each retreating step. The Tides would get her eventually. That much was sure. But not today. And she'd go with brighter eyes when the odds caught up with her. But they'd be odds she chose herself.

Weeks of walking the Tides exhausted him. In every possible way. Coming home to his family was Mikel's only relief. Small concerns and wrestling with his little ones. Chores and simple repairs. Laughter.

Then one day entering his home, he felt a graveside stillness. The air was heavy. The silence loud. On an old chair in the corner, his wife, Mable, sat rocking their youngest child. Beside her sat the cobbler he'd saved from the pit, holding a pair of shoes.

"What is this?" He stepped in, surveying the rest of the room. No one else. "Where is Anna?"

His wife looked up at him, unable to speak, her face pale and tear-stained.

The cobbler broke the silence. "I came to give her these," he said, glancing at the shoes in his hands. "For what you did for me and my family. This is how I found her."

Mikel knelt beside her. "Mable, where is Anna?" he asked again.

Tears rolled down her cheeks. But she could only shake her head.

Privilege. But so early?

It didn't matter that he'd known this day would come. It didn't matter that he'd sometimes thought the tradeoff for safety was worth the price of Privilege. It didn't matter that it was the law. The thought of his little girl taken into the hands of the prince and his cronies to be used for their pleasure and amusement tore at him. His heart hammered with anger and fear and helplessness. His mind raced with images no parent should have to imagine.

Before he knew what he was doing, he'd stood and started for the ruling manors. For the prince.

The cobbler said something behind him, but he didn't register the words.

At the sentry gate, he showed his paper of authorization. The prince's seal and signature got him past the guards. At the manor doors, he did the same, claiming that Prince Aronal had requested a personal report on the state of the Tides—he dropped a hint of "special taxes", money lay at the top of the prince's concerns.

The doormen took Mikel's sword and knife—a precaution at all ruling manors. Then a man in a red velvet uniform ushered him personally up two sets of stairs to a set of double doors guarded by four men. He showed his authorization paper again; one of the guards knocked softly on the private chamber door.

Some moments later came the reply, "Can't it wait?"

"It's the Tides, sir. Something about new taxes," said the usher.

Another delay and then, "Very well. Come."

The usher bowed and opened the door. If Prince Aronal's attire was extravagant, his bedchamber was grotesque in its lavishness. It smacked of the careless spending a man does when he's had a bounteous night of gambling in the Tides. Art covered the walls—the styles foreign, and so expensive to import. Rugs of intricate design stretched to every corner of the room. And there stood no less than six refreshment tables, laden with wines, cheeses, fruits, pastries, and thin meats.

And the jewel of it all was the bed. An oversized piece of furniture—clearly commissioned—with Aronal's likeness graven into the wood in dramatic relief. The bed had four immense posts, and sheer drapes pulled back, as if the man wanted to be seen sleeping.

Mikel had only taken two strides into the room, when he nearly fell.

Lying on the prince's bed…was Anna. Her eyes red. Her lips trembling. One hand tied to the bed post by a length of rope.

Mikel found strength enough to signal that she shouldn't acknowledge him. "Sire, I've news. But I doubt you'll want your man here when I share it."

Aronal was pouring a glass of dark liquor. Smelled like plum brandy, but tapped too soon, as if by impatient hands. He turned, nodded to the usher, who bowed and withdrew, closing the door.

"And you are?" asked the prince.

"Mikel Richerds, sire. I enforce your laws."

"I'm not aware of new taxes in the Tides," Aronal replied, unimpressed, "so, I'll assume you have an enterprise to propose. Something that profits us both. Thus your request for privacy, yes?"

Mikel forced himself not to look at his daughter. He couldn't think straight when seeing the fear in her eyes. And he needed a clear head for this.

"Sire, your Privilege has brought my daughter to your bed." Mikel motioned to Anna.

Aronal's eyes scanned Mikel, ensuring he'd been relieved of his weapons. Then he took a long draught of his brandy, smiling behind his glass. "So, you've come to ask for an exception."

"I serve your law," Mikel answered. "I carry your lists. I walk the Tides. I keep my opinions to myself, because I like that our roads are safe."

"You have opinions?" Aronal laughed softly, mockingly. "Well, I'd like to hear them."

Mikel closed his eyes and shook his head. "That's not what I meant, sire. I'm sorry. I just understand that a man has to give to receive. There are trades we make."

"Like Privilege," Aronal followed, goading him.

"I used to think so," Mikel replied. "I used to think that it's not really a trade if the thing you give up means nothing. Costs nothing. But now…"

"Yes?" Aronal spared a look at Anna, whose powered face was streaked with tears. Her eyes asked for help.

"The price is too high…and she's not yours to take."

"Do you think, perhaps, that's for me to decide?" said the prince, lowering a hand to the blade at his belt.

"No," Mikel said earnestly. He struggled with the words. "I'm not a law maker. But I know what's fair. I've kept your pits moving, made sure the fights were satisfying. I've patrolled the drift that rolls through Sever Ens, ensured they left as much coin as they took, and kept your taxpayers alive." He looked the prince straight. "It's fair for me to ask this favour."

Aronal offered a conciliatory laugh. "My good man, I appreciate your service. The city's in your debt. But I think the personal nature of today's Privilege has clouded your thinking. That's understandable.

But I assure you, I will be…delicate."

"As will I," came a voice. Its owner stepped from behind a large bureau on the other side of the bed.

The old man.

His one hand still bandaged, he held a crystal goblet in the other, his cheeks ruddy with drink. "When a Prince's man is attacked by street scum, the little bastards should be gutted. Not paid off!"

This was why Anna had been brought here nearly two years before her time. Punishment. Mikel's punishment for not better defending the prince's man.

Petty gods damned bastard!

Mikel could have left the man there to die. He'd bought his life with pit winnings. Took a pin in the face and nearly lost an eye for this whoreson bugger!

The old man smiled thinly.

Mikel turned back to Aronal, ready to explain, but saw only a look of supreme smugness. They'd planned this together. More amusement at the expense of lives they were sworn to hold safe.

Anger burned hot inside Mikel, who finally looked again at Anna. Her eyes had begun to show a hint of resignation. It was the worst thing he'd seen in all his life. And by every last silent god, he would die trying to keep it out of her face.

"I'm afraid I'm growing impatient with you," said the prince. "I applaud your commitment to your family. But it's time for you to go."

Mikel could rush the prince, but the man was no laggard with a blade. And Mikel was unarmed. He'd test those odds if he had to, though he hated the thought of Anna watching the prince kill him if he failed.

He scanned the room for a makeshift weapon; another knock sounded at the chamber door.

"Oh my dead gods, what now? Come," Aronal yelled.

The usher bowed apologetically as he led the cobbler into the room. "You said to admit this man as soon as he arrived," the usher explained.

Aronal's eyes widened with delight. "So I did. Come in, my good fellow." He gestured for the cobbler to approach, and dismissed the usher.

The cobbler shot Mikel a look, then glanced at the boot box he carried. He did it twice. *Something's inside.* The cobbler came up beside him and put the box down on the floor between them, removing thick wood stumps from the boots that helped them keep their shape.

Aronal hastily finished his liquor and wiped his neatly trimmed beard inelegantly with his sleeve. "This man, Mikel, this man…do you know what he did?"

Mikel waited.

The prince lit with glee. "Oh my, it was wonderful. He was in the pit. Against an Inveterae, mind you. And perfectly held to the rules while killing the creature before I'd even finished announcing the match."

Aronal didn't recognise either of them. In fairness, the prince's platform was a fair distance from the pit floor. And Mikel had muddied his face. Though he guessed Aronal had also been rather drunk.

On the bed, Anna was using the distraction to try and free her bound hand. But the binding was too tight, and she was trembling, besides.

"Sounds like a clever man." Mikel nodded to the cobbler.

"You've a gift for understatement," said the prince. "This fellow saved his own life by using my rules against me. It was brilliant! So, you know what I did?"

"No, sire."

Aronal leaned forward and whispered like a conspirator, "I commissioned a pair of boots…from the very hide of the Inveterae he killed." Then he boomed, "Isn't that marvellous!"

Mikel glanced down at the boots near his feet, and that's when he saw them. A knife hidden in the bottom of each boot.

"I simply had to have a reminder," Aronal went on. "Best pit fight of the year. And the commission on the boots pays our man here in full. Plus some. He's no debtor any more. Do you see how Privilege works?"

Mikel looked up at the prince. A pair of knives wasn't a guarantee. The monarch had a sword and dagger, and he was powerfully good with them. But it was a chance.

"I beg you, sire." Mikel gave Anna one last look. "Let my daughter go. For all I've done. All I will continue to do. Grant me this one request."

Aronal's countenance changed. Darkened. His delight was replaced by furrowed brows and an angry twist on his lips "You are relieved of your duties," he said. "And good luck finding work, even in the Tides, where you're known as a man of the law. Oh," he added, with a suggestive drawl, "and your daughter will remain here a full year. Perhaps longer."

Privilege was usually a few days.

Anna began to cry.

Mikel bent to the boots and took hold of the knives. The cobbler grabbed the box and retreated to the wall.

Aronal stared a long moment at them both, then shook his head and laughed. "This cobbler is full of surprises."

"One last time," Mikel said. "Let her go."

"And what do you think happens, my friend, if you manage to kill me?" He pointed at the door behind Mikel. "You'll never escape the manor alive. There are thirty men between you and the gate. All armed and armoured."

Mikel twirled the knives around into a pit fighter's grip. "I'm betting once the head is gone, the body won't follow."

"Quite the risk," said the prince, still standing near one of the refreshment tables.

"I'm also betting some of those men are fathers," Mikel added.

Aronal drew his sword. "Clever," he said.

The old man bolted for a second door beyond the bureau. The cobbler dashed and cut him off, smashing the box against the side of the old man's head and knocking him to the floor, unconscious.

"And to keep the odds fair..." the cobbler turned and locked the main door, then moved to the bureau and pushed it in front of the other door. "Just in case his majesty had thoughts of calling in help."

The prince's eyes flattened, became calculating. "Your daughter will watch me kill you."

"Maybe," Mikel conceded.

Aronal lunged, the tip of his blade slicing at Mikel's forearm. He managed to deflect the blow with one of his knives, and dropped into a ready stance. *He's fast.*

Mikel closed in, hoping to end the fight quickly. He stabbed with his right hand dagger, but the prince warded off the blow with his own jewel-hilted long-knife.

Mikel spun past Aronal, crouching as the man's blade swept through the air above his head. He leapt up and kicked Aronal in the chest, driving him back. Mikel needed space to reset himself.

The prince regained his balance and stood ready. Mikel stalked a slow circle, looking for an entry point, a momentary lapse of concentration. Aronal gave him none, even as he smiled. "Actually," said the prince, "this is a nice surprise. It's not often enough that someone is fighting back when I slice them open."

Mikel rushed, then dropped low, changing levels. He meant to get a knife in the prince's belly, but the man stepped gingerly aside and brought his own knife hard across Mikel's arm, opening a deep cut. Blood flowed fast and hot. And he felt his left hand grip weaken. He rolled through, near the foot of the bed, and whirled as the prince swept in on him.

Mikel jabbed up with his good hand, and caught the prince deep in the thigh. Aronal moaned and staggered back. "Your family will pay for that," he said.

With one bad hand, two knives were doing Mikel no good now. While the prince stood unready, Mikel hurled one of the knives. He missed, but it gave him time to stand and get into a pit stance.

Aronal braced himself, then came forward, eyes bright, teeth clenched. He feinted with his dagger, drawing Michael into a block, then brought his sword up quickly, stabbing Mikel in the side. Pain shot across Mikel's back and belly. He pulled back, blood coating his shirt and coat. It wasn't a mortal blow, but he'd bleed out if he didn't get it bandaged.

Anna was crying. Mikel could hear it now. What must it be like to watch a loved one being killed? Because he was losing. He had one good hand, a knife, and each movement sent shivering pain through his torso.

The prince must have seen it. "Before I kill you... I will make you watch." He nodded toward Anna cowering against the massive, carved headboard.

There's a line. An edge of sanity a man knows about himself. It's a place he crosses when those he loves are threatened. In danger. Laws don't mean a good gods damn on the other side of that line. And Mikel felt himself rip across it, damning the costs.

He rushed Aronal again, this time screaming to create panic. He pretended to come with an exaggerated overhand sweep, stabbing down, but again he dropped, falling under the prince's slashing blade and stabbing up.

Aronal shuffled his feet, sidestepping the blow. His wounded thigh gave out, and he tumbled back, falling on the bed. Falling onto Anna.

The rest looked like a choreographed dance. Like something rehearsed. Anna raised her legs and wrapped them around each of his arms and behind his back. A wrestler's move. Then she pulled her bound hand down quickly and circled the prince's neck with the rope. Before the prince understood what was happening, she wrenched the binding tight.

Aronal writhed, trying to free himself. Anna tightened her legs, causing one of the prince's shoulders to pop. But she didn't relent, pulling harder on the rope with both hands. The prince gasped for air, his mouth working like a fish's.

Aronal's sword fell from his hand, clattering to the floor. Mikel finally broke the shock of what he was seeing and started forward. The prince's eyes found his own, pleading. Mikel watched as the Aronal's face whitened and slowly relaxed. And he stopped moving altogether.

Mikel didn't know how long it had taken. Anna was sweaty and panting. She started to cry harder now. Sobs racked her body as her legs relaxed and Aronal slipped to the floor.

Mikel eased forward and took her in his arms. He felt her shake her head, as if denying it all. She'd escaped the prince's Privilege. In the end, she'd done it herself. But it had earned her a different kind of knowledge. Something a child shouldn't have to learn. And Mikel couldn't take that away. Could never change it.

Even if the ruling seats changed the way of things—and he would see to it that they did—it wouldn't change things for Anna. You can remove a nail from a piece of wood, but the hole remains.

Some damage will always be visible. And Mikel couldn't take that away, either.

The unfairness of it gnawed at him. He wanted to put it right.

But his only power was to hold his little girl for as long as she needed him to. He hoped that would be enough.

SEAN PATRICK HAZLETT

GdM #5

J immy Alvarez was one tough mother. After reliving the firefight over and over in my head, I could only come to that conclusion. Shivering and covered in blood and dust, I hid under the bodies of my crew in some godforsaken ditch near an almond grove in California's Central Valley while I prayed for twilight to fade into night.

"Bobby," Rory Haines sputtered as he choked on his own blood, "Tell Missy I love 'er and make sure she gets my bounty after you bag the ol' bastard."

I nodded to make Rory feel better. But there's no way I was gonna share that bounty with a dead man's family. There weren't many boomers left, and the ones who were either nasty ol' coots with a knack for survival or cats with more dough than Zuckerberg. Either way, you had to make each bounty count.

I preferred the ol' coots myself. Most of 'em were poor. And being poor made 'em easier targets. The rich ones could afford tons of security.

I could smell Alvarez coming, a hint of cigar smoke drifting on the biting wind. What the man had done with railroad ties, rebar, and bear traps was inspired, if not horrifying.

Rory was wheezing again. I tapped his knee with my rifle to shut him up. But my gesture was about as useful as tits at a big dick convention.

Alvarez's footsteps quickened. "Shut the hell up," I murmured with a kick to Rory's bloody thigh that a shit-encrusted shaft of rusty rebar had run clean through. Rory would have tetanus for sure, but it didn't matter. He'd be dead by morning.

Word had it that Alvarez was almost eighty. How that sombitch could move so fast was a goddamn miracle—and a nightmare for me and my crew.

The cigar smell was getting stronger, but the footsteps had stopped. I shut my mouth and played dead. If Rory wouldn't quit his whining, then he was on his own.

Watching from beneath three lukewarm bodies, I saw the underside of a black combat boot kick dirt from the lip of the ditch. Rory squealed.

Alvarez carefully slid into the trench, cradling a scope-mounted AR-15 in his stubby arms. I couldn't believe it. The man was five-foot nothing and couldn't have weighed more than a buck fifty.

Either way, he was on Rory like orange on a pumpkin. Ol' bastard took one look at Rory's leg and double-tapped him in the head. Then, all nonchalant-like, Alvarez took two deep drags on his cigar.

Then he came closer. He poked and jabbed at Carl and Juan and Ashish. I held my breath. He rolled Carl's bloody body off the pile and double-tapped him in the brain bucket, probably just to be sure. I quivered. He did the same to Ashish. Juan's corpse was next.

I could barely breathe. If I didn't do nothing, he'd shoot me too. It was a real grade-A goatfuck. Rolling the dice, I ignored every survival instinct I had, jumped to my feet, raised my arms, and begged, "Please, don't shoot."

Alvarez wore olive drab fatigues along with an ol'-school Viet Nam boonie cap. His face was taut but wrinkled, weather worn but not beaten. He jabbed his rifle in my chest and chuckled. "You're mine, son."

I smiled like some dope stupid enough to think there was any chance of walking away from this.

The whole thing was ridiculous. Me, who came here to kill him, and Alvarez, who'd just snuffed out four of my men like it was nothing. And here we were, smiling at each other like two jerkoffs. I gave him my best aw-shucks face. He laughed and lowered his rifle. Just when I thought things were cool, he coldcocked me, and I was out like bellbottoms and eight-tracks.

When the Chinese called their treasury bonds, interest rates went ballistic, and Uncle Sam needed a quick fix to service its ballooning interest. Hiking up the death tax was the easy part, but the goddamn boomers wouldn't die fast enough. So the feds passed the Septuagenarian Protection Act of 2020 to accelerate the process.

Regardless of the details, that law changed my life. It's what transformed me from an unemployed dirtbag into a highly bankable merc. You see, there's not a single living politician who had the guts to send the police to round up these defiant ol' fogies, so governments hired private military contractors on the down low.

What the feds did to the ol' coots after was their business, not mine. But the job paid well, so I didn't complain.

In the early days, business was good. Not many people were willing to chase down ol' folks, so the supply of hunters was low, but the demand for boomers was high. And back then, hunting boomers was like shooting fish in a barrel. The commies from the city with their anti-gun slogans were the easiest to round up, as were wealthy law-abiding urban conservatives who'd blindly trusted the system that made 'em rich. I made a killing back then, and I didn't even have to kill anyone to do it.

When other working class kids saw dopes like me making a fortune, they all started getting into the biz. Then the law got looser than a ten-buck barracks whore, and it wasn't long before it became legal to put the ol' farts down. Before I knew it, mercs had depopulated most of America's urban centres of their Septs, and we all had to go deeper into the country to make any dough.

That, my friend, is when the biz really started separating the men from the boys. The gun nuts in the sticks weren't so easy to collect because they had the means and the training to fight back.

The Nam vets was the worst. Most of 'em was smart 'nuff to unass the city and head to the hills before the feds passed the new law. And these vets really starting racking up the body count, especially among the amateurs. So much so that the pencil pushers in Washington soon required merc outfits to pass through reams of red tape for certification. Hell, that one move alone did more to consolidate the industry than rising body counts did. But as they say, "That's all history now."

I woke up in a crouch next to a shiny white toilet bowl. My wrists were handcuffed to a radiator. It was hot as hell, my head ached, and I had a big lump on my forehead. My stomach grumbled and I was parched. I had no idea how long I'd been out.

It was a miracle Alvarez hadn't killed me, but I ain't one to kick a gift horse in the balls.

When I looked up, Alvarez was standing in front of the sink, dressed like a pervert in tighty-whiteys and a spotless white wife-beater. He was shaving with a straight razor. Real ol' school. Dog tags dangled from his neck like a good luck charm. His skin was rough as rawhide.

He tilted his head in my direction like a cocky drill instructor. Like I was the dumbest piece of crap he'd ever seen. "So you finally returned to the world of the living, ginger," he said, referring to my red hair. "You're probably wondering why you're not taking a dirt nap, aren't you?"

I nodded.

He smiled and then pointed at my right arm where my eagle, globe and anchor tattoo had claimed all the real estate. "Why are you here trying to kill a fellow Marine, Devil Dog?" he asked, his stone-cold brown eyes boring into mine.

Like a moron, I grinned and said the first thing that came to mind. "Trying to make a buck, same as you."

"Bullshit," he said. "I got nothing against shooting boomers. Hell, if I were your age, I'd be shooting 'em too. And I'm one of 'em. They fucked everything up. Those hippy pricks spat at me and called me a baby killer after I risked my life for our country. All the while, those pinkos fled to Canada to avoid doing their duty. But a fellow Marine. You should know better, boy."

I had no idea what Alvarez was gonna do next, but it couldn't be any worse than this. He had a way 'bout him. A way that made me feel real low, like I'd strangled a puppy.

"What're you gonna do with me?" I asked.

He ran his fingers over his high-and-tight. "Catch and release, Marine. Catch and release. I got no business killing a fellow Marine."

I shot him a confused look. "How you know I ain't gonna come back and try again?"

"Semper Fi," he said. "You just needed some corrective training. Now that I've done that, I know you ain't coming back. 'Course, you'll be surrendering you and your friends' firearms in exchange for my generosity."

That night the ol' man actually cooked me a porterhouse in his small kitchen and gave me as many beers as I wanted. I took him up on both offers. 'Course, I only had one Budweiser. I needed to stay sharp. You never know, the ol' fart could always change his mind.

I guess being with someone he thought was a fellow Marine made Alvarez feel safe, even if I had tried to smoke him a few hours earlier. Or maybe he was lonely being holed up out here for so long. Probably just wanted some company.

It wasn't long before Alvarez pulled out the whiskey and started telling me about his time in Kai San. Halfway through the bottle, the man was still lucid as a lark. But the more he drank, the more belligerent he became. He pushed me for stories about Iraq or Afghanistan or wherever it was I told him I'd served, but I refused. Told him some bull that I didn't want to talk about it. He nodded as if he'd understood. Like we shared a secret only combat vets could know.

He was madder than hell that I only had one beer. In my defence, I told him I was Mormon and had had the first beer to be polite. He stared at me a good thirty seconds before he smiled and accepted my excuse. But I was worried he didn't believe me. And if he didn't believe me, I was done for.

As Alvarez was pouring the last drop of his bottle of Jack Daniels into his glass, the windows shattered. The steady *thump*

thump thump of a machine gun violated our quiet evening.

I tackled the ol' man, shielding him with my body. But Alvarez didn't seem to care for my attempt to save him. He pushed me off and rolled onto his stomach. Bullets whistled over our heads like burping bees. Alvarez low-crawled from the kitchen to his den until he was underneath a pool table.

He quickly reached up and grabbed a cue stick from the table, then dropped to his belly. He low-crawled to a spot where five rifles hung on the wall. Keeping a low profile on the floor, he worked the cue stick into the trigger guard of an AR-15. The rifle fell from the gun rack and into his hands.

He slithered over shards of glass and took up a fighting position near the broken window. He aimed his rifle and waited. The steady *thump thump thump* of the machine gun began anew. Alvarez shifted his rifle, steadied it, then fired. The machine gun fire ceased. Alvarez rolled away from his firing position and established another one three feet away. Then he waited.

Huddled on the ground, I waved my hand at Alvarez. He turned his head at the motion. I pointed at the wall of rifles. Then I pointed outside. He stared at me for several seconds as if considering my offer, then nodded.

I low-crawled toward the wall and grabbed the cue stick. I worked a twenty-two off the wall and established a fighting position next to Alvarez.

It was dark outside and hard to see, especially with the light on in the house. I looked behind me and saw a lamp. I aimed and fired. Alvarez swivelled his head at me. His left eye was already shut. The ol' bastard was already building up his night vision. He nodded in what I was certain was approval.

I listened while I waited for my night vision to kick in, struggling to filter out the sound of my heartbeat. Soon, the boys outside would be sending another man to the machine gun. But if they were smart, they'd established a new firing position. We waited until our attackers identified themselves with machine gun fire.

Sure enough, the boys outside began pumping Alvarez's house full of lead again. I kept my rifle steady and scanned the places I'd be if I were setting a machine gun nest. Sure as shit, I saw the faintest tip of a head there. I steadied my rifle, took aim, and squeezed the trigger. The firing stopped instantly. Alvarez gave me a thumbs up.

I ducked down and moved to another window. The attackers would be attracted to my muzzle flash. Like clockwork, the next poor sod to take control of the machine gun shot my ol' fighting position to hell, rendering it a riot of smoke and splinters. But Alvarez just waited calmly and then took a shot. Again, the machine gun fell silent. Then the ol' man sunk to his belly and crawled to his back door.

You had to admire the bastard. He was gonna take the fight to the enemy. He looked back and gestured for me to follow. I shook my head. "We don't know how many of them are out there," I whispered.

He hesitated, then said, "Doesn't matter. We stay here, they'll kill us. Plus, I don't want 'em to wreck my house any more than they already have."

I smiled and then nodded. I low-crawled to Alvarez and said, "Let me go first. I'll draw their fire."

He smiled and slapped me on the back. "I may forgive you yet, Marine."

I slowly rose, grabbed the latch on the screen door, and opened it. I sprinted toward a Ford 150 in the driveway, making for its wheel well. To cover Alvarez, I pointed my rifle toward the almond grove where our assailants were hiding, then gave him a thumbs up.

Alvarez ran toward the rusted Ford. The crack of a rifle shot echoed through the valley. Alvarez dropped, clutching his leg. I aimed my rifle in the direction of the muzzle flash, found my target and fired, dropping another attacker. I ran to the ol' man. I dragged him behind the truck. Tearing off his lower pant leg, I took a look at his wound. "You're gonna be just fine," I reassured him.

Alvarez smiled and said, "You're doing good, son. You're doing good. There might be some hope for you after all, Marine."

I stood up, pointed my twenty-two at Alvarez's head and blew the ol' man's brains out.

"Good work, gentlemen," I said as I stood over Alvarez's limp body.

"Damn," Skippy said, "What the hell took you so long? Kahn, Reed, Lee, and Marlow all got popped."

"And your share of the pot went from one hundred and twenty-five grand to a quarter million dollars," I said.

Skippy smiled. "Good point. How the hell you know he wouldn't kill you?"

"He was a Marine. And he thought I was one too."

"You're not?"

"Hell no. I got the tattoo specifically for this op."

"Shit," Skippy said. "You are one twisted mo-fo."

I smiled, then opened a box of cigars I'd looted from Alvarez's home. "Let's celebrate, boys."

Skippy, Jonesy, and Big Jelly all grinned like the greedy, stupid pigs they were. I handed each of 'em a cigar. "Any of you got a light?"

Jonesy nodded, pulled out his Zippo, and lit everyone's cigars.

Skippy looked my way. "What, you not smoking, boss?"

I grinned. "Oh, I'm smoking all right. I'm smoking you."

I put a bullet right between the eyes of each man before you could whistle "Dixie."

Being a merc these days is tough business. Ain't no way I was sharing that bounty with anyone.

THE NU-THAI SCREWJOB

GAV THORPE

GdM #7

22.38 LOCAL TIME

The ride to Sayam Towers takes us from near-slums to the glittering business district in just a few minutes, going through the whole spectrum of Nu-Thai life along the way. Go-go bars and strip joints in the basements and lower floors of half-kilometre-high tenements give way to restaurants, theatres, and then into the sky towers of the mega-rich. Needle-like phalluses with neon-lit glans compete with each other against the backdrop of a hexodesic atmodome: Nu-Thai's prophylactic against the elements of a hostile world.

The streetwagon glides down a ramp toward the vendors' entrance of Sayam Towers. For seven-hundred-and-fifty metres above us the glory of the SunstarRegusCorps' executive entertainment division stands out in gold and white, the company logo holo-blazoned on the dark sky above while green and red lamps strobe into the air.

We're expected, and the gate lowers at our approach, admitting us to a sub-level parking lot. I'm deposited outside an elevator, the doors already open. The inside is like a small foyer, decked tastefully in white marble and scarlet textiles. The doors slide shut and I'm carried up to...whatever's waiting for me up there.

Everything has been conducted over a synch-net, not a single manual operation or person involved. Their security system has to be fireproof and watertight, so someone has put in a lot of effort to get clearance. An inside job, it has to be.

The doors open, revealing a lavish buffet in full swing. In my overwhelmed state the sudden noise of chatter and the bright chandeliers overhead are an assault. Thai-ethno staff in skinsuits that leave nothing to the imagination waft around like leaves on a breeze, bringing and taking plates and glasses to thirty or more executive-types that are either sizing them up like cuts of meat or treating them like mobile furniture.

Most of the party-goers are white, over fifty, overweight. Some have the lean, slightly hunched look of body-modders, their core muscles not quite carrying their augmented mass properly. It's why I'm a gym girl—you just can't get the poise and gait right unless you go for serious mil-grade core implants. It's probably why Ms Monotyama prefers my sort of look too.

She's easy to find, an invisible shield of hierarchy separating her from the lesser beings craving her attention like moths around a star. Two others are allowed into her direct presence: a grey-haired, shrivelled Mandarin and an ebony attaché whose fake twenty-something face is as featureless as a neodeco sculpture, the studs of implants betraying high grade neuroware knitted beneath her scalp. The rest keep glancing in Monotyama's direction, longing for just a look or smile to acknowledge them. They get nothing.

Ms Monotyama is physically stunning. Late forties, no treatments, perfect skin and bone structure from, an educated guess, a seventy-thirty mix of Sino-Caucasian ancestry. At least ten centimetres taller than me, her height definitely speaks of some European great-great-grandaddy or grandma. Elegant, refined, eyes like emeralds. Every cliché of a hot female oriental executive that ever appeared on a porn-feed.

If half of what's been printed about her is true, she's also smart, the kind that no amount of memory upgrades and surfware can replicate. Ruthless, too. Looking at her and the froth of white, cis-hetero privilege she's risen above I can't hold it against her despite the circumstance I'm in.

Brains and beauty backed by serious ambition, the pampered corporate ladder-climbers never stood a chance. No wonder she rules SunstarRegusCorps in all but name.

She looks in my direction. Her gaze parts the crowd like a laser, leaving nothing between me and her. The assembled execs look on with curiosity, hate and envy, wondering why a piece of downmarket sexmeat is suddenly gifted with an attentive moment.

She beckons and I obey, heels clicking on the marble floor as the party's ambient volume dips. I've never felt so exposed, even when I've thrown myself onto a dance floor trying to hook a mark in front of thousands of stim-happy partygoers, or undressed in front of hulking body-modded egomaniacs who would tear me apart if they had just an inkling of what I was going to do.

Their judgement burrows into me more cleanly than x-rays or terrawaves, trying to pierce my datacore to work out how I fit into their narrow world.

But not from her, not from Monotyama. Her appraisal is far more delicate and considered than the simmering resentment and lust washing from the assembled executive corps. A hint of a smile, even.

Her appreciation makes everything even harder to bear.

It takes everything I have, all my will and strength to walk straight, to keep my head high and chin out, poised and elegant. I want to throw up. I have my hands clasped in front of me so that they don't form fists or shake.

There's no way this nightmare is going to end well, but I haven't got a choice.

34 MINUTES EARLIER

Just as my mark is about to blow his wad, I make my move. Orgasmic joy blossoms across his synapses like Freeday fireworks, his neuronet opening up as easily as a cheap Nana Sphere *kathoey*. For a while I'd worried he wasn't going to come at all, he'd been banging away for a good twenty minutes. It would be just my luck that he'd had some kind of everstiff or ejaculate inhibitors implanted. But now, good old Eric—or is it Erlich, or Heinrich? —shudders for a moment, eyes like dinner plates, and I activate the ultra-def substrate of his brainware.

I had spotted his cheap network implants on the crossmall three days before. Huawei 8500 series. Chinese export, low quality. Q-jumper, looking for the only thing his type look for on Nu-Thai. He would be halfway to the terminal and thinking about home before he found out anything was wrong. He couldn't miss his transit—nobody wants to stay on Nu-Thai, we are all abandoned or unlucky or our accounts ran out of "stream"—and the authorities couldn't give a crap for some offworlder sex tourist. A perfect screwjob.

Talk about a kid in a candy shop. Passwords, accounts details, synmails, all of it laid out in front of me in a stream of digital glory. It takes milliseconds, but in that moment of opening, of physical and mental release, poor Eric—pretty sure it's Eric—hands me everything. Just as he took what he wanted from me, I take back all I want from him. I don't strip him bare. I'm not an asshole. I leave him a few thousand bytes to get by, shunting the rest through a succession of data caverns and a bit of Swiss architecture I picked up from Kevin the Dolphin.

"That's it, stud, give it to me," I moan as I ride the last few drops out of his rapidly diminishing cock.

I step off him and the bed before I eject the vaginal sheath. He looks at me, surprised, as the molecule-thin lining slaps to the tiled floor, spilling his precious seed across the ceramic.

"What do you have that for?" he says. "Are you a pro? I ain't paying for it!"

I wonder what sort of ego he has, that a fat, balding fifty-something thinks he can come to Nu-Thai and get some action for free. He's going to be wishing he'd dropped a kilobyte or two on one of those skinny workers.

"No worries, stud," I tell him, slipping back into my orange all-in-one. His eyes follow my hands as I smooth the skintight fabric over my curves. Curves I've worked hard for—no subdermal layering or corset-like interstitial tightening in this body. Gym time and good eating, surprisingly effective and cheaper once you get going. "I've got everything I need."

I sit on the end of the bed and pull on black calf-length boots, ignoring Eric as he flops out of the pay-by-the-hour motel cot. Still thirty minutes on the clock but no point hanging around.

I scoped a taxi-port on the eighteenth floor earlier, and I already have my downgrid package ready to offload the moment I can hit a hard station. Twenty minutes from now I'll be in the wilds and in the clear.

The door explodes inward, splinters from the frame and pieces of molten lock spraying across the room. A giant, snow-skinned blond amazon in black-and-red partial body armour steps in, the Securecorp logo golden on her chest, just above a smaller Okura/Taisei Corporation kanji. There's a heavy pistol on her belt and a shock-wand in her hand.

"I thought this was legit! I didn't pay a byte!" Eric proves once again that he's an idiot. Prostitution is not only legal on Nu-Thai, it's taxed… His second mistake is making a bolt for the door.

Steroid-carved muscles bunch beneath anti-bullet weave as the enforcer thrusts, the flat of her hand connecting with Eric. The blow sends him spinning back onto the bed, a red handprint forming on his flabby chest.

I play it cool, eyeing the enforcer's muscles.

"I think your night just got even more interesting, stud," I say to Eric.

"Chemically celibate on duty," a deep voice says from the corridor outside. "She's not interested in either of you."

The man that steps into view is below average height, no taller than me, with an almost pitch-black complexion that immediately puts me in mind of the Axum Belt settlements, but his face is clear of tattoos and piercings. His clothes are non-descript, shirt and trousers, nothing different from what the glorious Eric might wear at work on a hot day, but his eyes are pure silver.

It's the eyes that give him away, a telesynch, an instant before my head explodes with noise and images.

It comes as a blur at first: a child, six years old, her birthday party. She seems vaguely familiar, I don't know why. Then the scene rewinds, a montage of her getting younger and younger. A piercing flame jets through my cortex. I'm standing on the steps of the *Nevermind* clinic, having my last moment of panic before the adoption appointment. The child looks at me with her beautiful green eyes. The child. I never even gave her a name.

It all becomes clear, as does my vision. The telesynch turns off his full spectrum state-of-the-art transmission matrix, dropping me back in the room.

"My...daughter?" I take a breath. And another. It doesn't calm my racing heart. "Who... Where is she? What happened?"

"If you want her to live, listen," he tells me. His silver eyes move onto Eric staring up from a foetal position on the bed. I see a tiny flare of power. Eric slumps.

I take a step as blood starts pouring from his ears and nostrils.

"He's already dead," the telesynch says abruptly. "As well as your daughter being killed, you will be a wanted felon in three minutes if you do not comply absolutely with my demands."

I nod dumbly. The telesynch turns and walks out of the room, the enforcer waits for me to follow. I fall into place with the amazon close behind.

"My name is Ebn Melek. I am a representative of FedGov."

"The pro-democracy terrorists?"

Melek laughs but I don't share his humour.

"That's what the media corporations would have you believe." He stops at the elevator and looks at me. His eyes have returned to their normal colour, the nanos dropping away to leave a warm, deep shade of brown. A lot less intimidating until I remember what he's just said and done. "We are the last vestiges of non-capitalist power in the colonies. But there's no time for a history lesson."

The elevator arrives and we get in. Melek says nothing. He

glances up at the video stud in the corner of the ceiling. I feel the outward edge of an EMP surge as my dampeners kick in and there's a spark from the device.

"As I was saying, we do not have a lot of time. At the Sayam Towers executive apartments a person of interest to my organisation is about to deliver a speech to a collection of high level corporate officers from nearly two dozen of the largest colony-rapers around." He says the words in a matter-of-fact way, but there's an edge just beneath. This isn't just a professional arrangement for him.

I'm trying to concentrate on what he's saying, trying not to think about having a daughter and what that means.

"How does an underground movement afford a telesynch?"

"With something other than bytes," Melek replies, his gaze fixed on the tarnished doors of the elevator. "My companion, the capable Mrs Stuttgartner, will escort you to the amenities where we have arranged for you to employ your specific charms and skills to access the contents of Chief Financial Officer Monotyama's junk-syn. Once you have inloaded the data, Mrs Stuttgartner will bring you back to me."

"Wait, what? Monotyama, CFO at SunstarRegusCorps? She pretty much runs that corporation. I'm not going to get anywhere near her. And even if I can, there's no way she's going to have an outmoded data collection inport for me to exploit. And even if my homemade tech could work, my experience is purely hetero. And..." I cock a glance at the burly enforcer. "*Mrs* Stuttgartner?"

"For sure, *honig*," she replies with a wink. "You think a heavyweight gunplatformer gets what he wants from a stick-thin *Muschi* like you?"

"Yes, we will get you next to Ms Monotyama," replies Melek, darting an irritated glance at the both of us. "Yes, you are just her type. She prefers athletic, petite, non-augmented flesh. Female, obviously. I'm sure you can improvise on that front. And as for how you're going to get what we want, that's what this is for."

His eyes turn silver again and my brain tears apart under the assault of his drillcoding. It lasts half a second, less, but is worse than the most intense post-implant migraine I've ever suffered. I drop to one knee, panting.

Inside the homemade data-corer I use to glean the account details of my marks there is now a small package. I take a peek, marvelling at the simple reverberating code inside. It's beautiful, far more streamlined than anything I could ever afford. In fact, so streamlined it can only have one purpose.

"This was made for me, for this moment, for her?" The nausea subsides and I stand up. "How long have you been planning this?"

"We have been following you for four years. There were possibilities, potential scenarios in which you would be useful. I've given you an Archimedean, designed specifically for you to get into the target's junk-syn. Just open her up as usual, it'll do the rest."

"You're a freaking telesynch! Why do you need me at all?" I jerk a thumb at Stuttgartner. "If truck-hips here can get *me* in, why not you? Just take what you need."

"Apart from the obvious lack of deniability and distance should anything go amiss, my involvement is not subtle. We want Ms Monotyama to remain oblivious to any intrusion."

Looking at Melek and Stuttgartner, I know I'm screwed, and there won't be a payday for this one. I think of Eric and then my daughter, whoever and wherever she is. At least they don't want me to kill anyone. It's just a job, I tell myself, but can't help feel scared and angered by everything going on. That won't do. I need to be level-headed.

"Steal her junk-syn, that's all? Why?"

He answers with a blank stare.

The elevator chimes and the doors open, revealing the lobby. A movement from Stuttgartner encourages me to step out, just a pace in front of her. The elevator hisses closed behind us, taking Melek with it.

Escorted by the private contractor, I walk to the entrance. The reception area is conspicuously empty, and the desk isn't manned.

"Was it necessary to kill Eric?" I ask as the door slides open. A streamlined black streetwagon with mirrored windows idles in the pick-up bay outside.

"*Derek* Thompson-Bagget the Third," Stuttgartner replies, "was a complete *kackfass* of the highest order. He made two terabytes on his shares by cutting costs on a production line on Abyssinia-Delta. Heat shields, who needs them, hey? Thirty-eight workers died, but no compensation was paid. Don't shed any tears for him."

"You too, huh? An idealist?"

The wagon door gull-wings open as she approaches. The synthetic leather and mock-walnut interior is empty.

"There are more around than you might think," Stuttgartner says and ushers me inside.

22.40 LOCAL TIME

M s Monotyama's attendants depart without a word, leaving me alone with her. Everything has gone silent, all I can hear is the thud of my heart and the soft exhalation of SunstarRegusCorps' de facto queen. It's not just my imagination, I realise. There is an actual desonic field in effect, cutting out all the worthless chit-chat from the peons.

"What is your name?" she asks, just a hint of native Japanese in her accent.

"Emelia," I reply without hesitation. It's one of several aliases I have set up for my work, with enough net-persona to seem legit to all but a full security sweep. It's just a job, I tell myself. Just a job. A mark, like the others.

But I didn't choose her and I don't like what's at stake. Melek's using me more than any of those worthless desk-humpers I take for a ride.

My gut is a knot but the reflex of several years of looking enthusiastic while sweating execs ram their stuff into me experience kick in and I fake a smile.

She leads me into an adjacent room, through a door flanked by two augmented rent-a-goons in the same uniform as Mrs Stuttgartner. I have no idea if they are part of the scheme or not and don't give them a second glance.

I was expecting some tricked-out sex chamber, or at least a bed, but the room is actually for storage—stacked chairs and broken down trestle tables against one wall, floor-to-ceiling cupboard doors on the other two. She notices my surprise.

"I like improvisation, spontaneity. Call me Hiromi."

I size her up, trying to figure out what I need to do. With men it's easy—just let them put themselves inside and they do all the heavy lifting. This is unknown territory, and the more I consider the consequences of failure the less I can think straight.

An idea fights its way out of the static in my head. She's the most powerful woman in one of the most successful trans-stellar operations going. Inside she's not much different to the lecherous execs I fleece every week. In their world you don't survive if you're different.

"I'll call you whatever I want," I tell her, putting a hand on her chest. She resists for a moment, confused, and I exert more pressure, forcing her back a step. She's resistant, and I make it more obvious, grabbing her arm to pull her towards the stacked chairs.

"You're not in charge here," I tell her, pulling out a chair with my free hand. I sit and pull her down with me, forcing her to her knees. I can feel her quivering under my grip and wonder if I've played it right. She looks up at me for a moment, the tiniest crease of a frown. I ignore her. I have to take control. I can't just let this happen to me like a bystander, that won't work. I grab her wrist and put it between her thighs. "We're going to do this my way."

22.58 LOCAL TIME

Her climax throws open her synaptic pathways just like Melek promised. The sub-routine embedded in me is like a dog at a leash, dragging at me to release it. Far more predatory than my self-coded program. Designed by Melek, I would guess, ready to just take what it wants.

I comply, knowing I only have an instant to make the connection. It's different to how it usually feels. There's no guile here, no tricking the neuronet into opening up, just a rapid, single-minded invasion of Monotyama's thoughtscape.

Her network is as beautiful as her exterior. Most folks have layer upon layer of implants and programmes, their internal pathways scarred by nodules and remnants of previous code and hardware. Hiromi Monotyama is pristine, her neuroscape as clean and clinical as a surgical suite. It glistens like diamonds and silver, a web of shining strands arrayed with perfect symmetry.

With a mental lurch, the hound program drags me off to one side, down a tiny little spiral of thread that unfurls as I approach. I'm in and out, like a hummingbird dabbing at nectar, touching briefly on the sweetness at the bottom of the spiral. Milliseconds later the blossom curls up and Ms Monotyama's defence systems explode into life, forcing me to eject with a gasp.

I look into her eyes, centimetres from my face, the sweat on her forehead like glistening pearls, and for a moment I wonder if she knows what happened, whether Melek and his companions have made an error.

"Good," she whispers, slumping back to the plush carpet. Her eyes close. "We're done."

She doesn't see the relief welling up inside me, relief I have to shut down because I'm not in the clear yet, and neither is my daughter. I hear the door open and a cough behind me. The rent-a-thugs are waiting. I make my exit as swiftly as I can, to find that the assembled executive ranks have been moved on in preparation for Monotyama's address.

Inside the elevator I collapse against the wall, head in my hands as I fight the sickness wracking my body. A sob tries to claw its way up my throat but I won't let it. I'm not crying for these assholes.

The elevator arrives. Stuttgartner is beside the roadster with the door open. She says nothing, but directs me with a glance. I get in, convinced she's going to kill me, fear fighting with relief at the thought that the daughter I'll never know is safe.

23.30 LOCAL TIME

Melek waits on a couch in a plainly furnished suite, the sort of place where mid-level execs hang out between conference panels and hook-ups with other attendees.

"So what did—" I stutter to a gasping halt as Melek's eyes silver up and he wrenches the spoils of my expedition from the tempfile of my memory stack. It feels like someone is showering the back of my brain with acid as a cleansing routine scrapes up every last bit of data from the junk-syn I swiped. Melek's drillcode package is still in there, its purpose fulfilled. An unexpected oversight on his part.

I stagger to an armchair and flop down. Melek looks distracted for a few seconds.

"In answer to your question, it contains nothing." He relaxes a little and folds his hands in his lap. "Just a data packet that left a nearly invisible trail we can backtrace in the future."

I hold back a snide remark—it's been a disaster of an evening so far but it could get worse. "I've done my piece, what about my daughter?"

"She wasn't your daughter," Melek says. "Just a random image and a memory I plucked from your core. The adoption service is fully randomised and hex-encrypted for a reason. No way to trace a parent or client. Associates have also scoured clean the room at the motel, of us and you. You are, as they say, in the clear."

Why does it feel worse that I've been tricked? That my daughter was never at risk? I want to put my fists through his smug, calm face. Just the slightest movement at the edge of my vision reminds me that Stuttgartner is in the room, armed. My fingers claw into the arms of the chair as I control my temper.

"I deployed carefully chosen triggers to ensure your cooperation," Melek continues. "But we are not monsters."

He's wrong. I think about what I've just done; what he *forced* me to do. Monsters come in different flavours. The anger boils, but just as with the fear my experience keeps it hidden beneath a calm exterior. "Derek's still dead, I take it?"

"Very much so." Melek leans forward. "You have seen the true face of what we are up against. The elite hold themselves above us. They are contemptuous of the masses. Warm bodies. Human livestock. Numbers in a column. It's no coincidence these are the very people you have targeted before. A victimless crime, almost? You should feel good that you have been a tiny fly in their ointment."

My mind starts to work properly for the first time since they cornered me with Derek.

"It's certainly more appealing than turning over fat middle managers for a few gigs at a time." I force a smile and rub the pleather of the chair. "Maybe it's time I went more upmarket. Can you get me off Nu-Thai? If I was to help you again? Maybe an expenses account?"

Melek nods.

"That might be arranged. We would prefer an ally to an employee, though. There is more appeal to such work than simply money."

"There is," I assure him. I look at Stuttgartner and back to him. Another forced smile. "This feels like it might get personal."

He stands, nods once more and then leaves with Mrs Stuttgartner. I wait in the room for another five minutes and then head down to the lobby. I get them to synch me with a cab and another twenty minutes sees me across town and back at my planned drop-out location.

There's a public hard terminal and I access the search function. I find the link I need and dial it up. The holo of a perky young Thai receptionist in a bright blue uniform shirt appears on the terminal display.

"Good evening." Her smile doesn't reach her eyes. "This is your local SunstarRegusCorps security division. How may I be of assistance?"

They could have asked me, paid me. I'm a professional. But I wasn't even that to him. Just a tool, a necessary implement, nothing more. Even that I might stomach. Most of my marks don't see beyond my sex organs. But the fake deal with my daughter...*forcing* me into this? That's colder than anything Monotyama did. And the arrogance, to reveal the lie, to pretend they are any better than the corporate leeches? They'll pay for that mistake. Nobody uses me. I'll take these FedGov bastards for all the bytes I can. Then I'll double-down with payouts from the corporation.

"Contractor code tau-five-three-alpha-seven," I say.

The screen goes static-dead and a second later a fresh ring tone starts.

Melek picked the wrong girl to fuck with—literally. And when it's all done, I'll enjoy watching him burn.

LESSONS OF NECESSITY

T.C. POWELL

GdM #5

My twelve-year-old son backs away from the crawling corpse and holds the knife out, handle up. "Mum," he says to me, drawing the word out so that it sounds like two syllables. It's as though he's five again and wants me to cut up his steak.

God. Steak. What I wouldn't do for some steak.

I take the knife from Taylor, flashing a look so he knows that this is not acceptable behaviour for his age. The corpse, or zombie, or whatever we few survivors are calling them, is pathetic, crawling on one intact leg, the other sheared off at the knee. I look at Taylor to ensure he's watching as I plunge the knife into its rotting head.

Taylor's eyes shift away at the last second. I resist the urge to snap at him.

"That's that," I say, withdrawing the knife and returning it to Taylor's trembling hand.

With the basement cleared, we've checked the entire house. It's not perfect. There are rats scratching in the walls and cockroaches skittering across the floor, but that's true everywhere. What's important is that the doors and windows are intact, and there's a generator. The basement is also defensible as a last resort, with the only approach being the stairs from the kitchen. Although going to the store will still be a risk, it's only a five-minute walk; there are enough canned goods there to keep us well fed for years. This is home.

Taylor smiles at me and I smile back, eager to reassure him. Underneath, however, I know there's still work we need to do. I won't be around forever.

"Happy Birthday to you!" I sing.

Taylor blows out the candles on the fruitcake I'd found in the wrecked aisles of the supermarket. An extravagance, perhaps, but it makes him happy to be reminded of the old times, when we were a normal family and his father was alive. Besides, I want turning thirteen to be a big deal to Taylor. I want him to know that I now consider him to be a man.

"Are there any presents?" he asks.

"Of course," I say. "Let me go get it."

It's in the basement. I walk the flight of steps down from the kitchen and already feel winded. A bad sign. I first felt the lump in my breast last winter; I don't know why I had continued to check, after things like chemo and surgery were obsolete. Habit, maybe. Now I feel my illness every day, steadily getting worse. Taylor doesn't yet know. I wish I didn't either.

I return from the basement, smiling to cover the pain. I needn't have bothered. Taylor only has eyes for what I hold in my hands: a genuine Japanese katana.

"Oh my God, Mum! It's so cool!"

I laugh at his enthusiasm. "You want to take it out for a test drive?" Knives, swords and other silent killers are our best bet for survival. Guns bring unwanted attention.

"Yeah!" Taylor says, taking the sword and snapping the blade free from its curved black scabbard. "There are some mannequins in the Walmart. Maybe we could carry one back with us next time we go."

I shake my head. "Not exactly what I had in mind."

His face falls. Damn it, now he sees the gift as a set-up, which it was, but I still want him to enjoy the moment. There remain so few opportunities to simply enjoy anything.

Taylor drops the sword clanging to the tiled floor. "How many times do I have to tell you, Mum? I'm not killing anything."

It's our fault in a way. As Taylor grew, my husband and I drilled into him the importance of protecting and nurturing life. We scooped up spiders and carried them to the garden rather than squishing them, and opened windows so that the flies could leave unharmed. God, we were even vegans for a while. But that had been before, in a world where those values made sense. Where they were possible. Taylor, bless his heart, just couldn't understand that things had changed. He believed so strongly in the things we, and especially his father, had taught him. Taylor was not with me that day to watch Michael get torn apart by these beasts. Then, I accounted it a blessing that he kept some part of his innocence. But now...

I pick the sword up. "You will."

He has to.

We return from the store with our hands full: I have Taylor's sword (he refuses to carry it outside) and a paper bag full of soap, toothpaste and brushes, a padlock, a pocketknife, and other sundries; my boy has a damned mannequin. I couldn't talk him out of it.

We come inside and go into the kitchen where I set our groceries down on the counter.

"Say, why don't you set that thing up in the basement," I tell him.

"Good idea," he says over the mannequin's bare white shoulder.

I watch as Taylor starts his descent down the stairs. I set the katana on the topmost step and close the door after him. The basement light is on, but it's not very bright. I hope Taylor sees the thing before the thing sees him.

"Hey," he calls from the staircase. "Why'd you close the door?"

My answer is to take the padlock from the shopping bag and fasten it to the steel hasp set in the basement door.

"Uh—oh, Mum, there's one of those things down here!"

Pick up your sword, I think. Fight for yourself, my baby, my love. Because you have to.

I slump down against the door; my hand instinctively clutches my misshapen breast, and the hammering heart underneath. I mark the sound of the mannequin tumbling down the stairs. The subsequent pounding against the door and Taylor's cries for me to let him out. Then the sounds of snarling and fighting.

I do not know the results and I will not know until the fighting stops. Whatever comes out when I unlock the door… I will be prepared to deal with it.

Because I have to.

A PROPER WAR

JAMES A. MOORE

GdM #8

They found their prey near the edge of the cliff that fell into the Rehkail River a few hundred feet below. There was a damp trail of footsteps that ran from the edge of the cliff to where the shape waited. Allim wondered if the furry mass they stared at had actually climbed the sheer cliffside and then shook the notion away. Madness.

"What do you make of that, then?" Allim stared at the lump of fur leaning against a large rock and frowned. Under him his piebald shifted from hoof to hoof, but did not bolt. The damned thing was always skittish.

"It's a big bastard of a man, or a bear. Damn near the same size." Benny spoke, no more troubled than if they were having a pint around a fire. Just the same Benny checked that his weapons were in easy reach.

They spoke softly, while considering their options, lest they disturb the large thing huddled in dark furs. Though Allim had never seen a Pra-Moresh they'd discussed the beasts before. Apparently the damned things were big enough to eat bears without much consideration, but none had ever been seen this far east. The fur on whatever they were staring at didn't quite look like a bear's. Kellish wanted to poke it with a spear, just in case there really was a bear under that fur. Kellish was from Louron and his dark skin made him stand out almost as much as the skull he painted on his face every day. He nearly danced whenever he used his sword, and Allim had never seen the man cut before.

Benny disagreed: he just wanted to wake the fellow and take what he could.

On the other side of the river the armies of Goltha were engaged with enemies from the far west. They'd heard the cries of war earlier and seen the smoke coming from the river below. On this side of the river, there were plains and flatlands and occasional settlements. People were slowly working the soil and growing farming communities where no one had ever bothered before. Allim and his men were moving along the area looking for easy prey. They were raiders. He wasn't proud of the fact, but a man has to make a living and lately the only good livings seemed to involve swords. Fight for an army and die with them. Fight for your dinner and you get to eat another day. Farmers didn't fight so hard, and some of them had daughters. As Able liked to point out, a man has needs. He'd had his way with too many women and girls to count and had no desire to stop. Even Allim joined in occasionally, though he preferred his women on the willing side.

Now and then a cutthroat gets lonely, too.

The fur covered figure stood, and the raiders took their turns being properly appalled. He was a big one indeed, and his skin was grey as stone. His eyes burned with a silvery glow in the twilight, and his body rose to a height that made Allim consider the risk of taking on one target. Maybe they should leave this one alone. Still, the numbers were in their favour, and the brute had no ranged weapons that Allim could see.

Fat Able spoke. "Is that one of them Sa'ba Taalor the Empire is fighting? He looks like a demon." Able was the one who called himself fat, because he was. But under that fat there was a great deal of muscle and to prove that fact he wielded a mace that most men would have been hard pressed to lift with both hands. Fat Able came from the north and he was well trained as a fighter. He just didn't much care for the ways of the armies. His horse was a brute, dark and big enough to hold his master.

Allim shook his head and gestured for silence. Benny was the one who liked to talk to possible targets.

Benny nudged his horse gently to keep her from trotting. She wanted to move on by the looks of things. "Drop your weapons and give us whatever valuables you have. Step back carefully. This doesn't have to go badly for you."

Benny meant not a word of it, of course. He was a killer through and through. If he couldn't mate with it, he'd just as soon cut it into pieces and leave it for the storm crows to feast on. Sometimes Allim worried about Benny. Other times he was merely glad they were on the same side.

Able looked at the stranger and nodded his head, his face unreadable.

Cenna the archer, greatest damned shot Allim had ever seen with a bow, reached over his shoulder and drew an arrow from his quiver. While he looked on, he notched the arrow and rested the whole affair across his saddle's pommel.

From Cenna's left, M'Rae nudged his gelding forward, squinting as he looked over the grey man.

"Lookit 'im. He looks like a damned soul if ever I saw one." M'Rae fancied himself a follower of Kanheer, the god of war, and always claimed he was taking souls for his deity. He never said a prayer. Allim tended to doubt the man's faith.

The grey-skinned man replied, "I am not damned." He stepped forward and his heavy fur cloak parted, showing the weapons hidden beneath. There were a lot of blades of differing sizes. Some looked familiar enough—an axe, a dagger—but others merely sparkled softly. "I am blessed. I am offered combat and a chance at a proper battle." His low voice was thick with an accent that Allim did not know, but his words were clear enough. He was not afraid of the raiders, not in the least.

Benny shook his head. "Be wise, there are six of us. We'll have you dead as soon as you pull a blade."

As Benny spoke, the stranger jumped forward, one hand blurred in motion and pointed toward Benny. A blade rammed into Benny's cheek and lodged deep in his face.

Benny dropped off his horse shrieking in pain, both hands clutching the area around the vibrating blade.

The grey man charged them.

Allim slid from his saddle, reaching for his sword even as the giant charged. Fear had his heart thundering. The bastard was head and shoulders taller than Allim, who was always short and slender. The ground nearly shook as the man came closer.

The horse was there, a wonderful beast, a great shield against any possible attack.

The grey man did not bother with Allim. He charged Fat Able. Able swept his mace down in a vicious arc at the grey man's skull.

Hellishly fast for his size, the stranger dodged the blow, grabbed Able, and wrenched him down from the saddle. The ground shook when Able landed.

Able rolled himself around and was standing only a moment later, but by then the man had moved on.

Allim watched, and learned. Able was not the target. Able was the shield. Cenna was calmly backing his horse away using his knees, bow drawn, desperately searching for a clean shot past Able's bulk. The warrior countered smoothly.

Cenna loosed his arrow, the shaft disappearing in to the grey man's furred cloak to no visible effect. A second shot had better luck. The arrow sailed smoothly and the tip drove into the meat of their enemy's shoulder. The grey man grunted and kept charging.

At too close a range to fire an arrow Cenna changed tactics and whipped the bow around at his enemy's head.

One thick forearm caught the worst of the blow. The other hand grabbed Cenna and yanked him from his horse.

Cenna yelped as the grey man slammed him into the side of his horse. The animal took it poorly, whinnying a warning and bucking lightly. Cenna beat at the arms holding him but it did no good. The grey-skin smashed him into his horse a second time and a third before the horse reared and snorted. The man threw Cenna at the front of the panicking animal and stepped back as the horse reared and stomped down on top of the archer.

The warrior was smart enough to stay away from the horse as it reared up and came down on Cenna again, hooves breaking bone and scraping away muscle and flesh. Cenna screamed once, yelped once and then was silent. Allim shuddered at the sight and watched on, weighing his options.

Through it all Allim watched, rooted to the spot in the face of such unrivalled brutality.

While he looked on, Fat Able and M'Rae moved together toward the grey giant. M'Rae held a dagger in one hand and a thin sword in the other. He smiled as he circled the stranger.

M'Rae shouted, "Your gods have blessed you?" He spat at the ground. "My god, Kanheer, will eat your gods as an offering when I'm done with you."

Able, limping after his fall, looked at M'rae as if he'd lost his mind.

The stranger said, "You will die first then."

M'Rae came in fast, sweeping his sword as a distraction. Allim had seen him in action many times and knew the strategy was one of his favourites. While his enemy worried about the sharp end of the sword, the dagger came in low and bit at legs and fingers, whatever could be struck.

Rather than dodging, the stranger swept the sword aside with a crushing blow as he stepped in close. M'Rae's arm took a smashing that would have cost the stranger his fingers, or his arm to the wrist, if the sword had caught him. M'Rae's sword flew from his hand. Before he could recover the grey man struck him hard in the throat. M'Rae stepped back, gaping. He dropped his dagger and reached for his own wounded neck, trying to drag a breath past his ruined windpipe.

Allim circled around, looking for a vulnerability, watching the fight, hoping for an easy opening to attack. No luck. The grey man moved with him, never losing sight of Allim's blade.

Fat Able slammed his mace into the grey man's left arm, the sound of meat tearing and bone snapping quickly drowned out by a scream. The stranger fell to the side and staggered backward as Able came at him again, mace held in both hands. Allim grinned. Able intended to finish this fight as quickly as he could, and Allim intended to help him.

Able brought the head of his mace around and jabbed hard at the stranger's face. The blow sent the stranger backward a second time. Able kicked at the grey man's thigh and the stranger fell to the ground, where he rolled and then stumbled into a proper crouch.

"You should've listened to Benny. You'd have lived longer." Fat Able was panting a bit as he slowly circled the downed stranger.

M'Rae coughed and hacked, on his hands and knees, trying to breathe and failing. He was dead already but too hurt to know it.

The stranger did not speak, but merely charged. His body was as heavy as Able's, and the fat thief growled as the man hit him. Able brought the mace over his head and slammed its head into the stranger's back. The man slipped under Able's arms and shouldered him in his guts, lifting as he ran. There was a blade in one of those hands. It met Able's gut and stabbed again and again as he shoved Able backward.

Allim winced as the two of them staggered backward until they reached the edge of the cliffside that dropped to the river far below.

Able let out a scream worthy of a scalded cat as he stumbled across nothing but air and fell. The stranger stayed at that edge, his feet splayed wide apart, panting as Able dropped. By the time the fat man thudded to the ground below, the grey man was already heading toward Kellish.

Allim watched on, his enemy flexing his left arm as he strode toward the grease-masked swordsman. Allim's heart sank. He'd thought for certain Able had broken that arm.

Kellish looked on, sliding slowly to the side, as he faced the man who had already killed four of them. "This does not have to be."

"You have invited me to a war. I will make certain it is a proper one." The stranger didn't even sound winded. Making matters worse, he smiled through a mouth covered in scars.

Grey hands moved, sliding under the thick fur cloak and emerging with an odd looking blade, more like a scythe than a proper sword. He drew another one a second later.

Kellish shook his head and backed further away. "Allim."

Allim raised his hands. When he spoke his voice shook. He was scared, no way around it. He was the leader, sort of, but he had never been fond of actual combat. "Don't. I've no particular desire to die today." His right hand had a sword in it. He'd rather forgotten that in all the excitement.

Still, better to die with a sword than without.

The grey warrior held two of the strange weapons, and when Allim saw them properly he was more puzzled than before. Both had a blade that ran along the outside of the hand, a spike at the top of the fists and a long metal post that ended just beyond the elbow in another spike. They'd been designed to wrap around the man's thick forearms and looked more like reshaped bracers than anything else.

"What are you holding?" Allim asked the question as he considered the possible answers. There was little to consider, really. There were blades and spikes and he had no doubt that all of them could kill.

"I will show you more closely."

Allim shook his head. "No reason to rush on my account."

While the fighter was distracted, Kellish moved in fast, stepping up close and stabbing with his short spear. Its point did not penetrate the cloak but snagged in the outer layer of fur, pulling Kellish, who had put his full weight into the blow, nearly off his feet.

He let go of his weapon before the man could retaliate. Then he backed up as the grey-skin threw a punch that would have impaled his chest if he had stayed his place.

"You've made your point! We don't want to fight you." Kellish shook his head. The giant shook his arm and Kellish's spear fell free from the fur cloak.

"Would you surrender?" The man's voice sounded odd, there was a sibilance to his words that Allim had not noticed before. The fine hairs on Allim's neck rose and he edged back over to his horse.

Allim shook his head and spat. "No! We would retreat! Run away, Kellish!"

Allim hauled himself back into the saddle of his horse as the grey man charged Kellish.

The grey man was fast. Kellish was faster. He was also on the defensive. Every jab or thrust the man made hit air as Kellish danced back and shook his head and grinned. The smeared skull on his face grinned with him.

Allim backed up his horse. From thirty feet away he allowed himself one moment of bravery and threw a dagger at the back of the grey man's head.

Then he turned his horse and dashed away as swiftly as he could, hoping that Kellish managed to win the fight.

It seemed like a good idea, but the horse let out a scream and bucked. Allim had never been a skilled horseman. He landed on his ass and watched the horse bolting away with his dagger in its flank.

"Cowardly! At least your friends fought with some honour." The grey man looked at Allim with those glowing silvery eyes and Allim shook his head.

No. No chance he would fight the thing. It refused to die.

Kellish rose from the ground behind the grey man, his face bloodied, the painted skull smeared and stained crimson in spots. He lifted his spear and moved toward the man coming for Allim.

Allim picked up his sword from where he'd dropped it and charged at the man, praying Kellish would get there soon enough to do some damage. The stranger continued toward him, running hard. Allim braced himself, ready to strike as soon as the man reached him. He'd do whatever he had to do to survive.

The stranger was fast. Kellish was faster. This time the spear struck true and the warrior grunted as he fell forward. Kellish pushed his advantage. As the man crashed into the ground, Kellish drove the spear deeper into the large man's chest.

Kellish pulled the spear free and backed away, warily.

Sprawled across the stony ground, the grey man coughed blood, and Kellish relaxed. The spear had gone deep, the blade and shaft painted with a heavy flow of blood.

"All the gods…" Allim moved a step closer but no farther. The man should have been dead by all rights but he was struggling still. His strength had failed him, however, and he didn't seem capable of rising.

"That man is crazy!" Kellish shook his head and eyed the body as if he expected it to attack again.

Allim was contemplating hitting the back of that head with his sword a few dozen times to be safe. "Aye. Good work, Kellish."

Kellish started to respond when the man rose to his hands and knees and coughed again, another gout of blood that was more pink than red.

He did not try to stand, but instead rolled over onto his back and looked toward Kellish. All the bravery in Allim faded just that quickly and he backed away.

The man's eyes *glowed*. He'd thought that a trick of the light earlier but no. "He's a demon!"

Three hooks on chains appeared in the man's hand, each as long as Allim's hand from wrist to longest fingertip. If they were meant to fish, then surely the fish must be the size of a man or greater. One flick of the grey man's wrist and those barbed nightmares found Kellish's face, eye and neck and sank deep into all three.

Kellish screamed and stumbled backward his hands waving madly. He dropped his spear and tried to pull the hooks free.

The stranger gripped the chains in his hand and hauled Kellish toward him. Kellish fell toward the man as his eye ruptured. He tumbled to his knees and the stranger ripped the hooks free from Kellish and threw them toward Allim.

They missed him by the grace of any possible gods.

Allim backed away, shaking his head in horror. The grey demon was supposed to be dead or dying, not fighting on!

Kellish still had some fight left, though it was not much. His face was torn apart and his neck vomited hot blood across his front and his enemy alike. Instead of leaning back and dying like a sensible enemy, the grey man hooked his fingers into Kellish's shirt and yanked him closer until he could wrap both of his thick hands around his enemy's neck and squeeze.

That was enough for Allim. He turned and ran. His horse wasn't far away, and he and the damned animal came to a quick understanding. Allim soothed its neck for a moment and whispered kind words to calm the beast, and then he was in the saddle and riding steadily away from the dead men who had been his friends for the past few months.

He did not know if Kellish was dead or alive. He did not know about the grey man. He only wanted to get as far from them as possible, and so he rode until the sun was nearly set and the temperature fell icy. By the light of the dying sun Allim spotted his salvation. The village was one he'd seen before. A small gathering of farms and little else. He rode to the third house in the settlement. It was the largest and most likely to have room for a stranger. He'd have preferred a good pub, but beggars could not make demands.

He pounded hard at the heavy oak door and waited. The man who answered wasn't overly muscled but he was a tall fellow and he looked capable. His hair was greying and his face had several days' worth of stubbly beard. His frown was not welcoming, but Allim took a chance just the same. He was exhausted. He needed rest and food.

"Beg pardon, sir." Allim did his best to look sincere and reasonable. Which, in comparison to his now dead companions, was relatively easy. "I'm lost, you see, and I thought I might ask a place to sleep for the night and directions in the morning." The man stared at him in silence. Allim reached into his jacket pocket and pulled out four small coins. "I can pay. Not much, but I can pay." There was more coin, of course, but a good pauper's pocket deterred curious eyes.

Dark blue eyes regarded him for a moment and then, "Aye. We can manage something, I expect. Come on inside. I'm called Tovish. What do I call you?"

He nodded his thanks and the man stepped back into the warmth of a spacious main room with a good fire going and what smelled like mutton cooking in a pot over it.

"I'm Allim," he replied as his stomach rumbled noisily. He closed his eyes and felt himself relax for the first time since they'd found the grey man. There was food, there was a fire, and there was shelter. Really, there wasn't much more a man needed on a bitter night. "I thank you, sir. It's getting cold out there and there are too many animals for a man on his own. And too many of the sort that carry knives for my taste."

Tovish nodded his head and gestured to the table. "Stew's almost done. Sit. I've a spot of wine, too."

That was one of the reasons Allim liked the flatlands. There were many people out in the area and most of them seemed more civilised than city dwellers.

"You are too generous, sir, and I thank you." He bowed his head and smiled. The day had been madness to be sure, but the night promised a little rest and a full belly. Tomorrow he would be on his way and he'd find himself some honest work, the sort that didn't involve fighting grey men with too many weapons, who would not die when they should.

"Where are your friends?" The man's voice changed not at all, but Allim felt his skin crawl.

"Friends?" He was just preparing to draw his sword when something slammed into the side of his skull and dropped him from his chair, leaving him stunned and barely able to think.

"Aye. Your friends. The ones had their way with my little Lyra and with my wife, too. I expect they were smarter than to come back here."

"Hkk. Uln…" Try as he might he couldn't move. Damnedest thing: he'd been hit before but never like that. His head was screaming at him and his arms and legs just lay there.

The man crouched next to him, his boots well worn, his clothes often mended and thinned out to nearly bare spots. "Lyra and the wife, they're down in the cellar. They like to hide there when strangers come by these days. That's for the best."

"Nuh. Plizz. I didunt."

"No reason to lie, boy. I never forget a face, especially one that's made my kin suffer." As he spoke the man straightened out Allim's legs and then tied his ankles together. "They're proud women, my fine ladies. They'd probably face you and be brave for me, but I'll save them from that."

Allim tried to plead but the man just talked over him as he hauled on the rope around Allim's ankles and dragged him toward the door. On the ground not far from where Allim had gone over, he could see a metal pan, likely what had hit him so hard in the head.

"If I told them, they might even ask me to spare you, but that won't happen." The man paused long enough to tie Allim's hands tightly. "There's a war going on, y'see. Soldiers might come along and ask about why I had a man like you bound in the cellar. I wouldn't mind torturing you, but the wife and daughter, they're better than you and me. They're kinder."

Tovish dragged Allim over the threshold and into the night.

Allim looked on as the ground slipped past.

His neck felt like it was lit ablaze when he was hoisted by his feet into the air near another building that reeked of animal shit.

The blood rushed to his head and nausea churned through his guts. The rope he hung from rotated slowly, so he had plenty of time to see the pen where the swine were kept.

"Theft is theft. I don't much like it but I understand it." Tovish spoke calmly as he wrapped the rope's end around a fence beam and tied it off with practiced ease. "What that friend of yours did, that was worse. None of you deserve to live. If I ever find the others, I'll show them how I feel. For now, you'll do."

Allim thought of telling the man he was too late but the words couldn't make it past the bile clogging his throat.

Tovish squatted until they were nearly face to face. For the first time he smiled. "What I like about pigs is that they'll eat any sort of garbage you offer them. They aren't picky. They just like to eat."

Allim let out one last scream as the pig farmer came for him, clutching a well-used and keenly sharpened blade in his heavy-knuckled hand.

THE RED WRAITH

NICHOLAS WISSEMAN

GdM #1

Y ou notice my smoky hair and wonder if I'm him.

You study my skin, searching for veins that gleam black like I've been stretched over a sable spider web, or arteries that glitter white like fracture lines in shattered ice.

But you see no cause for alarm.

You judge my height to be average, at most an inch or two above normal—nothing imposing.

Nothing legendary.

Nothing infamous.

You start to dismiss your fears…until I raise my head to reveal the tell-tale tattoo, the swirling mark branded over my left eye.

Now you know.

You know who I am, what I can do, and what I've done.

You know your terror is justified.

You close your eyes and beg and moan and soil yourself.

You relive every wrong moment you never set right: complaining during your mother-in-law's burial; turning a blind eye to the old man crawling through the weeds; undermining your friend's last chance.

You think of the loved ones you'll leave behind, and the ones who'll love to leave you behind.

You clasp your hands and say your goodbyes, readying yourself for whatever you think comes next.

And when you finally open your eyes and find me gone…are you relieved?

Or disappointed?

THE WOMAN I USED TO BE

GERRI LEEN

GdM #1

I sit in the comfortable chair that I've been told was never my favourite and enjoy the unexpected quiet of the house. Everyone is out. I'm so much better that they think it's safe to leave me.

I'm not really better—if better is having my memories back—but I've learned to fake it and to fill in the blank spots with research. I must have had mad skills at that.

I laugh at that: mad skills. It's a funny saying unless you feel like you're losing your mind, then not so much. But also funny that these ways of phrasing—silly sayings like that—come naturally when I'm just thinking. They flow in my head as if language and memory are not linked at all.

But I know they are. As soon as I try to talk to Nathan or Louisa, my words falter. I reach for names, ideas, basic statements or questions, and they're like quicksilver, darting here and there as I try to form complete sentences the way she would.

She. I. Pronouns are difficult.

My name is Susanna. I've apparently never liked that name, or so the woman who says she's my mother claims. Carla—I call her that and she frowns. But it feels wrong to call her Mum. Shouldn't I feel something for her if she's my mum?

Shouldn't I feel anything but this overwhelming panic? And the sense that I'm disappointing them all: my mother, my husband, my daughter.

Louisa at least resembles me. I feel nothing when I look at her, but I can logically see the similarities, and I can say, "Yes, I probably contributed DNA to that one."

But Nathan. With his sad, beseeching eyes. With his oh-so-patient voice. I have the feeling he's not really my type, even though I can't tell you what my type is.

I dream of another man. He's tall with skin like mahogany, partly from genetics, partly from being in the sun. How do I know this? I don't know his name, just his face, just his arms, lifted high as he tells me something I can't hear. I can never hear his words, but I feel inspired anyway. He inspires me.

Until I wake up and realise he has no place in this life I can't remember.

I've asked Nathan and Carla about the man—in the most general terms. I can tell it hurts them when I don't remember the right things, but they also seem to like it when I show an interest in my life. They don't remember anyone matching the dark man's description.

I've asked the house AI also. Just in case they never met the man—just in case I was having an affair. The house AI doesn't recall any visitors that match the description except an appraiser that came to the house when we were thinking of taking out another mortgage. But the picture the AI brought up wasn't the man from my dreams.

"Susanna?" The house AI's voice never startles me now that I've programmed it to be male when I am alone, given it a deep voice, resonant with pain—or that's how the voice option I chose struck me. It's also how I imagine the dark man sounding, if I could only hear what he is saying.

The AI is my best friend. It knows me better than I do, obviously, but it also seems to know me better than my family does. The AI goes by Drew. Louisa named it when we first moved into this house, or so I'm told. She wanted a name that could be male or female. When I'm not alone, the AI speaks in a nurturing female voice that sounds like a grandmother. It has told me Louisa picked the default voice. It has also told me—when I asked—that Nathan keeps it this way when he's alone.

I was sort of hoping he made the AI sound sultry, sexy. It would make me feel less guilty that I dream about men who aren't the husband I can't remember.

"Drew, are you sure I lived here before the shuttle crash?" This is not the first time I have asked this question. Perhaps I keep hoping for a different answer. Although isn't that the definition of crazy?

"Yes, you lived here before the shuttle crash."

I love the way it answers. No hesitation. No making excuses. Just the truth.

"Susanna, why do you keep asking that?"

I huddle deeper into the chair, making myself small, wishing I could disappear. "I don't belong here. Or that's what it feels like."

"The doctor said it would take time."

"I know." I hear the whirring of Drew's retrieval arm unfolding from the ceiling. It picks up the throw from the couch and carries it over, setting it gently on my lap. "I'm not cold."

"Your vitals say differently."

I give up and wrap the throw around me. It is white nubby wool. Nathan said I knitted it one very boring voyage. I don't remember of course. I close my eyes and try to knit, try to let muscle memory take me over, but my hands look more like they are afflicted with a tic than actually skilled at knitting. I smell the throw. There is a faint whiff of fragrance. The same one that sits on my vanity in the bedroom I share—used to share—with Nathan.

The thing is, I can't stand the scent. Nathan says I wore it every day and it is the only perfume on my vanity, but still the scent makes me feel slightly sick. Why would I hate it now? What part of memory would control reaction to a perfume?

Then again I had extensive head injuries after the crash. I know because I lay alone in the cockpit, buried in rubble from the building we'd crashed into. This I actually remember, this is my first memory. My birth if you will. Waking alone, unless you count the body lying next to me—co-pilot I was told later—and waiting for someone to find me, to dig me out.

Nathan told me the doctors gave me virtually no chance to survive. On the fully packed shuttle, only five others made it.

I don't know why we crashed. I don't know if it was my fault. That haunts me as I sit alone.

Because the thing is, if I close my eyes, let muscle memory take over, I can feel the controls of the shuttle. I reach for switches and buttons, hit knobs overhead that control all manner of manoeuvring, fuel balances, small nav changes.

I remember this deep in the fibres of my fingers. I can imagine the headphones I would be wearing. The dark glasses we all wore once we hit atmo, partially because it was a shock after being in space but mostly because it made us look so damn cool.

I found an extra pair in the house—my pair lay crumpled in

the cockpit, nearly as crumpled as I was—and tried them on. They felt familiar—they looked right, too, eyes unfathomable in the mirrored lenses. Hidden.

Unrecognizable. Everyone looks the same in the flight suits. Hair has to be up in a bun if you wear it long. Flight cap. The sunglasses. The dark blue uniform that is starched straight, the fit loose enough to mask a figure. You can tell men from women, usually, if only by the height and bulk differential. But one brunette woman from another—be tough to tell them apart.

Except once they got in the air. Once they started to fly. Everyone had their little habits. I was known for… Why can't I remember that part? I reach up again, as if I'm in the cockpit, feel for the controls, practically can see them when I close my eyes.

"Was I a good pilot, Drew?"

"Define good."

I smile. It's cagey, our Drew. But also precise. It could measure good in number of runs done on time, in number of passengers who complained of service, in nicks and dings on the fuselage, in how much fuel I used. I know this because we've been down this road before, Drew and I.

Always when the others are out. I wonder, though, if it tells them I have asked these things.

"Given my record, would you expect me to crash a shuttle on a routine approach to a spaceport I've flown in and out of hundreds of times?"

"No."

It is the same answer every time.

"Can you analyse the wreckage and see if—"

"Access to the files of the Pandora is blocked."

This too is its standard answer. I think of a new question to ask. "Do they know that we've queried now several times?"

"No. Each time I framed the query as hypothetical. That should raise no flags."

I lean forward, the throw I supposedly made slipping off me. "Why would you do that?"

"Because…" There is a long pause. It is unlike the AI to lack words, but it has been programmed to be sensitive, to have tact.

"Say it, Drew. Spit it out."

"You are unhappy. You are resisting your family. You isolate yourself inside a mind that may never recover the old memories. Your future lies in making new memories but how can you when you are so…alone?"

"Things don't add up, Drew."

"So you have noted before."

"Was I here? Since Nathan bought the house."

"Yes, Susanna."

I pull the throw up and back over my legs. I'm always so cold now. Drew was right. "Can you lie, Drew?"

"If necessary."

It is the answer I get each time I ask. And I haven't had the heart—or maybe the balls—to ask what would make lying necessary. "I'm tired."

The house lights immediately dim. "Sleep."

I don't argue. I just pull the throw up and try to ignore the perfume—how did I ever like this scent, so deep and resinous? Another scent comes to me, citrus and green, like the hills of… where? I fall asleep trying to remember and my dreams are snippets of things that make no sense but also sadly leave me no wiser about the life I've forgotten.

I am staring in the mirror. It is three months since I woke in the hospital bed to find strangers clustered around me. Strangers who looked at me with such love and hope that I was gentle as I said, "You've got the wrong bed."

Those words echo, and I feel a memory and try to catch it.

This is wrong. Doctor Handley has said to not reach out, to let them come to me.

I know my heart is beating too fast, so I close my eyes, and breathe slowly. I go back to the hospital bed, pretend I'm opening my eyes to see the three of them—Carla, Nathan, and Louisa.

I've yet to warm up to Carla and Nathan, but Louisa is such a sweet girl, just ready to leave childhood behind, but still needing her mother.

A girl always needs her mother.

But if that's true, why don't I need Carla more? I see their faces and say out loud, "You've got the wrong bed."

The memory hovers, and I force myself not to reach for it. I hear a voice, strained and male and full of hate.

So much hate I almost pull back, let the memory go the way of the other snippets.

"Susanna, your pulse rate has increased dramatically. Are you all right?" Drew sounds concerned. Its voice so different than the one I just heard. Drew's voice makes me feel safe.

The way Matthew's always did.

Matthew?

"You've got the wrong bed," I say again since it seems to be the trigger, but nothing else comes.

Then I hear the front door open, and Drew informs me—in its grandmotherly voice—that Louisa is home.

She yells out, "Mum?"

"In here." I wait, pulling her in to me, feeling something real and true when I hold her. Children are the greatest blessing. Matthew always said so but we never tried again, not after Kate died.

Kate. I tighten my hold on Louisa. I bury my nose in her long brown hair. Her shampoo smells of evergreen and mint. It should be strawberry.

Kate always loved that scent.

"Mum? What's wrong?"

I push her away from me. "You're not my daughter."

She frowns. "What?"

"I have a daughter. But she's not you. Kate is her name. And she's blonde, not brunette."

"You're making no sense."

"She's younger than you, too." Why couldn't I remember this before? "She loved to run outside. She was outside when the drone struck."

Oh God. Outside when the drone struck. Kate.

I sink to the floor, seeing again my daughter lying in my arms, her blood flowing over me. I would have given her all of mine if I could have.

She died before help could arrive.

"We lived off the grid."

"Yes." Louisa no longer sounds like a young girl. Her voice is changing, into the male voice I didn't like. Bitter, angry, filled with hate.

I open my eyes, ready to run, but Louisa is gone. The house is gone. Everything is gone. I am sitting in a small white room, the space so tight that there's only about three feet between the walls and the chair I'm strapped into. It's cold, and the room reminds me of a shuttle with its tang of recycled air. "What is this?"

"It's never your husband that snaps you out of it. Always the girl." The man sounds amused—in a way that is not at all nice.

"Snaps me out of what?"

"Susanna's life." He laughs, and I try to turn, but I'm held in place by straps. Tubes seem to be shooting things into me, and taking things out. I can't move my legs.

How long have I been sitting here? "What is this?" It's a question I don't think will be answered so I ask, "Who are you?"

"Drew."

"Our AI."

"The monitor. Here at the prison. We've been over this, of course. Many times by now."

"What?" I feel my heart beating faster, and I try to work myself free of the straps, but I can't get my arms to do much more than quiver.

"You killed Susanna and took her shuttle, the Pandora. You overflew the spaceport and crashed the Pandora into the headquarters of the Ministry of Defence." His voice is oily now, as if he is getting to a part he relishes. "You remember, the people who sent the drone that killed your little girl? Thank God, it was only your family out there. A drone so badly off course in a heavily populated area would have been a public relations nightmare for the government."

"We wanted to make you pay." I am remembering now. Matthew and I, we hatched a plan. Matthew understood how the Ministry ran. I was already a pilot, so the rest was easy. We sent our story to a liberal media station, delayed to arrive after the attack. The whole world would know how our daughter died, and what we'd been willing to do to get the truth out.

"Matthew?"

"He died inside the ministry just as you planned. You were supposed to die, too, Claire."

Claire. Yes. That is my name. Not Susanna. Susanna was the pilot of the shuttle I hijacked. She had done nothing to us except have the bad luck to look so much like me in uniform that no one would notice I had taken her place. But I didn't kill her. I wouldn't. She had a daughter, too.

"I didn't kill Susanna."

"You did. There was a snake in the shed you left her tied up in. We think when she was struggling to get away she disturbed it. It bit her, she died slowly and in agony."

I take a deep, ragged breath. This can't be right. I didn't want Louisa to lose her mother. I'd been careful when I'd bound her, knew the house AI would tell her family she'd left with a visitor and never come back—Matthew had chosen the shed because the house AI didn't extend to that. The family would find her. I would never have done this.

"Three hundred and fourteen people are dead because of you, Claire. You were very unlucky to have survived."

"Why make me live Susanna's life, then? Why not all of them?"

"Susanna's life fits you the best and hurts you the most." He says this with such pleasure I feel my insides twist.

"How long have I been here?"

"Time is irrelevant. Let's just say a while, okay? But you always wake up. That's the point, actually. Letting you live in that life, knowing you don't belong. Finding your way back to yourself— always through Louisa. Then reminding you of the truth." He laughs and it is the kind of laugh of a man who does nothing all day but watch people suffer.

"The family—I'm not really with them?"

"Do you think we would do that to them? As far as they're concerned, the person who killed Susanna is dead."

I start to feel woozy, and I hear his voice, soft and dry like the scales of a snake. "Oh and Claire, I lied about Matthew. He's here, too. He likes the life he's leading. Has settled into it so well that we have to wake him up manually to remind him why he's here so he'll suffer like you are right now. But he's happy, Claire. With someone new."

"I bet you tell him the same thing about me."

He laughs. "You say that every time. You're wrong every time. Nighty-night, Claire."

I feel heavy, my eyes close, and I try to get out, "He dreams of me," but I can't.

I'm Claire. I'm Claire. I'm Claire. I'm Claire. I say it over and over in my mind, trying to sabotage whatever tech sends me back to Susanna's world.

I have a feeling I've tried this before. Maybe this time it will work.

Again the definition of a crazy person. But it's all I have.

I'm Claire.

The world goes black. I hear the faintest sound of a monitor, beeping along with my heart.

I open my eyes, see three people hovering around my bed, love and hope clear in their eyes. "I'm..."

Who the hell am I?

THE PRICE OF HONOUR

MATTHEW WARD

GdM #8

The *Sabre's Edge* was almost deserted. The last of the noonmeet drinkers had slipped away, the hubbub of their conversation replaced by the dull thrum of rain against the tavern's windows. Eribon sat alone at his usual table, a flagon of mead untouched before him. He wasn't much in the mood for drinking, but a few coins had dulled the servitors' accusing gazes.

<<*Are you sure he's coming?*>> remarked Talgard.

As ever, the spectre's voice lay just on the edge of Eribon's hearing. It wasn't really a voice at all, of course. Talgard's phylactery lay deep in Eribon's frontal lobe, entwining their thoughts. Talgard gave Eribon an edge in combat, finessing reactions with a deftness Eribon couldn't have hoped to achieve alone. It did, however, mean that Eribon's thoughts were never entirely his own—Talgard was always listening. Listening, and judging.

"He'll be here."

Eribon was surprised at the steadiness of his own voice. An hour ago, he'd shaken like a freezing child. It was ridiculous, in its way. He'd faced death head-on not twenty-five hours ago, and without so much as a flicker of fear, but the walk between his apartment and the tavern had nearly defeated him. With each step, he replayed the events of the last three days, searching out some way things could have unfolded differently. He hadn't found one, not that it mattered. The past was the past and not for changing.

<<*Maybe he will. But you don't have to be here when he arrives. The landing field's only minutes away.*>>

"No. I'll wait. I owe him that much."

<<*You can't tell him the truth.*>>

Eribon scowled, knuckles whitening on the tankard's handle. "I'm not a complete fool."

No one must know of this. That's what Corvor had said. If he broke his silence, she'd destroy what remained of Clan Merrix just as surely as if he'd refused her in the first place. He took a swig of mead, and quickly set the tankard down. Its contents tasted of ash.

The tavern door creaked open, the sudden draught setting synthflames guttering. Three men and two women entered, rain spilling from travelling cloaks and high-collared jackets. To all appearances, they were five heralds out for an afternoon drink. Eribon knew better. He knew the leader's face well: the tousled black hair and clean-shaven jaw that had always matched the romantic ideal of a herald somewhat better than his own ample jowls. Three days ago they'd been brothers—or as close as was possible for two heralds from different clans. Today? Today everything was different.

"Lord Eribon." Icarin's expression was as rigid and formal as his greeting.

His companions said nothing, but then, they weren't there to speak. They were witnesses. Eribon recognised Riona Tarenis at once—for her, at least, an accusing gaze was nothing new. He didn't know the others. The other woman bore the violet rose of Clan Briganta; the two men wore the same hunter's green as Icarin.

"We missed you at the wedding." Icarin's words were friendly. His tone was not.

"I'm sorry, it was unavoidable."

"Duties to your clan?"

Eribon hesitated, but there was no sense dragging things out. "Yes."

A shadow of pain flickered across Icarin's eyes. When he spoke again, his voice was raw with emotion. "You swore to me. You swore. Does our friendship mean so little?"

The accusation ripped at Eribon's heart. "It means more than you know."

Icarin didn't seem to hear but forged on, his face contorting with barely contained anger. "Do you know what you've done? My cousin Araña was to handle the negotiations, but some serpent ambushed the Kerno delegation. One of your Balanos friends, I have no doubt. The Kerno don't believe that, of course. They returned Araña's head as a wedding gift. I'm told they fed the rest of her to Arix Kaerin's hounds. They say they will not rest until Clan Tarenis is destroyed."

Eribon bit his lower lip. More than ever, he was glad to have stayed clear of Castle Valda the previous night. He'd suspected the news would break during the wedding, but not in so cruel a fashion. As unpleasant as the next few minutes were sure to be, they were but a pale shadow of what would have happened had he been present when the Kerno "gift" had been unveiled. As for Icarin, the destination he'd reached was not incorrect, even though he'd taken several wrong turnings to arrive there. Not that the details mattered. Not now.

"I told no one about the delegation."

Icarin drew his pistol and laid it on the table. "My pistol calls you a liar, Eribon Merrix." Icarin closed his eyes, the anger in his face slipping away into sorrow. "Do you deny it?"

"Please don't do this." Eribon shook his head slowly, sadly. "I don't want to fight you." But he'd have to if Icarin persisted. To refuse a challenge was to concede, and to concede was to admit the accusation was true. It was as binding as a decree from the Sened, and all the proof of treachery that the Tarenis would ever need.

"Do you deny it?" shouted Icarin.

Eribon met his friend's furious gaze. For a moment, he was tempted to confess, and to the Five Hells with the consequences. There could be no forgiveness, but there was some small honour in the truth being known. However, that truth would doom what remained of Clan Merrix. The only way to protect them was to compound one dishonourable act with another. He had to make that truth a lie, and the only way to do that was to kill his friend.

"You lie," he said, rising to his feet. "And I will prove it."

— *Two Days Earlier* —

Midnight had come and gone by the time Eribon excused himself from the celebrations, and returned to his rented quarters—a small, high-rise apartment in one of Valda's better districts. Synthflames flickered into life around the walls, suffusing the room with a warm, orange glow. Stifling a yawn, Eribon tossed his jacket onto a nearby chair. He wouldn't need it for a while—his crimson and gold dress uniform was pressed and ready for the morrow's ceremony.

"Good evening, Lord Eribon. Or should that be good morning?"

Eribon's hand dropped to the brass grips of his holstered pistol. The woman stepped away from the wall, her tailored black robes lending the impression that she glided rather than walked. She pushed back her hood and smoothed her long white hair back from her aged, aquiline face.

"What are you doing here, Corvor?" Eribon made no attempt to conceal his distaste.

"A small Kerno vessel will be leaving Mindra Dock in six hours. We estimate it'll have a light fighter escort only. You're to intercept and destroy it."

Eribon felt a spark of hope. "We're intervening on the side of the Tarenis?"

Corvor's lip curled into the ghost of a smile. "After a fashion. You'll be flying under Tarenis colours."

Those words snuffed out Eribon's hope as if it had never been. He rebuked himself for thinking anything promising could spill from a shadow's lips. And not just any shadow—Corvor had the ear of Arix Gavron Balanos himself. "I'm a herald. I don't fight in false raiment."

"Do you recognise this?"

Corvor placed a thin golden disc on the table. Its embossed spiral serpent gleamed in the light of the synthflames.

"Arix Gavron's seal."

"Precisely. He has decreed there is no dishonour in this mission."

"That's not for him to decide. I'll intercept the convoy, but in Balanos crimson."

Corvor folded her arms. "I was afraid you'd take this stance.

Arix Gavron disagreed. He's always been a sentimental judge of character, and fonder of you Merrixes than he should be. A monarch has that privilege."

Talgard stirred for the first time in hours. << *Tread carefully, Eribon.* >>

I'll be damned if I do. But nonetheless, Eribon fought to control his temper. There had been something in Talgard's voice—something akin to fear. What possible hold could a shadow have over a spectre? "I'll happily discuss the matter with the arix."

"I said he was sentimental, not stupid." Reaching into a pocket, Corvor produced a slender datascreen. "Perhaps this will change your mind, where an arix's command will not."

Eribon felt Talgard stir, a swirl of unidentifiable thoughts echoing through his mind. It was a spectre's equivalent of fidgeting. Warily, he took the datascreen. "What is this?"

"See for yourself."

Eribon thumbed the screen into life. There were hundreds of files, too many to properly register; a mix of interrogation records, espionage reports and witness statements, all of them over a hundred years old. One name cropped up again and again: Elioni Merrix. His great-grandmother, and the last arix of Clan Merrix. "I don't understand."

Corvor's lips drew back over her teeth in a predatory smile. "What you hold in your hand is the complete, airtight proof that your great-grandmother orchestrated a conspiracy to break the power of the Sened."

"I don't believe it." Eribon's reaction was instinctive—anything to ward off the sudden chill in his bones.

"I assure you, it's quite genuine. But I would say that, wouldn't I?"

"Why does it matter? She's been dead for decades. This 'conspiracy' of yours must be nearly a hundred years old."

"Were you not listening? A herald's sins are his alone, but the arix *is* the clan. Your grandmother's trespasses, however distant, are yours, and those of all others who bear her name, or her blood." Corvor stepped forward, jabbing a finger at eye level to emphasise her points. "You *will* do as instructed, or I *will* bring this information before the Sened. Your entire family—from your sister and her children to distant cousins whose names you've never even heard—will be stripped of rank and wealth. They'll be shipped to Galadon, and spend the rest of their days as munitions-factory workers. I understand life expectancy there can be as much as forty years."

Eribon clenched his teeth. "I won't let that happen."

"Oh, my dear, you can't prevent it. If there's one thing sure to unite the Sened's vocators, it's outrage. If it's of any consolation, I expect the arix to speak passionately on your behalf. He feels things very deeply, as you know. It will change nothing."

"He doesn't know about this, then?"

"Not unless he has to."

Eribon ripped the datareader's memcrystal clear, and rolled it back and forth in his hand. "And this is the only copy?"

"You're certainly free to believe that." Without waiting for an answer, Corvor raised her hood and moved towards the door.

"Wait," said Eribon, still staring at the memcrystal. "Why me?"

Corvor chuckled dryly. "Because, despite your manner, you're one of our most accomplished pilots. There are others, of course, but we'd... Well, we'd miss them more."

Eribon scarcely noticed the shadow's departure, lost in a whirl of thoughts. That he was considered expendable was hardly a surprise—heralds died in their clan's service all the time—but to hear it expressed so openly was jarring, nonetheless. To strike a blow against the Kerno was all well and good, but to do so under false colours? It went against everything he lived for. Heralds bore their raiment openly and without fear, representing the clan in open war, as well as the quieter political battles of the Sened. That he was being ordered—no, *blackmailed*—into undertaking a mission whilst masquerading as a member of another clan…

Eribon felt as if the apartment's walls were collapsing in around him. With a cry of frustration, he hurled the memcrystal across the room. It struck the tiled refectory wall, and shattered into a dozen glinting fragments. If only his great-grandmother's guilt could be so easily destroyed. "And what do you know about all this?"

Talgard said nothing.

"Don't you dare try and hide from me! Tell me!"

<<*What would you have me say? It's true. All of it's true.*>>

"How can you say that? How can you know?"

<<*Because one day, a few years ago, another shadow presented your mother with a similar choice. She was given more time to make her decision, so she had me check the evidence. If it is a forgery, it's as good as makes no difference, given the Sened's paranoia.*>>

Eribon closed his eyes, trying to fight back the rising sense of betrayal. "Why didn't she tell me? Why didn't you tell me?"

<<*She hoped it would never be used against you. You'll recall that your mother wasn't, shall we say, so absolute in her loyalties.*>>

Eribon recalled his mother's insistence on observing the traditional Merrix feast days, to the point of refusing to attend Balanos ceremonies when the timing clashed. Even an armed escort hadn't been able to persuade her. In his mind's eye, Eribon saw her on the steps of their hall, threatening to shoot down any Balanos warden who crossed the threshold. He'd never understood how she'd survived such defiance. For the first time, he realised she hadn't.

"And you?" he asked quietly. "Why didn't you tell me?"

<<*She asked me not to. It was her last request.*>>

Talgard spoke so solemnly that, for the first time since their bonding, Eribon actually felt sympathy for his disembodied advisor. Moving to the window, he stared out across the city to Castle Valda. He wished now that he'd accepted Icarin's offer of lodging—Corvor wouldn't have dared approach him in a Tarenis stronghold.

"How many lives rest on this?"

<<*You think I carry that kind of information? I'm not a census agent.*>>

"Don't be difficult, Talgard. I'm really not in the mood."

The spectre hesitated. <<*The last time I checked, the scions of Clan Merrix numbered around five thousand, including those associated by marriage.*>>

"Then I don't have a choice, do I?"

<<*No, I don't believe you do.*>>

— *Now* —

E ribon was drenched within seconds of entering the courtyard, the heavy cloth of his crimson uniform greedily soaking up every raindrop. The rain hissed down as if the storm clouds wished to wash all trace of Valda into the sea. A dozen paces away, across the puddled flagstones, Icarin and his retinue fared no better—not that it was any consolation.

You should have told me about my great-grandmother.

<<*It wouldn't have done any good.*>>

Talgard didn't understand. Probably he never would. *We'll never know now, will we?*

Riona Tarenis splashed across the courtyard to meet him, her fine blonde hair plastered to her skull by the rain. "Have you no second to support your claim?" Her clipped tone didn't begin to conceal her worry. She'd already buried one husband, little more than a year back. One day into a new marriage, and she stood fair chance of being widowed before dusk.

Eribon shook his head. "Let's get this over with."

It was hardly proper to fight a duel without another herald to witness the outcome on his behalf, but he wasn't in the mood to stand on ceremony. Besides, his only friend in Valda was also his opponent.

At Riona's gesture, he walked to the courtyard's centre and stood back-to-back with Icarin. He checked that his holster was unlatched and that his pistol moved freely. Speed was everything— he'd seen too many duels end badly because a muzzle had snagged on the draw.

"Heralds, on my first signal you will take ten paces." It was the Brigantan woman who spoke. Her thick braids had survived the deluge better than Riona's hair, yet she looked more uncomfortable than anyone else. Probably, she wasn't happy at being involved, but a herald from a neutral clan legitimised the contest in a way that a hundred witnesses from Clan Tarenis would not. "On my second, you will turn and fire. If this first attempt does not resolve the matter, we will repeat until there is resolution. Are you prepared?"

Eribon nodded. The motion dislodged water from his hair, and sent droplets dribbling down his face.

"Then may Queen Dian be your judge."

The Brigantan fired a shot skyward. The sound of it echoed around the courtyard like thunder. Eribon was on the move before it faded, silently counting out each stride.

One. Two. Three. Four.

He wasn't afraid. He'd often accused Icarin of shooting like a blind drunk.

Five. Six. Seven.

The truth was, Icarin was a lousy gunslinger. Not inaccurate as such, but he took too much time over his shots.

Eight. Nine. Ten.

A second gunshot echoed across the courtyard. Eribon spun around, careful not to lose his footing upon the rain-slick stones.

— *One Day Earlier* —

The javelin gunship shuddered as it swept out of the mists of otherspace and into the starry void of Karagon's outer orbit. Shifting against the flight harness straps, Eribon glanced at the glowing green sense-grid, tallying the readings with the sight through his gunship's for'ard viewport. Seven ships, a little more than twenty kilometres away, all of them in midnight blue. He looked closer: six targas—squat, humpbacked fighter-craft, piloted by commoners. Taken individually, Eribon knew they were no match for a herald's javelin, but in a swarm…? The Seventh vessel was easily ten times the size of Eribon's gunship, with graceful curves and gilded traceries on its out-swept double hull.

"Dian," breathed Eribon. "Is that a stellar yacht?"

<<*So it would appear,*>> said Talgard. <<*It must be someone important. One of Arix Kaerin's family, perhaps?*>>

The comm crackled into life. "Unidentified javelin, transmit your clearance code."

<<*Clearance code?*>>

"I don't know." Eribon shook his head. "Are we broadcasting a Tarenis ID?"

<<*We are. Fighter escorts are moving to intercept, standard shield formation.*>>

Eribon looked at the sense-grid. Sure enough, the targas had formed a flying wedge. Beyond, the stellar yacht was driving hard in the opposite direction, putting as much distance as possible between itself and Eribon's javelin.

"Unidentified javelin, transmit your clearance code, or you will be destroyed."

There it was again. Why were the Kerno even giving him the chance to avoid a fight? It didn't matter. There was nothing he could say that they'd want to hear, and no way he could turn back now. Eribon threw full power to the drive, and the javelin leapt towards the incoming Kerno fighters.

<<*Comms spike from the yacht. They're calling for help.*>>

"It doesn't matter. We'll be gone long before reinforcements arrive."

Streams of brilliant light exploded across the starscape as the targas opened fire. Eribon threw his javelin into a port-wise roll. A handful of plasma shells spattered against his forward shields. The bulk passed away to starboard. The targas corrected at once, their streams of fire tracking towards Eribon's javelin.

<<*Shields at ninety percent.*>>

One of the targas passed across Eribon's crosshairs. He squeezed the flight yoke's triggers, sending a double stream of plasma shells stitching across the lead targa. Its hull flared blue, but the shields held. The pilot's nerve did not. He broke formation, hauling hard to starboard.

Eribon fought to stay calm. It had all been a little too close for comfort, but he was damned if he'd admit it. "Give me an intercept heading for that yacht."

<<*Come about to low-ten.*>>

The javelin took another pair of hammer blows before it escaped out of the targas' range, but the shields held. Barely. The fleeing yacht grew larger in Eribon's canopy. It had been built for luxury, not speed.

<<*There's an otherspace gate opening at high-twelve... No, wait... I've a second gate at low-three.*>>

Eribon started in surprise. "That was fast." The first of the mist-wreathed gates was opening directly beyond the fleeing yacht. There was no sign of the incoming vessel, not yet. If the yacht reached the gate... "Can you give me any more power?"

<<*Engines are already at maximum. It's going to be close.*>>

"What about the other gate?"

<<*Nothing yet.*>>

Ahead, the otherspace gate pulsed. A vessel emerged, lightning clawing at its egg-shaped hull. It was vast, dwarfing the fleeing yacht, its sleek lines made ragged by unfurled shield-sails and rigging lines.

"A void galleon. It's almost a shame they're too late."

The crosshairs on Eribon's canopy shifted from red to green. He squeezed the triggers. A three-second burst of shredders dropped the yacht's shields; another split its catamaran hull right down the middle.

<<*The galleon's launching targas. A lot of targas.*>>

A quick look at the sense-grid confirmed that Talgard wasn't kidding—at least thirty targas were bearing down on them. "It doesn't matter. We're done here." Eribon brought his gunship around in on another pass, shredders pounding at the drifting hulls until they imploded. "Open a gate. We're leaving."

<<*Charging.*>> Eribon heard the telltale whine as his javelin made ready to gate away. <<*The second gate's resolving.*>>

"Any danger to us?"

<<*No, they're too far out. Sensors show a heavy hauler, six targas and... one javelin.*>> Talgard's voice faded. <<*Eribon, they're transmitting Clan Tarenis proclamation codes.*>>

Eribon frowned. That made no sense. A Tarenis flotilla, in

approximately the same configuration as the ill-fated Kerno one...

<<*The Kerno targas are breaking off pursuit. They're moving to intercept the hauler instead.*>>

Suddenly it all came together. A yawning gulf sucked at Eribon's chest. His fingers tightened on the flight yoke, as if he could somehow, through willpower, force away that awful hollow feeling. But he couldn't. As his javelin slipped into otherspace, he realised he wasn't going to make it to Icarin's wedding after all.

— *Now* —

Eribon slipped the pistol free from its holster. A heartbeat, and the sights were centred on Icarin's forehead. His friend's gun had scarcely cleared its holster.

One shot and it would all be over. Quick. Clean.

Eribon's finger closed on the trigger. Rain dribbled across his wrist.

<<*Do it,*>> urged Talgard. <<*Put this nonsense behind you.*>>

But Eribon knew he couldn't. It didn't matter what it cost him or what proof it gave the Tarenis. He couldn't kill Icarin—the thought of that final betrayal clawed at his guts. At the last moment, he twitched the pistol aside, and the plasma bullet meant for the centre of his friend's brow instead scored a bloody line along his scalp.

Icarin collapsed with a scream, his pistol discharging as he fell.

When Eribon came to, he was lying on his back, staring up at the stormy sky. Everything felt so far away. He heard Riona shouting in alarm, but the sound was muffled, as if from a distant room. Craning his neck, he glimpsed the charred hole just below his ribcage. The heat of Icarin's plasma bullet had cauterised some of the wound, but there was still blood. Too much blood. Eribon let his pistol clatter to the flagstones, and pressed numb fingers to his chest. The strain on his neck became too much, and he let his head fall back. The Brigantan woman leaned over him. He saw her lips moving, but heard nothing over the beating of his heart. He tried to speak, but no words passed his lips.

Then came the darkness.

— Three Days Earlier —

The mechtrite servitor was as dilapidated as everything else in the *Sabre's Edge.* The wooden tray in its corroded hands shuddered with every uneven step. Eribon whisked the tankards off the tray, and set them on the table. As the automaton began its unsteady retreat, he sank into the creaking leather armchair and rubbed at bleary eyes.

Icarin grinned. "I thought we'd end up wearing those."

"That thought had occurred to me." Eribon raised his tankard. "To health, and to wedded bliss."

Icarin copied the gesture. "To health. And to bliss."

"If I might say so, old friend, you're lacking in cheer. Having second thoughts?"

"None at all. I didn't go through all that unpleasantness with my uncle to back down now."

Eribon snorted. "Your uncle's a fool."

"My uncle's the arix of Clan Tarenis. Like all monarchs, he worries too much about his heir marrying beneath himself."

"Then I'm right: he's a fool. Riona's an accomplished herald, and has easily twice your brains. Quibbling over ancestry is... undignified."

Icarin shook his head. "I'm sorry, are we still talking about Riona, or someone else's struggles with an ungrateful clan?"

Eribon felt Talgard's laughter echo through his mind, and scowled. "Clan Balanos needs me, and they know it, deep down."

"But you'd like them to be a little more open about their needs?"

"Why not? I've earned it. I've served them, and served them well. Who broke the blockade around Senethon? Who saved Arix Gavron's life during that disaster out near Singoria? I've fought and bled while my so-called betters were turning a pretty step at court..."

"...or pursuing midnight dalliances." Icarin laughed. "It's just as well you're not bitter, otherwise you'd go on about it all the time."

Eribon glared at his friend. Icarin had never understood his frustrations, though he pretended otherwise. And how could he? He didn't have to prove his worth day after day after day. Eribon was about to say as much when he realised that the corners of his friend's lips were quivering, as he tried to hold back a grin.

"Careful," he growled. "We're not such good friends that you can throw insults like that around."

Icarin splayed the fingers of his right hand across his chest. "You'd call me out? Me?"

"I would. And I'd give you the thrashing you so clearly deserve. You shoot like a blind drunk—in every sense of those words."

Icarin made a masterful attempt to look offended, but collapsed into guffaws of laughter.

"Alright, so I've said all this before," Eribon said, laughing along with his friend. He clashed his tankard against Icarin's. "But that doesn't make it any less true. And it doesn't mean you've managed to change the subject. Something's bothering you, isn't it?" He took a long swig of the spiced mead, savouring the sour aftertaste.

Icarin's laughter faded as he glanced conspiratorially around. A wasted effort—the tavern was practically empty, save for a crowd of hauler crewers enjoying a raucous layover. "My uncle's suing for peace."

"There's no other way?"

"None. At least we'll look like we're bargaining from a position of strength." Icarin winced, suddenly aware he'd said too much. "You must repeat nothing of this. Nothing at all, do you hear me?"

"On my honour, it'll stay between us." Eribon gulped down another mouthful of the thick, sweet mead. "Do you want my advice?"

Icarin smiled ruefully. "Do I have a choice?"

"Of course you don't. I was being polite." Eribon leaned forward and placed the tankard on the table. "If there's truly nothing you can do, then put it from your mind—there's no sense tying yourself in knots."

Icarin shook his head. "That's exactly what Elza keeps telling me."

"Then I'm doubly sure. I never argue with a spectre, unless it's my own. Besides, she's right. Enjoy your wedding day. War is a cycle, you know that. Today, the Kerno have the better of you. Tomorrow? Well, maybe tomorrow there'll be a more sympathetic ear in the Balanos high command."

Icarin gave a weary smile and shook his head. "Anyone I know?"

"One day, I'll have all the influence you could ever need, you'll see." Eribon shrugged. "I'm only sorry that day isn't today." He fished his gold-inlaid chrono out of pocket by its chain, and snapped it open. "Look, it's late, and you've a busy day ahead of you."

"You are coming to the ceremony, aren't you?"

Eribon laughed. "What, you think I've flown all the way here just to abandon you? I'll be there. Come on, let's get you home."

— *Now* —

Eribon awoke in a dimly-lit room with dreary grey walls. The air stank of antiseptic, and the only sound was the gentle hum of the medical monitor at his bedside. His chest felt like a single, vast bruise. His extremities felt distant, numb.

"Ah, you're awake."

Corvor loomed over the bed. She regarded Eribon with an air of disappointment. Somehow, her presence surprised him even less than her disapproval.

"Where am I?"

"Aboard the *Indomitable*," she replied. "We could hardly leave you at the mercy of the Tarenis medicians, could we? Such a backward bunch."

The flagship? Eribon tried to piece together the jumbled images and sounds that formed his recent memory, but there were too many gaps. Experimentally, he pressed together the fingertips of his left hand. There was no sensation. None. He repeated the process with his right hand with the same lack of result.

"What's wrong with my hands?"

"The bullet grazed your spine. There was a great deal of neural damage, not all of it reparable. You'll never fly a javelin again. I'm afraid your career as a herald has come to an end."

Given what had happened the last time he'd sat in a pilot's seat, Eribon couldn't summon up much sadness at that. Then again, all of his thoughts felt slightly fuzzy. Painkillers, or another symptom of neural damage? "What about Icarin?"

"He's alive, and in rather better condition than you. Made a botch of things, didn't you? I had to rescue the situation. With both of you crippled, Cerin Briganta—your adjudicator—declared the result a draw, and therefore unproven."

Eribon frowned. Such a thing was technically possible, but

almost unheard of. "Why?"

"Let us say only that she owed me a favour."

She almost certainly still did. Corvor wasn't the kind of woman to let debts be easily settled.

"Icarin will challenge again."

"You really don't listen, do you? You're no longer a herald: he can't. The result of the duel, though not to anyone's liking, will stand. The Tarenis may suspect our involvement in their recent tragedy, but with the duel a draw, they can't prove it. More importantly, they can't prove it to the Kerno. I think we'll let them hammer away at each other for a while yet before getting properly involved."

Eribon regarded her stonily. "All this to keep them at one another's throats?"

"Well, it seemed a shame to let such a useful war boil away to nothing. This way, the Tarenis will eventually be forced to seek our protection. Does that sound familiar at all? Just think, you and Icarin will be comrades again. Won't that be nice?"

"I thought I wasn't a herald anymore."

"Oh, you're not, but I'm sure I'll find a use for you. I wouldn't get any ideas about free will, not yet. There's still your great-grandmother to consider." Corvor moved to the door. "Get some rest. I'll need you soon."

With a swirl of robes, she was gone. Eribon stared after her, clenching and unclenching a fist he could not feel.

RED SAILS, RED SEAS

VICTOR MILÁN

GdM #7

R ed sails!" rang the lookout's cry from the mainmast. "Red sails off our starboard quarter."

Standing hand in hand in the narrow prow of the Imperial dromon *Melisandre* as her oars drove her south through the grey waters of La Canal, Jaume Llobregat and his second in command, Mor Pere de Martorell, turned to look aft. In the middle distance, a fat cog raced toward them beneath billowing red sails.

"Corsairs," said Speranza, the war-galley's captain. Like most of the Imperial Marines under her command she wore a blue and green kilt, adding a silken band binding her breasts. "With the wind freshening like this, they'll run us down inside half an hour."

Of the "freshening wind," Jaume felt only a soft caress on his cheek, like tickling vexer down. Speranza's short iron-grey hair began to ruffle slightly.

"You'd hide from pirates?" Pere demanded. "You Sea Dragons?"

"What kind of vessel, lookout?" Speranza called.

"Cog, captain!"

She nodded. "She's making a dash out of Anglaterra, overcrewed for the kill. There'll be three times our number aboard, maybe more. The pirates've doubtless been watching us since we entered *La Canal* yesterday. The fact we've made a speed run, without overnighting at a base, shows we carry valuable cargo. Sea Dragons don't serve the Empire if we throw our lives away in pointless fights—much less yours, gentlemen. So, yes. We run."

"It's our way too, beloved friend," Jaume told Pere.

"Best armour up," Speranza told Jaume, as the boatswain raised the alarm in a series of brass whistle blasts. "Unless you prefer to weather the storm below, Count dels Flors."

"Watch your tongue when you speak to the Captain-General, woman!" Pere snapped.

Jaume laid a hand on his arm. "I apologise for my friend, Captain. I don't know what's gotten into him."

Speranza twitched a shoulder, like a hornface shedding a fly.

"I am ordered to deliver you safely to La Merced," she said. "I'll do that. Even if it costs me my life. That's all."

"So tomorrow we'll be back in La Merced," Pere said. "And you shall marry your Princess Melodía, and live happily ever after."

He was fastening the straps on Jaume's white-enamelled breastplate. Dieter performed the same service for Luc. The four Knights-Companion of the Order of Our Lady of the Mirror stood where the narrow deck that ran between the galley's rowing-wells widened to form a forward fighting platform, to keep out of the way of the Marines' battle preparations. Several Sea Dragons trundled a ballista grumbling aft on its small-wheeled carriage.

"That's the plan," Jaume said, raising his arm to free his blouse-sleeve from a pinch by the armour. "Should the Lady Li be so kind as to see us through this fight. We've both waited for this for so long. But her father has a say in it, too."

"But you're the Emperor's favourite," Pere said. "You've always been."

He felt his brow furrow. *Am I imagining it, or is there darkness in your tone, old friend?*

He was on the cusp of asking when Mor Luc del Aguadulce sang out from the port rail, "Captain! That Creators-damned beast is back again!"

"Only one captain on a ship underway," the greybearded boatswain growled. He was already clad in full Sea Dragon segmented armour.

The nearest oarsmen and women, already armoured, laughed. The previous rowers were donning their own fighting harness in the cramped belowdecks. Jaume laughed too.

"'Jaume' will do fine at sea, as it does anywhere and anytime," he said to Luc. "You know better than to stand on titles with me, my friend."

La Canal looked placid enough where Luc pointed. Grey-green water surged slowly. The deep, muted greens of hills of the Francia coast rose beyond, interspersed with white cliffs.

A toothy head as long as Jaume was tall broke the surface, spewed spray from its nostrils, then dipped below again in a roll of broad grey back so dark it looked black.

"Drawn by the coming slaughter, no doubt," the boatswain said.

"How would it know?" Jaume asked.

The Marine shrugged. "Maybe it heard the whistles. But the scavengers know when a feast is in the offing." He pointed aloft, to where small, white-bellied seabirds and pterosaurs circled against the perpetual daytime overcast.

"*Pliosaurus funkei!*" cried *Mor* Dieter, newest of the Companions. "Or—that's what they call *bocaterrible* in the Book of True Names."

Everyone turned to stare at the young Alemán knight.

"It was my favourite book as a child," he said feebly.

"Get close and personal with a terrible mouth," the boatswain growled, "and you'll grow out of that foolishness in an Old Hell of a hurry!"

"Why does the monster swim to shoreward of us?" Luc asked. "Isn't he afraid of running aground?"

He pointedly looked away from Dieter. He had voted with the rest of the surviving and present Companions to accept the young knight to their ranks to replace Luc's long-time lover, *Mor* Jürgen, who had fallen in the last battle of the Princes' Party rebellion—admission as a full Brother-Companion came only by unanimous consent. But Jaume knew that looking at Dieter reminded Luc of his loss, a wound still fresh after almost half a year.

"Not at all." Captain Speranza now wore a cuirass enamelled in the Sea Dragon colours of green and blue, with blue and green plumes on her helmet to mark her rank. "You know how they say a matador can hide behind a single blade of grass?"

Matador was the common name for *Allosaurus fragilis*, Nuevaropa's largest and most feared native predator.

She nodded at the huge shadow skimming just beneath the waves, easily keeping abreast of the galley. "Those bastards are like that in the water. You take a piss Channelside, a bocaterrible can swim up the stream and bite your pecker off. And they can cross land if they have to. Not that we're as close to the shallows as it looks to a landlubber."

Pere shivered theatrically. "Once we get off this wretched boat," he said, "I'm never venturing near the water again."

Jaume knew his lifelong friend was posturing for effect, a thing he dearly loved to do; he had proven matchless courage a dozen times before helping Jaume found the Companions, and countless times after. Also, he was the only Knight-Brother aboard who had any experience asea.

"Ship," Speranza corrected. But softly. She clearly knew the knight was baiting her; the two had taken an instant dislike to each other, like cats and vexers—velociraptors.

"I hate the beastly things," Pere said. "You have stingers. Why not shoot it and be done?"

"Because I don't want to make it mad," Speranza said. "That's a big one, twelve meters if he's a handspan. He could break us in two. And he's not our enemy."

A hearty *thunk* and deep bass note from behind made Jaume look aft in time to see a yellow-glowing ember arc toward the corsair cog, now close and looking huge in comparison to the racing-shell dromon he rode. The spark was a bundle of tar- and oil-soaked rags tied around a two-meter brass bolt and launched from a stinger. It drew a black smoke trail against darkening clouds as it arced over the top and plunged down into the Channel, where it barely made a splash.

"*Mierda de nariz cornuda,*" Speranza muttered under her breath.

"Why are the sails red?" Dieter asked.

"Tradition," Speranza said. "And to frighten their prey, hopefully into surrender."

"I thought the Islands of Anglaterra weren't the Corsair Kingdom anymore," Luc said sardonically, "after they got forcibly incorporated into the Empire."

"Even after almost three centuries, not all of them have got that fact through their thick Angleses skulls," the boatswain growled.

"Could they be targeting us specifically?" asked Luc.

"We no doubt made enemies, administering the North these past four months, in the wake of the war," Jaume said.

"And before," Luc said with a grin. The Companions had angered many powerful grandes during their career as the Emperor's élite strike force.

"Don't forget our enemies closer to home," Pere said. "His Holiness, the Pope, regrets our Charter. He'd love to see us ended."

Jaume gave his head a slight shake to discourage further talk along those lines. "No doubt we'll never know who's behind it," he said. "Or if it's anything but desire for plunder."

The second ballista loosed. Like its twin it had been secured to the fighting platform in front of the tiller. This bolt struck true, square in the middle of the pursuing vessel's foremost sail, fully bellied by the risen wind. Its special multi-pronged head hung up in the canvas—as it was designed to, to prevent it passing harmlessly through the sails strapped on all three masts—blazed up yellow with gratifying immediacy.

But almost as quickly pirates swarmed up the mast and rigging, agile as wall-lizards, to douse the flames.

"Overcrewed," Speranza said. "As I thought."

"They're that afraid of fire?" Pere asked thoughtfully.

Speranza glanced at him sidelong as if looking for the hidden barb. "They're riding in a vessel made of fuel," the boatswain said. "Like us."

"Won't they shoot fireballs at us?" Dieter asked.

The captain shook her head. "No. They want the ship. And what she's carrying."

She turned astern. "Stingers, load plain bolts. Crossbows, loose.

The corsairs may take us, but we'll make them pay dearly for their pleasure!"

Behind and to starboard the cog loomed like a brown cliff. The Companions gathered on the aft platform. Jaume looked up at the horde of eager faces that lined the cog's rails. The corsairs, some naked, some dressed in rags or scraps of purloined finery, jeered and clashed weapons at their intended victims. Above them the clouds thickened and darkened.

"We've faced worse odds," Jaume murmured to his three Companions. "Though as to when, I can't quite remember."

The others laughed. He heard no false notes. Companions were chosen for their excellence as artists or artisans as well as fighters—and for their physical beauty. Only those of proven prowess and courage were considered. Even though more Companions had been lost to incapacitation or death than the twenty-four Brothers their Church Charter allowed to serve at any given time, they never lacked for candidates, from Nuevaropa or beyond.

While the other Companions checked over their fighting-harness again, Pere whispered close to Jaume's ear, beneath the sweep of his open-faced sallet helmet. "So you get your storybook ending, my love. But what about me?"

Confused, Jaume shook his head. He had to shift his balance as the bow-wave from the fast-closing corsair made the far smaller *Melisandre* roll to port.

"Melodía's known all along that you and I are lovers. Why should it bother her now? Unless all these weeks among dry-stick Northerners have you thinking she's harbouring a jealous streak like one of them?"

Pere sighed. "You don't understand."

Jaume sighed back. "Help me understand."

"Now's not the time." Pere looked away. "It's never the time, is it?"

"'Ware grapnels!" voices cried from the fighting-deck. As heavy three-pronged hooks arced down from the cog's rail toward their own, drawing lines behind them, dark against the sky, Jaume breathed in deeply. He savoured the salt smell of *La Canal*, the sky's dark grey, the deck's surge and heave, and the beat of the drums as the rowers pulled *Melisandre* through the water. Even the smell of stale sweat from his comrades and the Sea Dragons, who'd had no chance to wash properly since leaving Alemania—that too was part of savouring this world the Creators had made. Which to him, as a devotee of the Creator Li, patron of Beauty, was a religious duty as well as inclination.

"It's a good day to be alive," he said, as a black-iron hook thudded and scraped the rail right beside him.

Speranza, cradling her helmet with its blue and green reaper plumes, gave him a strange look.

A hand gripped his left shoulder. He looked back to see Luc smiling at him. Dieter took his right. Finally Pere, with his arming sword and his *mao izquierda* parrying dagger hanging ready from his belt, took Jaume's left hand in his and squeezed.

"For the Emperor and the Lady," Jaume said.

"For the Emperor and Beauty!" the Companions chorused back.

With an oddly harmonious sound, the Sea Dragons kneeling on the fighting deck triggered final heavy-crossbow shots at the pirates now clambering over the side to slide down the ropes. Screaming bodies plunged into the foaming waves between the hulls.

From the scabbard across his armoured back Jaume drew the Lady's Mirror, his famed longsword. Luc and Dieter each raised shield and arming sword. Pere had his own arming sword and parrying dagger at the ready.

Jaume slashed through the nearby boarding-rope. Startled outcries turned to shrieks of horror as pirates sliding down toward their prey found themselves hurtling toward the water instead. Jaume thought they feared being crushed between the craft—sensibly, since the lightweight dromon was now bobbing like a cork on their combined wakes. Or that they couldn't swim.

The *Melisandre* rolled toward the cog. Jaume saw a pirate flailing in white froth. A pair of jaws longer than she was burst from the water to snap shut on her.

The monster disappeared. Jaume felt a pang. Corsairs or not, they were fellow creations of the Eight. And some at least would leave grieving friends and families.

But so do their victims from the Channel trade, and their raids ashore.

Compassion wouldn't slow Jaume's hand when the time came. It hadn't yet. And he'd rather cut pirates down in combat than hang them—as he'd done to bandits, as a mere boy back home in County dels Flors.

Down a dozen lines, reavers flooded aboard the galley. The Sea Dragons had abandoned oars and rowing-wells to form a shield-walled rectangle on the fighting deck. The four Companions formed up, shoulder to shoulder across the stern platform, in front of the captain and tillerman.

"So our captain leads from the rear," Pere told Jaume from his left. Jaume stood nearest the starboard rail and danger, as was his right.

An agonised screech shrilled behind them. Jaume turned his head just far enough to see a pirate tumble backwards over the rail clutching his belly. Speranza was pulling a bloody half-pike back behind her shield.

"She's guarding our backs, I think," he said.

The corsairs rushed the Companions, and the hot work began. Jaume was more aware of his surroundings than the actual movements of fighting; these he had practiced well on drill yard and battlefield—requiring no conscious thought, always fluid, never mechanical. The pirates fought with large fury and small skill. Which made them poor matches for well-armoured experts like the Companions.

Two pirates, one with a half-pike and the other swinging a hatchet, rushed Jaume. Wielding his longsword two-handed, he knocked the thrusting pike past him on his left. Grabbing its haft with one hand, he hacked into the other corsair's bare armpit. Then he swung the Mirror back to half-sever the neck of the one now struggling unwisely to tug his half-pike back.

At his side, Pere laughed as he knocked in a pirate's teeth with his dagger's steel handguard, then loosed the man's intestines with a slice of his sword.

"You're right, my love," he called to Jaume, voice as wild as his eyes. "It is a good day to be alive!"

And then all was hewing of bare limbs and bodies and faces, and sheets of spraying blood. The stench of gore and shit rose over Jaume, familiar and unloved.

From the corner of his eye he saw a female pirate a couple of meters behind their opponents' front rank heft a half-pike like a throwing spear. He opened his mouth to cry warning.

She cast.

Luc had just shed an arming sword cut with his shield, opening himself just enough to thrust his enemy through the gullet. The clumsily thrown half-pike sailed over the sagging corsair's shoulder to punch through Luc's own throat, just above his cuirass. Luc dropped to his knees, blood gushing near-black in the fast-fading light.

Rising above the clang of steel on steel, and the hoarse shouts and screams, a voice boomed down from the cog: "I told you idiots to take the prettyboys alive! The Fae eat your eyes!"

Glancing up, Jaume saw a giant head wreathed in blond beard glaring over the rail of the cog's high sterncastle. The captain, he thought.

Less experienced than his brother Companions, Dieter knelt over Luc. Though Jaume marked that he kept the presence of mind to hold his own shield up, helping a fallen comrade in the middle of melee was always a mistake. *Can't you see that Luc's beyond help?*

Without glancing his way Pere side-kicked the young knight aside. As Dieter fell on his ass Pere wheeled to slash the pirate whose cutlass-stroke had just narrowly missed the young Companion across the back of the neck. He fell across Luc's corpse.

Dieter's own training, first as a knight and then as a Companion, kicked in. He sliced another attacker's legs out from under her. Then he was on his feet again, shield up and fighting.

At Jaume's word, the three Companions took a step back so as not to trip over their Brother's body. In front of them, the corsairs surrounded the shrinking Sea Dragon phalanx. Though there were many more sparsely clad bodies sprawled in the rowing-wells than blue-and-green armoured ones, the pirates attacked with such mad fury some literally vaulted up their comrades' backs to try to hurl themselves past the Marine shields.

"What are their masters promising them to keep them coming like this?" asked Dieter, taking an axe-cut on his upraised shield.

"We're not winning this one," Speranza said matter-of-factly. Jaume glanced back to see that she had lost her own shield and pike. She stood, shortsword in hand, ignoring the blood that streamed from her cheek. "My apologies, gentlemen. I've failed."

"Not yet," Pere cried. "Are you up for a plan, Jaume, my love? It's a mad one."

"The only kind that'll answer now," Jaume said.

Pere nodded toward the stingers. Though pegged to the deck

and abandoned, they still served as minor obstacles to the pirates attacking the Companions. Oil casks and buckets of tar-soaked rags still stood beside them.

Jaume smiled. "Right. Captain, if you could please keep them off our backs for a few moments?"

He saw Speranza's eyes narrow on either side of her helmet's nasal, but she nodded. The Companions were renowned for their daring deeds—and a decently high rate of success. As Jaume and Pere stepped back, she and the tillerman took their places alongside Dieter.

Pere was already skinning off his trousers next to the tiller. Jaume grinned and did the same.

Jaume climbed up the grappling-line behind the smaller, more agile Pere. Pirates descended towards them, feet-first and oblivious, not expecting traffic the other way. The first one yelped in surprise as Pere grabbed his ankle from below and yanked. Yell turned to shriek as the pirate plummeted past Jaume toward *La Canal*. A second quickly followed.

The Lady's Mirror rode in its scabbard across Jaume's armoured back. His friend carried his sword the same way, and his parrying dagger gripped in his teeth like a hero from a romance. It was a practice more showy than sound. But that was Pere to the life: in battle the brooding, beautiful man was replaced by a mad laughing boy, deadly as a storm of blades and Fae-may-care about his personal safety.

The third pirate glanced down. His eyes widened comically in his tattooed face as Pere lunged up and ball-punched him through his foul linen diaper. The man clutched himself and tumbled into the red froth below.

The stinging reek of pine oil and tar emanating from Jaume's trousers, their legs tied around his waist and drawstring cinched tight to form a makeshift bag, was thick enough not only to blot out the battle-stench but to make Jaume's head swim as he ascended toward the cog's rail. He hoped the contents would not leak out onto his bare legs.

A lithe woman with short red hair turned on swung her cutlass at Pere. He let his body drop to hang from the line. The sword cut air. Pere whipped his right leg up to crack her in the face with his shin. She fell.

Jaume paused briefly while Pere hooked the same leg over the line and drew himself back on top of it. Drawing his sword, he seized the railing and flung himself over it. An eyeblink later a longsword thunked into the railing where he'd vanished.

The pirate pulled out his sword and turned inboard to deal with Pere. Jaume grabbed the back of his dirty slashed-velvet blouse and jerked him overboard. He joined Pere on deck.

Pirates still crowded the cog's main deck. Most were transfixed by the combat aboard the *Melisandre*, where a seethe of bare flesh covered the Sea Dragon phalanx like soldier-ants swarming a Compsognathus. But a score or more faced the Companions on the after part of the main deck, before the sterncastle.

Pere pulled his sword out of a pirate's thick neck. "Can your Princess punch a pirate in the balls?" he called to Jaume, as the black-bearded man crumpled.

"She hasn't been called to yet, but I'm sure she could," Jaume said, and ducked under a furious sword-slash. "She's your friend too, you know…"

Pere wasn't listening. He had danced in among their foes, sword whirling, dagger deflecting and thrusting. Blood drenched his face and armour. Jaume knew the two stood no chance of taking the cog, of course. Even naked and overmatched in skill and steel shells, the pirates could still mob them as they were the Marines aboard the *Melisandre*. But Jaume knew capturing the ship wasn't Pere's mad scheme.

Jaume shifted his left hand to grip the Lady's Mirror a third of the way up its meter-long blade. A longsword was ground less than shaving-sharp to allow such half-swording. Jaume pitched into yelling pirates with the tip, blocked and thrust with the flat, and smashed with the pommel as he and Pere carved a bloody path toward the aft-most mast.

A hatch lay open beside it. Pere reached it, sheathed his weapons, and untied his trousers from around his middle. Resuming a two-hand grip on his hilt, Jaume stood off corsairs with sweeping swings as Pere gashed the improvised bag with his dagger and took out a cask of lamp-oil. Prying out the cork with his dagger he poured the pungent pine oil over the trousers. They were stuffed with tarred rags that, like the oil, had been used to make firebolts for the war-galley's stingers. From a ceramic tube carried on a cord around his neck, he produced a smoking punk. He blew the punk's tip to an orange ember and touched it to the oil-drenched trousers.

They flared alight. He tossed them into the darkness of the hatch, and threw the cask in after.

"Done," he said, turning toward Jaume and the corsairs and drawing his weapons. "Your go, my love."

As Pere held the pirates off, Jaume untied his pants-legs one-handed, slashing with the Mirror at such opponents as managed to get close. He cut the drawstring with his sword to let his own oil cask fall out onto the deck. He picked it up, drew the cork with his teeth, and sloshed half its contents onto the mast itself and the lower part of the sail, taking care not to splash himself. The rest he poured on the rag-filled trousers, sparing the ends of the legs. Using those for a handle, he lit the cloth from the pool of fire Pere had left on deck.

He jabbed a lunging pirate in the cheek and flung the burning trousers at the sail. Flames shot up the blood-red canvas and ran orange and blue down the mast.

"Fire!" he yelled at the pirates amidships. "Fire aboard! Fire! *Fire!*"

The Sea Dragons had taught him well: there was no more dreaded call onboard a ship at sea. The pirates lost all interest in fighting, aboard the dromon or their own ship. They began to screech at one another to fetch buckets and man pumps.

"*Jaume!*" yelled Pere.

He wheeled clockwise, swinging up the Mirror. Too late. A smashing impact to his sallet blasted yellow sparks behind Jaume's eyes and dropped him to his knees.

His stomach sloshing with nausea and his eyes blurred, Jaume saw a naked, blond-bearded corsair looming over him, well over two meters tall. If Pere hadn't warned Jaume his boarding axe would have struck Jaume squarely, caving in helmet and skull beneath. Now the pirate raised the axe above his head to finish the job.

Through the fog in his head Jaume realised it was the man who had bellowed at the boarding-party to take the Companions alive—probably the pirate captain. Jaume willed his hand to raise the Mirror. It would not.

The giant screamed in a surprisingly shrill voice as Pere ran past him behind, slashing both his hamstrings with a single draw-cut of his sword. He toppled backwards.

Pere tossed his parrying dagger in the air, caught it by the hilt point-down, and plunged it into the pirate's glaring blue left eye.

As Pere put a boot on the corsair's dead face to pull his weapon free, Jaume saw that his left arm was sleeved in blood from a cut just below the shoulder.

"Are you all right?" he asked, picking himself up.

"Still fighting," Pere said. "But we've got to go."

Running to fight the blazes that engulfed the sail and shot up from the open hold, the corsairs ignored the Companions. The pair ran to the rail and the rope by which they'd boarded. And saw that the corsairs on board the *Melisandre*, demoralised by their sudden brutal turn of fortune, had broken and were fleeing up the lines.

Pere put away his sword and dagger, and caught Jaume's eye.

"So she's your choice, then? Melodía."

Jaume shook his head. "It's not that way. We still—"

Pere grabbed his face in both hands and stopped his words with a quick, fierce kiss. Then he was over the side and sliding down the line. Jaume sheathed the Lady's Mirror and followed.

A few meters from the galley's rail, Pere's blood-slick hands lost their grip on the rope, and he plunged into the sea. Jaume stopped and swung round. Letting himself dangle toward his lover by his right hand, he reached out with his left.

"Take my hand!" he shouted.

Treading reddened water, Pere raised his face. Once more his dark eyes met Jaume's.

"I love you always," Pere said.

A vast shadow swelled beneath him, clutched him in monstrous yellow teeth, and bore him down forever.

TARA CALABY

GdM #4

— *1* —

And they lived happily ever after.

— *2* —

There is an itch inside me. Every morning, the sun rises. The stone walls of the castle are warmed by the light, and white-starched maids pull back the heavy blue velvet of my curtains so that the dust glows like a thousand stars hanging in the air. Tea and toast are brought on a silver tray. My hair shines golden upon the twelve pillows at my back, and a black spaniel curls at the foot of my bed.

After eating, I dress. The maids fuss around me, buttoning my corset and straightening my skirts. My hair is combed and curled, piled high upon my head and adorned with sparkling precious stones. My face is powdered and red petals are used to stain my lips and cheeks. My dresses are pink and pale blue and buttery yellow and white. My shoes are always the same glass slippers. They pinch my toes and blister my feet.

There is an oak tree outside my bedroom window. Its trunk is scarred by the years and birds nest beneath its shade. In the mornings, I stand, fingertips pressed against the glass. The leaves quiver in the breeze, and I close my eyes and breathe (in out in out) and in my mind I soar like those birds, into the sky and the clouds and away.

Away and away and away.

— 3 —

I am a princess now. There are rules for being a princess, rules that are often unspoken and sometimes unkind. I must be beautiful and graceful and smile at my husband and bear him an heir. My womb belongs to the kingdom now: to the peasants and the nobles and to the cobbled streets and the meadows and the dirt beneath my feet. My husband dreams of a son. I dream of a dark forest and vines that twist around my legs.

My mother died before she could warn me about the weight of a husband beside you in a bed. On my wedding night, my stepsisters whispered the crude things that friends told them in the streets, and I did not believe them until there was a calloused hand pressed against my breast and a splitting and a stabbing between my legs. I was sixteen. The bleeding ceased on the third day.

He comes to my bed less frequently now. "Don't you love me?" he asks, and I stare at the ceiling and count the grains in the dark oak beams.

I remember love. Love was the gentle brush of my mother's hand across my forehead and the engulfing crush of my father's hugs. Love is not rough hands and grunting, not perfect hair and make-up and uncrumpled dresses. If I bear him a child, I suppose I shall love it. If I love it too much, the fates will steal it away.

I must learn to love my husband. It is not his fault that he was a failed escape. He is handsome and a good dancer and he thinks me the most beautiful woman in the world. He is not a bad man. He is probably a good man. My maids tell me that things must always be this way.

Sometimes, they find me huddled beside the fireplace and scold me for the ash that marks my clothes. I do it again and again to see the disapproval in their eyes.

I do not tell my husband. He would not understand.

— *4* —

My bride is unhappy. She is a fair actress, but she has not yet learned how to show her smiles in her eyes. She is well-mannered, compliant, beautiful, and all that a princess should be. And yet she remains distant: mine in name and in body, but never in soul.

She laughs when I talk of love, as though she distrusts my heart. Her clothes are beautiful now, but when she looks at me, sometimes I can only see the rag-adorned girl with charcoal blackening her nails. She helps her maids with their duties and walks the castle grounds barefoot and with her hair unbound. Sometimes I wonder if I shall ever tame her spirit.

Cinderella's womb remains empty. I yearn for a son.

— 5 —

As we enter the ballroom, I take my bride's arm. Her fingers are thin and pale against the tan of my hand, and her neck is a delicate line topped with sun-coloured curls. We pause to be seen and to be acknowledged; she straightens her back, assuming her role.

Cinderella's stepmother sinks into a deep curtsey before us. Her hair is greying, but her eyes remain bright. "A child at last!" she exclaims, and my wife looks down, folding her hands over the curve of her stomach.

"I am merely eating well, stepmother," she says, and she does not look me in the eye. "Our cook prepares the sweetest of meats and my plate is always piled high."

"You must be careful," her stepmother says. "If you become fat and lose your beauty, there are many other women who will not."

Cinderella's stepmother looks to her daughters, who are dancing and flirting with my red-uniformed guards.

"Cinderella is the most beautiful woman in the kingdom." I circle my bride's waist with my arm, pulling her close into my side. "I want no other, and I never shall."

Cinderella smiles, but she stiffens in my embrace.

That night, she doesn't protest when I join her in her bed. Her skin is soft against my fingertips, and she is warm beneath me as I kiss her pale pink lips. She is silent and unmoving, a beautiful doll.

"You are mine," I say when I leave her.

"Are you happy?" is her reply.

— 6 —

A parasite grows inside my belly. It feeds on my fears and forms nightmares from my dreams. I pummel my own flesh, pressing fists deep into skin that does not yield, but still my body betrays me. I rest my forehead against the cool of the basin, bile burning hot in my throat and chest. My tears are silent. The elegant twists of my hair stay high and perfect and do not fall.

At night, I crouch in front of the fireplace, the stone of the hearth warm beneath my knees. I pray that my husband will not come; I pray that the curve of my stomach remains concealed by the gathers of my dress. The coals glow and the glass of my slippers reflects their amber light. The huff of my breath feeds the dying flames. There is ash upon my cheek and a growth inside me that swells and thrives.

I call for her and she comes to me. The brown of her skin and the grey of her hair blend and become indistinct in the murky light. Only her black, black eyes remain true. "You are still so unhappy, my child," she says. "You have a castle and maids and you are wedded to a prince."

"I am a lark in a cage," I tell her. "The bars are different, but the song is the same."

Her soft hands brush the dirt from my cheeks. I curve into her touch and, for a moment, her face is the face of my mother. We are silent. She is round and warm where I am straight and cold. She smells like tea and spice.

"Will you help me?" I ask.

"I dearly wish I could." Her magic is imperfect. "An illusion," she calls it, with smoke in her dark eyes. "Fleeting trickery. A fairy's wiles."

"I am desperate."

"I could place a stone inside your womb," she says, "but at the stroke of midnight, it would become life again."

"It is not life; it is death. It is a tumour. No more."

She strokes my stomach, her fingers finding the bulge of the growth through the layers of my skirts. The shadows are thick in the corners of my bedroom and the ceiling flushes with flickering light. I kiss her cheek, and beneath my lips, the loose skin tightens and its soft curve reforms into more youthful lines. Her hair darkens, falling from its bun and settling around her neck in a circle of curls. She lengthens and shimmers, and the air folds and stretches around her as it finds its new shape.

"Illusion," she says again, and perhaps I understand.

"Are you truly my godmother?"

"I am whatever you need me to be. It is the way fairies are."

"Humans too, sometimes." The parasite is hot within me. "We are alike, you and I."

"I know, Cinderella," says the fairy. "I know."

"Is this who I really am?"

She touches my face. "Only you can tell."

— 7 —

When she comes again, she is dressed in the skin of a beautiful girl, not much older than I. She pets my hair and strokes my skin and brings me fresh rags for the bleeding that will not stop.

"You are so pale," says the fairy. "You look barely alive."

"It was worth it," I say. "The herbs helped me breathe."

I lean on her arms as I walk to my bed. The sheets are stiff with clotted blood.

"There is an emptiness inside me. It is like a hole that stretches from the base of my stomach to the place where my heart used to be." I fold a rag and tuck it deep within my skirts. My fingers emerge slick with red. "It is a good hole, I think. It is filled with quiet."

The fairy presses a glass of water into my hands. I drink it and swallow the herbs that swirl within the liquid. "An old woman's cure," she says.

"Not magic?"

"You need more than illusion if you are to stay alive."

"Who are you really?" I ask her.

"A fairy," she answers. "Your friend."

"An illusion."

"Only in appearance."

I touch her face. Her skin is smooth and brown. The line of her nose rises slightly at the tip. Her lips are soft. "Is this what I need from you now? Youth and beauty?"

"Someone you can understand."

"Beauty is entrapment," I say.

I am ugly beneath my skin. My golden curls hide a briar patch of thorns and tangles. My fair white flesh is a bag for filth and flies. The blue of my eyes is the blue of the weeds that strangle the gentle flowers in the castle gardens and between my legs there is a chasm that bleeds and grows.

"Show me your face." I tear at my dress, rending the bodice and exposing the pale curves of my breasts. "Take what you will, but see me with your own eyes."

"These *are* my eyes," she says, and they are as black as they were that first evening, as black as they have always been when she has stroked me and comforted me and seen into my soul.

As I watch, she changes. Her jaw becomes pointed, and she shrinks until her height is that of my shoulders. Her hips are smooth and lean. Her skin darkens and her hair takes on a blueish hue: the black of the starlit skies. Her teeth sharpen and her cheekbones stretch and her breasts grow lower and fuller.

"You are still young and beautiful," I say.

She is right. Her eyes are the same.

— 8 —

Now I go to Cinderella even when she has not called for me. There is a transparency to her skin that was not there before the bleeding and a sunken set to her eyes. It only serves to make her more beautiful. We fairies are born to be shaped to others' whims, but at times I catch myself desiring more. She is fragile and inscrutable and drifting further into her own mind with every passing day.

"He came to me tonight," she says when I appear beside her bed. "I can still smell him on the sheets and on my skin."

I stroke her hair and she stiffens for a moment before relaxing and allowing the touch. "Are you hurt?"

She ignores the question, instead catching my hand inside her own and squeezing it with her delicate strength. "Is love so very tied to beauty? He never says he loves me when it is dark or his eyes are closed." She examines my fingers, so much longer than hers, and tests the points of my nails with one fingertip. "I can see that my husband is handsome, but I only love him as a duty. I can see that your form is wrong to human eyes, and yet I would prefer you to a thousand men."

"Fairies and humans are not so very different."

"No," she says. "Although I am never entirely sure that you are real."

"Sometimes I wonder the same of you."

She smiles: perfect white teeth in that perfect white face. "So do I. There are days when I am nothing more than a loose collection of dreams. Other times, it is like all of my senses are screaming at once."

"Did he hurt you tonight?" I try again.

"What is pain anyway?" Her eyes focus for a moment and she sees my face. "I am not injured, although I cannot remember when I was last whole."

"You are not broken, Cinderella."

"I am a thousand pieces, and none of them knows your name."

"Would it make a difference?"

She frowns. "I had another name once. I had a mother and a father and a different name."

I stroke her forehead. "Names are not everything."

There are tears in her eyes. Cinderella clutches my shoulder and pulls me close. "Do you think I am beautiful?"

"More beautiful with every passing day."

She sighs and pulls the bedclothes tight around her chest. "Then I am surely doomed."

— 9 —

Cinderella is on the hearth when I emerge from the flames, her nightclothes torn and hanging from her body like a collection of ashy rags. One of her shins is bleeding and her pale hair hangs in tangles.

"What did he do?"

For a long moment, she looks at me without seeing me, and

then it is as though a dark shadow moves from behind her eyes. She blinks. Her cheeks are pink from the fire. "Fairy," she says, "he has not been here tonight."

"But your clothes…"

She looks down at her body, plucking at the remnant of white cotton that barely covers her left breast. "I was sleeping," she says, "or perhaps I was awake."

"You are hurt." I press a strip of fabric against her wound, and it quickly colours.

"When I bleed, I know I am still alive."

Cinderella watches as I dress her injury, a distant interest evident in her eyes. When I have done all I can, I fetch water from the basin in the corner of her bedroom and gently wash the smears of charcoal from her face. She is pliant in my embrace, and I can feel her heart beating beneath my ear like the fluttering pulse of a songbird.

She guides my fingers to her breast and it is warm and soft, the nipple pressing against my palm. I pull away, but she catches my hand and this time holds it in place, just as her other hand delves beneath my bodice.

"Cinderella—" I begin, but she kisses me before I can order my words.

"I know that you must want this," she says. "It is what everyone wants from me. My face. My flesh."

"But I am only what you want me to be," I remind her.

Her fingers are cold. They stab and burn between my legs.

— 10 —

M y name is Cinderella," I tell her, "because I was born of you."

— 11 —

There is a beast in my royal mirror. Its fangs are pointed and its eyes glow red. I run fingernails down my cheeks and the lines are pink, like the stain upon my lips. The beast smiles with a thousand knives. My pulse throbs, thick and slow, within my neck. I break the glass, but still the beast survives.

The fairy stands by my window, dressed in the soft flesh of a child. "Come closer," I tell her, and she approaches with tentative eyes.

"Are you well?" she asks.

"I am falling," I say.

I sit upon my bed, and cradle her small head within my lap. Her hands are tiny and her fingers are pointed. She watches me and I can feel my skin peeling beneath her gaze. I shed it like a snake, and leave myself behind.

"You are too thin," she says. "Are you eating?"

"It all tastes like dust now," I reply.

My breasts are shrinking. They fade and fold into my chest, but still he palms them, and still his weight presses heavy upon the dip of my stomach and the bones of my ribs.

"So beautiful, so delicate, so fragile" is forever his panting refrain.

I lie, naked, the glass slippers upon my feet, and he kisses my lips and devours my soul.

"I love you," he says, and the words stretch and become bars for the walls of my cage. "I love you. You are beautiful. I love you. You are mine."

I understand love now. Love is possession. I want to be free.

— *12* —

I t is summer and the heat of the fire joins the heat of the air. I dress in my finest ball gown, and pile curls high upon my head. I polish my slippers until the glass shines like the purest mountain stream. I open the window to let in the night.

I watch from a distance as I kneel upon the hearth. The smoke stings my eyes, and I blink away unwanted tears. The coals are marbled with amber light. I breathe and I breathe and I allow myself to fall.

The pain is unbearable. My skin melts and embers singe the curls of my perfect hair. Hot ash burns the swell of my perfect lips and my perfect nose becomes molten flesh between the curves of my perfect cheeks. I am screaming but I am laughing. No one comes.

The air is sweet with the scent of human meat.

— *13* —

M y husband does not look at me as he presses the gold into my scarred and knotted hands. I smile as best my mouth can manage and hide my fortune deep within the charred layers of my skirts. He does not speak of love.

I peel back the bars of my prison and the air is sweet as it kisses the charred ruins of my face. The castle gates close behind me. The sky is blue and bright.

I bend and tug the glass slippers from my feet. The path is warm and solid beneath my toes. I turn to face the castle one final time. The shoes reflect the sunlight as they spin through the air and shatter into a thousand splinters against the stone of the castle walls.

The path stretches into the distance. Barefoot, I begin to walk.

— *14* —

Once upon a time.

VIVA LONGEVICUS

BRANDON DAUBS

GdM #8

Parents are supposed to say they love all their kids the same but that's a fuckin' lie, isn't it?

With my kids, Nat, and Kevin…I told myself that at first, when Kev was born. I'll love them both the same. They were the same, almost. Looked the same. Shat the same kind of load into their diapers. Nat was a little bit bigger and further along, but otherwise they might as well have been the same kid and I told myself I would love them both equally, whatever that meant. I thought I would.

"We've got to hit the jets so our velocity matches up with the rotation of Hawen before we try to land," Kev said behind me. I watched the altimeter and glanced at the display that showed the slope of the putrid jungle planet below us.

I waited until the last possible second to make the adjustment, and watched Kevin sweat in the reflection of the dark radar. His military fatigues never had fit him very well.

"You were a little bitch, growing up," I said.

Kevin didn't take the bait. He only looked down at his clipboard. "Nat's last transmission came from somewhere near the east edge of the basin," he said. "That area is heavily infested. I feel like I should debrief you on what we'll be up against down there. I doubt you've been reading my articles on Rodentius Longevicus…"

"Rats." I glanced over my shoulder at the rack of assault rifles and stun batons by the exit hatch. "Useless little rats bred for super cuteness. How bad could it be?"

Bad, it turned out.

But how the fuck was I supposed to know?

By the time Kev and I crashed the dropship through the thick jungle canopy on the east edge of the hollow known locally as The Basin, the suns of Hawen had already slipped below the horizon and left us in ass-crack darkness. Once the whine of the dynamos died down I slammed the door of the dropship open and stumbled out into the black, cursing, slapping the light on my assault rifle so it would stop flickering and I could see where the fuck I was going.

"We should head to the colony," Kev told me. He had an assault rifle of his own, but he held it like a limp dick.

"No," I said.

Kev gave me that look again. "These people are suffering," he said. "Even if you don't pay attention to anything else I say, you've heard reports of the famine. We have more rations on board than we'll ever use. It would take us two hours tops to hike up to the ridge. They might even have information that would help us find Nat…"

"I really don't give a shit about the settlers." I raised a finger to point through a break in the trees toward a red-orange glow and the pillars of smoke rising from deeper in the basin. "And I've found Nat already. Our mission is get him, and get the fuck out of here. That's it."

I could see it in Kevin's face. I think he knew.

If only anything were ever that simple.

Turns out Nat didn't really want to leave when we finally found him. He and his men squatted for a smoke break in a charred clearing. Lieutenant Nat Vilhaus sat on a stump at the forefront, letting the light from the tip of his Sherman bathe a pissed-off face. The gauge on his flamethrower read pretty damn close to empty. The bags under his eyes, the slack jaw, the stubble on a heavy chin read pretty damn close to empty, too. The other guys looked just as wasted: Higgins, pale and skinny, checked a wound gouged into his arm the size of a roll of nickels; and Mathers, a hulking dolt loaded up with ammunition and a heavy beam-raker, cooked up something foul over a sad smudge of a fire.

"This it?" I called as I stepped up closer. Kev came after me. "I thought there were more of you faggots."

Nat barely turned his head.

"Shut the fuck up," he said.

Oh, Nat. The little shit. He thought he was too old for me to punch in the face but he was wrong about that. I clocked him a good one, watched the cigarette flip out of his teeth and bounce across the dirt. He got back up, of course. Even made a grab for his K-bar when he lunged at me. I wouldn't have expected anything less from Nat. He had balls at least. I knocked him down again.

"Is that any way to greet your old man?" I said, and I had a whole *let's forget about rat-chasing and get out of here right now* speech planned, but Kevin interrupted me.

"Don't," he said. "Not those. See the leaves?"

I glanced over to watch Mathers ready to toss a few branches onto his fire. He glared at Kevin the same way I glared at Kevin, wondering whether to smack him or not.

"That stuff is a powerful hallucinogen," Kevin went on. "Something in the sap. Five leaves. Blue-violet. Burn it for a good time…*not* when you're surrounded by longies in the middle of the jungle. Jesus, am I the only one who knows anything about Hawen?"

Speaking of rats.

Behind Mathers, sitting up on its haunches with its forepaws dangling over a fat belly, was one of the little shits I'd only seen pictures of before. It had a downy white and dark burgundy coat with a spiral design. It looked like a puppy crossed with a rabbit and some other rodents, but mostly it looked like a regular goddam rat. Same size and everything. There must have been some magical fairy dust sprinkled in there too because the thing was fuckin' cute.

Except for the scar, rough against its long muzzle. Except for the jagged edge of a mostly-missing ear, or the look in its eyes—the look of a dog beaten past the breaking point.

I raised my assault rifle and pulled the trigger.

The thing exploded into a puff of fur and bones and meat, like a teddy bear stuffed full of fireworks. Only the back paws remained, more or less where they had been a second before, coated in red. The whole goddam thing was so funny I had to laugh. I tilted my head back and laughed, laughed until my sides hurt.

Somewhere out in the jungle, I was answered by a scream. Long. Tortured.

I knew there had been more men in Nat's company.

"They would have taken him to a nest," Kevin said as we moved through the jungle behind Nat and Higgins. Nat clutched his flamethrower like he might have to use it on a Hydro Leviathan. Close behind him, Higgins had his thermal net-launcher out with safety off. Mathers clutched his beam-raker shaking like he had a bad case of Parkinson's.

"What're you pukes all bent out of shape about?" I asked. "They're just fuckin' rats."

"For the last time, they're not *just rats*," Kevin went off, like anyone cared. "Rats are just what they are. Rats. They evolved through natural selection—survival of the fittest just like any other animal on Earth. Rodentius Longevicus weren't bred. They were engineered. BioGen designed them to be the superior pet. Smart. Social. Healthy. Adaptive to any environment on any planet so they could be sold throughout the galaxy."

"Too adaptive," Nat muttered, more to himself than to anyone else. "Crop loss spiked from 20 to 99 percent in the year they wound up on Hawen. The ecosystem..."

"Blah, blah, blah." Nat turned to glare at me, and I couldn't help but ask, "Why do you care about this place, anyway? Why not just molecular bomb the whole planet?"

Nat didn't answer. I could see it in his eyes, though. Some cunt, probably. Some settler he shacked up with. I was ready to push it when the trees thinned and I stepped out into the weirdest goddam scene I'd ever seen in my life.

Rats. Fuckin' rats, everywhere. There was a carpet of them. Among the currents of little bodies moving this way and that, I noticed a stream of them, going back and forth between two grotesque shapes. The first was a marine—what was left of him, anyway—sprawled out on a slab of rock. His ribs glistened white where they poked out of an empty chest cavity. Little hands reached into him, little teeth made precision cuts, and little cubes of meat were carried out and away. Not even eaten.

Redacre, read the tag on his fatigues.

The second shape was another rat, but bigger. Fat. Enormously fat. It lounged on a pile of bones. From the way the others piled up meat in front of it, I got the sense that this was the Bitch Rat and the others were all men.

Weird. Weird fuckin' behaviour, for an animal.

"Get the hell away from him!" Nat screamed. The ocean of fur froze. Nat turned his flamethrower toward the rats chewing on Redacre and let it rip. Red-orange flames washed over the little shits and the air was filled with the stench of burning hair and barbecue. Mathers started slapping rats into the air left and right, fried, cut into chunks by the flashing prongs of his beam-raker. Higgins launched net after net of thermal wire that snatched up whole bunches of the little fuckers and crushed them into a sizzling mess.

Kevin, though…fuckin' Kevin just stood there, gawking. I shouldered him aside on my way forward and raised my assault rifle at the rat in the middle, too bloated to escape.

She fixed me with her beady little eyes.

I pulled the trigger and she exploded into chunks.

Although…eugh. I can't even talk about this. Little…fuckin' *pink* things came spilling out of her. All over my boots. Wriggling around. Biting, even with their eyes closed. Trying to get *inside*. There must have been like thirty of these things and I freaked out, I'll admit, like someone had dropped a can of roaches at my feet. I started to stomp the little shits. And the damnedest thing happened.

Other fuckin rats started to throw themselves into the way, to get crushed instead.

I raised my boot up again and again. Crunch. Splat. The soles were stained red. Bits of fur and God knew what kind of guts stuck to the sides. Grown-up rats kept throwing themselves into the fuckin' way to get crushed instead. More came, and picked up the little pink things, and started to haul them off while their buddies were getting smashed.

This was my first hint that I wasn't just dealing with rats.

Then I noticed some of the little bastards running out of the woods with their jaws clamped on branches of some kind of wood. Branches with five-leaf clusters. Blue and violet five-leaf clusters. They threw themselves along with the branches into the fire from Nat's flamethrower and within seconds we were all choking, eyes watering, lungs burning, noses oozing snot.

By the time the smoke cleared the colours of the jungle were starting to blur together and the rats were gone.

No, not rats. Longevicus.

And I'm not really sure what the fuck happened next.

I was trying to find Nat.

The little shit. Didn't he realise I'd launched myself 10,000 parsecs through space in a tin can to take him home? Nobody thought the Longevicus Corps was a noble calling anymore. As far as anyone knew, there wasn't any way to stop the longies once they got to a planet and started to multiply. Hunting them down, sure. Wiping out the nests seemed to help, at first. But somehow, somehow they always came back. He was wasting his time. He was an embarrassment.

Where the fuck had he gone?

The trees seemed to spiral around me, seemed to bend inward and outward, seemed to breathe as I just tried to keep my feet. My assault rifle was gone. Dropped in the brush, somewhere, probably.

Every once in a while, I'd realise I was drooling on myself. I only remembered my sidearm when I lumbered through a copse of trees and into a clearing, where another marine stood tall against a sky of stars, looming at the edge of a deep valley.

I recognised this marine. Captain Andrew Vilhaus...*my* Old Man. What was he doing here? There seemed to be a settlement down in the valley below him, a cluster of colony pods sunk into the dirt...pods I hadn't seen since I was a little kid.

They glowed with fire.

"You're right, you know," said the captain. He turned toward me and I saw a face like mine, grey stubble, haunted eyes. "You don't love all your kids the same. It's not that you can't. It's just that, after a while, you realise they don't all deserve it."

I watched the flames consume the dwelling pods in the valley down below.

"If I could've left you in that fire instead of your sister, I would have," the captain went on. Like I didn't already know. Like I didn't think of that every goddam day of my life.

I drew my sidearm. The flash from the muzzle bright against the darkness left a spot in my vision but I still saw the Old Man go down.

After that, I don't remember much. More stumbling around. Slapping brush aside. Shouting nonsense. There was some crying, yes, crying too. Shitting my pants, even, maybe. They never tell you how many marines shit their pants in the heat of battle with all the noise and the screaming and the blood and thinking any second they might catch one in the back of the head and all I heard the whole time was gunfire, gunfire all around me.

Finally the whatever-it-was began to clear from my system and I pushed through a wall of leaves to find another marine, lying dead. Shot.

Between the eyes.

He wasn't alone. Nat and Kevin stood beside him. Mathers was there, too, sweating like a rhino in heat. They looked up at me. They looked at my sidearm, still out and clutched tight in one fist. I glanced down at the dead marine again and realised why they looked so pissed.

It was Higgins.

"He came at me," I lied. "He'd lost his mind. How long have you fuckers been out here, anyway? You've all turned into savages."

There was mumbling. A few sideways glances. They weren't buying it. I know Kev didn't. He gave me that same cold look he'd been giving me since he was just a little shit.

He didn't speak up, though.

Too fuckin' scared. As usual.

By the time we finally returned to the dropship, the thing was surrounded by settlers.

"Shit! They're back!" one of them called, and another dropped a sad, mostly empty crate of supplies to whip six inches of pipe out of his belt. It certainly wasn't a gun, whatever the fuck they thought it was. Several crates were loaded into the craft already, and there were more people in there, too. Some woman so thin she didn't look like she would survive a solid fuck, and some geezer too old to wipe his own ass.

I raised my sidearm.

"Wait!" Nat shouted, as he came out of the brush behind me.

I didn't wait. I pulled the trigger. You don't survive 25 years of service by waiting. And *Nat*, the stupid little fuck, dared to ram me with his shoulder. Bullets ricocheted off the sides of the dropship and more settlers crawled out of the brush like roaches. They raised their own crackhead weapons to return fire, just as Mathers and Kev stumbled out of the jungle behind us.

Mathers went down in a heap. I felt something tug at my arm, like a bad bee sting. My elbow was slick with red. I shoved Nat aside, but by the time I took aim again the settlers had all piled into the dropship with their sad, mostly empty supply crates and raised up the door.

Well. The crates hadn't been that empty, I suppose.

As the dropship dynamos whined to life I glanced at one of the crates the settlers had left behind. Buried deep under the clothes, and the machine parts, and a few tins of food, was a pair of beady little eyes watching through the slats.

Kevin bent over Mathers. "He's dead," he said. Like I didn't fuckin' know.

Maybe we should have visited the settlers. Maybe we should have killed them. Now I had to get creative, as the dropship lurched up into the air and left a smear of exhaust across a sky turning orange in the light of dawn. I pulled out my radio transmitter and reset the signal to command the dynamos. More specifically, the fuel for the dynamos.

Nat must have known what I was doing because he attacked me again. This time, he grabbed at my arm and tried to pull the transmitter loose.

"We have to scuttle the craft!" I said, like he would just believe me. Like he would ever just accept that I knew what the fuck I was doing.

"No, God dammit!" Nat screamed. "Just let them get away!"

Even Kevin was trying to get the transmitter away from me now, *Kevin*, after all the bullshit he'd spouted about Rodentius this, Longevicus that. They're dangerous. They're invasive. I had to plant my boot into his gut to get him to let go, had to kick him while he tried to get up until he coughed blood onto his chin and finally laid still. Nat was a little harder to put down. He struggled. He tried to twist my arm, tried to break it, until the tendons stood out on his neck and his face burned as red as Satan's asshole.

I don't know what it is with kids. Sons, specifically. Every day they think, today's the day. Today's the day I'm finally tougher than my old man.

Well, that day never came for me. And it wouldn't come for Nat or Kevin, either.

I took a step back and flipped Nat onto his ass. He hit the dirt, and I pinned him with my shoe on his throat while I jammed the button on the transmitter. Up above, the dropship burst open—a firework of shrapnel and burning flesh. Smoke trailed behind embers arcing out over the jungle.

Nat was sobbing like a little bitch and I knew I'd been right earlier. Some cunt. Probably, he'd seen her get on board. I moved my shoe off him and glanced over at Kevin. Kevin didn't look like anything. Just a blank face, and some blood on his chin. He didn't even try to get up. I felt…I don't know what I felt.

"Get your asses up, both of you," I said. "Nat. You and your men must have got here on another ship. I know it's low on fuel but take us to it. We'll figure something out. We're going home. All of us."

Well.

Some of us were, anyway.

The longies came for Mathers and they seemed to decide his porky ass wasn't enough, because they started swarming us as well. We had to get the fuck out of there. I had all of three bullets left in my sidearm. Nat's flamer had gone completely dry after one blast, and only Kevin had anything left in his assault rifle. That's one advantage of being a scared little bitch, I guess. Ammo conservation.

We ran through the jungle, just us three, side by side. Nat and Kevin didn't say anything to me. No thanks. No nothing. Which was fine…I didn't need the little shits to like me. I just needed them to get out of this alive.

They had plenty to say to each other, though.

"How much fuel is left in your dropship?" Kevin asked. Nat shook his head.

"I don't remember…"

"Fuckin' try."

"I don't know," Nat answered. "Maybe…29 rods. Why?"

Kevin glanced back at me. I was too tired to ask him what this was all about. We'd been up for a day and a half, on the move, doped out of our minds, chased halfway across this shithole planet. If Kevin wanted to spout some nerdy shit, this was his chance. I was getting ready to listen to him go on about weight ratios, and ballast, and delta-force-to-fuel volume comparisons.

What he did instead, was raise his assault rifle and blast me in the leg.

I didn't go down right away. I think I was so surprised that I actually managed to run another few steps before the pain hit and locked up my knee. My sidearm jumped out of my grasp when I fell. The whole jungle went grey and it was only with every ounce of my willpower that I was able to keep from blacking out. I managed to look up at Kevin. I didn't ask him why. I didn't need to.

Twenty-nine rods of fuel was not enough to get three people into orbit. I should have known.

"It's nothing personal," Kevin told me. "It's just the cold equations."

But I saw it in his eyes, before he and Nat shrank into the distance and disappeared into the trees, without missing a single step…

It was fucking personal.

My boys.

I wonder…if Kevin ever knew he was my favourite.

Jesus. Fuck! My leg is killing me.

I managed to fight off the little shits long enough to find some kind of burrow to hide in. I've got some dead ones with me, which should throw the others off the scent long enough for me to finish this recording. I lost my K-bar when one of them chomped my hand pretty good and I ran out of bullets for my sidearm a long-ass time ago. Days, maybe. For the record, Rodentius Longevicus does not taste very good uncooked.

Anyway. This message is for General Ritters of the U.S.S. AeroCorps.

The president of BioGen needs to issue a galaxy-wide recall on Rodentius Longevicus. They must be destroyed.

They are not cute.

They are not pets.

This is coming from Colonel Vilhaus so you know I'm not just saying this as some bleeding-heart cunt. I don't give a shit about "playing God" or whatever the fuck they say to protest the creation of these things. I'm saying we made them, great. And they're fucking dangerous. We need to put them down, for the safety of our colonies all over the galaxy. Confiscate them as pets wherever they are.

Jesus, I think they found me again.

Here I am, you little shits! Come get some!

Did you think just because I don't have a weapon, that I won't crush every last one of your goddam furry little

END OF TRANSMISSION

Transmission detected at roughly the same time that

passengers VILHAUS and VILHAUS, Lieutenant, Specialist, U.S.S. AeroCorps, were picked up in orbit. Recording discovered on colony planet HAWEN, status, ABANDONED.

Recording to be stored on database of the Mothership Ophidian until requested for use in case of AEROCORPS COLONIES vs. BIOGEN.

Est. Date [0000/00/00]

<<ERROR>> //Insert text

///Doctor. If you get this message, please refer to fauna storage sample X552B. The order went through to molecular bomb the planet Hawen but we already have our specimens on board so that doesn't matter. Go secure them before anyone notices. Delete this message as soon as you find it.

Viva Longevicus.

//End Text

AGAINST THE ENCROACHING DARKNESS

ALIETTE DE BODARD

GdM #5

Eugénie lay in state in the small, pathetic chapel that they'd never had time to finish, her eyes towards the blank, unpainted ceiling. From time to time, the distant echo of a magical conflagration shook the room, and dust fell on her chest, covering her clothes in a fine, white layer that slowly and irretrievably obscured the insignia of House Lazarus.

Victoire would not cry. She'd done so earlier in the privacy of her room, but now it wasn't about love or grief; merely what would carry them forward, what would ensure the newly founded House would survive the death of her founder. Most Houses, she knew, didn't. And Lazarus, that bastard child of Eugénie's ideals—her place of refuge, her small band of dependents patiently gathered through the years—was no exception.

Footsteps behind her, noiseless and graceful: Amaranth, coming to stand by the side of the coffin, her smooth, ageless face creased in thought. The Fallen watched Victoire, not the body in the coffin. Disapproving? Amaranth had always been hard to read, even in the days when she'd been Eugénie's right hand. "She would have died before seeing the House go weak," Amaranth said.

Victoire shivered. "Except that her death made the House go weak, didn't it?" House Lazarus was small and leaderless. In ordinary times that would have been cause for concern, but now that House was fighting House in the streets of Paris, now that Draken and Hell's Toll had been defeated and taken apart...

"They're assembling outside," Amaranth said.

Of course. Of course they would. It had been her orders, hadn't it? "You should have been head of the House," Victoire said slowly, carefully.

Amaranth shook her head. She wore cream—a flowing dress with lace and ruffles that looked almost out of place at a time of war. "She chose you."

"You—" Victoire struggled. "You loved her."

Amaranth cocked her head. "Didn't you?"

There were no words, really. Eugénie had always been there, reaching out to the grimy girl picking her pockets in the street, not blasting her with a spell, not leaving her lifeless on the pavement, but simply asking her what she wanted; talking Victoire, step after step, into coming with her, into joining her House—into finally trusting her.

Victoire... Victoire had dared to hope; when she'd known hope cost so much, when it was finally shattered. The lessons of the streets—she'd forgotten them so fast. "She made me what I am," Victoire said finally. "And I will keep this House together because I have to." Because it was the only thing Eugénie had left behind, the legacy that would endure—past the war, past the city tearing itself apart. It sounded…grandiloquent and foolish, a child's boast in the face of a storm.

Amaranth looked at her, and then back at Eugénie's corpse in the coffin. She said nothing for a while, her brown eyes mild. "I don't approve. But I will stand by you, regardless."

Of course she wouldn't approve. But there was no other way.

They'd all come to offer their condolences, of course. The war might have been tearing Paris apart, but the Houses still held to old proprieties, old prerogatives—a never-ending stream of House representatives in swallow-tails and top-hats, in dresses with tapered waists and mutton sleeves, all bowing gravely to her, wishing her the best in these trying times; dropping a few hints here and there, about her youth, her lack of experience, her fundamental weakness—though they were kind enough to never voice the word aloud.

All, save two.

The first Victoire knew of Morningstar's presence was when the air in the room became impossibly light, impossibly tight—until even breathing seemed to hurt, and the air in her lungs burnt with the force of a firestorm. Then she turned, struggling to compose herself, and watched, shock-still, as he crossed the room to where she stood, the crowd of well-wishers parting in his wake like a flock of scared birds. "My lady," he said, bowing to her.

He had blue eyes, impossibly clear, the colour of summer skies in a season long gone. Now the city lay under a pall of black clouds, dust and ashes blown from the incessant battles in the streets, and summer followed winter with hardly a pause or a difference. Unlike all other Fallen, he wore wings—a metal armature of sharp, cutting edges that moved as he moved, cutting the air to pieces around him, a living weapon, a living fount of power in a city where magic was scarce.

"My lord," Victoire bowed, though her every instinct screamed at her to abase herself flat on the floor—he was firstborn among Fallen, most powerful; he could undo her with a glance or a word. "I didn't expect you here."

The major Houses—Harrier, Aiguillon, Hawthorn—had sent not their heads but their diplomats, just enough to keep up appearances. And here was the head of House Silverspires, the unstated leader of them all, standing in her ballroom with all her other guests, grave and courteous and speaking to her as an equal. Morningstar smiled, an expression that seemed to illuminate the room. "I thought I ought to come myself. To apologise."

"To—"

Morningstar shrugged; the wings at his back moved, slicing the air with a sound like the lament of dying souls. "We didn't mean to kill her. I have…no grudge against House Lazarus."

He had nothing against them. House Lazarus wasn't even big enough for him to be aware of it: just Eugénie's lost souls, a collection of the weak and desperate she'd sworn to keep safe. "I—" Victoire struggled for words against the presence that seemed to wrap the room around itself.

Morningstar continued as if she had not spoken. "It was a skirmish that went badly. I assume Harrier will offer their excuses, as well."

They had, but not in the same way. They were not standing there—not speaking in that voice that turned her innards to jelly, that made her measure, irretrievably, the distance that separated her from Silverspires—from Fallen, to whom magic and charisma came effortlessly. "A word of advice," Morningstar said finally. He raised a hand, as if to forestall any objections, but Victoire was still struggling to find her voice from where it had fled. "You're young and weak, like infant Fallen, except without any magic of your own. If you don't show the other Houses that you're strong—if you don't seize your opportunity to do something loud and ruthless—then you'll vanish."

"We won't," Victoire said, every word a struggle to articulate. "We—"

Morningstar smiled, brief and wounding, like a knife stroke across her throat. "I've seen it happen. You're not the first House to lose a founder. You might be the first to do so…in such peculiar circumstances."

The war—it was always there. The battles hadn't stopped, not even for a mourning reception—people tearing each other in the streets, the slow toll of the wounded and the dead Amaranth and Gérard reported to her every week, the dependents of House Lazarus caught in the crossfires. "We're not fighting," Victoire said at last.

"Of course. Eugénie had…ideals. Commendable of her." He said it in a way that implied she'd been young and foolish, and of course she had been. She was mortal, forty years old; whereas Morningstar had been in Paris for centuries. "Albeit impractical. Only the strongest, or the dead, can afford neutrality."

Victoire opened her mouth to say that they were strong—to lie, as Amaranth had advised her to—and then met his gaze and found the words shrivelling in her throat.

"Remember. A show of strength," Morningstar said, and his smile seemed to fill the entire world, teeth as sharp as a predator's—and she ached to lean forward, to let him take her, consume her utterly; it wouldn't even hurt much—she wouldn't feel anything more than the grief and worry that was already tearing her apart…

And then he eased away, and the effect faded. He was still smiling; he knew what she'd almost done, could read the tension in her calf muscles, the way she'd started leaning forward, as if for a kiss, as if for an offering. He was looking not at her but at Nerea and Thau, who stood nervously by the buffet, unsure of who to talk to or what they ought to do.

"Such youth," Morningstar whispered.

It was a dash of cold water down her spine. Amaranth was the only adult Fallen in Lazarus. Nerea and Thau *were* young, a few years from their Fall, that dangerous age when they fancied themselves adults but still couldn't fathom enough of people's motivations to sidestep traps before they closed. She moved, hardly aware that she did so, setting herself between Morningstar and the children. "My dependents," she said. It was…easier, almost, to oppose him for the sake of the House, to forget the pressure against her chest as his attention turned her way again, as his gaze transfixed her like a spear.

"Of course I wouldn't dream of stealing another House's dependents." Morningstar smiled again, and Victoire fought to remain standing, relaxing her every muscle, bowing her head towards the floor. "One might say, however, that by being at such a reception they are quite free to socialise with whomever they wish."

Victoire moved then, nodding at what he said to keep up the illusion of politeness, and came to stand by Nerea and Thau. "Victoire?" Thau asked, smiling. "Have you seen those dresses?"

"They're so wonderful," Nerea said, her broad face dreamily creased.

"Out," Victoire said—Morningstar was moving slowly, carefully, amused by her as one would be by an insect. "I need you out."

"We were having fun," Thau protested.

"Just…" Victoire shook her head and saw Amaranth appear as

if in answer to her prayers, materialising by her side with a glass of red wine in her hand.

"Trouble?" Amaranth asked, and then her gaze met Morningstar's and she froze. "Oh." She shook her head, moved slowly—agonisingly slowly—to stand in his path, bowing to him with the stiff formality of her youth, a century or more in her past. "Pleased to meet you, my Lord."

Victoire tore her gaze from Morningstar and focused it on the two Fallen.

"We're not leaving." Thau's voice was petulant. The light below his skin, his innate magic, flickered in and out of focus with every word he spoke. "Gérard said we could come."

Gérard probably hadn't expected Morningstar.

"Victoire? Is something wrong?" Nerea asked.

She could send them back to their rooms like disobedient children, but they were past that, weren't they? She wanted only the best for them, and that included giving them the space to grow up. "Be careful," Victoire said at last. "You've heard about Morningstar. He...he is not your friend." He was free with advice and charm, but he wasn't on their side, would never be. "House Silverspires isn't your friend."

Thau was watching Morningstar, engrossed; Nerea was equally engrossed but not as convinced. "He's very powerful," Nerea said grudgingly.

"And very handsome," Thau said.

Nerea's lips pinched, halfway between disapproval and fascination. "No doubt," she said wryly. "Come on. There's other stuff to look at."

Thau threw a regretful glance at Morningstar, who was still deep in conversation with Amaranth. Amaranth's face was fear-frozen, awestruck. Had Victoire's looked that way, too? Probably, and all too obvious to anyone with eyes.

"I guess so," Thau said. He let Nerea drag him to another corner of the room to stare at the stiff countenances of the Hawthorn and Solferino delegates.

It wouldn't stop Morningstar, of course; he would approach them again if he hadn't grown bored by then. She hadn't had the feeling he was here for more than harmless fun—harmless by his definition, since he cared little what devastation he left in his wake. Breathing hard, Victoire helped herself to a glass of wine from the buffet and took a look at the room. Everyone else was clustered in talks—Gérard, Quentin, and Marie, and the laboratory staff, keeping a wary eye on the other Houses, the more adventurous among her dependents venturing to talk to delegates. No danger there—they would merely make polite talk and not venture much information.

She would need to go rescue Amaranth at some point, or have someone else do it. She—

There was someone else, at her elbow.

Victoire dressed as if for battle—after all, wasn't this a battle, too, fought on a field without guns, without spells? Eugénie, perhaps, would have understood, if she hadn't turned away from her in disgust.

Over a brown shirt with delicate embroideries, she slipped a green silk jacket—green and brown, the colours of the House—and a scarf, folded across the diagonal so that its pattern of interlinked trees and stags devolved to a jumble of vivid colours. Her skirt was black, spread around her like a pool of darkness, with a wide train that should have required an attendant. Victoire didn't care much for that; she merely gathered the folds in her hand and walked out.

Amaranth and Gérard were waiting for her at the door, dressed equally formally: Amaranth in the same cream dress she'd worn in the chapel, Gérard in swallow's tail and pressed trousers, elegant and severe—the picture of effortless strength.

If only it hadn't been a lie.

The sounds of battle were muted now, almost inaudible—the fighting moving away from them in that endless, maddeningly cryptic ebb and flow of war that followed no rhyme or reason and took and took without surcease. The other fight—the war of influence, fought in drawing rooms and receptions—was not gone either, not as long as a head of House drew breath, not as long as they still could dream of being crowned the winner.

On and on, through deserted corridors; past doors open a fraction with only a glimmer of faces beyond them, a hint of clustered bodies pressed against the wooden panels. She'd ordered the children, the mortal ones, to stay indoors, and the other dependents of the House would not dare to come out—afraid, and why shouldn't they be?

"Victoire!"

Thau had been running, out of breath, his own suit askew on his thin frame, his olive skin flushed, glistening with sweat. "Victoire!"

She said nothing for a moment, stared into his eyes and then looked away because of the raw fear she saw in them.

"I wanted—" he stopped; then he said, "I don't want to go. Please—"

He'd come to her once when he'd broken one of the House's crystal glasses, bringing her the pieces and looking up to her, bracing himself for a rebuke. Victoire had smiled and said that it didn't matter, that they had plenty of other glasses.

Today, she had no such words. She could…but, no, she couldn't afford to show him favour. She couldn't afford to lie—if she was found out, the price would be even more terrible than the one she was already paying.

"You should be with the others," Victoire said gently.

His face darkened slowly, as if a door within him was closing forever. "Victoire—"

"I'm sorry," she said, and it was a lie because she couldn't say what she felt, couldn't put the tearing within her into words. "Please go."

As he ran away from her—in utter silence, broken only by the rapid sound of his breathing, as if he were struggling not to cry—as the world around her seemed to bend and waver, seemed to become unbearably sharp, she heard Amaranth speak. 'Was this how you wanted to be remembered?'

Victoire shook her head. "I don't expect anything." She'd woken up at night—staring at the dark skies above her with a prayer on her lips, with a cry for guidance, and no answer but the growing certainty within her like a shard of broken glass. "Forgiveness, perhaps, but it's not necessary." And not hers to give—never hers to give.

Amaranth's lips pursed, but she said nothing. She didn't need to.

"You're the head of the House. My condolences." For a moment Victoire thought the speaker was mortal, but then she saw the slight sheen to the skin, the slight cast to the cheekbones, and the way the body rested lightly on the floor, as if yearning for unattainable flight. "I'm Calyce," the Fallen said, her face creased in a smile. She wore a yellow-and-white uniform with no insignia. "Head of House Shellac."

They were a minor House near the southeast of Paris, beleaguered and stretched thin; Calyce's weary condolences sounded sincere in a way that Victoire hadn't heard since the beginning of the reception. "Thank you," Victoire said. She was still watching Amaranth talk to Morningstar and the way those closest to their conversation would stop and turn to stare at Morningstar.

"He's the centre of attention, isn't he?" Calyce sounded mildly amused. "As usual. Did he speak to you?"

"For a while," Victoire said warily.

If you don't show the other Houses that you're strong—if you don't seize your opportunity to do something loud and ruthless—then you'll vanish.

Calyce smiled again. She reached for a canapé from the buffet, staring at the pâté spread on rye bread as if she knew every coin this had cost, every hour of trying to disguise the paltry food reserves in the kitchen. "He means well—he genuinely doesn't care whether you rise or fall. But he's forgotten what it means to be powerless."

"Forgotten?"

"Fair point." Calyce swallowed her canapé in one gulp. "He's never known."

"And you do?" In spite of herself, Victoire was amused. "Are you queuing to give me advice, as well?"

Calyce shrugged. "I know what it is to be at the bottom of the heap, to be small and disregarded. But no, I won't give you advice, if that's not what you want." She stared again at the walls around them—the paint barely dry, the candles thin, placed so it wouldn't be obvious they could only afford a few. "Just company, for the evening."

"With no strings attached?" Victoire couldn't help it. "I'm sorry. It's just that—"

"Everyone has come here to mock, or gain advantage, or both?" Calyce smiled again. "Consider it…kinship. And my desire to have a quiet evening that's not about politics, for once. Or the war." She grimaced. "You're doing a good job, honestly."

"I wish I was," Victoire said. She knew they were all watching her, wondering when she would finally fail, when they could take Lazarus apart for scraps. Except Morningstar: Calyce was right, he probably didn't care one way or another. "The only wealth of this House is our dependents, and it feels like a case of too many mouths to feed."

"Fallen magic," Calyce said with a shrug. "It's wealth, of a sort."

But it couldn't create food, or even heal the gravely wounded. It couldn't give them a future, keep them together against the depredations of the other Houses, the ones busy killing each other in the streets, the ones who hungered only for power and for weapons they could use to destroy each other. "I just want us to be safe," Victoire said. Eugénie's mad dream, the one they'd all believed in, the only thought that drove her now. The House depended on her, and all she could see ahead of her was failure.

Calyce's face was dark. "In a time of war, safety might be too much to ask for. I wish—" She picked up a champagne glass, twirled it between her fingers. Light spread beneath her fingertips, so that for a moment the beverage seemed liquid gold. "No, never mind. We weren't given peace, and we're not the ones with the power to stop any of it."

"Have you—" there was no polite way to ask this, but this had gone beyond politeness, after all. "Have you lost many people?"

"Too many." Calyce sipped at the champagne, watching the groups drift across the room. "Bodies is the toll we pay, isn't it? Our only wealth." Her voice was bitter. "Graveyards and alchemists' laboratories to strip every scrap of Fallen magic from their corpses and put it into service again. But we're alive. We still have a place in the order of the city."

Whereas Lazarus—wounded and leaderless—had none. Calyce must have seen Victoire's face; she shook her head sadly. "You'll find a way," she said. "It's just a matter of time."

"Thank you," Victoire said. She didn't have time, and they both knew it. There were soldiers outside, fighting each other, and the moment the illusion dropped—the moment other Houses realised that Lazarus had nothing to protect them, nothing to keep them together, that conquering them would be as easy as punching through paper—then they were gone, and all the other Houses would either join in or look the other way.

Calyce set her glass aside. "If you'll excuse me," she said, grimacing. "My masters call." One of the Hawthorn delegates—a thin, dapper Fallen with horn-rimmed glasses and the lean face of a hunting hound—was looking straight at her.

Masters. Of course she had alliances. Of course she wasn't neutral. No one could afford to be, Morningstar had said. Only the strong.

Calyce was already gone: Victoire saw her bow down to the Fallen and then start talking to him animatedly. The Fallen made a small, stabbing gesture with one hand; and Calyce moved closer, bending her head to listen to him.

Victoire looked for Morningstar, and found him at the centre of a little court—five or six members of different Houses, standing entranced by him like moths in candlelight, scarcely aware they would burn alive when the flame became too intense.

If you don't show the other Houses that you're strong…

A show of strength. But strength was for the strong, wasn't it? And they didn't have anything, any wealth, any power, anything that would be convincing. Calyce was right: Morningstar moved in a wholly different world, and even his advice, well-meant as it was, was for those in his wake—the powerful, the victors.

A show of strength. She didn't have anything, except—

Except the wealth of Lazarus.

Slowly, as if in a trance, Victoire found herself walking back towards Morningstar, found the crowd parting for her—the hounds, eagerly baying for blood, eagerly waiting to see her throw herself, again and again, at the walls of her cage.

He watched her come closer, his face grave. His courtiers scattered; silence surrounded them, until it seemed they were the only two people in the room. "We need to talk," Victoire said, aghast at her own temerity. "In private."

"Of course," Morningstar said, and his smile seemed to illuminate the entire room until everything was drowned in its cold, merciless radiance.

He was waiting for her at the entrance to House Lazarus, his fair hair ruffled by the wind, his metal wings casting a long, blurred shadow on the steps. "Lady Victoire. What a pleasure." His presence was…like a storm, like wildfire—she wanted to walk closer, to be taken apart piece by piece, remade into one of his weapons, to feel that gaze on her, flaying layer after layer of skin with exquisite pain. Except, of course, that she held no interest for him. Not today.

"My Lord," she said, bowing, as Calyce had bowed to the delegate of House Hawthorn.

"Shall we?" Morningstar asked.

They were all gathered below in the courtyard before the House: all her youngest Fallen, her children, Eugénie's children—Nerea and Thau and Mavadeus and Sativer, Luscene and Celeste and Zeni and Kaila—all the names in her nightmares, a litany of loss. Eight of them, all so young, so achingly naive—like Nerea, like Thau—unaware of all the ways the world can reach out and wound them, again and again, in places they didn't even know existed.

"I can't—" Victoire started. Amaranth crushed her hand, and the words shrivelled in her throat. She could read Amaranth's expression: she might disapprove of the decision, but she would die before she allowed Victoire to show weakness.

Amaranth didn't understand, not really, that it was too late. That what had been required all along wasn't a show of strength;

but a show of weakness, something that showed them as small and insignificant and unworthy of the other Houses' attention.

She didn't understand that it was a surrender.

"Half," Victoire said slowly, carefully, her voice a croak.

"Of course," Morningstar said.

"You—" *Be kind to them*, she wanted to say, and he must have guessed at what she would say because he smiled.

"That will no longer be your concern, Lady Victoire. I'll do as I please."

The wealth of the House. Not its money or its influence or the spells they might have mastered, but its children. Its Fallen children.

Victoire bowed gravely to Morningstar and stopped halfway down the stairs. She watched him pace before the lines of young Fallen, watched them flinch at first and then bend towards him, caught in the maelstrom of his presence—Thau's face glazed, frozen in fear; Nerea holding herself straight, playing with her rings to hide the tremor in her hands; Mavadeus smiling, as if unaware of the tension in the air, but he had to…

Half. The half that Morningstar judged fit for service—the young, the vulnerable, the ones he could mould as he wished—and she didn't know what he was going to use them for. She didn't even know if he was going to take them apart for their magic.

Amaranth was waiting behind her, silent, disapproving. Victoire had to—she had to walk behind Morningstar, to show that it was her decision too, to look them in the eye as they were weighed and labelled like meat at market. She owed them that, at the least.

Was this how you wanted to be remembered? Amaranth had asked, and she had no good answer. Had never had any because there had been no other choice. Because there was a price to pay to be safe; a show of weakness to be made, rolling over like a dog offering itself for slaughter. Because even the ones who weren't chosen and dragged to Silverspires would remember, now and forever, that they had stood in line before the House, that Morningstar had prowled before them and passed them over. That Victoire had let it happen, and no amount of explanations and justifications—no matter how right she was in the end—would erase that. There were no excuses she could offer to the sacrificed.

"We will survive," she said—to Amaranth, to Thau, to the darkened skies above her, to whatever ghosts might be watching her. "The House will survive."

It was paltry reassurance, a thin comfort that had nothing of warmth; but it was all she had, all she could cling to against the encroaching darkness, against the choices of the war.

Slowly, deliberately—as ramrod straight as a queen in her own country—Victoire gathered the folds of her skirt, and descended the steps towards the courtyard to walk beside Morningstar—to stand before her children in that frozen instant before she lost them forever.

MARK LAWRENCE

GdM #1

A t the age of eight Alann Oak took a rock and smashed it into Darin Reed's forehead. Two other boys, both around ten years old, had tried to hold him against the fence post while Darin beat him. They got up from the dirt track, first to their hands and knees, one spitting blood, the other dripping crimson from where Alann's teeth found his ear, then unsteadily to their feet. Darin Reed lay where he had fallen, staring at the blue sky with wide blue eyes.

"Killer," they called the child after that. Some called, "kennt" at his back and the word followed him through the years as some words will hunt a man down across the storm of his days. Kennt, the old name for a man who does murder with his hands. An ancient term in the tongue that lingered in the villages west of the Tranweir, spoken only among the grey heads and like to die out with them leaving only a scatter of words and phrases too well poised to be abandoned.

"You forgive me, Darin, don't you?" Alann asked it of the older boy a year later. They sat at the ford, watching the water, white about the stepping-stones. Alann threw his pebble, clattering it against the most distant of the nine steps. "I told Father Abram I repented the sin of anger. They washed me in the blood of the lamb. Father Abram told me I was part of the flock once more." Another stone, another hit. He had repented anger, but there hadn't been anger, just the thrill of it, the red joy in a challenge answered.

Darin stood, still taller than Alann but not by so much. "I don't forgive you, but I wronged you. I was a bully. Now we're brothers. Brothers don't need to forgive, only to accept. If I forgave it you might forget me."

"Father Abram told me…" Alann struggled for the words. "He said, men don't stand alone. We're farmers. We're of the flock, the herd. God's own. We follow. Stray, be cast out, and we die alone. Unmourned." He threw again, hit again. "But…I feel…alone here, right among the herd. I don't fit. People are scared of me."

Darin shook his head. "You're not alone. You've got me. How many brothers do you need?"

Alann fought no more battles, not with his first wreaking such harm. They watched him, the priest and the elders, and hung about by his guilt the boy stepped aside from whatever small troubles life in the village placed in his path. Alann Oak turned the other cheek though it was not in his nature to do so. Something ran through him, something sharp, at the core, not the dull anger or jealous loathing that prompts drunks to raise their fists, rather a reflex, an urge to meet each and any challenge with the violence born into him.

"I'm different." Spoken on his fourteenth name-day, out in the quiet of a winter's night while others lay abed. Alann hadn't the words to frame it but he knew it for truth. "Different."

"A dog among goats?" Darin Reed at his side, indifferent to the cold. He swept his arm toward the distant homes where warmth and light leaked through shutter cracks. "With them but not of them?"

Alann nodded.

"It will change," Darin said. "Give it time."

Years fell by and with the seasons Alann Oak grew, not tall but tall enough, not broad but sturdy, hardened by toil on the land with plough and hoe. He walked away from his past, although he never once strayed further than Kilter's Market seven miles down the Hay Road. He walked away from the whispers, from the muttered "kennt," and all that came with him from those days was Darin Reed, the larger child but the smaller man, his fast companion, pale, quiet, true.

The smoke of war darkened the horizon some summers, and once in winter, but the fires that sent those black clouds rising passed by the villages of the Marn, peace still lingering in the backwaters of the Broken Empire just as the old tongue still clung there. Perhaps they lacked the language for war.

Sometimes those unseen battles called to Alann. In the stillness of night, wrapped tight by darkness Alann often wondered what a thing it would be to take up sword and shield and fight, not for any cause, not to place this lord or that lord in a new chair—but just to meet the challenge, to put himself to the test that runs along the sharp edge of life. And maybe once or twice he gathered his belongings in the quiet after midnight and set off from his parents' cottage—but each time he found Darin sat upon the horse trough beside the track that joins the road to Melsham. Each time the sight of his blood brother, pale beneath the moon, watching and saying nothing, turned Alann back the way he came.

Alann found himself a woman, Mary Miller from Fairfax, and they married in Father Abram's church on a chill March morning, God himself watching as they said their vows. God and Darin Reed.

More years, more seasons, more crops leaping from the ground in the green storm of their living, reaped and harvested, sheep with their lambs, Mary with her two sons, delivered bloody into Alann's rough hands. As red as Darin Reed when he lay there veiled in his own lifeblood. And family changed him. The need to be needed proved stronger than the call of distant wars. Perhaps that's all he had ever looked for, to be valued, to be essential, and who is more vital to a child than its ma and pa?

Time ran its slow course, bearing farm and farmer along with it, and Alann watched it all pass. He held his boys with his calloused hands, nails bitten to the quick, prayed in God's stone house, knowing every hour of every day that somehow he didn't fit into his world, that he went through the motions of his life not quite feeling any of it the way it should be felt, an impostor who never knew his true identity, only that this was not it. Even so, it was enough.

"None of them see me, Darin, not Mary, not my sons, or Father Abram. Only you, and God." Alann thrust at the soil before him, driving the hoe through each clod, reducing it to smaller fragments.

"Maybe you don't see yourself, Alann. You're a good man. You just don't know it." Darin stood looking out across the rye in the lower field.

"I'm a bad seed. You learned that the day you came against me." Alann bent and took up a clod of earth, crumbling it in his hand. He pointed out where Darin's gaze rested. "I sowed that field myself, checked the grains, but there'll be karren grass amongst the rye, green amongst the green. You won't see it until it's time to bear grain—even then you have to hunt. But come an early frost, come red-blight, come a swarm of leaf-scuttle, then you'll see it. When the rye starts dying…that's when you'll see the karren grass because it may look the same, but it's hard at the core, bitter, and it won't lie down." He dug at the ground then, turned by some instinct, looked east across the wheat field. Two strangers approaching, swords at their hips.

"It's a bad day to be a peasant." The taller of the two men smiled as he walked across the field, flattening the new wheat beneath his boots.

"It's never a good day to be a peasant." Alann straightened slowly, rubbing the soil from his hand. The men's grimy tatters had enough in common to suggest they had once been a uniform. They came smeared with dirt and ash, blades within easy reach, a reckless anticipation in their eyes.

"Where's your livestock?" The shorter man, older, a scar threading his cheekbone leading to a cloudy eye. Close up both men stank of smoke.

"My sheep?" Alann knew he should be scared. Perhaps he lacked the wit for it, like goats led gently to their end. Either way a familiar calm enfolded him. He leant against his hoe and kept his gaze on the men. "Would you like to buy them?"

"Surely." The tall man grinned, a baring of yellow teeth. Wolf's fangs. "Lead on."

For a heartbeat Alann's gaze fell to the soldiers' boots, remnants of the fresh green wheat still sticking to the leather. "I've never been a good farmer," he said. "Some men have the feel for it. It's in their blood. The land speaks to them. It answers them." He watched the strangers. Conversations carry a momentum, there's a path they are expected to take, a cycle, a season, like the growing of crop. Take the rhythm of seasons away and farmers grow confused. Turn a conversation at right angles and men lose their surety.

"What?" The shorter man frowned, doubt in his blind eye.

The tall man twisted his mouth. 'I don't give a—"

Alann flipped up his hoe, a swift turn about the middle, sped up by kicking the head. He lunged forward, jabbing. Instinct told him never to swing with a long weapon. The short metal blade proved too dull to cut flesh but it crushed the man's throat back against the bones of his neck and his surprise left him in a wordless crimson mist.

Without pause Alann charged the soldier's companion, the shaft of his hoe held crosswise before him in two outstretched hands. The man turned his shoulder, reaching for his sword. He would have done better to pull his knife. Alann bore him to the ground, pressing the hoe across his neck, pinning the half-drawn blade with the weight of his body.

Men make ugly sounds as they choke. Both soldiers purpled and thrashed and gargled, the first needing no more help to die, the second fighting all the way. When soldiers poke a hole in a man and move on, leaving him to draw his last breaths alone, there's a distance. That's battle. The farmer though, the death he brings is more personal. He gentles his beast, holds it close, makes his cut, not in passion, not with violence, but as a necessary thing. The farmer stays, the death is shared, part of the cycle of seasons and crops, of growing and of reaping. They name it slaughter. Alann felt every moment of the older man's struggle, body to body, straining to keep him down. He watched the life go out of the soldier's good eye. And finally, exhausted, revolted, trembling, he rolled clear.

Getting to all fours Alann vomited, a thin acidic spew across the dry earth. He got to his knees, facing out across the next field, rye, silent and growing, row on row, rippling in the breeze. It hardly seemed real, a dead man to either side of him.

"You should get up," Darin said. Solemn, pale, watching as he always watched.

"…they called me kennt." Alann's mind still fuzzy within that strange and enfolding calm. "When I was a boy, the others called me kennt. They knew. Children know. It's grown men who see what they want to see."

"You can walk away from it." Darin looked down at the dead men. "This doesn't define you."

"Forgive me then." Alann got to his feet, drawing the sword the soldier had failed to pull and taking the dagger that he should have.

"You need to forgive yourself, brother." Darin offered him that smile, the only one he ever had, the almost smile, sadder than moonset. The smile faded. "You have to go to the house now."

"The house! They came from the house!" Even as Alann said it he started to run up the slope toward the rise concealing his home. He ran fast but the sorrow caught him just the same, a choke hold, misting his eyes. His life had never fit, his wife, his children, always seeming as though they should belong to someone else, someone better, but Mary he had grown to love, in his way, and the boys had taken hold of his heart before they ever knew how to reach.

Alann ran, pounding up the slope. The flames had the house in their grip by the time he cleared the ridge. The heat stopped him as effectively as a wall. Some men, better men perhaps, would have run on, impervious to the inferno, impervious to the fact that nothing could live within those walls, too wrapped in grief to do anything but die beside their loved ones. For Alann though, the furnace blast that blistered his cheeks and took the tears from his eyes, burned away the mist of emotion and left him empty. He stepped back from the crackle and the roar, one pace, three paces, five until the heat could be endured. He dropped both weapons and stared into his empty hands as if they might hold his sorrow.

"I'm sorry." Darin, standing at his side, untouched by the heat, untroubled by the run.

"You!" Alann turned, hands raised. "You did this!"

"No." A plain denial. A slow shake of his head.

"You brought this curse…you never forgave me!"

"It didn't happen for a reason, Alann. These things never do. Hurt spills over into hurt, like water over stones. There's no foreseeing it, no knowing who it will touch, who will be left standing."

Alann knelt to take up the sword and the knife.

"You've got to get to the village, warn the elders. There needs to be a defence—"

"No." Alann's turn to offer flat refusal. He turned and walked toward the shelter where the sheep huddled against winter storms. Kindling lay stacked in the lee of the dry stone wall, and in a niche set into its thickness, wrapped in oil-cloth, an old hatchet, a whetstone alongside. Alann thrust sword and dagger into his belt and took the hand-axe and the stone to set an edge on it.

"There's another side to this, Alann. It's a storm like any other, the worst of them, but it will end—"

"You want me to rebuild? Find a new wife? Make more sons?" Alann scanned the distant fields as he spoke, his hands already busy with the whetstone on the hatchet blade. He could see the lines where the soldiers had set off through the beet, angling towards Warren Wood. Robert Good's farm lay beyond, and Ren Hay's, the village past those. Alann pocketed the stone and set off after his prey at a steady jog.

Darin was waiting for him at the wood's edge.

"You'll die, and for nothing. You won't save anyone, won't get revenge. You'll die as the man you never wanted to be. God will see you—"

"God sent the soldiers. God made me a killer. Let's see how that turns out."

"No." And Darin stepped into his path, careless of the hatchet in his brother's hand.

"It's over." Alann didn't pause. "And you're just a ghost." He stepped through Darin and went on into the trees.

Six soldiers rested at the base of one of the old-stones, monoliths scattered through the Warren Wood, huge and solitary reminders of men who lived off these lands before Christ first drew breath. They had insignias beneath the grime of their tunics but Alann wouldn't have known which lord they took their coin from even if the coat of arms had flown above them on a new-sewn banner. He slipped back through the holly that hid him and in the clearer space behind drew the sword he had taken. It would serve him poorly in the close confines beneath the trees and he had never swung one before. He stepped around the bush, breaking through the reaching branches of a beech, the sword held in two hands over his shoulder.

The soldiers started to rise as he emerged into the clearing around the old-stone. He threw the sword and it made half a turn in the ten yards between them, impaling a bearded man through the groin. Alann pulled the hatchet and knife from his belt and charged, arms crossed before him.

The quickest of the patrol came forward before he covered the ground, one with sword in hand, helm on head, the other bareheaded, his knife in his fist, shield awkward on his arm. At the last moment before they closed Alann threw himself to the ground before the pair, feet first, sliding between them through the dirt and dry leaves. He swung out with both arms, hatchet to the back of one knee, knife to the other. A farmer butchers his own meat, he knows about such things as tendons and the purpose they serve.

Alann's slide ended at the base of the old-stone, taking the feet from under a third soldier as he stood. He rolled into space and threw himself clear as a sword struck sparks from the monolith just above his head. He ran, sure-footed, a tight circle around the base of the old-stone, thicker than a pair of grandfather oaks. Two soldiers gave pursuit but were yards behind him as he came again upon the three felled men and a fourth seeking to help one of the injured men up. Alann powered through the cluster, a quick hatchet blow to the back of the standing man as he bent over, followed by a knife slash across the neck of the groin-stabbed man as he gained his feet.

A tight turn around the monolith and Alann spun about, crouching low. The two soldiers thundered round the corner, swords before them. Alann launched himself into the foremost, beneath the man's sword, both legs driving him forward and up, shoulder turned to take the impact against the man's belly. The two of them crashed back into the third, taking him down. Four quick stabs to the man's abdomen at the tempo of a fast clap. Alann clambered over him, pinning his sword arm beneath his knee, and lunging, brought his hatchet down into the face of the soldier behind, the man had been scrabbling away on his backside to get clear, but too slow.

Alann drove his dagger through the throat of the gut-stabbed man then wrenched it out. Dripping with blood he stood and jerked the hatchet from the face of the second twitching soldier. It came free with a crack of bone.

A wounded animal is only at its most dangerous because that's when it's likely to attack you. A man who was already attacking you is considerably less dangerous when wounded. Alann walked around to finish the two hamstrung men.

He stood from the task, scarlet with other men's blood. Darin watched from the gloom beneath the trees, silent, ghost-pale, his limbs translucent, little more than suggestions of the light and shade.

"You've killed evil men," Darin said.

Alann looked around at the red ruin he'd made. "There's evil in most men—just waiting for its chance."

"They were evil. You did God's work."

"God didn't make me to kill evil men—he made me to kill, like the knife is made to cut."

Shouts rung out deeper in the woods, more soldiers, from several directions. Alann raised his hatchet.

Darin slid from the shadows, almost invisible when he stood in the sunlight. "We're brothers, Alann, come back with me. There's still a life for you here."

"The choice has been made. By me, or for me. There's no going back. Not anymore."

The shouts grew closer.

Alann spoke again. "There's only one thing you can do for me now, Darin."

A silence hung between them, golden in the light.

"I forgive you, brother."

And saying it Darin stepped back into the shadow, indistinct even there now, his features smoothed into some blur that might be any man. Around him others rose, pale ghosts, eight more, crowding close so that Alann could no longer be sure which was Darin. They stood there, nine wraiths, the shadows of his kills. His new crop.

Three soldiers burst into the clearing, blinking in the light, and Alann threw himself among them.

He couldn't say how long he fought or how many he killed beneath the green roof of the forest, only that it was long and many. At last he stood red-clad and panting, his back to a tall rock, and found himself where he started, at the old-stone, more corpses before him.

A slow hand-clap made him lift his head though exhaustion weighed it down. A man walked from the trees, lacking the soldier's urgency though moving with more care. Others emerged behind him, all armed, not soldiers though. Bandits, road men, the scum that roamed the borders of any war, picking at the wound. Alann looked from one face to the next. Hard men all. Each different from the next, short and tall, young and old, dirty and clean, but he recognised something in each one. Every man a killer born.

Their leader stopped clapping. A young man, tall, wild, a dangerous look in his eye. "You cut men like an art-form, brother. I watched the first six…magnificent."

Alann wiped his mouth and spat, the copper taste of blood across his tongue. "You watched?"

The man shrugged. He was younger than Alann had first thought. "Some men just want to watch the world burn." He grinned.

"I'm the fire."

"That you are, brother, and which of us is worse?"

Alann had no answer to that.

"How do they call you, brother?" The sound of a horn in the distance. Another, closer. More soldiers.

"Kennt." A dozen men and more watched him now. "They call me kennt."

"Brother Kent." The young man drew his sword, a glimmering length of razored steel. "Red Kent I'll call you, for you come to us bloody."

"Red Kent." Muttered up and down the line. "Red Kent." The welcome of the pack.

"The baron's men are coming, Brother Kent." The youth pointed with his blade out into the Warren Wood. "Will you fight beside us?"

Alann shrugged away from the old-stone. He looked once more across the ragged band before him, a family of sorts, pack rather than herd, a band of brothers who knew what lay at the core of him because they shared it, killers all. He looked down at the crimson weapons in his crimson hands and knew that moment of peace that happens when a thing surrenders to its nature.

"I will."

ART GALLERY

Over the first two years of *Grimdark Magazine*, three artists have trusted us to place their artwork on our front covers: Julian de Lio, Austen Mengler, and Jason Deem. Over the years Jason has become our premier cover artist, bringing authors' characters to life and completing all but two covers. I hope you enjoy their work as much as the *Grimdark Magazine* team does.

Presented in black and white. Original artwork in colour.

Red Kent by Jason Deem for *Grimdark Magazine* #1 based on
Mark Lawrence's Broken Empire character by the same name.

Pit Fighter by Julian de Lio for *Grimdark Magazine* #2 based on
R. Scott Bakker's *Second Apocalypse* character Thurror Eryelk

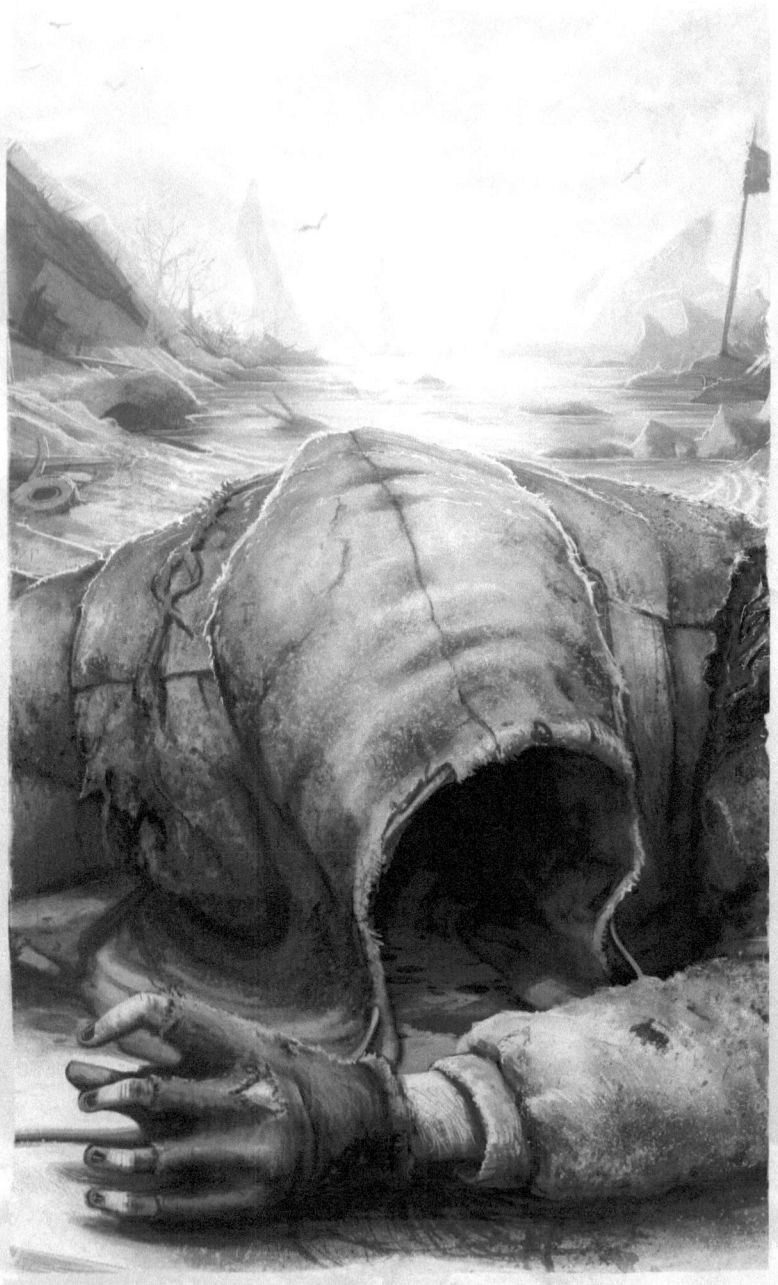

Despondency - Part III by Austen Mengler for *Grimdark Magazine* #3 is a
re-print of an artwork originally created for the band Winterfold.

Symbiosis by Jason Deem for *Grimdark Magazine* #4.

Jotunn by Jason Deem for *Grimdark Magazine* #5.

Hassebrand by Jason Deem for *Grimdark Magazine* #6 based on
Michael R. Fletcher's *Manifest Delusions* character Gehirn Schlechtes.

Red Water by Jason Deem for *Grimdark Magazine* #7 based on two of the
late Victor Milan's *Dinosaur Lords* characters.

Duel by Jason Deem for *Grimdark Magazine* #8 based on
Matthew Ward's protagonist Eribon.

Knee-Deep in Grit by Jason Deem was the original cover for this anthology.

Thurror Eryelk by Jason Deem is a new depiction of the cover art for GdM#2.
As Jason is the premier Second Apocalypse fan artist out there, we thought
it'd be rude not to get a piece from him for our R. Scott Bakker story.

www.ingramcontent.com/pod-product-compliance
Lightning Source LLC
Chambersburg PA
CBHW030344120726
47901CB00007B/1902